Lucas's body ached for Sloan. His mind was in turmoil, his harmony completely gone.

The old medicine man was watching him. "Tell me, my son, how long have you wanted to look after this white woman's sheep?"

"Sloan Baron doesn't have any sheep, my grandfather," Lucas said irritably.

"Where is her man?"

"I don't know," Lucas said.

"Maybe she hasn't got one."

"I don't know," Lucas said again, increasingly uncomfortable.

"Maybe you should find out. The People think all the whites are the same. This one *isn't* the same."

Lucas made no reply. He didn't have to. He knew precisely what the old man meant.

"No sheep," the medicine man mused sadly. "Ah, well," he added sagely, "perhaps Sloan Baron has something *else* for you to look after...."

Dear Reader,

Welcome to Silhouette **Special Edition**...welcome to romance.

The lazy, hazy days and nights of August are perfect for romantic summer stories. These wonderful books are sure to take your mind off the heat but still warm your heart.

This month's THAT SPECIAL WOMAN! selection is by Rita Award-winner Cheryl Reavis. *One of Our Own* takes us to the hot plains of Northern Arizona for a tale of destiny and love, as a family comes together in the land of the Navajo.

And this month also features two exciting spin-offs from favorite authors. Erica Spindler returns with *Baby, Come Back,* her follow-up to *Baby Mine,* and Pamela Toth tells Daniel Sixkiller's story in *The Wedding Knot*—you first met Daniel in Pamela's last Silhouette **Special Edition** novel, *Walk Away, Joe.* And not to be missed are terrific books by Lucy Gordon, Patricia McLinn and Trisha Alexander.

I hope you enjoy this book, and the rest of the summer!

Sincerely,

Tara Gavin
Senior Editor

Please address questions and book requests to:
Silhouette Reader Service
U.S.: 3010 Walden Ave., P.O. Box 1325, Buffalo, NY 14269
Canadian: P.O. Box 609, Fort Erie, Ont. L2A 5X3

CHERYL REAVIS

ONE OF OUR OWN

Silhouette®

SPECIAL EDITION®

Published by Silhouette Books
America's Publisher of Contemporary Romance

To the "boys" at the Health Department,
heroines all and my longtime companions
in surviving the crazymakers of this world.

 SILHOUETTE BOOKS

ISBN 0-373-09901-0

ONE OF OUR OWN

Copyright © 1994 by Cheryl Reavis

This edition published by arrangement with Harlequin Enterprises B. V.

® and TM are trademarks of Harlequin Enterprises B. V., used under
license. Trademarks indicated with ® are registered in the United States
Patent and Trademark Office, the Canadian Trade Marks Office and in
other countries.

Printed in U.S.A.

Books by Cheryl Reavis

Silhouette Special Edition

A Crime of the Heart #487
Patrick Gallagher's Widow #627
One of Our Own #901

CHERYL REAVIS,

public health nurse, short-story author and award-winning romance novelist who also writes under the name of Cinda Richards, says she is a writer of emotions. "I want to feel all the joys and the sorrows and everything in between. Then, with just the right word, the right turn of phrase, I hope to take the reader by the hand and make her feel them, too." Her Silhouette Special Edition novel *A Crime of the Heart* reached millions of readers in *Good Housekeeping* magazine. Both *A Crime of the Heart* and *Patrick Gallagher's Widow* won the Romance Writers of America's coveted Rita Award for Best Long Contemporary Series Romance the year they were published. Cheryl currently makes her home in North Carolina with her husband and teenage son.

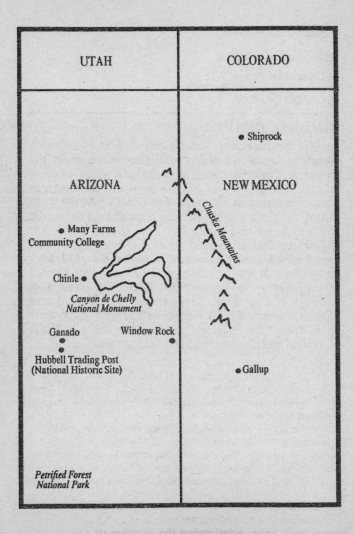

Chapter One

What is that old proverb—a journey of a thousand miles begins with a single step?

No, she thought. It begins with a telephone call from a stranger in the middle of the night.

"Are you still there, Ms. Baron?" the caller asked.

"Yes," she said. She took a deep breath, trying to remember who the woman had said she was. "I'm—I don't—" She closed her eyes for a moment, then started again. "Tell me what I need to do," she said, her voice sounding husky and strange to her. She was fully aware that her hands trembled.

"Your brother will be moved to the trauma center at the University of New Mexico Hospital in Albuquerque as soon as his condition is stable. Unless—"

The woman didn't continue, making the tacit possibility—perhaps likelihood—of Mark's dying all the more real. She wasn't having a bad dream. She was completely awake and talking to this minimally informed social worker about Mark, who had been seriously injured in a car accident on some back road in New Mexico.

"Can you at least tell me if my brother is conscious?"

"Your name and address were on a letter in his wallet," the woman said, either sidestepping the question or giving the only information she had. And, at this point, it would have been difficult for Sloan Baron to say which would have been more surprising—that Mark might have asked someone to notify her or that he actually carried one of her many unanswered letters around in his wallet. She hadn't really heard from him in nearly four years. He had always been a poor correspondent, but she had stopped writing only when her letters could no longer be delivered. He hadn't sent her a new address. He hadn't telephoned. He hadn't bothered to send any cards at Christmas. There had been nothing from him but a sporadic series of money orders with no return address, their arrival as unpredictable as the amount.

"Actually, we could only read your last name on the envelope," the woman said. "Would you give me your full name for our records?"

"Sloan Baron," she said, her voice trailing away as a barrage of questions began to surface in her mind.

My God, what was he doing in New Mexico?

But she knew perfectly well that Mark had never needed a reason for anything he did. He'd spent his whole life chasing one whim after another until the novelty wore off, then he moved on to something else. Truthfully, both she and their mother had expected a call like this ever since Mark had been a boy, some stranger's voice in the middle of the night saying that he was hurt or in jail or dead.

"Is there a doctor there I could speak to?" Sloan asked abruptly, because she needed to know more than this woman was telling her.

"No," the woman said. "I'm sorry."

"A nurse who was in the emergency room then? *Someone* who knows the medical—"

"I'm sorry," the woman said again.

"Look! I have specific questions I want answered. I want to know exactly what my brother's condition is."

"I'm sorry, Ms. Baron, that isn't possible. I'm no longer at the clinic where your brother was taken. I'm at the law enforcement building in Window Rock. The clinic is a very small facility and it's been extremely busy there this evening. There is no one to talk to you right now—that's why I'm calling, and I've told you all I know. I also wanted to reassure you that you don't have to worry about the little boy. We'll make arrangements for him to stay at our children's receiving home for now. The people who staff the home are very good with children—"

"Wait a minute," Sloan interrupted. "What little boy?"

There was silence on the other end of the line.

"I don't understand," Sloan said. "What little boy?"

"Your brother's three-year-old son, Ms. Baron," the woman answered.

Sloan could feel the woman waiting for some kind of response, but her incredulity had left her speechless.

The incredulity rapidly gave way to anger and then to an overwhelming sadness. The boy—Mark's son, for God's sake—was three years old and she hadn't known he existed. How could Mark not have told her?

"Ms. Baron, are you still there?" the woman asked.

"Yes. I'm sorry. I...haven't spoken to my brother in some time. I didn't know. He—the boy is all right? He wasn't hurt?"

I don't even know his name!

"He wasn't with his father at the time of the accident. He was staying with some of your brother's friends from one of our community colleges. Your brother was teaching there."

What could Mark possibly be teaching? she almost said. But she took a deep breath and tried to formulate a more reasonable question. This woman was already privy to enough of the Baron family's dysfunction.

"What about the child's mother?"

"I understand she's been absent from the home for some time. We will make some effort to find her if we can."

Absent from the home. Sloan was familiar enough with that particular social services euphemism. It meant separation, divorce, abandonment—anything with a negative impact on the family as a whole.

"Is anyone there? Her family?"

"We haven't been able to contact anyone except you. The only information I have is from one of your brother's friends. I gather the boy's mother is estranged from her family, too."

Too, Sloan thought. She sensed a certain amount of reproach in the woman's voice, but she made no comment. She tried instead to absorb the information she'd been given. Mark had remarried—or perhaps not. But, in any event, he was the father of a three-year-old son.

"Ms. Baron, your brother's injuries are...extensive. That's why we've decided to intervene on the boy's behalf. If Mr. Baron's recovery was expected to be short-term, then the boy could be left in the care of his father's friends. As it is, you understand that we—"

"Are you talking about putting him in foster care?"

"Not precisely. The receiving home is just—"

"I know about receiving homes," Sloan interrupted. "I have to make some arrangements here—please give me a number where I can reach you. I'll let you know in the morning when I'll arrive."

The woman didn't immediately respond.

"Can you give me a number?" Sloan repeated.

She scribbled hastily as the woman finally answered her, twice having to ask her to spell her last name, because it was completely unfamiliar. Inez Yazzie.

"I'd like for you to make sure the boy knows about me," Sloan said. "Please tell him that he has an aunt and that I'm coming and that he shouldn't be afraid. And tell him— God, I don't even know his name."

"His name is William," Inez Yazzie said. "I understand everyone calls him Will."

William, Sloan thought. *Master William Baron.*

She gave a quiet sigh. "Thank you for your help. I know these kinds of calls are . . . difficult. You'll hear from me later this morning."

Sloan hung up the phone and sat on the side of the bed, staring at the pad where she'd written the Yazzie woman's name. But she saw nothing. It was simply too much to absorb at once. Mark's not telling her that he had this child was completely irresponsible—even for him.

Damn it, Mark. What have you done to yourself now? What have you done to me!

She abruptly stood up. She had no time to waste feeling sorry for herself. She had to think. She had to make plans. And she had to go downstairs now and face the monumental task of telling Mark's *other* children.

Lucas Singer waited by his desk for Inez Yazzie to hang up the telephone. She didn't. She sat holding the receiver, her mind a thousand miles away.

"If you want that thing to talk some more, you have to punch those little buttons," he said when she glanced in his direction.

"You are *very* funny, Officer Singer," she said. She abruptly hung up the receiver.

"Inez, I told you I'd make the call to the family," he said as she stuffed papers into her briefcase.

"You were busy," she said shortly, but he took no offense. He had first met Inez Yazzie when they were both new in their jobs, both green and a little scared and far too idealistic. It pleased him to note that practically none of those three qualities remained—in himself, at any rate. He admired Inez immensely. She was at least his mother's age, and she'd gone back to college late in her life, after her husband had died of tuberculosis and her grown son had been killed in a drunken brawl in a dark alleyway in Gallup. Incredibly, she had decided that she would have to have a thankless social services job of trying to straighten out the troubles The People got themselves into if she was going to bring her own life back into harmony. Harmony was very important to the Navajo. One must live in harmony in order to walk in beauty. Even a sometime traditionalist like himself wanted life to be beautiful.

"Did you find a relative?" he asked.

"Yes."

"It was a woman? Mother? Sister? Aunt?"

"*Yes,*" she said pointedly, clearly still annoyed by his earlier assertion that the handwriting on the envelope and in the letter could not be masculine. He had been very definite about it, precisely because he knew that such unfounded male opinions irritated her—very un-Navajo of them both. The Navajo way was moderation in all things. The fewer emotional peaks and valleys, the better. Allowing oneself to become irritated, allowing oneself to provoke irritation was undesirable, particularly since he'd only been guessing about the handwriting.

"Which?" he asked.

"Which what?"

"Mother or sister or aunt?"

"Sister."

"So what is this woman like?"

"Lucas, why are you asking all these questions? This has nothing to do with the tribal police."

"I'm asking for my mother. She'll be very disappointed if I don't know everything there is to know." It wasn't quite the truth. Certainly, his mother would hear about the bad accident on State 264 by morning. News always traveled fast on the reservation, and this particular mishap was grisly enough to draw detailed comment—even more so since the victim was a community college teacher. There would be much talk about whether or not this teacher had died and whether his ghost, his *chindi,* had been trapped in his wrecked car and left behind to do evil there on 264.

The real truth was that he himself was curious. He had discovered what was left of Baron's car on his way back from a court testimony in Santa Fe. The accident itself hadn't disturbed him. It wasn't the first car crash he'd happened upon and it wouldn't be the last. Such things were a part of the natural pattern of his life as a Navajo tribal policeman and therefore acceptable to him. He was as comfortable with the dead and dying as was possible for a Navajo who had been hogan-raised. He no longer believed in *chindis*, in the evil ghost every dead person left behind. If such beings could cause trouble for the living, he had never seen it. It was his opinion that those who created the most difficulty—in his own life or in anyone else's—were always unerringly alive.

It was Mark Baron himself who didn't fit the natural pattern. He wasn't an exhausted traveler or a lost-in-the-dark tourist. He wasn't one of The People who had had too much bootleg whiskey, or a fleeing archaeologist grave robber. He wasn't one of the superficially concerned young doctors paying back a government loan by practicing in the Indian health service. And, by all accounts, Baron wasn't one of the bleeding heart Indian lovers, religious or otherwise, who arrived from time to time hell-bent on making it up to the tribe for more than a century of what amounted to government-sanctioned genocide. Lucas could see *no* reason Mark Baron would have been on the reservation—certainly not for community college teacher pay, and he found the man's presence, even learning of it after the fact, jarring.

"So what can I tell my mother?" Lucas said, still determined to glean whatever information he could.

"Your mother is a busybody, Lucas," Inez said. "She has no business trying to get confidential information out of a policeman."

He smiled. "That's true. But she may be taking care of the little boy if he's coming to the receiving home. She's been working there lately."

"Has she now?" Inez said, obviously pleased. "Your mother, busybody or not, has a way with homeless things. I remember people used to bring her their runt lambs to take care of. She's the reason you're no more insufferable than you are."

He laughed, enjoying the banter, but he still wanted to know about Mark Baron's relative. "You didn't tell me what the Baron woman is like," he reminded her.

"Bossy," she said. "Like all *belagani* women."

He wasn't ready to concede that *all* white women were bossy, any more than he was willing to concede that they were all liars, though he could have easily done so on both counts. He knew most of the white women on the reservation to be assertive—boarding school teachers, missionaries, medical clinic personnel. And he knew at least one rich, white doctor of anthropology to be a consummate liar. His experience with her had brought him as close to self-destruction as he ever wanted to come.

He still cringed at the memory of his own stupidity and arrogance. He had been so stupid and so arrogant as to believe that he could marry her. He hadn't learned from the white girls who had pursued him when he was a student at the University of New Mexico that there were some of them who tried on sexual encounters in the same way others tried on hats. It had nothing to do with need or even curiosity. It was done entirely for effect. He had been barely sixteen years old the first time he recognized the not so subtle sexual question in a white woman's eyes—*What are you? Are you a real man? Would I like it?* That he understood. *That* he could have accepted and enjoyed—if the white anthropologist could have just let it go at that. But she hadn't. In the beginning, he had had no great expectations. It was she who had insisted she wanted their relationship to be more, and for what reason, he still didn't know.

Of course he himself was not without blame. He had come to her willingly. Because he had craved the pleasure she could give him, he had let himself believe every lie, every flattery, not realizing that he was, at the very most, embodying the need she had to flaunt her wild but unearned independence in the face of her wealthy father. And he hadn't realized that her abrupt departure would leave him with an emotional pain of such magnitude that in his worst nightmares he couldn't have imagined it. That, and the humiliation of having everyone on the reservation know what a fool he'd been, and the sorrow of having a child aborted by a woman he thought he loved. In the final analysis, he had mattered so little to her that she hadn't even told him she was pregnant, much less what she planned to do about it.

As the investigating officer, he had read Mark Baron's letter from North Carolina. Regardless of Inez's appraisal, the woman who had written it had not seemed "bossy." She had seemed . . . resigned was perhaps the best word, as if she was writing a letter to someone who would never read it, much less keep it in his wallet. Family news mostly. Meggie had been enrolled in a Catholic school because of her ongoing problem with reading—the classes were small and no one seemed to mind that she was Protestant. Patrick was learning to drive and had backed over the lilac bush. And reminiscences about a Christmas spent in a beach house in Crescent Beach. Lucas had difficulty imagining a kind of Christmas that involved a beach. He was perplexed enough by the hoopla of the Christmas celebration itself. He hadn't been introduced to the white custom of decorated trees and gift-giving until his first year at a reservation boarding school. Then, a small boy far from home and scared half witless, he'd had no idea what the fuss was about—brightly wrapped offerings to some kind of tree god? He still didn't understand the observance precisely. The reason for the celebration—the birth of the savior of the world—seemed to have nothing to do with the commercial gaudiness of the celebration itself. Or perhaps it was trying to imagine the beach part of it that gave him the trouble. Except for movies and television, and pictures in books or magazines or newspapers, he'd had no experience with beaches.

It interested him, too, that Mark Baron and his sister had apparently been in this part of the country before. Still reminiscing, the Baron woman had written about a cross-country automobile trip when she and her brother were children—Route 66 and wigwam motels, rattlesnake pits at the tourist traps and ant bites in the Painted Desert. Both the Baron children had cried, and Lucas didn't blame them. Ant bites in the desert were no laughing matter.

Inez was halfway out the door.

"Where are you off to now?" he called after her.

"I've got to get that little boy to a receiving home," she said over her shoulder.

"Tonight?"

She stopped and turned to look at him. "There's no point in waiting. You saw that boy's father, Lucas. Besides that, who knows what kind of person he left the child with—probably some addled teenager with one of those loud music things stuck in her ears. Mark Baron was one of *our* employees. The tribe has a responsibility to his child."

"Are you bringing him back to the receiving home here?"

"Yes, Lucas," she said patiently. "I'm bringing the boy here. Your mother can get her hands on him tomorrow."

"Try to keep it under a hundred, Inez," he called unnecessarily as she went down the hallway. She gave him a shooing motion with her hand and kept going. Inez Yazzie drove the same way she did everything else—the Navajo way—carefully and with great purpose. He smiled a bit at the irony of her comment about the Baron woman. Inez Yazzie was not only bossy, she was ruthless when something needed to be done—to, with, or for The People.

He expected her to go through the outside door to the parking lot, but she turned the corner toward the dispatcher instead. He sat down at his desk and stared at the unfinished paperwork that still surrounded Mark Baron's car accident. He despised the bureaucracy of his job. Endless paperwork was one legacy from the white man he could have easily done without.

The bitter always comes with the sweet, he thought, or so his mother had always told him. She had worked very hard to teach him the proper frame of mind for Navajo life. *How could we enjoy this good food,* she would say, *if we never went hungry? How could we be so happy around this warm fire if there was no winter snow?*

Unbidden, another memory surfaced—one of the white woman anthropologist's face the first time she had seen the battered oil drum stove in his mother's winter hogan. He pushed it aside. He was tired. He'd had a long day and he needed coffee badly.

The telephone on his desk rang as he was about to go get it.

"Singer," he said into the receiver.

"Becenti here," the familiar voice said, surprising him because Captain Becenti had gone home hours ago. "I want you to take Inez wherever she needs to go tonight," he said. "You can come in two hours later in the morning."

"Yes, sir," Lucas said, but he wasn't happy about it. Of course, he was the likely choice to chauffeur Inez, long day or not. The oncoming shift had their assignments and were already gone. It was a simpler matter to send him.

He gave his cluttered desk a backward glance on his way out. He was happy not to have to labor over the accident report, but he hated having to forgo the coffee—not because he particularly liked it, but because he associated coffee drinking with his own personal ritual for rediscovering his mental quietude. One could drink coffee and think and not have to justify the apparent inactivity. He counted himself fortunate that, unlike some of his other weaknesses, this particular one was neither illegal nor overtly harmful.

Inez was waiting for him in the parking lot, standing beside her generic white sedan with the Navajo tribal emblem emblazoned on the door. There was a slight wind stirring, a dry, dusty wind because the rainy season hadn't begun yet. He could smell cigarette smoke nearby—a white man sitting in a dirty black car and smoking and not looking in their direction.

"You called Becenti at home," he said to Inez as he approached. "Just like that."

"Actually, I had the dispatcher do it," she said without remorse.

"I underestimated your clout, Inez. You and Becenti don't even belong to the same clan."

"I've known Johnny Becenti since we both used to look after our mother's sheep in the big canyon. The way I see it, he and I are still trying to keep our sheep out of harm's way."

"I wouldn't call him at home if the whole damn flock was going over a cliff," he said, and she laughed. "Over there," he said, directing her to the tribal police car Becenti had put at her disposal. "Are you going to tell me what's going on?" he asked as he unlocked the door on the passenger side for her. He had accompanied social workers before to take some orphaned or abused child into protective custody, but this was not a situation that was likely to require the authority of the tribal police—on the surface.

"Did you pass the sergeant's exam?" she asked.

"I don't know yet, and don't change the subject."

"I think you'll pass. You're an intelligent man, Lucas. You're college educated and you're a good policeman. You care about The People. You don't persecute them just because you can. You should have taken that sergeant's exam long before now. You have to let your personal disappointments inspire you, Lucas, not drag you down."

"Are you going to tell me what's going on or not?" he said, ignoring her allusion to his failed love affair and to the fact that his response to a "personal disappointment" hadn't been nearly so positive as hers. She had started a new career; he had nearly ruined his. It occurred to him that she was likely the only person he knew—except for Becenti—who would have dared mention it to him, even obliquely. As far as he was concerned, the white woman anthropologist was dead, and the Navajo never talked about the dead, lest their *chindi* come and haunt them.

Inez waited until they were well down the road before she answered his question.

"The boy, Baron's son, is one of ours."

Sloan Baron sat quietly at the gazebo end of the long porch. The night was cool. A breeze fluttered the leaves on the maple trees that in daylight would have shaded nearly the entire porch. She could hear traffic in the distance, a random car now and then, an indicator of how late it was, or how early. She had no idea how long she'd been out here. She should be inside, doing what needed to be done, instead of sitting out here crying like some overgrown abandoned child.

She looked around as the hinges on the screen door squeaked open—Meggie and Patrick, coming to look for her. They must have heard the phone ring or her crying. She wiped furtively at her eyes in case one of them turned on the porch light.

"I guess we're bothering you," Patrick said lamely. His face was in shadow, but she could hear the anxiety in his voice. Meggie stood behind him, clutching the back of his T-shirt.

"No," Sloan said. "It's all right. Come here—both of you. We have to talk." Her voice broke, and she waited a moment before she continued. "Come sit down."

They both sat down awkwardly in the swing—close to her, but not too close. She had always tried to be truthful with them, but until now she had kept her private moments of despair exactly that—private. It was apparent to her that they must have heard her crying and that a crying Sloan was something that neither of them knew what to do about.

"I got a telephone call a little while ago," she said.

"I heard the phone ring," Meggie said, her voice trailing into a quiet sigh. Mark's children would always expect the worse, Sloan thought, and she was about to give it to them.

"The call was from a social worker in New Mexico. Your father has been in a car accident—"

"Is he dead or what?" Patrick interrupted.

"I think it's very... bad. I don't have many details. I didn't know he was in New Mexico—"

"Yeah, well, join the club," Patrick said, interrupting again.

"We're going out there," Sloan said, ignoring his sarcasm because it wasn't directed at her. It was directed at his absent father whom he seemed to miss more and more of late, instead of less.

"Not me," he said.

"We're going," Sloan said again, in the same quiet voice she hoped both children had learned meant that she expected no arguments.

"Why?" Patrick demanded. "It's nothing to me. I don't want to see him."

"Because *I* want to see him. I need you to help me, Patrick. I can't—*won't*—go and leave you and Meggie here alone. I can't afford for all of us to fly. The only way is to drive. I need you to help me with the driving so I can get there before... before your father dies."

"I don't want to see the son of a bitch!"

"Patrick, I've told you before. None of us has any control over the way other people behave. It's a useless, painful waste of time to let someone else's behavior, even if it happens to be your father's, affect your life to the point that you become no better than they are. I need your help. I'm not asking you to do anything but be a participating member of this family. Whether or not you see him once we get there is up to you."

Patrick abruptly got up from the swing and headed for the screen door.

"There's more," Sloan said sharply.

"For God's sake, what!" Patrick said angrily. "What did he do—kill somebody? No, I know. He robbed a bank, didn't he? He wanted to buy Meggie and me a really great present to make up for all the Christmases and birthdays he's missed. And he cracked up his car making a getaway. Right? *Right?*"

Meggie got up from the swing and squeezed into the wicker chair next to Sloan. She pressed her head into Sloan's shoulder, shivering as Sloan put her arm around her.

"We have to go get your three-year-old brother," Sloan said quietly.

She could hear Patrick's sharp intake of breath.

"My father has another *wife?*" he asked after a moment.

"I don't know."

"You want to go all the way to New Mexico to get his—his *bastard?*" he said incredulously.

"I don't know if the child is a bastard or not, Patrick!"

"You didn't even ask if he got married?"

"No. I didn't. It doesn't matter. The only thing that matters is that the child's mother isn't around and apparently there's nobody else to look after him. He's your and Meggie's half brother. He's my nephew. There isn't anybody else to do it. Now, I need you to help me!"

"I want to go get him," Meggie said. "Well, I do!" she said when Patrick threw up his hands.

"Yeah, well, you would," Patrick said. "That's just what we need around here. Another one of your strays—"

"He's not a stray, he's a *brother!* Almost anyway. And I want to see *him,* too. My... dad. I want to see him, Patrick. I want to see him really bad."

Patrick stalked inside the house, the screen door slamming hard on whatever comment he made.

"Patrick's mad," Meggie said unnecessarily.

"Not at us," Sloan said, getting out of the chair. "The person he's angry with is your dad."

"Are you angry with him, too?" Meggie asked, catching Sloan's hand as they walked across the porch.

"It's a waste of time to ever be angry with Mark, Meggie," Sloan said as she pulled the screen door open. If she'd learned anything in her life, she'd learned that. She reached to turn on a small lamp in the foyer. They had all done enough stumbling around in the dark for one night.

"Are you going to have to take another job?" Meggie asked.

"Another job?" Sloan asked, not understanding. The child's offhand tone of voice completely belied the distress Sloan saw on her face.

"You have to work two jobs to take care of me and Patrick. If there's going to be three of us, are you going to have to have *three* jobs?"

Sloan forced a smile. "No, honey," she said, lifting a strand of hair out of Meggie's eyes. Her hair was red and thick and too curly to do anything but fly in every direction. Both Meggie and Patrick were redheads, courtesy of Mark's first wife. Sloan *had* met her, but only briefly, a plain young woman completely dazzled by Mark's good looks and charm. "I don't plan to work the two jobs forever. Just until we get ahead a little bit."

"Sloan, is my dad going to die?" Meggie asked quietly.

The stereo in Patrick's room abruptly came on, blaring some hard-driving rap song through his closed door. Sloan didn't try to avoid the question, regardless of the gauntlet Patrick had just thrown down. "I don't know, Meggie. But I'm afraid he is."

"Didn't he love *my* mother—mine and Patrick's?"

"Yes. I think he loved her very much. He was very sad when she died."

The music from Patrick's room suddenly got louder, not because he'd turned up the volume, but because his door had cracked open.

"Go on to bed, now," Sloan said. "I have to talk to Patrick."

Meggie sighed heavily. "I feel like crying, Sloan."

"I know," Sloan said, giving her a hug. "Do you want to come in after I've talked to Patrick?"

She shook her head.

"Are you sure you're all right?"

"Well, I kind of wish it was a sister," she said, glancing at Patrick's door, "instead of another *brother*. It won't do any good to worry, will it? About my dad, I mean."

"No."

"I'm not worried about the three-year-old, even if he is a brother. He can't be as bad as Patrick." She sighed again. "I guess I'll just say some really good prayers then—I'm glad I'm in the summer room tonight," she whispered when Sloan hugged her again, and Sloan smiled. Meggie and her "summer room." The old sun room was made almost entirely of nine-over-nine glass windows, the room Meggie had moved into as soon as school was out because she could see the moon and the stars and because she could pretend to be a princess in a castle of glass or a space voyager and not have to worry about things like indifferent, perhaps dying fathers and new, sight-unseen half brothers.

The door to Patrick's room opened wider. Meggie seemed about to say something to him, then apparently thought better of it, giving Sloan a small wave before she disappeared into the sun room.

Sloan took a deep breath and quietly knocked on Patrick's already open door. She understood the need to tread lightly. She realized that he wanted to talk to her and that the half open door was as much of an overture as he would allow himself to make.

"Can I come in?" she asked.

He shrugged, and she went inside, stepping over the size-twelve athletic shoes he'd dropped in the middle of the floor. She expected his silence to continue, expected to have to work at getting him to say whatever it was he wanted to say, but he asked the question almost immediately.

"Am I like him?" he said.

Sloan could barely hear him over the music. She pointed to her ear, and surprisingly he reached to turn the stereo down.

"Sloan, am I like my father?" he asked again without looking at her.

"No, not very much," she said. She moved closer because she couldn't see his face.

"Good. Because I don't ever want anybody to hate me the way I hate him."

He looked around at her then, and she already knew what she would see. Yet another Baron child who felt desperately like crying.

Chapter Two

Every bootlegger, every sheep rustler and pickpocket and grave robber in the district seemed to have made himself and his illegal doings flagrantly visible. Coming in to work two hours later than usual was *not* helpful. Lucas hated finding himself thrust in the middle of things. It was contrary to his Navajo conditioning, to the belief that everything had to be done in an orderly fashion, "sunwise," east to south to west and finally northward. This morning the entire law enforcement building seemed to be awash in counterdirectional activity, not the least of which was trying to identify suspected federal agents who were apparently at work on the reservation, but whose superiors hadn't deemed it necessary to notify the Navajo Tribal Police. No one seemed to have any idea who they were or what they were doing. Drug enforcement? FBI? Serious felonies on the reservation came under the jurisdiction of the United States government. That was simple enough if one didn't happen to step on the jurisdiction of a county sheriff or the New Mexico State Police or the Arizona Highway Patrol or the Bureau of Indian Affairs. Federal agencies were not known for using the numerous local law enforcement people for anything other than holding the Lone Ranger's horse. Even so, Captain Becenti considered it a breach of interagency etiquette to completely exclude his office. It became a matter of ethnic pride to do whatever he could to become enlightened.

"You're sure they were feds?" Lucas heard him ask one of the newer officers, Carlos Johnson.

"Yes, sir, I'm sure. I was spotting federal agents before I could walk."

And he probably was, too, Lucas thought. This particular officer's grandfather had been notorious for trafficking bootleg whiskey. The old man was the reason Carlos was never assigned to anything pertaining to alcohol control now.

"Got some messages, Lucas," the dispatcher said as Lucas tried to get to his desk without being trampled in the abrupt grand exodus of the on-duty police.

He took the slips of paper Mary Skeets handed him, trying not to spill his coffee while he looked through them. One caught his eye immediately. Just a name and a return telephone number. He didn't recognize the area code, but he recognized the name—or part of it. Baron. Sloan Baron.

Mark Baron's sister? Sloan seemed an odd name for a woman, but anything was possible among the whites, though why she would be calling him, he had no idea.

He walked back to the dispatcher. Mary Skeets had been with the department for nearly three years, but she had her own concept of what taking telephone messages entailed. He handed her the slip of paper with Sloan Baron's name on it, politely waiting for her to read it before he asked the question.

"What did this person want?" he asked when she looked up.

She looked at the slip again. "This message is for Inez Yazzie."

Again, he waited, observing Navajo decorum by not pressing her to say more until she was ready. He took another sip of coffee.

"Then why did you give it to me?" he asked when there seemed to be no more information forthcoming.

"Captain Becenti said you drove Inez wherever she was going last night and you might know where she is this morning."

Logical, he thought—except that he didn't know.

"Mary, don't you think you should have put at least some of that on this little piece of paper?"

"I knew you would ask," she said reasonably.

"What if you weren't here?"

"I'm always here."

"Yes, but what if you weren't? What if you'd run off to Flagstaff with the vending machine man? Who would I ask then?"

She giggled and turned to answer the telephone.

Hopeless, he thought as he reached to take the message back. His need for orderliness had made it his lot in life to always try to restore the natural pattern—to return the stolen sheep, to get the bootleg whiskey off the reservation, to sober up the drunken man. Clearly, this curse extended to his phone messages, but there *was* no pattern where Mary Skeets was concerned.

He walked to his desk and sat down. He tossed the rest of the messages aside and stared at the one from Sloan Baron. If this call was for Inez, it must be Mark Baron's sister. After a few moments, his curiosity got the better of him, and, ignoring Becenti's latest memo about curtailing unnecessary long distance phone calls, he punched in the number. He could justify this particular expense by the fact that Becenti was the one who had routed the message to him.

Someone answered on the third ring.

"I'd like to speak to Sloan Baron, please," he said. "This is Officer Lucas Singer, Navajo Tribal Police."

"Just a minute, please," the child who answered said politely.

He could hear noise in the background—running feet, rock music, a door banging. Without much success, he tried to visualize what this place in North Carolina looked like.

"Tell Patrick to turn that music down or die," a woman's voice said.

Inez was right, he thought. This woman was definitely bossy. And it seemed effectively so, because, after a moment, the music subsided.

"Who did he say he was?" the woman said next.

"Officer Lucas Singer," the child said, the second syllable of "Lucas" clearly added as soon as she remembered that it wasn't just plain Luke.

"This is Sloan Baron," the woman said into the receiver.

"This is Officer Lucas Singer. Navajo Tribal Police. You left a message for Inez Yazzie—"

"Is this about my brother? Is he—"

"No," Lucas said quickly, mentally kicking himself for not realizing she would jump to that conclusion. "I haven't heard anything about Mr. Baron this morning. I just wanted to return your call. Apparently, Inez gave you this telephone number so we could track her down. Is there a message I can give her?"

"I just wanted to tell Ms. Yazzie—"

"Yazzie," he said, giving the "a" its correct "ah" sound. It was impolite, but the mispronunciation of Navajo names had always been a source of irritation to him, particularly when it never seemed to occur to white people that there *was* a right and a wrong way.

"Ms. Yazzie," Sloan Baron acknowledged, immediately assuaging his pique. "I just wanted her to know that I'm leaving this afternoon. We'll have to drive out. It'll take us at least two days to get there."

"Ms. Baron, I think it would be better if you flew."

She didn't respond immediately. "I see," she said finally, seeming to understand what he didn't say. "You saw my brother?"

"I was the investigating officer at the accident."

He could hear her give a soft sigh.

"There are three of us," she said. "And there will be four of us coming back—regardless of what happens. It's not possible for us to fly."

He didn't say anything, but he was thinking that, unlike the white anthropologist, this woman was *not* rich.

"Officer Singer, do you know anything about my nephew, William?"

"Inez and I transported him to the receiving home last night. He slept all the way, so I haven't really seen him awake. He didn't seem upset or frightened. I would say he's used to...change."

"Yes. Living with Mark, he would be. I...wonder if I could ask you a favor."

Here it comes, Lucas thought. White people always wanted something.

"I've already called the hospital in Albuquerque," she said. She lowered her voice, as if she didn't want whoever else was there to hear. "All I can get from them is the standard nonanswer. All I can find out is that they're still assessing his injuries. If my brother...dies before we can get there, I'd like to know. Some hospitals—and I think this is one of them—feel it's more...humane not to notify a family, not to tell them bad news on the phone. But I don't want to take Mark's children into the hospital not knowing what I'll find. This is very hard on them. I think it would be better if I knew beforehand so I can prepare them. Could you ask the hospital to notify your office if there's any change in Mark's condition? I think they'd do that, if you officially requested it. Then I could call there to find out."

"Mr. Baron has other children?" he asked. It wasn't precisely a police officer question. It was more a son-who-takes-after-his-busybody-mother question.

"He has a daughter who is nearly nine and a son who's seventeen."

Meggie, who had trouble reading, and Patrick, who backed over lilac bushes, Lucas thought.

"I'll see what I can do," he said, making up his mind quickly. It was beyond the call of duty, certainly, but not unreasonable. He could manage it with only one more unauthorized long distance call. Sloan Baron apparently didn't like to approach a situation from the middle, either.

"Thank you, Officer Singer. Thank you very much. It's..."

"Whatever I can arrange, I'll leave word with the dispatcher here," Lucas said quickly because he thought she was going to cry. "You can call back later to find out."

"Thank you," she said again.

He listened to her hang up the phone, then reached for the gray metal box of index cards on his desk and flipped through them until he found the hospital number. The entire process was amazingly simple, ending with a nurse's promise to flag Mark Baron's chart with the notification request and Lucas's name and the tribal police telephone number.

Then he sat and stared at his desktop. So, he thought. Sloan Baron expected to take her brother's child back with her. He wondered exactly how much she knew about the little boy. Inez had said that she hadn't known he existed. And if that was so, she wouldn't know he was half Navajo—unless she knew something about her brother's relationship with the boy's mother, in which case she might suspect. Lucas realized that as far as Inez was concerned, this child belonged to the tribe and that technically he was already under lock and key.

Last night, he had cajoled Inez into telling him precisely, by clan, *which* Margaret Madman was Will Baron's mother. He remembered the girl she described very well. He had arrested her for solicitation at the Navajo Fair in Shiprock several years ago. Margaret Madman had had a long and unbrilliant career. Prostitution. Bootlegging. Petty theft among the summer tourists. Not the motherly type and not the type to become involved with an underpaid community college teacher. He hadn't asked Inez if Baron and Margaret Madman were legally married. It didn't matter. The boy was Margaret's child and therefore a member of her clan. And he was beginning to see the potential for a great deal of disharmony for everyone involved. Driving all the way across country for a *belagana* nephew was one thing. Driving all the way for one who was half Navajo was something else again. And even if Sloan Baron did want the child, so, most likely, would Margaret's people. And there was still Inez and the Indian Child Welfare Act.

Thankfully, none of it had anything to do with him.

His mind went to the last time he'd seen Margaret Madman. She had still been pretty enough to attract whatever man she wanted, still confident enough of her prettiness to try to persuade him to let her go. Except for not having a rich father and a PhD, he suspected that she was very much like the white woman anthropologist.

He abruptly stood up. His coffee was cold. He went to warm it and to try to explain to Mary Skeets the call-in arrangement he'd made with the Trauma Center and Sloan Baron.

Nothing was going right. The day grew more and more overcast. When she was halfway home from the automatic teller window at the bank, a heavy rain began to fall. It did nothing to lighten the despair Sloan had felt all morning. Quite the contrary. With the first few raindrops, she wanted to put her head down on the steering wheel and cry. She needed more cash than she could get out of a bank machine on a Sunday. She needed clear skies and dry pavement so she wouldn't have to worry so much about letting a teenage boy drive. She needed *not* to have to work two jobs. It was hard enough to tell one employer their staff shortage was about to be compounded by her unexpected trip to New Mexico, much less two. She had been mentally and physically exhausted before she heard about Mark. In the cold light of day, the task of trying to get to Albuquerque seemed insurmountable.

And she'd had no idea that Meggie had understood their financial situation so perfectly. If Sloan had to take two jobs to support two Baron children, then it was only logical to Meggie she'd have to have three to support yet another one. Sloan supposed Meggie had also realized that her father sent practically no money for her and Patrick—not so surprising, if he had another family. Sloan was lucky, she supposed, that nurses were in such demand, but she was so tired of worrying about money. She hated moonlighting in a hospital emergency room, regardless of the sizable supplement to her income. She didn't like the emotional coldness one had to adopt in order to function where the sum total of a human being came down to whatever was bleeding or broken. In life-or-death matters, there was no time for anything else. She preferred the more leisurely pace of working with families as a whole.

Her mind went to the telephone conversation she'd had with the policeman from New Mexico, Singer. She couldn't place his accent at all. The words were pronounced very distinctly with the *R*s clearly defined. She had understood what he *didn't* say about Mark's condition, and she believed that he would do whatever he could to keep her informed.

Oh, Mark! she thought, fighting down the urge to cry again. He was so charming and likable, and so damned unreliable. It was incredible to her that he apparently had a steady job. She wanted to find some excuse for his neglecting Patrick and Meggie, but whether he'd acquired a third child or not, there was none. Money was a poor substitute for a father, but it would have been better than nothing. She was afraid of what lay ahead. Another child of Mark's to raise? She was more afraid than she had ever been in her life.

Yet she understood only too well how much she was to blame for Mark's continued bad behavior. Their mother and father, by their perpetual forgiveness, had established the pattern, and, after their deaths, she, though a younger sister, had taken up exactly where they left off, killing the fatted calf every time the prodigal brother returned, letting him charm his way back into her good graces, because by then he had two children whom she adored. Her reward for all that acceptance and understanding had been that Mark had essentially given Meggie and Patrick to her.

She had *known*, when she agreed to let the children stay with her for a few weeks so he could follow yet another rumor of a "really great job," that she was likely taking them forever. Those few weeks had stretched into months and then a year, until Mark had disengaged himself from their lives completely. And it had been hard. The day-to-day struggle with childhood illnesses and single parenting and undependable day care had left her feeling persecuted and completely abandoned. She had had no respite from the responsibility. She knew that Patrick and Meggie's other grandparents were alive somewhere, but not where or how to contact them—or even if she should. No grandparents were surely better than bad ones, and Mark's children had had enough rejection. She didn't even know if they were aware that they *had* grandchildren. Mark had never wanted to talk about his wife or her family. He hadn't wanted to talk about his wife's death, regardless of the fact that Sloan had asked him point-blank how she had died. Mark had walked away from her without answering. It had been one of the few times in her life she'd ever seen him cry.

"Later," he'd told her. "Please, Sloan, not now."

But later had never come, and seeing what she believed to be his genuine grief and distress, she hadn't asked for specifics again.

Apparently his grief had abated enough for him to get himself another son.

The truth was that she was tired of everything. She saw herself as emotionally bankrupt, because it had taken everything she had to keep what was left of the Baron family together. Yes, she loved Patrick and Meggie with all her heart. Yes, it was better now that they were older, even if Patrick was constantly enmeshed in the multiple traumas of being a teenage boy. But how could she start all over again with a three-year-old? She refused to even consider what kind of prolonged care might be involved in Mark's prognosis—if he had one.

Terrible person or not, she wanted *her* life now. She wanted children of her own with a man she loved, despite the fact that, realistically speaking, in the past four years, she hadn't met a man she even considered a possibility. The lament of her generation. Where have all the good men gone? Knights in shining armor were few and far between these days, and the grand deed she required was particularly difficult—commitment to somebody else's children. She had no interest in the bitterly divorced, or the permanently unattached, or the regretfully married. And she was beginning to consider herself an old maid. She was thirty-one years old, and regardless of some enthusiastic advances, she was still sexually inexperienced. She supposed she had Mark to blame for that, too, or to thank, depending on the point of view. And not because he'd burdened her with his children and thereby ruined any chance she might have had for a personal life. The truth was that she had simply never wanted a man, not even when she was a girl. She had always wanted *the* man, the one she could respect and trust. The one who would be neither indifferent to nor careless of the love she had for him.

Growing up with Mark, dealing with him all her life, she had developed a keen sense of whether or not a man was sincere. She recognized a man's intent, regardless of what he said, and she was only a short distance away from believing that all men were liars—the ones who lied deliberately and the ones, like Mark, who never seemed to know they were lying at the time.

But, regardless of his shortcomings, one undeniable fact remained. All their lives Mark had done nothing but disappoint her, and yet she couldn't bear the thought of his dying. She still wanted him in her life. He was her brother. He was the only person in this world who shared the same memories as she. It hurt too much to even consider that he might be irrevocably gone.

Patrick was waiting impatiently on the porch when she turned into the driveway.

"Where have you been, Sloan?" he said as she got out. "I thought you wanted to get the car packed before noon. What's the matter *now?*"

"Nothing. Everything's all right, more or less."

She glanced at him. Patrick was growing into a handsome young man, in spite of his gangliness and his freckles and his unruly red hair. He had one of those fad, short-to-long haircuts, the kind that suggested that the barber must have abruptly left the shop before he finished the back side. Ordinarily, Patrick was witty and cheerful, but she could see the chip on his shoulder before she got out of the car. She could see the adolescent need in him to go head to head with the first authority figure he could find. Unfortunately, that happened to be her, and she felt just upset enough to give him exactly the confrontation he wanted—and then some.

"Yeah, well, you look like you've been pulled through a keyhole backward," he said.

"I can't help that. This is as good as it gets." She held his gaze, forcing him to look her in the eye if he intended to provoke her. He abruptly looked away, and after a moment she reached up—way up—and tapped him on his bottom lip.

"What's this?" she asked.

"What's what?" he said, dodging.

"This," she said, trying to do it again.

"Quit, Sloan—"

"You'd better get that pout back in, boy. You leave that thing stuck out there like that and a chicken's liable to come along and perch on your bottom lip."

"Very funny. Ha. *Ha,*" he said. His tone of voice was pure teenage sarcastic, but a grin worked at the corners of his mouth, and he laughed in spite of himself. "Where do you *get* all these dumb sayings?"

"Oh, I don't know—been passed down through the family for generations, I guess. You can use them with your children."

"I'm not having any children."

"You should. You know a lot about what *not* to do, don't you?"

He frowned.

"How's the packing going?" she asked, because, regardless of her comment, she didn't want to get into a discussion about Mark's parenting skills now.

"We've packed the clothes you said to pack. Meggie cleaned out the refrigerator. We made sandwiches out of everything we could—all that stuff is in the cooler. I put the porch furniture back into the garage, and I sent Meggie to take a house key to the neighbors next door— What?'' he said when she suddenly reached toward him.

"Thank you, Patrick," she said, hugging him fiercely. They had started off badly last night, but she had told him the truth. He was *not*, thank God, another Mark.

"Jeez, Sloan—you know I hate that hugging stuff!"

"Yes, and I told you when you were a little boy—"

"Yeah, yeah, I get hugged even if I get so big you have to stand on a chair."

"Exactly," she said, letting him go and starting up the porch steps.

"Sloan," he said as she opened the screen door. "I still don't want to see him."

"I understand," she said truthfully. When everything was said and done, a brother's indifference was one thing. A father's indifference was quite something else again.

It took nearly two more hours of checking and double-checking before they were finally ready to leave. Sloan had a headache by then and an intense desire just to lie down—and Meggie kept dawdling until she'd disappeared altogether.

Sloan found her sitting on the floor beside Mark's old high school shop project bookcase in the back of the wide center hallway.

"Meggie, come on! We have to leave now."

"I just wanted to look one more time," she said. "I might not recognize him." She had the family photo album in her lap, the one with all the pictures of her father.

"Meggie..."

"I know he won't know who *I* am. I was just five when he left me here. I don't look anything like I did then. He won't know me, will he?" she asked as Sloan knelt down on the floor beside her.

"I think he will," Sloan said. She didn't say how much Meggie was turning into a pretty version of her mother. It was true that Meggie had changed, but not just physically. She'd been so shy at first, it had taken Sloan a week to get her to smile. Now she was outgoing and warm and loving. Most children brought home stray animals at one time or another. Meggie had always brought home stray people—the little boy in her class whose mother was in prison for welfare fraud, the only child in the entire school who was Vietnamese. Who but Meggie would know the town's alcoholic homeless by their first names and speak to them all every time she saw them? Meggie was the perfect child for someone like Mark to have, compassionate, forgiving. It was his great loss that he had chosen not to be a part of her life.

"Let's go," Sloan said, getting up off the floor. "You can bring the album with you."

"Sloan? I'm scared, Sloan."

"Me, too, kid," she said, pulling Meggie into a standing position.

She let Patrick drive, rain or no rain, because he needed to know she meant it when she said she needed his help. And she gave Meggie the road atlas and the magnifying glass and let her sit up front beside him. Reading problem or not, she wanted both Mark's children to feel needed.

"Okay," she said, trying to fit into the only small space left in the back seat. "Let's go—and don't play fast and loose with the speed limit, Patrick."

"Who me?" he said in mock surprise.

"Yes, you."

"Can I pick up wild women?"

"Sure. If you think they won't mind riding on the roof."

"Nah, we'll put old Megan on the roof."

"That's not funny, Patrick," Meggie said, giving him a push.

"Did you see that? Did you see that?" Patrick turned around to ask. "Flagrant interfering with the driver—"

"Please!" Sloan said. "Both of you! Let's go! And remember—I have no qualms whatsoever about beating children."

They both grinned at her token threat. Sloan watched the house through the back window as Patrick finally pulled out of the driveway. How sad and empty it looked in the rain. It occurred to her that this was the second time in her life she'd left this house to begin the same long journey. She'd been about Meggie's age then, and she'd had no premonition that she would repeat the trip long after her parents had died, and with Mark's children instead of Mark himself. That time it had been a great adventure. This time it would be an ordeal.

She tried to relax, tried not to back-seat drive. They had a long way to go and Patrick was doing fine—with the driving, at least. She thought of Mark's other son. The people who fared the worst in Mark's life were the ones who couldn't defend themselves. She imagined the little boy in a county facility somewhere in New Mexico, alone and not understanding why his father didn't come for him.

Oh, God, she nearly said out loud. Then she closed her eyes and tried not to think at all.

Chapter Three

Mary Skeets handed Lucas two messages. Both of them were from his mother.

"When did she call?" he asked, because there was no time written on either of them.

"While you were out," Mary said with her usual logic, mimicking the heading on the message forms without realizing it.

While I was out, Lucas thought, walking to his desk. That narrowed it down to about five hours. He sat down and punched in the children's receiving home number, and he noted that apparently there were no messages from Sloan Baron or from the trauma center.

The telephone at the receiving home rang a long time. He glanced at his watch. It was time for the evening meal. He knew that his mother and everyone else would be busy with that, but he let it ring. Eventually someone answered, another volunteer who'd been instructed to tell Dolly Singer's son to come to the receiving home when his shift ended. He smiled slightly as he hung up the phone. Like Inez Yazzie, his mother left very little to chance. Likely, everyone in the place old enough to pick up the receiver had been advised what to say to him. And like Inez, he was glad she had volunteered to help with these uprooted children.

With the leaving of her last child—Lucas's younger brother, Tommy—Dolly Singer had suffered a great deal from a lack of harmony, in spite of the fact that she had done everything exactly as it was supposed to have been done. She had diligently taught her children the Navajo way, and she had buried their placentas under her hogan doorstep so that they would always come home again.

But Lucas hadn't lived with the Singer extended family since the white woman anthropologist went back East. And his only sister, Lillian, had returned only briefly to the reservation in the last three years. She was a lawyer who wasted her considerable legal talent working as an aide and who-knew-what-else to a married member of the New Mexico legislature. If she ever left his side at all, she didn't come to Window Rock.

But it had been Tommy's decision not to come home this summer from the University of Pennsylvania that had been more than his mother could endure. Lucas suspected that his mother thought Tommy might be following in *his* footsteps and gotten himself involved with some unworthy *belagana* woman. She had consulted a crystal gazer for the cause of her melancholy and she had been sent to the Navajo Peacemaker Court for the cure. Peacemaker Court wasn't a standard remedy for his mother's kind of problem, but the peacemaker was a wise man. His solution had been for her to turn to *other* children who needed her, for in helping The People, she would help herself.

Lucas had another hour of paperwork to complete before he could leave. He used some of that time to reread Mark Baron's accident report and to make yet another unauthorized long distance call. He had lived with racial prejudices long enough to know that there were those who would consider a request for notification from a Native American police agency of no consequence.

The intensive care unit nurse advised him that there had been no change for better or worse in Mark Baron's condition. Baron was still alive, and he was still on the critical list. His family was en route from North Carolina, she said, and he'd had two visitors who'd made inquiries and left.

Interesting, he thought as he left the building. Who were the two visitors who had already gone to see Mark Baron? He had asked for specifics. Two men—white men, the nurse had said. She didn't know anything more. Someone from the community college perhaps? He would have expected Baron's first visitor to have been Margaret Madman, though her interest would likely be in finding

out whether or not the father of her child had any life insurance
and if she was the beneficiary.

He was hungry, but he decided to postpone his supper until after he'd seen his mother. The structure the tribal council had set
aside for a receiving home was not far away. It was one of the
many post World War Two building projects the United States
government had seen fit to inflict upon the Navajo Nation. Low-
pitched roof. Ugly. But the government had been so pleased with
what it had done that it built hundreds more just like it. It was
difficult to see anything harmonious or beautiful in these struc-
tures, though a certain amount of landscaping with Russian ol-
ives and some wooden fencing helped soften the austere, low-
income look of the receiving home somewhat. That and the swing
set and the two picnic tables out back.

He parked in the nearly empty parking lot, looking at the sky
again as he walked to the front door—still no rain. He looked
forward to the rainy season, because he always felt renewed as the
earth was renewed. When he went inside the building, he could
immediately smell the pine-scented disinfectant that had been used
to mop the worn tile floors and the mutton stew that had been
served for the children's evening meal.

He could hear voices in the big dayroom off to his right, and he
went in that direction, finding his mother just inside the dayroom doorway.

Dolly Singer was a small woman, and she had given up traditional Navajo dress except for her turquoise jewelry. It was going
to take Lucas some time to get used to seeing her in a green volunteer's smock with her name sewn on the pocket, almost as long
as it would take him to get used to the fact that she now lived in
town, staying in a small house in Window Rock instead of in the
canyon and mesa hogans and following the sheep from winter to
summer pasture. He could see immediately that she was worried
about something, but he waited as he'd been taught, letting her tell
him whatever she wished him to know whenever she wished him
to know it.

There were a few children about, several watching *Leave It To
Beaver* on the one portable television and one small boy he immediately recognized sitting alone in the corner on a child-size
molded plastic chair.

When Lucas looked at his mother, she was ready for him to
know why she had asked him to come. In keeping with another
fine point of his Navajo upbringing, he turned his gaze away so
that he would not be staring directly into her face when she spoke.

"This child, the one born to Margaret Madman's clan, the one whose father is white," she said in Navajo. "He doesn't eat. He cries all the time."

"He isn't crying now," Lucas said, glancing from the boy to her.

"Not here," his mother said, lightly touching her eyes. "Here." She touched her heart. "The older boys have told him he has no relatives. He is Navajo enough to understand the insult. They have told him he has no one to teach him the Beauty Way and so everyone will *know* he has no relatives. They have made him ashamed. I want my son the policeman to do something about this crying child."

Lucas abruptly looked at her, then away again. That his mother should make a request of him did not surprise him. Navajo society was a matriarchy. She had no son-in-law and no prospect of one. It was right and proper that she should ask her older, unmarried son for whatever she needed. But, until now, her requests had always been reasonable. What could he possibly do for this essentially orphaned half-white boy?

"Think about what should be done," his mother said, apparently sensing his resistance.

But his mind was already working on the problem. He crossed the room to speak to William Baron. The boy was still sitting in the same place in the corner, perhaps watching Beaver Cleaver and his troubles, perhaps not. He fidgeted in the chair from time to time, but he made no attempt to get up. Instead, he transferred his restlessness to a yellow apple that someone had left for him on the small table next to his chair, toying with the stem but making no move to eat it.

Lucas pulled up another small chair, reaching into his pants pocket for his knife before he sat down. The knife had two blades that folded into a silver casing inlaid with turquoise. It had been a gift from his uncle when he was not much older than this small boy.

"I have a knife," Lucas said to him as he sat down. "It's a really good knife. I could peel that apple for you. What do you think?"

The boy's gaze shifted from the apple to the knife and back again. After a moment, he nodded, and, without Lucas asking, he picked up the apple and handed it to him.

"When I was a boy," Lucas said, "my uncle used to peel apples for me. He took the whole peeling off in one long piece. I wonder if I can do that?" He opened the knife, pulling out the larger, sharper blade, feeling the boy's interest. "Do you like apples?"

Again, the boy nodded.

"This is a good kind you've got here—sweet."

"Dolly brought it in here," he said, twisting in his chair as he watched Lucas work.

"She did? Well, that means she likes you. This is a fine apple, so she must like you a lot." He kept cutting around and around the apple, making the peeling grow longer and longer.

"Does she...give you a apple?" the boy asked.

"Well, not since I was a little boy like you—"

"I'm not a *little* boy. I'm *big*. I'm a *big* boy!"

Lucas stopped peeling long enough to give him an appraising look. "Yes," he decided. "You are a big boy. I didn't notice before. Such big boys are going to need a big piece of this apple."

The long, curling peel suddenly broke and plopped on the floor.

"Whup!" the boy cried, clapping his hands together in delight. "It fell down!"

"So now what are we going to do with this?" Lucas said as he picked up the peel and laid it aside on the small table.

"Feed it to George," the boy said. "George likes peelings."

"He does? Where is he?"

"In the *goat pen,*" the boy said pointedly, and Lucas laughed.

"In that case, George must be a goat."

"A *big* goat!" the boy said, taking the slice of peeled apple Lucas offered him. He grinned broadly and bit off a piece. "A good apple!" he pronounced it. "You eat some. You eat *that* piece."

Lucas obliged, eating the second piece he'd cut off. They continued to share the apple until it was all gone, then they went into the backyard to give the peeling to the goat George, an aged creature apparently consigned to live out the rest of his days as a mascot and garbage disposal for homeless children. Will Baron was talking more now, little-boy observations about goats and apple peelings. On their way inside, the child trustingly took Lucas's hand, still talking and looking up at him from time to time.

Navajo and not Navajo, Lucas thought. Would the child he and the white anthropologist made have looked like this one?

"Have you got a name?" the boy asked next.

"Officer Lucas Singer," Lucas said. "You can call me Lucas."

"Have you got a boy like me?"

"No. No boys or girls."

"Do you know my daddy?"

"No," Lucas said, which was technically the truth. Finding a man in the worst possible of medical conditions didn't constitute an introduction.

"I want to go find him."

"I know. But I think it's better that you stay where *he* can find *you*."

"Is he looking for me?"

"Not yet. His car ran off the road and he was hurt. When he feels better, he can come here," Lucas said, picking his words carefully so as to reassure but not give false hope. "Did Dolly and Inez tell you that?"

The boy sighed and didn't answer.

"Did he hurt his head?" he asked after a moment. "I hurt my head one time—right on here." He pointed to his forehead. "Did he hurt his face? Did he hurt his nose?"

"Will," Lucas interrupted. "There's another reason you need to stay here."

"Why?"

"So your aunt can find you."

"I don't got a aunt. I don't got a mother and I don't got a aunt."

"You have an aunt. Her name is Sloan Baron. I talked to her today on the telephone."

"Where is she?"

"She's coming in her car—all the way from North Carolina. It's a long way for her to drive, so she won't be here for a while yet. But she's coming. Your North Carolina family is coming."

"Mine?"

"Yes. Yours. *Your* family."

"Lucas," Inez Yazzie said behind them. He hadn't seen her arrive and it startled him somewhat that she was so close.

"Run inside now, Will," she said to the boy. "Dolly will give you some milk to drink."

The boy went off happily—or at least more happily than he'd been when Lucas first arrived.

"Lucas, you shouldn't have told him that," Inez said.

"Why not? And while we're at it, why did you give Mark Baron's sister the tribal police telephone number?"

"I shouldn't have to explain this to you, of all people. You know what white people are like, what white *women* are like. Suppose this Baron woman changes her mind about coming? What then? And what's she going to do when she sees him? That little boy will be even more disappointed. The less he has to do with them, the better."

"She's on her way, Inez."

"How do you know that?"

"I talked to her on the telephone. You gave her the tribal police number, remember?"

"Just don't tell the boy anything else about the Barons, all right?"

"I don't know, Inez. If it keeps the older boys from making him miserable, what can it hurt for him to know the truth?"

"It can hurt, Lucas. I've already talked to a couple of people from Margaret Madman's clan. Nobody seems to know where she is, not that she's fit to have the child if we could locate her. If Mark Baron dies, his sister is not going to want that boy." She turned to go inside. "I just hope he didn't understand what you told him."

Lucas gave a sharp sigh. All this was not *his* business, regardless of his mother's concern. He would not let his thoughts dwell on these people. He would not let himself be reminded of the half-Navajo child he had lost. It had taken him too long to find his own harmony again; he wouldn't waste it on strangers.

But Will Baron *did* understand. He understood perfectly. There was a commotion in the dayroom. Fists clenched and feet planted, the boy was assuring them all that he did indeed have relatives and that *they* would teach him the Beauty Way.

For Sloan, the entire journey had come down to arguments, interstates and mindless fatigue. She had to keep taking small town exits, looking for the right kind of automatic teller machine so she could tap her savings account and chain grocery stores so she could buy enough bread and cold cuts and orange juice to put together cheap meals. Late afternoon driving was the worst, when she had to fight the sun in her eyes. She began to lose all track of time, she wasn't certain what day it was, and she could feel the movement of the car even when she was out of it.

Twenty miles out of Albuquerque she called the Navajo police station in Window Rock. Mary Skeets was on duty as usual, and she assured Sloan that there had been no news from the trauma center. It was a relief to know that there had apparently been no change, but the worry Sloan had kept at bay by the struggle to get this far threatened to overwhelm her the closer they got to their destination. She thought that Patrick and Meggie must be feeling the same as she did, because their squabbling ceased, both of them sitting in uneasy silence.

They arrived in Albuquerque in the early evening, exhausted, hungry, and with a full moon rising over the city. The Sandia Crest was one of the few landmarks Sloan actually recognized from her cross-country trip as a child. The city lights and the huge mountain range backdrop matched her memory as nothing else she'd seen along the highway. She got onto neon-lit Central Avenue as Mary Skeets suggested, looking for the more reasonable hotels and motels that were supposed to be along the old Los Angeles to Chicago highway. And by now she had no qualms whatsoever about walking into a lobby and asking the room rates and walking right out again if the place was too expensive.

They eventually found a family motel she could afford, one with a neon sign out front that actually had all its colorful tubes working and a nearby fast-food restaurant.

But she didn't take the time for amenities like food and a bath. She and Meggie left immediately for the hospital, and surprisingly, Patrick accompanied them, taking over the driving again because she was so tired. In a very short time, however, she was wishing vehemently that he'd stayed in the motel room.

"I don't want to see him," he said for the third time since they left the motel parking lot.

"All right!" Sloan said sharply, wondering if he was trying to convince her or himself. "Turn here."

He made the turn into the hospital parking lot too sharply.

"Patrick!"

"And if you and Meggie are going to go in there and bawl all over him, you can just count me out," he added.

"You're being stupid, Patrick," Meggie said. "That's all boys are. Stupid!"

"I'm not being stupid!"

"You are! And you want to be mean to Will Baron just because he got to stay with Dad and we didn't—"

"What do you know about it, Megan! You're just a kid!"

"You're mean, Patrick! You're mean to our dad and you're mean to a *baby!* You call him a bastard and everything—"

"Enough!" Sloan yelled into the middle of the argument. "Patrick, watch where you're going!" she cried, because he nearly hit a light pole.

She got out of the car before it stopped, regardless of her overwhelming sense of dread.

I can't do this, she thought. *I can't! I can't go in there and watch Mark die.*

She stood staring at the building where Mark was supposed to be. It took everything she had not to break into a run in the opposite direction.

"Are we going in or not?" Meggie said beside her.

She sighed heavily. "Yes," she said after a moment. She was going in for the same reason she'd done everything else these last four years. Because there was no one else to do it.

Chapter Four

Lucas had been looking forward to Wednesday morning so he could get his much-needed paycheck.

"She's here," Mary Skeets told him as soon as he walked through the front door.

"Who?"

"Mark Baron's sister."

"Here?" Lucas asked because he never knew when Mary was generalizing or being specific, and he'd never been able to fathom her logic well enough to second-guess her.

"Albuquerque. She called last night. There's nothing from the trauma center, so I guess her brother is still alive."

"Does Inez know?"

"I called her. She didn't say if she was going to go see the sister or not," Mary said, for once answering a question before he had to ask. "Somebody ought to. Mark Baron worked for us and the little boy is here."

She was looking at him with obvious expectation.

"Somebody from the community college will go," he said.

"They won't know as much about the accident as you do," Mary said.

"I don't have anything to tell her."

"People would rather hear nothing from somebody who was there than from somebody who wasn't, Lucas. It makes them feel better."

"Mary, this—"

"Your mother thinks so, too."

"Oh, she does? And what else have the two of you decided?"

"Nothing," Mary said, clearly insulted. "This isn't *our* business."

"You could have fooled me," he said on his way to his desk.

"The little boy is waiting for his aunt," Mary called after him.

Yes, Lucas thought. And Inez was likely still upset about it. He supposed that if Mary and his mother were discussing the situation, then so must half the reservation be forming some kind of opinion. And, regardless of Inez's misgivings, it would seem that Mark Skeets and Dolly Singer wanted to expedite the arrival of a Baron relative—whether she was white or not.

"Lucas!" Captain Becenti called when he walked past the captain's open door.

"Yes, sir," Lucas said, sticking his head in.

"I want you to go to Albuquerque—"

"Somehow I thought you might."

"What?"

"Nothing, sir," Lucas said, waiting to be told what he likely already knew. In his mind's eye he could imagine Mary, his mother and *Mrs.* Becenti in deep discussion and at some point deciding how they wanted the captain to handle the Baron situation.

"Come in and sit down. Is that old college roommate of yours still with the FBI in Albuquerque? What's his name again?"

"Nicholas Wager. He's there as far as I know," Lucas said, surprised. "We keep in touch but I haven't talked to him in a long time." He came in and sat down, but he would just as soon not have. He didn't like being summoned to Becenti's office, and he didn't like talking about Nicholas Wager. He remembered only too well the last time Nick had been a topic of conversation with Becenti. It had been when Lucas had been faced with the very real possibility of being dismissed from the Navajo Tribal Police Force. And he would have deserved it. He had been wallowing in self-pity for months after the anthropologist left, and his job performance had deteriorated into nothing. He came in late to work, or not at all. He bungled the simplest of assignments or he forgot them altogether. He'd been drunk and disorderly on a number of occasions.

But Becenti had given him the option of telling him everything that had led up to his shameful behavior—and he meant everything—or turning in his badge and revolver that very day. Becenti was a fair man, but he had no intention of giving second chances to a recalcitrant officer without knowing the details. Lucas had swallowed what little had been left of his pride and told him. He left out nothing. It was a relief to finally say the words. He even told Becenti about his old college friend, Nicholas Wager, who had introduced him to Sara Catherine McCay and who had had to tell him about the abortion. In the end, Becenti must have thought Lucas Singer was worth salvaging.

"You think you can get anything out of him?" Becenti asked now.

"Like what?"

"Like what the hell two of their agents think they're doing here on the reservation."

"I don't know. I can try."

"I got four calls at home this morning before I even finished my coffee, all of them apparently about the same two guys. You put it to Wager this way. You tell him it looks like the bureau has got two loose cannons out here who have stepped way out of line. You tell him the day has come and gone when we'll sit still for it. If they've got two agents who are too extreme for polite white society, they don't need to think they can just transfer them out here and let them run wild. You tell him to tell *his* superior I'm letting you bring the complaint through the back door first—but if that doesn't do it, there's going to be hell to pay because I know *exactly* whose cage to rattle."

"Anything else?" Lucas asked as he stood up to go. He was expecting to be assigned to do public relations for the tribe and Mark Baron's family.

"No," Becenti said. "Yes. Don't blow your paycheck on Central Avenue."

Lucas was still smiling at Becenti's small joke when he left the building. At certain times of the year, Central Avenue ran hot with prostitutes, and Lucas's amusement came from the fact that the captain's admonishment to stay away from them was the same remark he might have made to any of his officers—not just the ones notorious for their woman troubles. Perhaps he was going to get past his history with Sara Catherine McCay after all.

He telephoned Nick as soon as he got to Albuquerque, clearly taking him aback with his out-of-the-blue invitation for lunch. Lucas had first met Nicholas Wager when they were eighteen-year-old freshmen at the University of New Mexico, and as unlikely as it might have seemed, he had become fast friends with this sensitive bookworm of a white boy, taking Nick home with him countless numbers of times during their four years at school, teaching him to eat fry bread and to dip sheep and to ride a horse well enough to impress Nick's extremely unimpressionable father. Lucas had understood Nick's situation perfectly. He knew only too well how hard it was to make oneself fit white male society's idea of what a "real" man should be. Lucas wondered if Nick's father had mellowed enough to be pleased that Nick worked for the FBI. Probably not. Nick's job was computer programming and not field work. The macho senior Wager likely had no use for a son who didn't arrest or kill somebody regularly.

He and Nick agreed to meet at the Country Bar-B-Q, a favorite place for both of them when they'd been at the university. Nick was already waiting when Lucas arrived, a changed, older-looking Nick than when they'd last talked face-to-face nearly two years ago. Lucas forced aside that particular memory, one of Nick worried and upset and trying to be kind, trying to break it to him gently that Sara Catherine McCay wanted nothing more to do with him and that his persistence had become an embarrassment to her. And, finally, that what would have been a baby, *his* baby, was long gone.

"My God, look at you!" Nick said, slapping him hard on the back, entirely oblivious to the restaurant onlookers. "How is it you look just like you did in college and I look like my old man?"

"You don't eat enough mutton stew and fry bread, Wager. I tried to tell you that years ago."

"Years," Nick said, shaking his head. "How many—fourteen? God, has it been that long since we started our great academic adventure? Can you belive it? Where did the time go? You're still with the tribal police, I see. How's the family? How's Dolly?"

"Fine," Lucas managed to squeeze in. He had forgotten that talking to Nick could be all rapid-fire questions.

"So what brings you to Albuquerque? Business or pleasure? How long are you going to be here?"

"I need a favor," Lucas said.

"What kind of favor?" Nick asked, his hand stopping midreach for the menu. Lucas realized immediately that Nick expected the favor to have something to do with Sara.

"It's a reservation problem—but let's order first and then I'll tell you."

The food came, delicious as always. Lucas filled Nick in on the doings of the Singer clan, waiting until they were nearly done eating before he gave him the message from Becenti as word for word as he could make it.

"I'll pass it on, Lucas," Nick said. "But the bureau is pretty arrogant. You and Becenti both know that. I doubt it's going to do any good."

"Yeah, well, Becenti wanted to give the back door approach a shot. All you can do is tell them he's pissed—and with good reason, I gather."

They sat for a while in silence, Lucas finishing the last of his coffee.

"You aren't going to ask me about her, are you?" Nick said finally.

"No."

"She's asked about you."

Lucas made no comment, and once again the silence lengthened.

"I . . . went home a few months ago," Nick said. "A vacation with the whole Wager family at Cape Cod. Her family was at their place. I saw her at church."

"Church?" Lucas said, laughing.

"Stranger things have happened."

"I doubt it."

"She wanted to know if you were . . . all right."

"She wanted to know if I was over her," Lucas said. "She wanted to know if she could ever come back here to do more research or whatever the hell she's doing now—without being annoyed by some lovesick Indian. She wanted to know if I'd gotten all this into the proper perspective, so that if she *did* come back and found herself in the mood some night, she could call on me and not have to worry about the emotional consequences."

Nick stared at him across the table. He had no guile and never had had. He would never have made a poker player or an FBI field agent. The truth of what Lucas had said was clearly reflected in his eyes.

"I've got to get back to Window Rock. It was good seeing you again, man," Lucas said. He picked up the check and stood up.

"Lucas, there's one other thing. If you hadn't called, I would have come out to Window Rock to see you. I wanted to give you some news. Good news—at least I think so. I'm . . . getting married in the fall."

"That's great!" Lucas said sincerely. "Who's the lucky girl?"

"It's Sara, Lucas."

"Sara," Lucas repeated, for the briefest of moments not grasping the significance of the name.

My Sara? he almost said when he did.

"We've been seeing a lot of each other since the vacation on the Cape. I fly back East almost every weekend. She's changed, Lucas—"

"Yeah, right."

"We grew up together, Lucas. I know everything there is to know about her. I accept it. She doesn't have to pretend with me."

"For your sake, Nick, I sure to God hope so. I have to go. I—"

He abruptly walked away, his mind in turmoil. He had paid the check before he realized that he had the opportunity to behave with some dignity. And he was going to do it, if it killed him. He was *not* the same wreck of a man he'd been two years ago.

He walked back to the table. Nick was still sitting there.

"I don't want you to send me an invitation," Lucas said when Nick looked up. "You were always a good friend to me. I...hope the two of you will be happy."

Nick smiled the same smile he'd had at eighteen, the one of relief and gratitude when something turned out not to be the hell he expected. "Thanks, Lucas. Thanks, man—"

But Lucas was already on his way out again, and he didn't look back. He got inside the Navajo Tribal Police vehicle and sat there. He was coming unraveled, and he tried reaching deep inside himself for the calmness, for the harmony he'd always been taught should be his goal. It wasn't there. It had been replaced by jealousy and anger and a sense of betrayal that was akin to physical pain. Nicholas Wager was his friend, had always been his friend, and he was marrying Sara Catherine McCay.

"Damn it!" he shouted, pounding the steering wheel hard once with his fist before he started the engine and recklessly drove away.

He tried not to think about her, but memory after memory fell into his consciousness like stones. Sara, his lover. *His* lover. Sara, eager for him and whispering his name.

Sara...

Was it the same with her and Nick?

He waited until the last possible moment to make a decision about getting onto the highway, deliberately passing the first three access ramps.

You don't know everything about her, Nick! Not everything!

Or perhaps he did. Perhaps Sara had given him every minute detail.

He couldn't face the long drive to Window Rock with nothing to keep his mind off Nick's announcement. He abruptly made a turn, causing the driver behind him to slam on brakes, and he headed back in the direction he'd come—toward the University of New Mexico Hospital trauma center.

Sloan gradually became aware that someone was seated nearby, someone who turned the pages of a magazine from time to time and drank coffee. She could smell the coffee, and she shifted her position slightly in the corner of the waiting room sofa, letting the full realization of where she was and why wash over her before she opened her eyes. It wasn't time for visitors to be let into the intensive care unit again. It was too quiet. She had stayed the night and most of the day at the hospital, and already she was sensitive to the sounds of the ICU routine—elevator doors opening again and again, and a murmur of voices when it was time for the friends and family to gather for the fifteen minutes allotted them with a patient.

"Ms. Baron?" a voice said, and she jumped violently.

"I'm sorry," he said. "I thought you were awake."

"I was," she said, trying to focus on the man who had spoken. "And I wasn't." She sat up and painfully straightened her legs. She had learned to nap in small places when she was in nursing school, a skill that had been of great use to her in the years since. The less room one took up, the less likely someone was to interrupt precious sleeping time—but it was agony on the knee joints.

"I'm Officer Lucas Singer," he said. "Navajo Tribal Police."

"Oh," she said, looking up from rubbing her aching knees. "We spoke on the telephone. Sloan Baron," she said, extending her hand.

At first, she thought he wasn't going to take it, but then he did, his handshake warm and firm, regardless of his initial hesitancy. She noted that he must be left-handed, because he wore his watch on his right wrist, but she immediately changed her mind because the gun and holster was on his right hip. He had black hair, cut very short, and he wore a khaki police uniform with all the usual police paraphernalia and pouches hanging from his belt.

"I'm sorry about your brother," he said. "Has there been any change?"

"No," she said tiredly. "Well, he's begun to fight the ventilator, but they don't think that's a good sign."

Lucas noted the slight emphasis on the word "they." She disagreed with the person who had made the observation about the ventilator. Where did this arrogance in *belagana* women come from? he wondered. Why did they seem to be so damned sure about everything? Sara had been the same way.

His mind went abruptly to the restaurant.

I'm . . . getting married, Lucas.

It's Sara, Lucas—

Damn, Nick! She'll eat you alive!

He forced himself to look at Sloan Baron. This wasn't working. He had wanted to occupy himself with some task, but he shouldn't have come here. He was too agitated, too out of harmony, to deal with a white woman now. When she offered him her hand, he hadn't wanted to touch her. He hadn't wanted anything to do with her. He was careful not to meet her eyes. He didn't want to see the same silent question white women always asked.

What are you? Are you a man?

Sloan Baron was neither pretty nor ugly to him. She was small and fragile-looking. Her hair was light brown and pulled back from her face into some kind of complicated braid that started at the crown of her head. She'd had a restless night. It was coming undone in places. She looked disheveled and exhausted. She needed clean clothes and a bath.

The silence grew uncomfortably long. Sloan glanced at him. He seemed to be waiting, for what, she had no idea. She read the insignia on his uniform sleeve, realizing that it hadn't really occurred to her when she talked to him that an officer from the Navajo Tribal Police would actually be Navajo—or at least she assumed he was Navajo.

"You were the investigating officer," she said finally. "Do you know what happened to Mark?"

"Not really," he said. "There were skid marks, so he didn't fall asleep."

"I see. What about my nephew? I've tried to reach Inez Yazzie several times today. She hasn't returned any of my calls."

"Your nephew is being well taken care of. You don't have to worry about him."

She frowned slightly at his tone of voice—not defensive, exactly, or belligerent, but enough of *something* for her to realize that he was finding this hospital visit not at all to his liking. She stared at him until he met her eyes. He didn't immediately look away, but she could feel how much he wanted to.

"When can I see him?" she asked.

"The boy's in Window Rock," he answered—as if he was pointing out the obvious to someone particularly dull-witted.

"How far away is that?"

"A hundred and fifty miles."

"Or more," she said sarcastically and not quite under her breath.

"Yes," he agreed, as if he knew she meant for him to hear her.

"Will you be seeing Inez Yazzie any time soon?"

"I don't know."

"Could you make an effort to see her?"

He stared at her for a moment before he answered. "I could do that."

"Good. I want to talk to her. There is a lot I want to know. And I want to see William as soon as possible."

"I've told you he's—"

"I know what you told me," Sloan said. "Look, Officer Singer, I can see you have things you'd much rather be doing. You've made your token visit or whatever this is and we're beginning to get on each other's nerves. I have enough to worry about—" she stood up, and the room swayed "—to worry about—" she repeated before her knees buckled.

He had her by both forearms. "Sit down," he said. "Put your head down."

"I know what to do," she said irritably, her head flopping forward onto her knees whether she wanted it to or not. "Oh—"

"How long since you've had anything to eat?" she heard him ask, his voice seeming to come from far away and his tone suggesting that he already knew she'd been stupid enough to have gone a long time without food.

"Here, take a whiff of this," another voice said. The crushed ampoule of ammonia that passed under her nose nearly took the top of her head off.

"I'm all right!" Sloan said, trying to get away from the ammonia fumes.

"Yeah, the officer and I can see that, can't we, Officer Singer?"

Sloan lifted her head. One of the ICU nurses stood ready to give her another whiff. "Enough," she said. "I'm all right."

"No, you aren't," the nurse said. "You need to call somebody to come and get you right now."

"I have to be here."

"No, you don't," the nurse said. "Look, honey," she said, putting her cool hand on the side of Sloan's face. "You're one of us. You *know* we don't have time to look after you, too. I want you to go back to the motel for a while. Eat something. Sleep a couple of hours and then come back. I'll call you if anything changes with Mark. I swear. Okay?"

Sloan didn't say anything.

"Are you on a time clock, Officer Singer?" the nurse asked.

"No," he answered. "I'll take her."

"I don't—" Sloan began.

"Please!" the nurse said. "Give me a break here, will you? I've already got a Baron to take care of—I don't need *two*."

"All right," Sloan said after a moment. "I'll go. You'll call me?"

"Swear to God," the nurse said. "We've got your motel number on the chart. One of us will call if you need to get back here. Can you stand up now?"

"Yes," Sloan answered, but her knees were still wobbly. "I'm okay," she said to Singer. "I don't want to bother you. I can call Patrick."

"I'll drive you to the motel, Ms. Baron. Do you want to take a quick look at your brother before you go?"

The empathy that his question suggested surprised her. "Yes," she said. She walked with the nurse to the double doors of the intensive care unit, slipping quietly inside and going to the cubicle where Mark lay. She stayed only a moment, just long enough to assess the cardiac monitor and the drip of the intravenous fluids and to touch his hand. Meggie had braved seeing her father like this—several times. Patrick had absolutely refused, staying in the waiting room or the cafeteria or the snack bar until she'd sent them both back to the motel. She felt completely overwhelmed. She'd been functioning on nothing but nerves for days now, and she had just about reached her limit.

Singer was waiting for her when she came out.

"I'm all right," she said, because she could feel him trying to decide. Her voice was husky, and she was afraid she was going to cry. She didn't want him to do this errand of mercy, or whatever it was, for her, but she no longer had the strength to argue.

He watched her carefully as they rode down in the elevator, and when they crossed the main lobby on the way outside, he took her firmly by the arm.

"I'm not going to fold up again," she assured him, but he didn't let go. "Great," she said. "Led out by a policeman. Everybody's going to think I robbed a bank."

"I took responsibility for you," he said. "If you fall and get hurt, I don't want to get sued."

She looked at him. He meant it.

"What time is it?" she asked.

"Almost three o'clock."

The short walk across the parking lot to where he'd parked his official-looking police vehicle left her completely breathless. After only a few steps, she was glad he had her by the arm.

"I—don't know—what's wrong with me," she said.

"The altitude is part of it," he said as he hunted for the key to unlock the truck door. "Albuquerque is a mile high. You probably aren't used to it. How high is your part of North Carolina?"

"About as high as the downtown curb—did I say I was from North Carolina?"

"Somebody did," he answered.

Three men and a woman, who were apparently on their way into the trauma center, walked by. Singer still had her by the arm, and all of them stared curiously.

"I think you're right," he said.

"About what?"

"About people thinking you robbed a bank."

She laughed. Her laughter was short-lived and it made her head hurt, but it was genuine. As miserable and worried as she felt, this puzzling man had made her laugh, something he seemed to have an aversion to doing himself. No laughter. No smiles. Only a kind of grave intensity she couldn't penetrate with meager conversation.

Except for asking the name of the motel, he didn't talk to her on the way there. She sat quietly against the door as he turned onto Central Avenue, trying her best to conquer the fatigue and the sadness that threatened to roll over her. She could feel her control slipping. She bit down on her lip and clasped her hands tightly in her lap. A tear slid down her cheek anyway. She turned her face away and stared out the side window, seeing nothing.

After a moment, something brushed her arm—a box of tissues Singer produced from somewhere and held out to her. She took one. He indicated with the box that she was being too conservative, so she took another. And another.

"Sorry," she said as she wiped her eyes, her voice barely a whisper.

He set the box of tissues on the seat between them.

"I can make it from here," she said when he pulled into the motel parking lot.

He made a sound that could have been yes or no or maybe, and he got out of the vehicle and came around to her side before her feet had touched the ground.

"Have you got your key?" he asked.

She had it in her jeans pocket, and she had a lot of trouble getting it out. He waited patiently, silently holding his hand out when she finally produced it.

Patrick opened the motel room door before he got a chance to use it.

"Jeez, Sloan," he said, his face filled with worry. "What's wrong?"

"What's wrong?" Meggie echoed behind him.

"Nothing. Officer Singer offered to drive me back—"

"Your aunt is exhausted," Singer interrupted. "She nearly fainted at the hospital. She needs to eat something and she needs to sleep for a while. Can the two of you manage that?"

"Officer Singer—" Sloan said.

"They need to know what happened, Ms. Baron. You won't do them any good if you fall on your face. Sit down. Please."

"I can run get a milk shake from the fast-food place," Meggie said. "I've been there twice already, haven't I, Patrick?"

"Yeah, yeah," Patrick said, obviously still worried, thanks to Singer. "Here, take this money."

"You don't have to run, Meggie," Sloan said, but Meggie was already out the door.

Sloan stayed where she was on the only chair. Patrick and Singer moved out of her line of vision. She could hear them talking, but she was too tired to make any sense of what they said. She closed her eyes and took a deep breath, and she must have nodded off to sleep, because she jumped when the door flew open—Meggie with the milk shake.

The milk shake was basic vanilla, and she was hungrier than she thought. She finished it entirely, not worrying about manners and the fact that she was the only one eating.

"I'm going now," Singer said to her. "I've spoken with Patrick and Meggie. They know what to do if they need—"

"What did you do? Tell them to call 911?"

"Yes," he said frankly. "Look. I realize you must be used to looking after everything yourself, but you need to let go for a little while. It's not good to—"

"Thank you for your help," Sloan interrupted. "I appreciate everything you've done."

His eyes held hers for a moment. "Fine," he said, and he turned to go.

She immediately stretched out on the bed behind her, and she was asleep before she heard the door close.

Chapter Five

As much as Sloan needed to sleep, she had slept too long. She woke up with the sun shining through a crack in the motel room drapes, and rather than feeling refreshed, she felt as if she was in some kind of stupor. It took a great effort for her to think, much less get herself and Meggie ready to return to the hospital. If Patrick had been anything but completely cooperative, she wouldn't have made it.

When they entered the hospital lobby, she was acutely aware of the air of quiet desperation that seemed to permeate everything. Outside the intensive care unit, among the family members who chatted and occasionally laughed, the sense of desperation intensified. She wasn't immediately allowed in to see Mark because of some procedure that was being done, and she waited impatiently in the hall, her anxiety rising.

"Are you worrying?" Meggie asked beside her.

"Yes."

"About my dad and Will, too, right?"

"Yes," she said again, looking down at Meggie and wondering if her policy of always trying to be truthful was a good one.

"Me, too," Meggie said.

They had to move out of the way of a volunteer with a flower cart.

"Well, I guess that's better than the two of us worrying all by ourselves," Sloan said. "Where did Patrick go?"

Meggie shrugged; they both sighed.

"I'm trying not to worry," Meggie said. "Officer Singer said it didn't help and it upset my harmony—but I don't know what I'm supposed to do. If you're worried, you're worried."

"When did you talk to Officer Singer?" Sloan said, surprised.

"While you were asleep. I asked him some things about . . . my dad. We sat outside on the steps so we wouldn't bother you."

"What kind of things?"

Meggie gave another small shrug. "It was personal."

"I see," Sloan said, a little miffed.

"Officer Singer said it was all right to ask him whatever I wanted to know," Meggie said defensively.

"Well, it was, if he said so. Did he answer your questions?"

"Some he did. Some he didn't know the answer. He said maybe nobody knew the answer except my father. And I'd have to ask him if I got the chance. I like Officer Singer. *He* doesn't treat me like a dumb kid."

Sloan frowned, but she made no comment. As much as she disliked Meggie's discussing their private family matters with Singer, she didn't ask anything else. She decided to leave another message for Inez Yazzie instead, walking a short distance away from the waiting area to use a more isolated pay telephone. The people in the waiting room were desperate for something to take their minds off their ordeal, and she didn't want to make a telephone call to Window Rock with a rapt audience.

"Do you have *any* idea where I can reach her?" she asked Mary Skeets, because, as usual, Inez was nowhere to be found.

"No, Ms. Baron, I'm sorry. Inez is never in one place for very long. I'm not allowed to give out her home number, but I'll make sure she gets your message if she stops in. How is your brother?"

"I haven't seen him yet this morning," Sloan said. "But thank you for asking." She had to swallow several times to keep from crying. It was becoming all too clear that whether she'd slept longer than she'd intended or not, it hadn't been enough to re-store her self-control. "I've taken enough of your time," she said after a moment. "I really do need to speak to Mrs. Yazzie. I need to know about my nephew. If he's alone, he must be—"

"You don't have to worry about him," Mary Skeets said. "He's being well taken care of."

So you and Lucas Singer keep telling me, Sloan thought. But Mary sounded sincere enough, and a lot less annoyed that Sloan might be concerned than Lucas Singer had.

She glanced down the hallway. Meggie was waving frantically for her to hurry. Sloan said goodbye and walked toward the waiting room. How many messages had she left for Inez Yazzie? Three? Four? She could think of no legitimate reason the woman hadn't returned any of her calls. She had left the motel number and the number of the pay phone in the waiting area—regardless of the audience. How busy could this woman be?

The same nurse—the one named Kelly who had been here yesterday, waited outside the double doors of the intensive care unit.

"Good news, honey," she said as soon as Sloan walked up. "He's off the ventilator. He gave them hell fighting that thing last night. The doctor took him off about four this morning. And so far so good—except he's running an abnormal strip. Has he had heart problems before? The doctor's not sure if this is something he's had or something caused by the accident."

"I don't know," Sloan said. "I haven't seen him in some time."

"Well, he's breathing on his own and he's been asking for you. And that's good. How long you can stay depends on how excited he gets, okay? And Number One Daughter here gets to sit this one out," Kelly said to Meggie. "You can come in later, baby."

"Have I *got* to wait in the waiting room?" Meggie asked.

"Yes," both Sloan and the nurse answered.

"I've looked at every magazine in there five hundred times," she complained, but she went. "Patrick's in here," she called when she reached the door.

"Then stay with him," Sloan said. "And in the waiting area so I can find you," she added to keep from having to look all over the hospital for them when she came out.

She took a deep breath before she followed Kelly through the double doors, hesitating before she approached Mark's bed. The last thing she wanted to do was cry.

Mark knew she was there even before she took his hand.

"Sloan," he whispered, his voice dry and raspy and pained. His face was swollen past the point of recognition, and the fact that she hadn't seen him in so long didn't help. His fingers squeezed hers. "Sloan."

"I'm here, Mark," she said, bending down close. "Don't try to talk."

"Patrick—and Meggie—"

"They're outside. Try to rest now. You can see them later."

"No, no," he said, his fingers digging into hers. "Sloan—go home. Take my—kids and—go—home."

"Mark, it's all right," she said, searching his face for some overt sign of mental confusion. All she saw was her brother—in anguish. "Mark, you don't have to—"

"Do it—Sloan! William—before it's—"

He abruptly closed his eyes.

"Mark? What about William, Mark?"

"Come on," Kelly said at her elbow. "This is too much for him. He's throwing some PVCs. Come on, let him settle down."

"Mark, I'll come back later," Sloan said, near tears.

"No," he said distinctly. "No."

She stood for a moment longer before she gave in to the nurse's insistent pulling at her sleeve.

"Hang in there," Kelly whispered as she walked with her to the double doors. "He may not be coherent. You know how it goes."

Yes, Sloan thought. She knew. She looked at Mark once before she stepped out into the hallway. Had he been lucid? She couldn't tell with any certainty. But surely he hadn't meant that he wanted her to leave with Meggie and Patrick *now*. If he had been in his right mind, then she didn't understand any of this.

She stood for a moment before she went looking for Meggie and Patrick. More visitors had arrived since she went in to see Mark. The waiting area was crowded, Meggie had been reduced to sitting on the edge of the low table that held all the magazines she'd complained of having looked at five hundred times. But she wasn't looking at magazines now. She was talking to Lucas Singer.

Lucas saw Sloan as soon as she came out of the intensive care unit. She looked every bit as beleaguered today as she had yesterday. He watched her walk in his direction, then pause for a moment to regain her composure. She didn't want the little girl, Meggie, to see how distressed she was, a considerate if useless gesture, Lucas thought. Meggie Baron was astute for a child. He doubted that very much escaped her. And, regardless of what he felt about white women, he was reasonably certain that this one cared about her brother's children. Or at least his white children.

"Can I go in now?" Meggie asked immediately.

"No," Sloan said, her eyes on Lucas. "No more visitors right now."

"Sloan..." Meggie protested.

"Meggie, that's the way it is. I'm sorry. Where is Patrick?"

"Around somewhere," Meggie said vaguely. "He said he was hungry and he was tired of sitting."

"I told him to stay with you."

"No, you told *me* to stay with him. And you said not to leave here, so Officer Singer is baby-sitting me."

"Officer Singer," Sloan Baron said, finally acknowledging him.

Lucas met her eyes, though it took a certain amount of effort. She seemed to always be listening for what he meant, regardless of what he said. He could feel her waiting for him to say what he was doing here again today, an unusual thing in a white person. It had been his experience that white people rarely waited for anything.

The truth of the matter was that he was here because Becenti had finally made it his assignment. He had had to stay the night in Albuquerque, because he followed yet another of Becenti's cost-effective memos. All officers were supposed to check in before they returned from a distant assignment. In the past, it had been a fruitless gesture on Lucas's part. This time he had two urgent messages, both of them from Nicholas Wager. Becenti ordered him to stay in Albuquerque to follow up on Nick's telephone calls and to justify the delay in his return by making a courtesy call on Mark Baron's family. Lucas didn't mention that Nick's urgency likely had more to do with his wedding plans than with their talk about overly zealous FBI agents, and he didn't mention that he'd already made the courtesy call. He simply let these latest developments become part of the natural pattern, pulling into an economy motel near Interstate 40 and lying for hours in the dark while he waited for his harmony to return.

He kept thinking about the *hataalii* Becenti had sent him to see when he'd come so close to ruining his career. Lucas had believed in very little then, and certainly not in the powers of a decrepit Navajo healer to cure him. He hadn't particularly wanted to be cured. He had wallowed in his misery so long he couldn't remember what it had felt like to be in harmony. But he'd gone to see the old man, fully aware that Becenti's cost-cutting policies extended to him, too. It was considerably cheaper to rehabilitate an already trained and seasoned officer than to have to start over with a new one.

The old *hataalii*, Hosteen Martin Anagal, had looked at the horizon for a long time and had asked him nothing. Lucas had waited, quietly and with a respect he didn't feel.

"You cannot destroy the pain with liquor or obliging women, my son," the old man finally said in a voice as brittle and dry as the desert itself. "You cannot hide from it. You cannot run from it. You have let your pain take you from the Beauty Way. Your pain is very strong. The road out—the road to beauty—is always the same road. You must turn around and face this pain. You must go *through* the pain. You must feel it and know that the Beauty

Way is just on the other side. You must face what you have let
yourself become."

What *he* had let himself become. In spite of his college educa-
tion. In spite of his mother's prayers.

Undependable. Worthless. Drunken. A living, breathing ex-
ample of the white man's racial prejudice, and all because a white
woman had rejected him. He had faced it. He had felt the pain.
And, with Hosteen Anagal and the ancient healing rituals of The
People, he had let the pain become only a memory. The old man
had set him firmly on the way to finding himself again, but he had
failed to mention that a memory could hurt as much as the real
thing.

But he was better this morning, he thought. When he had finally slept, he slept well. It was as if he had been kicked and kicked
hard in an old, healed-over wound. At first it had hurt as badly as
when the injury was done, but the scar had held, and now the pain
seemed to be receding.

"Officer Singer," Sloan Baron said again, though this time it
was a prelude to something.

"How is your brother this morning?" he asked instead of
waiting to hear what she wanted to say, an act of rudeness on his
part that a white woman from North Carolina wouldn't notice.

Her eyes immediately welled with tears, and she looked away.
"He's awake," she said. "And off the ventilator. He...knows me.
I think." She took a deep breath; her mouth trembled slightly. She
abruptly looked at him. "Is Inez Yazzie trying to avoid me?" she
asked bluntly.

Lucas hesitated before he answered. His earlier assessment had
been correct. This woman was no better off now than when he'd
left her at the motel. She was still upset about her brother, off the
ventilator or not, and now she intended to further disrupt her
harmony by confronting him about Inez.

"Meggie says the two of you haven't eaten yet this morning,"
he said, because it was obvious to him that Sloan Baron had
learned nothing from her fainting episode yesterday afternoon.
"Do you want to go to the cafeteria? We can talk there."

Sloan stared at him for a moment, then nodded. She understood perfectly what he didn't say.

This child needs to eat whether you starve yourself or not.

And she didn't need his prompting to take care of Meggie. She
had planned for all of them to have breakfast as soon as she'd seen
Mark. She made no excuses for Meggie's unfed state, because she
didn't owe this man any explanations.

"Don't you and Miss Meggie worry," one of the men who always seemed to be in the waiting room said. "I'll tell them where you are if they come looking for you."

"Thanks, Mr. Fred," Meggie said. "He calls me Miss Meggie—I call him Mr. Fred," she said to Singer.

Sloan smiled her gratitude. "Would you tell my nephew Patrick, too, if he shows up? He's the tall boy with red hair."

"Will do," the man said. "Enjoy."

The cafeteria was nearly empty and noticeably quiet except for an occasional clatter of dishes and pans. And cheap, Sloan noted with a certain amount of relief. She could smell brewed coffee and bacon as she moved down the line of food, and she had to dodge a few latecomers, harried hospital personnel, who were accustomed to grabbing what they wanted and going around the visitors who invariably held up the line. She noted with mild interest that Lucas Singer bypassed the usual bacon and egg breakfast she would have expected a working man to choose. She thought perhaps he'd already eaten—until he reached the pancakes and muffins.

"I'm hungry," he said to Meggie, who giggled at the pile on his plate.

"I was just about almost ready to guess that," Meggie said.

They sat down in a far corner, and they ate in silence. Or at least Sloan ate in silence. Meggie and Singer carried the conversation entirely, and if he minded her inquisitiveness, it didn't show.

"Can I go look at the pictures?" Meggie asked as soon as she'd finished her own pile of pancakes, because there was a large display of photographs—an employees' costume charity event of some kind.

"Yes," Sloan said. She waited until Meggie was out of earshot. "Are you going to answer my question?" she asked Singer. "Is Inez Yazzie trying to avoid me?"

"Yes," he said simply.

"Yes, you'll answer the question or yes, she's avoiding me."

"I think Inez is avoiding you," he said.

"Why?"

"I don't know. I can say I think she's trying to avoid you, because I believe it's true. You would have to ask *her* to know why."

"If I could ever find her," she said, more to herself than to him. She looked at him. "William is a surprise to me. I didn't know Mark had another son. Did Inez tell you that?"

"Yes."

"Is that the reason, then? Because I didn't know? Does she think I'm some kind of horrible person because Mark didn't tell me? I'm not. I don't know why he didn't bother to let me know he had another child. He certainly didn't mind leaving his other two children with me. I know *you* think I never feed anybody, including myself, but I do take good care of Meggie and Patrick. It hasn't been easy—" She abruptly stopped. "I'm sorry. I..." She forced herself to stop talking. She refused to let the fact that he seemed to be listening make her forget her earlier assessment of him. This man did *not* want to be here.

He finished the cup of coffee he was drinking. "Don't leave," he said, getting up from the table.

Sloan watched him walk to the pay phone on the opposite side of the cafeteria. He was lean, his leanness accentuated by the cut of the khaki uniform. He was taller than she—close to six feet, she guessed, but not more. He had a very precise, military way of walking and standing. Perhaps he *was* ex-military, or perhaps he'd learned it in whatever police academy he'd attended. She had no doubt that he had attended one. He had that same I-am-in-charge-here air about him police officers always affected.

He dialed a number and spoke to someone, then waited for a time, then spoke to someone again. Then he motioned for her to come over. She went.

"Inez Yazzie?" she asked when he held out the receiver, because she believed him able to locate the elusive Mrs. Yazzie, if he wanted.

"No. William Baron."

"William?" she said incredulously.

"Do you want to talk to him?"

"Yes!" she said.

"Will," he said into the receiver, listening for a moment. "Here she is."

"He knows about me?" she asked as she took the phone.

"I told him."

"Will?" she said. "Hello. This is your Aunt Sloan—he's telling somebody there's a lady talking to him," she whispered to Singer.

"My mother," Singer said, and Sloan looked at him in surprise. No wonder he'd gotten the child on the telephone so easily, she thought. And no wonder he had been so touchy when she'd been concerned about the kind of care her nephew might be getting.

"Will?" she said again. "Are you there? This is your Aunt Sloan."

"I don't got a aunt," Will Baron told her. "She's in her car."

"Yes, you do. That's me. I'm your aunt. I came in a car from North Carolina."

"Do you got a name?" he wanted to know.

"Sloan," she told him. "My name is Sloan. Can you say that—Sloan? No," she whispered to Lucas.

"Have you got a boy?" Will asked.

"No, no boys, only nephews. A big nephew named Patrick Baron. And another big nephew named Will Baron—"

"Me!" he cried.

"Yes, you," Sloan assured him. "You are my other big nephew." She looked at Lucas and smiled.

Lucas resisted the urge to smile in return. He would not smile and he would not be impressed that she was savvy enough about three-year-old boys to know better than to call Will Baron little. He had intended only to relieve some of this woman's sadness and worry, but the sudden transformation in her, a transformation he essentially had brought about, left him feeling perplexed and uneasy.

Sloan glanced away from him, wondering if she'd done something to offend him. Perhaps it was some kind of cultural thing, she thought, to always be so intense and grim.

"Are you a family?" she thought Will asked next. "I'm *your* family," she said, hoping she was answering what the child wanted to know.

"Do you know any coyote stories?"

"Coyote story?" she said, now completely lost. "No. You'll have to tell me the coyote story—"

"Bye-bye, sweet sugar!" Will cried suddenly, and Sloan laughed out loud. There was a loud clunking noise in her ear and then a soft female voice in a language she didn't understand.

"I think he's through talking," she said, handing Lucas the receiver. "And I think this is for you."

He took the receiver, and she waited while he spoke to the woman in what apparently was his second language. Or his first. She stood nearby and frankly listened. His side of the conversation was mostly monosyllables that seemed to be the English equivalent of "Yes, I see" and "Is that so?"

She waited until he'd hung up the phone.

"Thank you," she said when he turned around.

"My mother..." Lucas began, but he lost his train of thought, because he realized suddenly why he'd made the telephone call to the receiving home in Window Rock. He wanted to see this woman smile again, the way she had when he'd made that stupid remark yesterday about her being mistaken for a bank robber and the way she was smiling now. He had wanted to see her smile, and worse, he'd wanted to be the reason for it. What was this weakness he had for needy white women? In her own way, Sara had been just as needy as Sloan Baron. Sara had a penchant for shocking the establishment, and he'd been only too happy to oblige. Sloan Baron needed a reason to smile, and he'd been ready to oblige her, as well.

"Your mother?" Sloan prompted.

He reached into his shirt pocket and brought out a small notepad and pencil, scribbling on the top sheet and tearing it off. "This is the receiving home telephone number. My mother asks that you call again. About the same time of the morning would be good. She says that you've made a little boy very happy today."

"It was mutual. Thank you," she said again. She took the slip of paper he gave her and put it into her purse. She felt awkward suddenly, and she looked around for Meggie. Meggie was still at the display of photographs, but Patrick had arrived, for once seeming to listen to whatever Meggie was telling him instead of ignoring her.

Sloan walked over to them.

"Did I miss the boat?" Patrick asked.

"He's already eaten one time, I bet," Meggie said, rolling her eyes.

"I got room for more—hey! Officer Singer!" Patrick said around Sloan, leaning out and giving Lucas Singer the kind of masculine, knuckle-punching greeting that had always fascinated her, because these secret-handshake, male-bonding rituals seemed to be universally understood—among males. She supposed that Patrick's enthusiasm at seeing Singer must be because he, too, had sat on the motel steps yesterday and talked to the man.

"I need to get back," Sloan said.

"Fine by me," Patrick said.

She looked at him for a moment. This was neither the time nor the place for an argument. "Patrick, I just don't want you to do anything you're going to regret," she said, trying to keep the peace and still say what needed saying.

He shrugged. "I'm still hungry, Sloan. Can I have some money?"

She hesitated, then gave him a five-dollar bill. She couldn't force him to see his father. She couldn't force him to pretend to be a dutiful son. She had no idea what to do about him—or for him.

"Hey, Officer Singer," Patrick said. "Some lady with a clipboard was looking for you."

"Lady with a clipboard?" Lucas said.

"One of those hospital women who run around with clipboards and act like a seating hostess in a restaurant. You're supposed to call the operator."

"Where's the house phone?" Lucas asked the nearest cafeteria worker.

"Over there," a woman in a hairnet said, pointing with a serving spoon.

Lucas walked to the telephone she indicated. "Officer Lucas Singer," he said when the operator answered.

"Hold please."

There was a series of clicks. "Lucas?" Nick Wager said. "Damn, man, you're hard to track. You know how long I've been holding—"

The rest of whatever Nick said was lost in a sudden blare of background noise—car horns and traffic.

"Nick, where are you? I can't hear you."

"I'm at a pay phone. I didn't want to call you from anywhere in the building. Can you hear me now?"

"I can hear you."

"Well, I thought I'd check on that matter we discussed," Nick said, apparently still cautious. "I mean before I brought it up—so I could nose around a little first. I managed to get part of a list."

"What kind of list?"

"Surveillance list. I'll read you the names I got before I had to shut it down."

Lucas listened. There was only one name he recognized. Margaret Madman. "Do you know why they're watching these people?"

"No, but that's not all. There's one more name, Lucas."

"Whose?"

"Yours, man."

Sloan watched Lucas Singer suddenly swing around toward the wall as if he didn't want anyone to hear what he said.

"Let's go," she said to Meggie. "I don't want to wait for Patrick to eat breakfast again. Did you get enough pancakes?"

"Yes. Can I say goodbye to Officer Singer?"

"I think he's busy with whoever that is on the phone," she said, moving Meggie along. "Guess who I talked to?"

She told Meggie about her brief conversation with Will as they got on the elevator.

"Aw, Sloan, I wanted to talk to him, too," Meggie said, obviously disappointed.

"Next time," she said, resting her hand on Meggie's shoulder. "He didn't talk long. You kind of have to catch three-year-old boys on the run."

"When can we go get him?"

"As soon as we know your father's getting better, and I can find out exactly where he is."

They stepped off the elevator. A neatly dressed woman wearing high-heeled shoes and a University of New Mexico Hospital identification picture—the woman with the clipboard—approached them immediately.

"May I ask who you are here to see?" she said pleasantly.

Sloan realized something was wrong the moment she said Mark's name. She realized that all those plans, all those phone calls to the Navajo Tribal Police as she traveled across the country, and her arrangement with Mr. Fred to advise the intensive care unit staff of her whereabouts had been for nothing. She had walked into this—now—completely unaware.

The woman excused herself and went immediately through the intensive care unit double doors. Sloan managed to smile at Meggie while they waited, but the woman didn't return. She glanced at the clock on the wall. Three minutes. Five. The elevator doors behind them opened and closed at regular intervals. More and more people got off, family members arriving for their brief visitations. Sloan stood there, her hands icy cold with dread. She felt light-headed. She wanted to sit down somewhere, anywhere. But most of all, she wanted to escape the terrible news that someone behind those doors was about to bring her.

But the message bearer came from an altogether different direction.

"The Mark Baron family?" a young doctor in a green scrub suit said somewhere behind her.

"Here," Sloan answered, taking Meggie's hand and making her way to where he stood. The doctor looked tired and distracted. He, too, carried a clipboard, and his attention kept darting between it and a point somewhere above her head.

They don't teach them, she thought. *They never teach them how to do this.*

He led her off to the side, to a small room that had no other purpose than to hide the families who received bad news from the ones who still had hope. He introduced himself. He even shook Meggie's hand. Some part of her watched all this with complete detachment. Some part of her wondered whether to send Meggie to bring Patrick.

But the young doctor gave her no time to decide.

"I'm very sorry, Ms. Baron, to have to tell you that your brother expired at 9:25 a.m."

Chapter Six

"**P**atrick wants to drive back to the motel."

Sloan looked up, forcing herself to pay attention to Lucas Singer's quiet voice. She hadn't heard him come into the small side room, hadn't realized he was there until he spoke.

I can't just sit here, she thought. *I have to decide what to do.*

But the decisions she needed to make were too numerous and too obscure. She felt numb, disoriented. Meggie clung to her. And Lucas Singer stood waiting.

"Has Patrick come back?" she said, making an effort to disengage herself from Meggie so that she could stand up. "I have to tell him about Mark."

"He knows, Ms. Baron," Lucas said. "He wants to drive back to the motel now."

"No, I need him here."

"The boy needs some time alone, Ms. Baron. He's going to cry. He doesn't want you to see him."

And just how would you know that? Sloan nearly asked him, but then she realized that it didn't matter. What mattered was that she believed him.

"I've told him that I'll bring you and Meggie to the motel when you're done here," he went on in that quiet way he had. "If you'll give me the car keys, I'll take them to him."

She abruptly reached for her purse and found the keys. "Tell him to—tell him—" She shook her head in defeat. She had no instructions to give him. There were none, for this. And what kind of surrogate parent had she been if Patrick didn't want her comfort now? She took a deep breath. "Tell him Meggie and I will be there as soon as we can."

Lucas nodded and took the keys, his fingers unavoidably brushing hers. Her hand was icy cold.

"I have a call in to Mary Skeets. She's going to try to reach the people at the community college where your brother worked. He had friends there. I think they can help you."

She looked at him, her incredulity at his suggestion that anyone would be able to help clearly visible in her eyes.

"I'm very sorry about your loss," he said.

She made a feeble attempt to respond, but he didn't wait to hear it. He could at least relieve her of having to be civil to a stranger. He looked at her once before he went out, watching as she put her arms around Meggie.

Patrick was standing at the far end of the hospital corridor.

"I didn't think she'd do it," he said when Lucas handed him the keys.

"She understands," Lucas said, because he believed that to be true. If Sloan Baron hadn't understood this boy's need, she wouldn't have given him the keys.

Patrick kept glancing around him, as if he was afraid someone from the waiting area would come and ask him about his father. His mouth trembled with the effort not to cry. It struck Lucas how many times he'd seen young men—boys—in this same struggle not to give in to their emotional pain. Ones who'd been beaten half senseless by a drunken father. Ones who had killed or maimed a rival over some indifferent, worthless girl. And the bitter ones who couldn't stay on the right side of the law and who had to face yet another time when they had brought themselves and their families nothing but shame. He had recognized Patrick Baron's estrangement from his father early on—and his feigned lack of concern. Unlike Meggie, the boy hadn't been able to find it in himself to forgive whatever wrong had been done. Lucas didn't ask him if he was all right—to do so would have unraveled the boy completely.

"Drive carefully, Patrick," he said instead. "Your family has had enough grief today. Sloan says to tell you she and Meggie will come to the motel as soon as they can."

Patrick nodded and walked away. Lucas waited until he'd gotten onto the elevator before he went looking for a pay telephone.

He needed to call in to Window Rock and he needed some time and space to digest the information Nick had given him. He had no idea why his name would be on an FBI surveillance list. He'd never done anything against a federal law. Admittedly, he'd been drunk and disorderly in that bleak time after Sara's leaving, but that came under tribal jurisdiction. His only association with Margaret Madman had been that he'd arrested her once in Shiprock. There was also the possibility that she wasn't the same Margaret Madman as the one on the list, and that he wasn't the same Lucas Singer. Duplicate names were the curse of the Navajo tribe, and consequently, the curse of any Navajo policeman who had to sort through them to do his job.

Besides that, the death of the teacher from the community college had been unsettling in a way he hadn't expected. Perhaps it was because he'd walked hand in hand with the little boy, Will. He couldn't deny that his concern for the dead teacher's family far exceeded what he intended. He thought that Sloan Baron and Sara Catherine McCay, on the surface at least, were nothing alike, and yet he was clearly unable to think of one without thinking of the other. He seemed to need to compare them, as if he expected the hard lesson he'd learned from Sara to be validated somehow in Sloan Baron. It made no more sense to him than Nicholas Wager's list.

He found a telephone not in use and dialed the Navajo Tribal Police number in Window Rock.

"Anything from the community college?" he asked Mary Skeets when she answered.

"Nothing. Are you still at the trauma center?"

"For right now. I need the information from the community college, Mary."

"Captain Becenti wants to know if you called in about the FBI thing."

"I'll talk to him later," Lucas said.

"You *don't* want to talk to him now," Mary said, her tone of voice communicating clearly that the captain would not be happy to hear it and that she would be the one who would have to deal with him.

"I'll call back later when I've got more time. And see if you can hurry up that inquiry to the community college, will you?"

He made sure she had the number and hung up the phone, surprised to find Sloan Baron and Meggie standing nearby.

"Is Patrick all right?" Sloan asked immediately.

"He's upset and trying to hide it," Lucas said. "But I think he's all right. I think he needs some time by himself."

"Is that what he said? That he wanted some time alone?"

"No," Lucas said patiently. "That's what I think."

He could see the fatigue and the sorrow plainly on her face, but she seemed all right physically, in spite of the fact that Meggie clung to her so hard she was all but having to carry her.

"I have to sign some…things," she said vaguely. "I don't know how long it will take."

"I'm still waiting for Mary to call me back," he said. "I'll be here when you're ready to go."

She nodded and looked at him. "I . . . seem to always be saying this to you, but I want you to know that I—that Meggie and I—thank you for your help."

She turned and walked with Meggie to the small room where she was supposed to stay until the bureaucracy surrounding her brother's death had been satisfied. Lucas continued to wait by the telephone, wishing that he could go get coffee and that he had a cigarette. He would have given a great deal for either at that moment. Or both. And he was feeling sorry for the Baron family again. He should be back in Window Rock, doing his job, minding his own business, and all the while he was thinking how different Sloan Baron looked in a dress. Yesterday, in jeans, she'd looked small and boyish. Today, in spite of her ordeal, she looked soft and womanly in a yellow cotton dress.

The pay phone rang softly, and he immediately picked it up.

"Officer Lucas Singer, please," a woman's voice said. "He should be close by."

"Inez?" he said, surprised because the reservation grapevine was working even better than usual.

"Lucas, I've heard about the teacher from the college," she said. "We think it's best that the family be brought to his house near Chinle until the—"

"I don't know if she'll want to do that, Inez," he said. Unless he'd misjudged Sloan Baron completely, she would want to go to Window Rock to see her nephew as soon as possible.

"She'll need to go through her brother's belongings, Lucas, and she has to go to Chinle to do that. She might as well stay at the house he used until everything is settled. This is a courtesy the tribe will extend her. She'll be better off there than having to pay for a motel."

Lucas agreed—in principle. But he didn't miss the fact that this arrangement would keep Sloan Baron well away from Window Rock. He wondered, too, if the tribe knew what courtesies it was extending at Inez Yazzie's behest.

"I don't think she'll go," Lucas said again.

"She'll have to if she wants her brother's things," Inez repeated.

"And I'm supposed to tell her that."

"Yes, Lucas. You are. We feel this is the best way."

"I'll give her the information, Inez. But that's all I'll do."

"That's all I want you to do, Lucas. Do you have something to write on? I want to give you some names and telephone numbers—the people you asked Mary Skeets to find out about. She needs to talk to them, I guess. And she needs to make the funeral arrangements. She may want to take the body back home with her—white people worry about things like that."

Yes, Lucas thought. They seemed to worry a great deal about where and how to put a body after it was dead and empty. And a being in the womb caused at least one of them no concern at all.

He pushed the thought aside. He would not think about that. Sara was Nick Wager's problem now.

He wrote down the names and the telephone numbers. Then he went to the side room where Sloan Baron waited. He knocked quietly on the door, not wanting to intrude if she needed privacy. The door opened almost immediately.

"Excuse me, Officer Singer," Meggie said, sliding past him into the corridor.

"Is she all right?" he asked because the child had looked so pale.

"She's going to get something to drink," Sloan said. "To tell you the truth, I don't know if she's all right or not. Meggie is very...optimistic. I think she thought her father would be just fine and somehow he'd turn into Super Dad and we'd all go home and live happily ever after." She opened the door wider to let him in. "They still haven't brought the papers I need to sign. Please. Don't think you have to wait. Meggie and I can get back to the motel."

"Are you prepared to go to Chinle?" he said, ignoring the opportunity she had given him to withdraw his offer of help.

"To where? I don't have any idea where Chinle is. No, I'm not prepared. I'm not prepared to do anything except go home as soon as possible."

"Your brother lived in a reservation-owned house there. I've been advised to tell you that the tribe has authorized your use of it until everything is settled."

"Is Chinle close to Window Rock?" she asked.

"No."

"I see," she said quietly, and Lucas suspected that she did see, that Inez's machinations were as apparent to her as they had been to him.

But she didn't say anything else. She wandered aimlessly around the small room, picking up a magazine here and there only to put it down again. He waited a long time for her to speak, even by Navajo standards.

"I have some telephone numbers," he said finally. "People who can help you make arrangements."

"You know I used to think that Mark couldn't possibly complicate my life any more than he already had," she said abruptly, as if she hadn't heard him. "I was wrong." She took a deep breath and held out her hand. "Could I have the numbers?"

He gave them to her, and he stepped outside again while she made the telephone calls. Meggie stood in the hallway, empty-handed.

"Did you get something to drink?" he asked her, because that seemed a safe enough question.

She shook her head. "Changed my mind," she said. She made no attempt to go into the room with her aunt. She was still very pale, but she wasn't crying, as far as Lucas could tell.

"Are you worried about Patrick?" Lucas asked.

She sighed. "It doesn't do any good to worry about Patrick," she said matter-of-factly. "He's a hardheaded, teenage boy."

Lucas couldn't keep from smiling. "Well, if that's so, he'll grow out of it."

"I don't know," Meggie said, sighing again. "My dad never did. Never." She looked at Lucas. "My harmony is all gone, Officer Singer."

"Yes," Lucas answered, because it was obvious and because it couldn't be otherwise.

"I don't think I can ever get it back."

"You can, Meggie. It's hard sometimes, but that's what makes it worth having. If you want it and you wait, it'll come back."

"Are you sure, Officer Singer?"

"I'm sure."

"Have you ever lost your harmony?"

"Many times."

"And it always came back."

"Yes," Lucas said, regardless of how precarious his own emotional equilibrium had been these last two days.

"I didn't get to ask my dad the question, Officer Singer—the one you said I should ask him. I didn't get to." She was close to tears. "I wanted him to see how big I am now. I wanted him to see

I wasn't a little kid—it's not fair!'' She stood with her arms folded tightly over her chest. After a moment, she bowed her head. ''Why can't things ever go like you want them to?'' she said.

She suddenly looked at him as if she expected him to answer. ''Why can't they?'' she repeated, her voice wavering.

His first impulse was to send her to her aunt. It was Sloan Baron's place to give this child whatever philosophy she wanted her to have. But Meggie was looking at him so earnestly.

''My people, the Navajo, believe it's Coyote who makes everything go wrong,'' he said.

Meggie wiped furtively at her eyes. ''Coyote?''

''Coyote is the cause of all the mischief in the world. Just when you think things are going to work out the way you want them to, and they don't, it's Coyote's fault, because he's always watching us humans, always looking for the chance to upset things.''

''He sounds awful.''

''He is—but in the end, *we* are smarter than he is, because we learn from him. We listen to the stories about him—stories the grandfathers and the grandmothers pass down to the little children—and we learn not to behave foolishly and get into trouble all the time like he does. You see? Any mischief Coyote does, if we learn a lesson from it, then it's not such a bad thing.''

He waited while Meggie thought this over.

''It's his *job* to make things go wrong?'' she asked after a moment. ''For everybody, no matter who it is?''

''Something like that.''

''And he's always watching—''

The door behind them opened.

Sloan Baron looked from one of them to the other. ''I have to go to Window Rock,'' she said.

Except for the road signs, Sloan perceived little of the trip to the town where Mark's child was supposed to be. It was as if she had developed a kind of tunnel vision that let her see only what she needed to see. She was aware of Patrick and Meggie, and Lucas Singer's unobtrusive help in getting things together so that they could leave Albuquerque shortly after noon. But she felt nothing.

Lucas Singer's main concern had been why he had been told one thing about where Mark Baron's family should go and she another. She had no answer for that, except that the person she'd spoken to, the coworker of Mark's, had assumed that she would be coming to Window Rock and had given her the directions to a place where she and Mark's children would be expected. Unlike Singer, she found the change in travel plans neither curious nor annoying. She needed to be in Window Rock. The thing she found impossible to understand was that there were no funeral arrangements for her to make, because Mark had already made them.

She drove to Window Rock without difficulty, letting Meggie sit in front with her and read aloud Lucas Singer's list of places to make turns. Patrick slept the entire trip, snoring and oblivious in the back seat, determined to convince her and himself that his father's dying meant nothing to him.

She was pleasantly surprised that Lucas was waiting at the house when they arrived. Though he hadn't specifically said so, she had thought when he left the motel this afternoon that she wouldn't see him again. As she and Meggie got out of the car, several women came from the small cement block house—one of them Dolly Singer.

"My mother," Lucas said when he introduced her.

"Yes," Sloan said, pleased to meet the woman who was taking care of William. "It was very kind of you to let me speak to my nephew this morning. Is he—does he know about Mark?"

Dolly Singer said something to her son, but Lucas chose not to translate it, regardless of Sloan's questioning look.

She let herself be directed into the house, let Singer take on the problem of getting Patrick awake enough to get him out of the car. She was immensely grateful for the presence of these people, strangers or not. She'd been alone so long, responsible so long. The quietly voiced condolences and the dishes of wonderful-smelling food that had been brought in and now lined the kitchen counters were very much like what she would have encountered if she'd been at home. For a little while at least, she could relinquish having to take care of everything and everyone. She let Dolly Singer and the other women take over the feeding of Patrick and Meggie, and she stepped outside for a moment, standing alone in the front yard of the house and watching the sun go down.

How strange this place is, she thought. The raw landscape was almost surreal to someone who had grown up in rolling hills of hardwood and pine forests and field after field of nothing but green. She remembered the Painted Desert and the Petrified Forest from her long-ago trip. This place was quite different and strikingly beautiful in its own rugged way. But she could see nothing here that might have appealed to Mark. Perhaps it wasn't the place, she thought. Perhaps it was a person—young Will's mother, or some other woman who had taken her place.

Will's mother was absent from the home, according to Inez Yazzie. Was anyone looking for her? Did she even know what had happened to Mark?

"I have to go," Lucas Singer said behind her. "Please let one of the women know if you need anything. And my mother wants to know if you'll eat now."

She glanced over her shoulder at him. "Yes," she said.

He made a monosyllabic comment of some kind. "I just told her you never eat," he said in a tone she might have called teasing—if the situation was different and if the remark hadn't come from Lucas Singer.

She managed a small smile. "I wouldn't *not* eat when people have gone to so much trouble."

"It wouldn't be polite where you come from," he suggested.

"No. Not polite at all."

He took a piece of paper from his breast pocket and handed it to her. "The burial is tomorrow at ten-thirty," he said. "Someone from the community college will come and take you where it will be. I'm told your brother didn't want any kind of service."

"I don't understand," she said, looking down at the paper he'd given her. "I don't understand at all. Mark never planned any farther ahead than his next meal. He was completely irresponsible. He can't have made his own funeral arrangements."

"Apparently he did," Lucas said.

"But why? That's what I don't understand."

Lucas noted that she was looking at him in much the same way Meggie had, as if she fully expected him to explain the unexplainable. Coyote had definitely been at work today meddling in the business of humans. In Meggie's fervent wish to ask her father if she could be his daughter again. In Inez's plan to keep Sloan Baron away from Window Rock. And in his own desire to be left alone.

"It may have been done as a courtesy to The People," he said.

"What people?"

He made a gesture with one hand, already regretting that he was about to embark on yet another anthropology lecture. "The Navajo," he said. "We call ourselves *Diné*—The People. Death is a very old and very strict taboo for us. We have a great fear of the dead, no matter how enlightened we become. Your brother may have wanted to spare his Navajo friends having to deal with anything associated with his dying."

"Is that why you never mention Mark by name? And why your mother looked so startled when I said his name just now?"

"Yes," he said, once again more impressed than he wanted to be that she had immediately grasped the situation.

"Did . . . my brother have friends here?"

"So I'm told," Lucas said.

"Yes, he must have," she said tiredly. "He wanted to be buried here on the reservation. He didn't want to come home again." She looked at him. No remnant of the smile he'd seen earlier remained.

"The food is waiting," he said.

"I haven't forgotten," she said, turning to go inside.

He watched her walk away. He expected to feel a certain amount of relief. He had seen to it that the dead teacher's family had been properly met when they arrived in Window Rock, and that they had food, and that Sloan Baron knew when and where the burial would be. His job here was finished. He would not have to concern himself with these people again.

But he didn't feel anything akin to relief, and Coyote was still at hand.

"Ms. Baron," he said as she reached the front door. "If you want to see your nephew tomorrow, I'll take you."

Chapter Seven

In spite of Mark's aversion to anything that reminded him of his army days, he had arranged to have a military funeral. Sloan expected the cemetery to look like the National Cemetery at home. It didn't. In fact, but for the familiar military-type headstones scattered among the other grave markers and a few tattered American flags flying, she wouldn't have recognized it as a burial place for veterans at all. There were no shade trees, no manicured grass, no precisely laid out paths and flower beds. The graves had simply been set down in this dry and rocky place, all of them nearly overrun by the haphazard growth of desert weeds. She got out of the car and stood where she was directed to stand, trying not to mind so much that Mark, by his own choice, would be here always. She took Meggie's hand, smiling at her sadly as they waited for the other cars to arrive—not that there were that many cars coming. Singer had said that Mark had friends here. Perhaps. But they didn't attend funerals.

The wind blew hard across the open expanse of ground, whipping the dust into her face. She kept hoping at the last moment that Patrick would arrive. Even as an elderly Navajo woman finished singing the last a cappella verse of "Precious Memories," she hoped to see him.

But he didn't come. She and Meggie stood essentially alone as a small group of World War Two veterans conducted this final rite of passage. And they did it with nearly more dignity than she could bear—elderly men all of them, former Marines, according to their VFW caps. She tried not to flinch when the rifle salute was fired, tried not to sob out loud when an old ex-Marine reverently placed one of the spent cartridges in her hand. She held her body rigid to keep from trembling as she received the folded flag. The mournful strains of "Taps" floated upward and away in the stiff wind, and she kept reminding herself that Mark had wanted this. She looked away from the grave and out over the lonely, barren land around her. *This.*

"You got any reason to think you're being watched?" Becenti asked when Lucas had given him Nick Wager's information in its entirety. Lucas had toyed briefly with the idea of not telling Becenti about his own name being on the surveillance list and avoiding this very question, but at the last minute, good sense had prevailed. If he had learned anything in his bumpy career, he'd learned to keep Becenti informed or suffer the consequences.

"I haven't seen anybody," Lucas said, not precisely answering the question. The question wasn't whether or not Lucas had seen anybody. The question was whether or not he'd done anything to annoy the FBI. "I may not be the name on the list."

"Or you're on the list and they just haven't gotten around to you yet. Or you haven't been paying attention."

There was a time when the latter possibility would have been a likelihood, but not now. "I haven't seen anybody," Lucas said again, feeling his irritation rise. He covered a lot of open territory in the course of his job, and there were only so many places for some covert observer to hide. He would know if he'd been followed, watched.

"Well, I want to know if you do," Becenti said. "And I think we'd better find Margaret Madman. She's the one who'll know what's going on if anybody does."

"I thought I'd go check out her family the first chance I get. On the quiet—no questions about Margaret around here until I talk to them. I don't want her clan to know I'm looking for her until I get there."

"Or the FBI," Becenti said.

When Lucas came out of Becenti's office, he was surprised to see someone other than Mary Skeets working as dispatcher. "Where's Mary today?" he asked one of the officers in the hall.

"Gone to the funeral of the teacher from the community college," the man said.

Lucas got coffee and went to his desk to read his phone messages, such as they were. He actually understood all of them, for a change, but there was nothing that needed his immediate attention. His mind went to the Baron family—to Sloan Baron. He had deliberately stayed away from the funeral. The tribe was being officially represented by people from the community college. There was no reason for him to attend, absolutely none, except that the thought of Sloan Baron having to bury her brother alone left him filled with a disquiet he would have been hard pressed to explain. He tapped a pencil absently on the desktop. There was nothing he could do to help her. Sloan Baron wouldn't want his help, and he should have more sense than to want to offer it.

He glanced at his watch. He would go to the house later, and regardless of Inez's wishes, he would take Sloan Baron to see her nephew. He looked at his watch again and stood up, immediately revising his plans. He would go to the house now. He wanted to get this ordeal behind him. It occurred to him as he went out of the building that the world was an unhappy place when taking a woman to her first meeting with her brother's child could only be described as an ordeal.

Sloan Baron's car was in the drive when he got to the reservation house. Patrick was sitting in it with the driver side door open, his head spinning sharply around at the sight of the tribal police car. Lucas got out and walked toward him, expecting to hear music coming from the car radio. But Patrick wasn't listening to music, and he wasn't dressed as if he'd just come from his father's funeral. He was barefoot and he had on a rock concert T-shirt and cutoff jeans, the kind that had been strategically shredded in places and probably cost far more than any discerning person ought to pay for mostly strings.

"You leaving?" Lucas asked as he walked up.

"No keys," Patrick said. His eyes were red and puffy and he looked away to keep Lucas from noticing.

The lack of keys explained the silent radio, Lucas thought. He doubted if it was humanly possible for a boy this age to sit in a vehicle with a working radio and not have it blaring as loud as it would go. "Is Ms. Baron here?" he asked.

"No," Patrick said—with no elaboration of any kind.

"Do you know when she'll be back?"

Patrick glanced at him. "I don't know how long these things take."

Lucas was beginning to get the picture. The boy hadn't gone to the funeral, and in the wake of that decision, he didn't have any idea what to do with himself.

He waited for a moment to see if Patrick wanted to say anything else. "You hungry?" Lucas asked when it was obvious that he didn't.

"There's stuff here."

"I'm going to eat chili. You want to come?"

"No money."

"I'm buying."

"Did *she* tell you to come over here?"

"Who?" Lucas said obtusely.

"Sloan—you know who. Look, man, I'm not a charity case, and I don't need a damn baby-sitter."

"Well, that's good, because I'm not looking for the job. What I am looking for is Ms. Baron. Since she's not here and it's past noon, I want to go eat chili. And since I'm coming back here afterward anyway, I thought you might like to go along—because the chili's good and hot and because at least two of the waitresses are about your age."

Patrick looked up at him, squinting in the sun. "Are they good and hot, too?"

"I don't know," Lucas said pointedly. "And neither one of us is going to find out any time soon. Go get your shoes."

Patrick gave a short laugh, cutting it off quickly as if it had taken him by surprise. "Okay," he said, getting out of the car. "I like hot chili—not as much as I like hot waitresses, of course," he added with just enough mischief to make Lucas smile.

"Leave a note for your aunt," Lucas said as the boy walked gingerly over the uneven ground toward the house.

"Hey, I'm not a kid, either," Patrick protested. "I don't have to leave Sloan a note."

"*I* have to leave her a note," Lucas said. "And hurry up so we can beat the crowd."

Lucas didn't press Patrick for conversation, other than to explain that the meatless, beanless red and green chili dish Lucas wanted might not be what Patrick had in mind. And he didn't ask the obvious question— *Why didn't you go to your father's funeral?* In spite of Patrick's initial bravado, Lucas could see that the boy was hurting, and he suspected his pain was intensified by the knowledge that he had failed both his sister and his aunt when they needed him. The only thing Lucas could do was feed him, and give him some respite from having to sit and wait for the two people he had disappointed most to return. Lucas knew from personal experience how difficult that kind of encounter could be.

The chili lived up to its reputation. They were halfway through their second order before Patrick began to relax, though Lucas guessed that it was more the very unsubtle admiration Patrick was getting from several of the waitresses than the food.

"How come you were looking for Sloan?" Patrick asked him at one point.

"I'm going to take her to the receiving home today," Lucas said. "To meet your half brother."

Patrick looked at him sharply, but whatever remark he was about to make, he apparently thought better of it and left it unsaid. He went back to eating.

"What is the kid like?" he asked after a time, his eyes staying carefully on the chili. "I guess he's a pain in the butt. I know he is if he's like my—his old man."

"He's like most three-year-old boys," Lucas said. "He likes to talk. He likes apples. And goats."

"Goats?" Patrick said, looking up from the last of his chili.

"I'm afraid so," Lucas said, his eyes scanning the other patrons for possible FBI agents. He'd been looking over his shoulder ever since he'd talked to Nick in Albuquerque, and it made him feel ridiculous. There *were* no agents, regardless of Nick's list, and certainly there were none in here. The place was filled with working people and knowledgeable tourists and several groups of rowdy teenagers, particularly a table of boys—perhaps Navajo, Native American, certainly—just to the left of the cashier and the front door. Patrick had looked around several times at some remark one or the other of them had made in his general direction. Apparently none of them was particularly pleased with Patrick's affinity for giggling waitresses. It was obvious they thought Patrick was trespassing.

Patrick had to walk by them on the way out, and Lucas had already witnessed enough territorial posturing from both sides to be on his guard. Boys this age weren't good for a damn thing, he decided as he waited to pay his check—except giving tribal police officers indigestion.

He thought at first that Patrick was going to make it out the door without incident. He was wrong. One of the boys, the one wearing a "Custer Got What He Deserved" T-shirt, reached out and grabbed Patrick's arm.

"What's the matter, White Eyes," the boy said. "You don't like the shirt?"

"Hey!" Patrick said, deftly peeling the boy's hand off. "Don't start with *me,* Cochise. My great-great-great-granddaddy was a Stanly County Yankee hunter. He spent four years of his life trying to take Custer out. If he'd been a better shot, *your* people wouldn't have had to worry about him. Whose Jimmy is that outside?"

Happily for Lucas, the topic of the conversation immediately turned to trucks and sports utility vehicles and four-wheel drives. One other thing boys this age were good for, he thought as he held out his hand for his change, was knowing exactly who had arrived in which vehicle. He should take one of them along with him the next time he had to go to some big gathering to make an arrest.

The group of boys abruptly adjourned and were exchanging automotive white lies in the parking lot when Lucas walked outside. Patrick was right in the middle of it.

"See you guys around," he said to the group when he saw Lucas.

"You get enough to eat?" Lucas asked him.

"Oh, yeah. Thanks, Officer Singer. That was some good food."

Lucas started the patrol car, and they rode for several blocks in silence.

"I'm . . . sorry about what I said earlier—about not needing a baby-sitter," Patrick said abruptly. He glanced at Lucas. "I didn't go to the funeral," he added in a rush. "Sloan's going to be pissed. She is going to be *really* pissed."

"I doubt it," Lucas said, surprised at his willingness to second-guess Sloan Baron's reaction. He made a left turn onto the street that would take him to the reservation house the Barons were using. "It's not that kind of situation, is it? The kind where she'd be mad just because you didn't do something you were supposed to do. We're not talking about forgetting to feed the dog or not carrying out the trash. I don't think she'll be angry that you didn't go, Patrick, but I think you can count on her—and Meggie—being hurt. And sometimes that's worse."

Patrick sighed heavily. "She's back," he said as Lucas stopped in front of the house.

Sloan Baron was indeed back, and she'd been home for a while—long enough to change from her funeral clothes into jeans and T-shirt and athletic shoes. She looked small and vulnerable, and Patrick had been quite right in his anticipation of her state of mind. She wasn't visibly upset, but Lucas was certain she was angry. She stood waiting by the car until Lucas and Patrick got out.

"So," she said to Patrick, her voice quiet. "Where have you been?"

"You didn't leave a note," Lucas said to him.

"No, hey, I left a note," Patrick said. "Well, I did!" he insisted.

Sloan held up one finger, then carefully removed a piece of paper from her pocket and unfolded it. She turned it around so that both Lucas and Patrick could see. The so-called note was succinct and borderline truthful. Very borderline.

Gone: ? Back: ?. P.

"Is Patrick in any kind of trouble?" Sloan asked Lucas.

"He's in trouble," Lucas said looking at Patrick hard, "but not the kind you think." He understood now why Patrick was so certain Sloan Baron would be angry—because he, Patrick, regardless of how distressed Sloan must be today, had done his damnedest to provoke her.

She crumpled the note in her hand. "Am I going to be able to see Will this afternoon?" she asked Lucas.

"Yes," he said, turning his attention to her.

"When?"

"Now, if you want."

She nodded. "Patrick, Meggie is asleep. She's exhausted and I want you to stay with her while I go to the receiving home. I don't want her disturbed, do you understand? No loud anything. And when I get back, I want you to give me twenty-four hours. I buried my brother today, and it's going to take me at least that long before I can endure any more of your being cute. I have to get my purse," she said to Lucas.

Patrick stood by miserably as Sloan went inside the house.

"Nice going, kid," Lucas said to him.

Sloan waited until she was in the patrol car to look at Patrick, and her heart sank.

"Please—wait," she said when Singer was about to drive away.

She got out of the car again and walked to where Patrick stood so forlornly.

"This isn't for you," she said to him. "This is for me." She gave him a brief hard hug, the kind he claimed he hated, the kind they both needed, regardless of the friction between them. She didn't say anything else. She was too upset with him to talk now, even if she couldn't bear to see him so miserable.

She got into the patrol car, and she could feel Lucas Singer's glance as they drove away. She was becoming accustomed to this man, to the fact that just because he didn't verbalize a question didn't mean it wasn't there.

"What?" she asked pointedly when she couldn't tolerate the lack of inquiry any longer.

"Nothing," he said. "Sometimes white people . . . amaze me."

Sloan frowned. She had no idea what he meant, but she might have taken exception to a remark like that if she hadn't had other things on her mind. She could only think about Will Baron, and she was grateful to Lucas that he'd arranged for her to talk to him. She refused to anticipate all the many things that could go wrong at this first meeting—that he might be afraid of her or simply not like her or, worse, that he might be so distressed about his father she wouldn't be able to establish any kind of rapport with him at all.

She abruptly gave a sharp sigh, precipitating another of Singer's glances.

"Does my nephew know about . . . his father?" she asked him since she already had his attention, remembering at the last moment that it would be uncomfortable for Singer if she called Mark by name.

"I don't know. We can find out before you see him."

"Is your mother going to be there?"

"Probably."

In a short while, he turned into an unpaved parking area beside a low-pitched, cement-block building.

"This is it," he said, pulling the car under the shade of a tree.

"I'm . . . scared, Singer," she confessed, looking at him. She hadn't known she was going to make such an admission, especially to him, but there it was.

"Yes," he agreed, and oddly enough it made her feel better. Of course she should feel afraid in this situation.

He got out of the car. She waited a moment, then took a deep breath and opened the car door, feeling the hot, dry wind on her skin. She was so tired suddenly. She glanced at Lucas Singer. He was waiting quietly for her, and he was neither impatient nor irritated as far as she could tell. She wondered idly if he was still amazed.

You can do this, she told herself as she got out, repeating the litany that had come to rule her life of late. She tried not to think of Mark and the desolate place where he'd been buried this morning.

She looked at the sky. Nothing but blue scattered with high, white clouds. A memory surfaced suddenly in her mind, one of that long-ago trip she'd made with Mark when they were children, one of a sky like this, where the blue overhead had seemed to be a great, cloud-filled corridor that went on and on as far as the eye could see. Skies never looked like this at home. North Carolina skies were claustrophobic compared to the great expanse she saw now.

Lucas seemed about to say something to her as they walked to the front door, but he didn't, holding the screen door open for her instead. She stepped inside, giving her eyes a moment to adjust to the darkness.

Dolly Singer came immediately, as if she'd been watching for their arrival. Lucas said something to her in Navajo—to which she made a rather lengthy response.

"My mother says Will was told yesterday about his father," Lucas said. "She says that he's—" He stopped, seeming to search for an English equivalent of what Dolly Singer had said. "He's like most small children," Lucas went on finally. "They understand and they don't."

Sloan nodded. That a parent wasn't going to return—for whatever reason—was a difficult concept for a child. She'd been through it on some level already with Patrick and Meggie.

"Does he know I'm coming?" Sloan asked.

"Yes," Lucas said. "My mother thought it would be better if he knew, so that he wouldn't worry that he had no relatives."

"Where is he?"

"In the dayroom, the room behind you," Lucas said. "Do you want my mother to go in first?"

"No," Sloan said. "I think I'd rather go alone."

She looked from one of the Singers to the other, wondering why they both looked so grim. "This room?" she asked, turning toward the doorway he'd indicated.

Lucas walked along with her, and once again she was struck by the notion that he was about to say something.

She stopped just outside the door. She could see several Navajo children in the room, most of them watching television at the far end, some kind of cartoon show with numerous loud explosions.

"I don't see him," she said, staring around the room.

"He's the one sitting at the table," Lucas said. "The one playing with blocks."

Sloan looked into the room, toward the low, kindergarten-type table, toward the only child who sat there. The Navajo child.

"Where is—" she started to say, but then the realization hit her. Lucas Singer hadn't made a mistake. *This* boy was Mark's son.

She looked around at Singer. His face was completely impassive, but not his eyes. She stared into them, trying to understand. A hundred questions clamored in her mind, but only one of them mattered.

Why didn't you tell me Will's mother was Navajo?

"Ms. Baron," he said, but she stepped away from him. The little boy—Will—was looking expectantly in her direction. He was her nephew and he was alone. The last thing she wanted him to see was the turmoil she was feeling now.

She walked toward him quietly, and as she did, the tower of blocks he'd been working on toppled. She knelt down beside the table to pick up the ones that had fallen on the floor, handing them to him, first one and then another.

He took each block solemnly, giving her a shy glance, but he made no attempt to stack them again. He sat holding the last block she'd given him and he simply waited.

"Are you Will Baron?" Sloan asked kindly. She stayed on the floor, sitting back on her feet so that they were nearly eye-to-eye.

He nodded.

"Do you know who I am? I've come a long way to see you. I'm—"

She never got the chance to say who she was. The boy flung himself out of his chair and into her arms, clinging to her, his face pressed into her shoulder. She rocked him gently, fighting down the rush of tears that threatened to overwhelm her, tears she hadn't shed for Mark, or for Meggie and Patrick, or for herself. And most of all, tears she hadn't shed for this small boy.

"Sweet boy," she whispered to him, her mouth trembling. "It's all right. I'm so glad to see you."

Sloan looked toward the door. Lucas Singer stood watching, and another woman she hadn't seen before, a woman who was carrying a briefcase and who was *not* happy. Her throat ached and her eyes burned. Tears streamed down her face in spite of all she could do. She wiped them away with the heel of her hand.

"You didn't tell me if you know who I am," she said with a brightness she didn't feel, leaning back so she could see Will's face. "Who am I?"

"An' Swone," he said with his finger in his mouth.

"Right! And who are you?"

"Will Baron," he said dutifully.

"Right again!" she said, teasing him gently, smiling so that he would know she was teasing. "What a smart boy you are. Am I lucky or what? This big nephew of mine is smart *and* handsome. And who are *we*?"

"Aunt Swone and Will Baron," he said, grinning.

"That's us, all right. Give me another hug. Terrific!" she said when he immediately complied. "Just what I needed—a genuine Will Baron hug."

She suddenly noticed how hot the child felt. "Have you got a fever?" she said, leaning back to touch his forehead and his face.

"He has an ear infection," a woman's voice said behind her.

Sloan looked up to see the woman with the briefcase.

"The doctor has prescribed an antibiotic for him," she went on. "Go out to the kitchen with Dolly," she said to the boy. "It's time to take some more medicine."

But Will Baron had other ideas. He rested his hands on Sloan's shoulders and looked directly into her eyes.

"Is my daddy coming?" he asked her.

"No, Will," she answered, determined not to avoid the question. This was the only aspect of her first encounter with Will Baron she was prepared to deal with. She knew he would have questions about his father's death and likely the same questions he'd already asked someone else. "Your daddy isn't coming."

"Why?"

She glanced at the woman with the briefcase. "Because he died, Will."

The boy continued to watch her face. "Are you sad?"

"Yes," she said. "Very sad."

"Why?"

"Because your daddy was my brother and I loved him."

Will thought about this for a moment. "Is he coming tomorrow?" he asked.

"No, Will."

"My daddy died."

"Yes," Sloan said.

"Can I go find him?"

"No."

He gave a small sigh. "I got to take my medicine," he said.

"I know. There's Dolly looking for you."

But he had more questions, and he hung on to her T-shirt to make certain he got to ask them. "If I don't take my medicine, will I die?"

"Your medicine is for your ear, Will, so it won't hurt and you won't be sick."

"Was my daddy sick?"

"No. He was—"

"Lucas said it," he interrupted. "Lucas said my daddy was hurt."

"Lucas was right," Sloan said, glancing around to see if Lucas Singer was still here. He stood just behind her. "Go take your medicine, sweet boy."

Will giggled. "You called me *sweet boy!*"

"I know," Sloan said, smiling and ruffling his hair. "I can't help it."

He trotted off with Dolly Singer, and Sloan got up from the floor.

"Well?" she said looking from Lucas to the woman with the briefcase. "Did I pass?"

"I . . . don't understand," the woman said.

"This was some kind of test, wasn't it? You were trying to find out about my racial prejudices. I'm sorry," she said to the woman, "I don't know who you are."

"I'm Inez Yazzie," the woman said.

"Of course," Sloan said, shaking her head in defeat. "Look. I know that in a perfect world you shouldn't *have* to announce that a child is half anything, but this isn't a perfect world. You should have told me the boy is Navajo. I could have been the worst kind of bigot, or even if I wasn't, the surprise alone could have made me say something—do something—that would have hurt that child. Or do you prefer to see outsiders floundering? I'm surprised you didn't sell tickets. What is wrong with you people? Singer here had every opportunity to tell me my brother's child might not quite be what I was expecting. Both of you knew that I didn't know this little boy existed until a few days ago. But at least *you* had the excuse of being *unavailable,*" she said to Inez Yazzie. "You know, I wouldn't have minded knowing that Will was sick, either—*before* I got here, novel as that concept may be."

"Excuse me, Inez," a young girl said from the doorway. "The new boy is here."

"Yes, thank you. I can see you're upset now," Inez said to Sloan.

"Upset?" Sloan said incredulously. "Yes. I'm upset."

"I have to see about this new arrival." She said something to Lucas in Navajo, an act of rudeness Sloan found even more difficult to tolerate. "We can talk later," she said to Sloan.

"If I can find you," Sloan said.

"You'll be able to find me, Ms. Baron," Inez said over her shoulder. "I'll come to the reservation house to see you tomorrow."

Sloan turned her attention to Lucas. "Aren't you going to say anything?" she asked, knowing that if he apologized for any inconvenience he'd caused her she'd probably hit him, police officer or not. She needed to understand this situation, and he was doing absolutely nothing to bring that about.

"Yes," he answered.

"What is it?" She looked into his eyes. The look caught and held.

"You . . . passed the test."

Chapter Eight

The boy cried when Sloan Baron left. Lucas stood on the sidelines and watched her say her goodbyes with the calm assurance of a woman experienced at leaving a weeping child behind. As Patrick and Meggie's surrogate and only parent, she must have done it many times, he supposed. It was only after she was outside the building that her composure slid away.

The afternoon shadows had grown longer, and the wind had died. He sat behind the wheel for a moment before he started the patrol car, feeling both her distress and her sense of helplessness. "Is there anything I can do for you?" he asked.

"No, Officer Singer," she said, her voice husky in her determination not to cry. "I just want to get all of us back home as soon as I can. I should be able to tell if Will is well enough to travel by tomorrow—"

"Sloan," Lucas interrupted, and she looked at him. He had never called her by her given name, a fact that didn't go unnoticed on her part and clearly made her wary.

"What is it?" she said. "Some other small detail I missed?"

"You can't take Will," he said. He saw no point in giving her anything but the bottom line, and that was it.

Sloan pursed her mouth to protest, then didn't, giving a quiet, wavering sigh instead.

Please, Singer, don't make things worse, she thought. *Not today. I need twenty-four hours from you, too.*

"Why?" she asked, but she didn't look at him. She looked out the window toward the receiving home instead. A child, a Navajo boy about Meggie's age, stood on the other side of the screen door watching.

"Will Baron is not yours to take."

"He's my nephew. Inez told me she didn't know where his mother was. Apparently that situation hasn't changed. I'm willing to do whatever I need to do to satisfy the Department of Social Services, but I can't stay here and I certainly can't leave him in a receiving home. I *have* to take him back to North Carolina with me."

"Legally, you can't do that."

"One of us is not listening here. He's my brother's child."

"He belongs to the tribe. There was a law passed in 1978—the Indian Child Welfare Act. It came after years and years of having Indian children forcibly taken off the reservation so that they could be raised white. Will's mother is Navajo. We have a matrilineal society. He belongs to the tribe. The tribe has custody. You, as a white person, can't just take him, do you understand?"

"I understand the *words*. I can't just go off and leave him, either. How can I do that, for God's sake! He's as much mine as Patrick and Meggie—"

The boy on the other side of the screen door suddenly stepped outside.

"I need to talk to this kid," Lucas said, getting out of the car.

Sloan waited, pressing the point of pain between her eyes with her fingertips. The conversation between Lucas and the boy appeared very intense, and after a moment Lucas walked him into the receiving home.

"Is he the new arrival?" Sloan asked when Lucas came back, primarily because she thought the child was close to making a run for it.

"Yes," Lucas answered.

"Is he all right?"

Lucas looked at her for a moment before he answered.

"I'm not just making conversation, Singer. I'd like to know."

"I think he's all right," Lucas said finally. "It's hard to tell how much is fear and how much is not wanting to stay in a place that has rules."

"Why is he here?"

"His old man beats him when he gets drunk. He's got five kids, but he only beats this one." He started the patrol car and drove out of the parking lot. "You need to talk to Inez," he said.

"Talk to Inez," Sloan said. "Now there's a novel idea."

"She'll come by to see you tomorrow."

"Will she?"

He didn't answer her question, and Sloan noted that he clearly wasn't going to let her drag him into any kind of purposeless bickering. She noted, too, how much she wanted to bicker, how much she wanted to rail against the injustice of this situation and throw things.

Instead, she sat in silence the rest of the way to the reservation house, trying to force herself to sort out the things she needed to do first, when, like the newest arrival at the receiving home, she really wanted to run, as far away and as fast as possible.

Patrick and Meggie were sitting waiting for her on the front steps, both of them looking as uncertain as she felt. She would have been hard-pressed to say who she felt the more sorry for, Mark's children—*all* of Mark's children—or herself.

"Thank you, Officer Singer," she said as she opened the car door. "I appreciate your arranging for me to see Will, even if I don't understand why you . . ." She didn't say any more.

"It wasn't what you think," he said when she was about to get out. She looked at him, and she realized how much she had wanted this man's respect, regardless of the fact that she'd known him such a short time. It had hurt her to realize that he had made some kind of sweeping generalization about her, and once that generalization had been made, he had given her no chance to defend herself.

"It was exactly what I think, Singer," she said.

"I didn't tell you the boy was Navajo—"

"Because you were sure I was a racist."

"No," he said firmly. "It's not that simple. What you said earlier is true. In a perfect world no one should have to say what a person is or isn't. But it's not a perfect world and I've spent a lot of years trying to deal with the imperfections. Indian people resent—*I* resent—having to prepare you white people for our existence. I didn't want to tell you Will Baron isn't white. Me—not Inez. I didn't know she was going to be at the receiving home, and she wouldn't have been there if Jackie Begaye hadn't been brought in this afternoon. I wasn't thinking about Will and I wasn't thinking about you. I wasn't thinking about what kind of telling information Inez could get from the situation. I was thinking how much it would annoy *me* to have to say the boy is half Navajo. Do you understand?''

"Not entirely," she said. "But I'll work on it." She got out of the car and slammed the door closed, looking at him once on her way to where Meggie and Patrick still sat on the front steps. The afternoon had been filled with revelations. Aside from the obvious things she'd learned about Will and the things Lucas Singer had deigned to tell her about the boy's stay at the receiving home, she now knew that Singer resented white people—and he knew that she was afraid.

"Ms. Baron," Lucas called after her, and she turned. "Maybe tomorrow will be better," he said, and she gave a short laugh.

"I doubt it," she said, and she stood staring after him as he backed the patrol car around and drove away.

"Jeez, now what's the matter?" Patrick said, standing up.

"Nothing," she said.

"Yeah, right. We don't see the kind of face you're wearing now for 'nothing,' do we?" he asked Meggie, poking her in the ribs with his elbow.

"No," Meggie said. She gave a resigned sigh.

"Well, you should know, Patrick," Sloan said tiredly. "You're the one most likely to put some kind of face on me." She made sure that she met his eyes. She was still upset with him and would be for a while—but she had a new crisis, and he and Meggie might as well know about it. "All right. Nothing is . . . an understatement. I think we'd better have a family meeting."

"Didn't you get to see the kid?" Patrick asked.

"I saw him."

"He's not the kid, Patrick," Meggie said to him. "He's our half brother."

"Yeah, well, how do *we* know that?"

"We *know*," Meggie said pointedly, "because our dad was looking after him. If he wouldn't look after you and me, he wouldn't look after somebody else's kid."

"Depends on what was in it for him," Patrick said. "That's *my* guess."

Sloan led the way inside, and she stayed out of the discussion of Mark's shortcomings. The memory surfaced of the last time she'd seen Mark alive. He'd been so distressed, so adamant that she leave. She wondered if she would ever be able to put his dying into perspective, if she would be able to find the time to remember Mark fondly and to grieve. All of these feelings, hers and Patrick's and Meggie's, had to be addressed at some point—just not now.

She was surprised to find the small kitchen table set with three places and the house filled with the smell of something warming in the oven.

"We were waiting for you to get back," Meggie said.

"It looks good," Sloan said, trying to be more pleasant than she felt.

"So what's the deal?" Patrick said.

Sloan pulled out a chair and sat down at the table, waiting until Patrick and Meggie were both seated before she began.

"Patrick wants to tell you he's sorry," Meggie said.

"Do you mind if I do my own talking here?" he said irritably.

"Well, do it," Meggie said.

"If I worried you, I'm sorry," Patrick said.

"If?" Sloan said, not letting him off with some halfhearted, token gesture, the kind she'd always accepted from Mark. "Patrick, you've lived with me for enough years to know exactly what will and will not worry me. *If* I was worried, it was because you chose to behave in a way that would do it."

He fiddled with the saltshaker and didn't look at her. "Yeah, I guess," he said finally. He looked up at her. "I'm sorry."

"For what?" she asked.

"For worrying you. When I could have left a better note."

"I'm sorry, too," Sloan said. "For forgetting that you're seventeen years old and that your father's going off and leaving you the way he did hurt you a lot more than it hurt me. I think that I asked too much of you when I expected you to put all of that aside and—"

She stopped because she thought he was going to cry. "Meggie, did you want to say anything?"

"I want to see Will Baron," she said simply. "I don't want to just hear about him."

"I need to tell you some things about Will," Sloan said. They were both looking at her. "I learned a lot of things about him today. First, he's been scared and he's been worried because he was taken to the receiving home and he couldn't see his—your—father. And Lucas Singer tells me he's had a hard time there because he didn't think he had any relatives."

"He's got us," Meggie said.

"But he didn't know that, not really. I'd only talked to him once on the phone and not for very long. His mother and her family are somewhere on the reservation, I think, but so far, none of them has come around. He's been more or less abandoned, and the other boys at the home have been teasing him because of it."

"Why would they do that?" Meggie wanted to know, and, typically for Meggie, she was already indignant. "A kid can't help it when he gets dumped."

"Children can be very cruel to each other," Sloan said. "All the children at the receiving home believe that not having relatives to teach you how to behave is a shameful thing."

"It is," Meggie said glumly.

"In this case I understand it's a specific Navajo belief. Will learned about it from living here and from his mother. Will's mother is Navajo."

Meggie and Patrick continued to stare at her, but she didn't go on.

"You mean the kid's an Indian?" Patrick said finally.

"Yes," Sloan said. "Half," she qualified.

"He's an Indian," Patrick said, looking at Meggie.

"Yes," Sloan said again.

"Does he look like an Indian?" Meggie asked.

"Yes," Sloan answered.

"Neat!" Meggie said.

Patrick frowned. "You mean to tell me my half brother is half Navajo Indian?"

"Yes, Patrick. That's exactly what I mean to tell you. And I want you to make whatever remarks you're going to make now, because tomorrow all three of us will go to the receiving home to see him." She had to fight hard not to say *or else* and unravel the tenuous peace she and Patrick had just established. "Will isn't alone, and the sooner he knows that the better."

"Well, this is just great," Patrick said loudly. "How come you didn't tell us before *now?*"

"Because I didn't know until now. Nobody mentioned it. I didn't think to ask."

"Well, maybe you should have," Patrick said.

"The next time anyone calls about an abandoned nephew, I will," she assured him in a tone that should have left little doubt that her invitation to make whatever remarks he wanted to make was token at best. "I don't have anything else to tell you now except that he's sick. He has an ear infection, fever, that kind of thing. He didn't want me to leave but I couldn't get around the visiting hours—and I needed to come talk to the two of you. I know this is hard. But I just want you to remember that we're a family—the two of you, and Will, and me, all right? The truth is that you could have easily been in his situation yourselves, and I want you to try to understand what it's like to think you've been left alone."

"Did you tell him about us—Patrick and me?" Meggie wanted to know.

"Yes."

"Is he glad or anything?"

"He's very glad, Meggie. I let him keep the picture of the two of you I had in my wallet. Now, if there's nothing else you want to ask, I'm going to eat a little supper and I'm going to bed before I fall on my face." She didn't want to get into the 1978 Indian Child Welfare Act, at least not until she knew precisely what it entailed.

They ate in silence. Sloan hugged both of them before she went into the small back bedroom she'd slept in the night before. Except that she hadn't slept, and she expected another restless night. Lord knows, she had even more to worry about.

Will Baron isn't yours to take.

How could she not be given custody of Mark's child if she wanted it, if she petitioned legally for it? She was a responsible person. She was employed. She was already taking care of Mark's other children.

But Lucas Singer had sounded so definite. She had believed him, just as she had when he'd told her in the hospital that Patrick had wanted the privacy to cry.

She washed her face and brushed her teeth and put on her nightgown. Then she lay in the darkness letting the conversation she'd had with Lucas play over and over in her mind, hearing him say in that unapologetic way, "*I* resent—"

She had sensed that in him, certainly, but she still would have said that he seemed more resigned than resentful, as if he was working all the time to overcome some experience, presumably unpleasant, or some preconceived idea that caused him to be unfair where she was concerned.

She fell asleep without finding any kind of solution to the problem of what to do about Will, or how to comprehend the complexities of Lucas Singer. And she awoke to daylight and the aroma of coffee, which delighted Meggie, because Sloan was lured to the kitchen just like the coffee-craving people on the television commercials.

"Patrick made it. If it's any good it'll be a miracle. See, I told you she'd wake up, Patrick. He said you were too tired. Are we going to the receiving home this morning?" Meggie said as Sloan poured and tasted.

"The coffee is great," she said, lifting her cup in Patrick's direction. "Yes, we're going as—"

"Some woman's coming to the door," Patrick interrupted.

But it wasn't some woman. It was Inez Yazzie, apparently as good as her word.

Inez had the alert and officious look of a person who had already been at work for some time. Sloan introduced Patrick and Meggie. She even offered the woman coffee, marveling as she poured it that Patrick had actually recognized her need for privacy and had taken Meggie and himself outside. Sloan felt much more able to cope this morning, but she still recognized that she was at a distinct disadvantage. How could she hold her own in some kind of bureaucratic procedure when she didn't know the rules and she didn't have enough money to learn them? The only things she knew were the stakes—a little boy who hugged her as tightly as he could and called her "Aunt Swone."

"I need to make sure you understand the situation," Inez said as she accepted the steaming cup. She waved away Sloan's offer of milk and sugar.

"I understand more than you think," Sloan said. "I know about the law—the one that says I can't take Will home with me, the one that made it unnecessary for you to have to return any of my phone calls."

"My first concern is always the child," Inez said, taking another sip of coffee. "Communication on the reservation isn't as simple as it is where you come from. Many times I am nowhere near a telephone."

"Well, that must come in handy when you want to give somebody the bureaucratic runaround."

"It does," Inez said, unperturbed. "I think you're forgetting something. You're not the first one in line here, Ms. Baron. There is still Will's mother, Margaret Madman. She has to be located. She has to be notified of your brother's death. Then both you and she—or her family—will be given the opportunity to speak before the tribal judges so that the matter of Will's custody can be settled. All of which takes time."

"And if I get tired of waiting and go on home without causing any complications, all the better."

"Regardless of what you think, I'm not trying to discourage you or wear you down," Inez said. "I have no idea how long it will take. You must understand that the law regarding Indian children is neither cruel nor unjust. It has the child's best interest at heart. It's usually better for a child to stay with his own kind."

"His own kind? My brother was the one who was taking care of Will. *I* am his own kind!" Sloan abruptly threw up her hands. "This is pointless. I don't have to convince you—I have to convince a court. If I can make my money last long enough to do that."

Inez didn't respond immediately. She was staring at her coffee cup. "Are you willing to do something?" she finally asked.

"I beg your pardon?"

"I understand from Lucas Singer that you're a nurse. Are you willing to work while you wait for the custody hearing regarding your brother's child?"

"Thank you, I already have two jobs."

"But you still need money," Inez said. "And you don't want to abandon the child."

"Yes," Sloan admitted.

"Then why not work while you're waiting? There's a good chance that housing would be provided with the job—this house or something like it."

Sloan understood what Inez Yazzie *didn't* say perfectly. The Barons' current free housing was about to be terminated. "I take it you have something definite in mind."

Inez smiled, a response that Sloan would have heretofore considered impossible for the woman. "I have The People in mind, Ms. Baron. They are always in need of improved medical care. I'm assuming that your participation in their health care system would be an improvement. I'll need the number of a valid nursing license and the telephone numbers of your current place of employment—both places."

Sloan suppressed the ridiculous urge to laugh. Inez Yazzie was nothing if not manipulative. She was a virtual steamroller at accomplishing what she perceived needed to be done. Sloan was about to be coerced into working on an Indian reservation—but only if her references were good and her nursing license valid. And she had the distinct impression that Inez had had a lengthy discussion with someone about all of this before she got here. Who? Sloan wondered. Lucas Singer?

"Do you want to make the best of the time you have to spend waiting or not?" Inez said. There was a light emphasis on the word *have*.

"Yes," Sloan said. "But I—"

"I don't know if there's anything available. If there is, I'll get back to you."

This time Sloan did laugh. "Great," she said. "You make it impossible for me to say no and then you tell me you don't know if there's a job."

"First things first," Inez said, drinking the last of her coffee. "I like to find out if the sheep are thirsty before I dig the well."

Sloan chose to ignore the sheep analogy, regardless of how much she felt like one—all hemmed up and driven in a direction she didn't want to go. "If I did work, there's Meggie. Patrick's old enough to stay by himself, but I wouldn't want to—"

"We can cross that bridge when we come to it."

"Somewhere after the first things first," Sloan suggested.

"Exactly. Now if you'll give me the numbers I need."

Sloan got her nursing license out of her wallet. She wrote down the number and the expiration date, then the two telephone numbers and the names of the people who could give Inez the information she needed.

Inez looked at her watch. "I have to be in court. I'll let you know something soon."

"Should I make plans to move out of the free housing in the meantime?"

"No, no," Inez assured her. They looked at each other, and Inez extended her hand. Her handshake was much like herself—brisk and firm.

"I plan to see my nephew as often as possible," Sloan said by way of warning.

Once again Inez smiled—almost. "You know, I think we understand each other," she said. On her way out, she nearly tripped over Patrick and Meggie both, who had been blatantly eavesdropping outside the door.

"Are we going?" Meggie asked Sloan immediately.

"Are we staying here?" Patrick asked.

"Yes," Sloan answered, because she knew Meggie meant the receiving home and Patrick meant Window Rock.

Meggie and Patrick looked at each other.

"Yes," Sloan said again. "We have to get to know Will and we're not going off and leaving him."

"I think you better get real here, Sloan," Patrick said. "I'd like to know what you think we're going to do with a half Navajo kid in North Carolina."

"You ask me that again—*after* you've met him."

It was clear that Will had been watching for their arrival. He met them at the door, exuberant and shy in turn. He seemed to be feeling better, but he was by no means well. His eyes were glassy and fever-bright. Sloan had already warned Patrick and Meggie that he might ask them about their father as if he was still alive and that she wanted them to answer him truthfully. She had told them that it was all right to say the word *died* and that euphemisms like *gone away* or *sleeping* would only add to his confusion.

"Who is that?" he asked Sloan, hiding behind her.

"That's Patrick and Meggie," she said.

"I got their picture. I got your picture!" he said to them. He let go of Sloan's jeans leg and stood toe-to-toe with Patrick, his eyes traveling up the length of his tall half brother until they reached his face.

"Come up here, short stuff," Patrick said, holding out his hands. "You're too low to the ground."

"I'm not *short stuff!*" Will protested, but he lifted his arms so Patrick could pick him up.

"Well, now you're not," Patrick said as he lifted him. "Now you're up here with us tall guys."

"I'm a tall guy!" Will said, clearly delighted with his new vantage point and his new brother. Impulsively, he gave Patrick a hug.

"Me, too," Meggie said. "I get a hug, too!"

Will promptly hugged her—with a little help from Patrick to get low enough to reach her neck. Patrick would have put Will down altogether, but the little boy wasn't about to turn him loose.

"Are you a brother?" Will asked him.

"Yep," Patrick said. "Are you a brother?"

"Yep," Will said, giggling.

"So who is *she?*" Patrick asked, thumping Meggie on the head.

"She's a girl brother," Will advised him.

"A girl brother, huh?" he said, winking at Sloan. "Let's make that a girl *sister,* okay? Just to keep things neat. So where's the goat?"

Sloan had heard all about George yesterday. She had no idea how the goat's fame had reached Patrick.

"Out there," Will said, indicating with an over-the-shoulder, backhand point. "Let's go!"

"Are you going to walk?" Patrick asked.

"No!" Will said, clinging hard in case the question was a prelude to being set down on the ground again. "I'm a tall guy!"

"You mean I got to *wear* you all day?"

"Yep!" Will assured him. "Come on, Meggie! Come see the goat!" he said as Patrick walked in the direction he'd pointed. He leaned down and grabbed her hand, causing a bottleneck in the doorway as they went outside.

Sloan watched the three of them, her eyes welling.

Bless you, Patrick, she thought. *Bless you and Meggie both. It's going to be all right. It's really going to be all right.*

"He's been up waiting since dawn," the Navajo woman who had let them in said.

"I would have been here sooner if I'd known," Sloan said, turning her attention away from the doorway Mark's children had gone through.

"That wasn't meant as a criticism, Ms. Baron. You came at just the right time. Why don't you go outside with the children? There's nothing planned until lunchtime. Enjoy the goat," the woman added, smiling.

Sloan smiled in return. "Yes," she said. "I think I will." She wondered if Dolly Singer was working today, but she didn't ask. She supposed that the resentment Singer felt must be echoed by his mother.

She went into the backyard, finding the goat tour over and all three of them sitting at the picnic table. Meggie was telling the "Billy Goats Gruff" story—with Patrick and Will making the proper goat noises when she cued them. Sloan made a mental note to see if she could arrange some kind of family outing for Will as soon as he was well again. Perhaps she could take him for a weekend, or a Saturday night, at least.

Will reached for her as soon as she sat down, sitting in her lap for a moment before he went back to Patrick. She held him close, savoring his little boy smell, and he kept touching each of them, as if he couldn't quite believe they were real.

Meggie was well into the Billy Goats Gruff when a tribal police car drove into the dirt parking lot. Sloan watched as the officer got out and walked toward them.

Not Lucas Singer, Sloan thought, surprised at the disappointment she felt. This officer was younger, and clearly worried, she decided.

"Ma'am" he said, as he walked up, and that was all. He didn't say what he wanted, if anything, and he didn't go inside. He didn't come close enough to intrude, exactly, just close enough to make Sloan uncomfortable.

"Would you like to sit down, Officer?" she asked after a moment. Whatever it was he was doing, he might as well do it sitting.

"No, ma'am," he assured her. "This is fine."

"Are you looking for someone?"

"No, ma'am," he said again.

Whatever, Sloan thought, still puzzled.

"Are you ready to hear the end of the story?" Meggie asked Will, and they were all immediately immersed in continued goat drama complete with sound effects. The tribal police officer stood by.

The back door to the receiving home opened, and the young girl Sloan remembered from yesterday came out carrying a tray with five cups of grape juice.

"Purple mustaches all around," she said as she set the tray on the picnic table. She said something in Navajo to the young police officer, who demurred then took the cup she offered. She chatted with him for a moment, then went back inside.

Will was the first to acquire the dreaded purple mustache, and Sloan smiled and wiped his mouth with a tissue she had in her pocket. She glanced at the young officer, then back again, because he suddenly seemed to have an intense need to get rid of his cup.

Lucas Singer was coming out of the receiving home back door. He was in uniform, and he looked tired and rumpled, she thought, as if he had worked all night and was still working. He nodded in her direction, but he went directly to the young officer, engaging him in a conversation Sloan couldn't hear.

After a moment, the young officer left, taking his cup with him, and Lucas walked over to the table.

"I was beginning to worry about him," Sloan said of the young officer.

"Meggie, Patrick," Lucas said, acknowledging them. He picked up Will in response to the child's raised arms. "I need to speak to you," he said to Sloan without prelude.

"All right," Sloan said, and he would have handed Will back to Patrick.

"Have you seen my daddy?" Will asked, holding on to Lucas's shirt.

"No, Will," Lucas said. "I haven't seen him."

The boy put his head down on Lucas's shoulder, and Lucas spoke to him softly in Navajo. Will responded in kind, taking Sloan by surprise. She hadn't even considered that the boy might be bilingual.

"It's time for his medicine, Patrick," Lucas said. "Could you and Meggie take him inside?"

They went—with Patrick giving Sloan pointed looks over his shoulder all the way into the back door.

Lucas sat down on the picnic table bench next to her, leaning forward with his arms resting on his thighs. Up close, his uniform looked as if he'd been rolling in the dirt. One pants leg was torn just above the knee.

"How much longer have you got?" Sloan said because he didn't immediately say anything.

He looked up at her. "What?"

"Until you can go home. You have the look of a man who's been deprived of his sleep."

"I have," he said, "and that depends on you."

"On me?" She gave a slight smile. "I don't understand."

"No, you don't, because Martinez didn't tell you."

"Martinez?" Sloan repeated.

"The officer you were worried about. The one with the grape juice."

"I see," she said, but she didn't see at all.

"Is today better than yesterday?" he asked, looking at the sky in a way she'd seen her farmer grandfather do a thousand times. *Is it going to rain or isn't it?*

"Yes, why? Singer, will you get to the bottom line here?"

He let his eyes meet hers. "I've taken Martinez's place. I can't leave until you do. Your visits with Will have to be supervised."

Yes, she thought, picking up one of the empty grape juice cups and immediately setting it down again. That was precisely what young Martinez was doing. Supervising.

She could feel Lucas waiting, feel his eyes on her. She was so tired suddenly, but not too tired to be angry.

"What will you do, Singer?" she asked, looking into his eyes again. "What will you do if I try to take him? Shoot me?"

"This has to be done to protect The People," he said.

She abruptly got up and walked toward the entrance of the receiving home.

"Sloan, there's something else," he called.

"For God's sake, what!" she said, whirling around to face him.

"Inez says to tell you you've got a job."

Chapter Nine

Once again Lucas made a concentrated effort to put Sloan Baron and her troubles out of his mind. He invented no pretext to go by the reservation house to see her, or to the Indian health service where she'd been working for the last few days. He didn't go to the receiving home, except when he knew she wouldn't be there. His mother had told him that Sloan and Meggie and Patrick had come to see Will Baron every day after Sloan finished work, that Sloan had made arrangements with the staff to come at that time so the supervising police officer could be on hand and the receiving home routine wouldn't be disrupted. Lucas hadn't asked for the information. His mother had decided that he needed to know these things and she had told him, and anything else about the Barons that came her way. And she wasn't the only one with a penchant to keep him informed. Mary Skeets had offered him all the latest gossip about Sloan, even though he was certain he'd given no indication whatsoever that he wanted to hear it. Sloan Baron was filling in at the Indian health service for a nurse who'd broken her ankle when she stepped in a hole in the parking lot of a country music dance club in Gallup. Sloan Baron understood practically nothing about the Navajo Way, but she wasn't disrespectful or lazy. And Sloan Baron always smiled at children.

Lucky children, he thought idly, because he'd been on the receiving end of one of those smiles a time or two. It must be difficult for her now, he thought, when she had so little to smile about.

His shift today had been essentially quiet. No running around in the desert looking for bootleggers half the night. No lost tourists or missing sheep. Even so, he was more than ready to go to the small house he rented on 264 West out of Window Rock. He needed some solitude and a decent night's sleep. He needed not to think about—anything.

But he wanted to go by to see his mother at the receiving home first, because he knew that she was worrying about him and he wanted to put her mind at rest. It was one of those ESP mother things, as far as he could tell. He hadn't consciously done anything to precipitate her worrying. He hadn't gone to work late, in recent memory. He was staying sober. He was trying to keep himself in harmony.

And because he was trying to keep himself in harmony, he arrived at the receiving home well ahead of the time Sloan Baron might be there. He noted immediately that he was both relieved and disappointed her car wasn't in the parking lot.

It was only natural, he told himself as he got out of the car, that he would be curious about how she and her family were managing. He had been an interested observer in her situation from the beginning. Curiosity was fine, acceptable, especially in a police officer. And the fact that he was curious and must have shown it shouldn't by any stretch of the imagination cause his mother any kind of distress.

He went into the building quietly, because the younger children would likely be napping. The place was quiet and essentially deserted—except for Meggie Baron, who was sitting at one of the tables in the dayroom. She was talking to Jackie Begaye. Lucas could hear part of the conversation from where he stood outside the door. Meggie must have asked Jackie how he came to be in the receiving home.

"My father hates me when he's drunk," Jackie said with the calm acceptance of a child who had had to deal with that hard truth for years.

"You're lucky," Meggie told him. "My father hated me all the time."

Lucas wanted to interrupt, to make some kind of objection to Meggie's revelation. He had to work hard to overcome the impulse to interfere. He didn't know the truth of what Meggie said. For all he knew, the dead schoolteacher *had* hated his daughter. He reminded himself that Meggie's confession was for Jackie Begaye, not him. Perhaps she'd only wanted to give Jackie some kind of comfort. And he might have convinced himself of that fact if he hadn't seen the look on Meggie's face.

But it was not his business.

He kept telling himself that, and he kept right on ignoring it. He walked over to the table.

"Meggie," he said, and she looked around, smiling broadly. "Where's the rest of the family?" he asked.

"Will's taking his nap," she said. "Patrick is at home with a cold. And Sloan is working. I'm staying here because she didn't know how late she'd be and she didn't want Will not to have a visit from at least one of us today. Did you know we were going to a *Kenaalda?* Me and Patrick and Sloan. Not Will—he can't leave the receiving home. Sloan has to work at the *Kenaalda*. Patrick might not go unless his cold is better—he says it's not a cold, it's his allergy. Sloan says time will tell. But we get to go with her if we behave and be respectful. We said we would."

"When are you going?"

"Tomorrow. We have to go on the third day when everybody else goes, so Sloan can see whoever she needs to see. Dolly told me about the *Kenaalda*. It's just to honor girls and it's special, kind of like going to church. I think I'm going to like it."

"My mother speaks to you in English?" Lucas asked, completely surprised by that piece of information.

"She has to, Officer Singer," Meggie said matter-of-factly. "I can't speak Navajo. She says it makes her face hurt to speak English, but she has to tell me things so I can help Will."

Lucas smiled. He tried to think of another person his mother had ever spoken to in English. No one came to mind.

"I'm trying to teach her some words," Jackie said, and it was clear to Lucas that the boy reveled in Meggie's apparent desire to learn.

"That's fine," Lucas said. "Then you can talk to Will in two languages."

"I'm not very good," Meggie admitted. "Officer Singer, do you know a priest?"

"A priest? Not personally. Why?"

"I want to have a Mass for my dad. I've been going to Catholic school for a while and I like Mass. Could you tell me where a Catholic church is?"

"Meggie, does Sloan know you want to have a Mass?"

"No," she said thoughtfully. "But she wouldn't mind. If she didn't get mad at Patrick for staying away from the funeral, she wouldn't be mad at me for wanting to have a Mass."

Lucas wasn't quite sure what one thing had to do with the other, but Meggie knew her aunt much better than he did. He looked up because his mother was standing in the doorway, and he made a decision. He knew about the scheduled coming-of-age ceremony, the *Kenaalda*. At Becenti's suggestion, he had already planned to attend, because there would likely be relatives of Margaret Madman there. And he rather enjoyed the fact that the ceremony would be held on a part of the reservation that was difficult to find. If he was the Lucas Singer on the FBI list, then let them use up their big budget trying to follow him. It was, however, no place for an outsider like Sloan Baron.

"Meggie, tell Sloan I'll stop by this evening. I need to talk to her about the *Kenaalda*."

"Okay," Meggie said. "She's been wondering."

"Wondering what?" he asked, because his resolve not to concern himself about Sloan Baron was completely useless. The fact that he had insisted on taking Martinez's place at the receiving home the other day told him that. He still wasn't sure why he'd sent Martinez away—except that he didn't want Sloan to hear more bad news from someone who didn't mind giving it.

"If you were coming to see us again," Meggie said.

She said that? he almost asked. But it was a boy's question, and he wasn't a boy. He was a grown man who should know better, particularly with his history with white women. "Don't forget," he said instead.

"I won't."

Lucas walked to where his mother stood, noting as he approached that her face looked much like his own must look. Out of harmony.

"The white teacher who died," he said to her when he was close enough. He touched his heart. "The white teacher left *all* his children crying."

"Officer Singer is coming to see you," Meggie said.

Sloan looked at her and then at Lucas Singer, who stood by a battered truck in the driveway.

"You don't say," she said dryly, and Meggie giggled.

"I forgot to tell you," Meggie said sheepishly.

"You don't say," Sloan said again. Twice since she'd come to Window Rock, she had decided that she wouldn't be seeing this man again, and yet here he was. She got out of the car wondering, What in the world now?

Except for his face, he didn't appear to be here on an official visit. The wary look he always seemed to have was definitely in place, but he wasn't wearing his tribal police uniform. Lucas Singer in jeans and Western boots and blue denim shirt took a bit of getting used to.

She gave the small bag of groceries she'd bought to Meggie to take inside, fully aware of two things. She was no longer angry at Lucas Singer. He had only tried to keep her informed, and it was pointless to want to kill the messenger. And she was glad to see him.

"Officer Singer wants to talk to you about the *Kenaalda*," Meggie called over her shoulder as she went inside.

"Why?" Sloan said to him.

"I want to know how you're going to get there," he said, and Sloan noted a faint reproach in his voice, just as she had the first time they met.

Perhaps she wasn't done being angry with him, after all.

"I'm not gate-crashing, Singer," she said with a patience she didn't feel. "It's my job to go. I've been assigned—"

"How are you going to get there?" he said again. "Is anybody going to go with you?"

"I—no. I'm going to drive. I have directions."

"Sloan, there are no directions to this place. The only way you can get there is with somebody who's been there a couple hundred times or was born there—and then it's iffy."

"So," she said, giving up on trying to be civil. "It's one of *those* kinds of visits, is it? Let's straighten out this incredibly uninformed white woman, right? Officer Singer, going to the *Kenaalda* is *not* something I thought up in a moment of intense boredom. I'm *supposed* to go. It's my job. I never wanted a job, but there you are. Why would the health service send me to a place I can't get to?"

"Federal agencies have a tendency to overestimate themselves out here," Lucas said.

"Federal agencies have a tendency to overestimate themselves everywhere."

"If you get lost, it's a tribal police problem."

"Yes, I'm beginning to see that," Sloan interrupted. "What, pray tell, do you suggest I do?"

"I'll take you," he said, ignoring her sarcasm.

"You'll take— Fine," Sloan immediately decided. "What time?"

He looked as startled by her acceptance as she had been by his offer.

"Well, what did you think, Singer? I'm not *that* headstrong. As much as it pains me to admit a weakness, I don't know how to get around out here. I probably *would* get lost, and since I'll have Patrick and Meggie with me and I'm not completely irresponsible, I bow to your superior judgment. What time?"

Lucas was smiling, a truly unguarded smile that made her smile, as well. "About four," he said.

"In the morning?"

"Exactly," he advised her.

She sighed. "So. Have you had supper?"

"Yes," Lucas said, almost as a defensive reflex. "No," he amended, because he immediately realized how much he was enjoying himself, regardless of the fact that he'd made her angry again. If an invitation was forthcoming, he wanted it. He stood there, looking into her eyes, and he tried to think why he enjoyed this woman. It wasn't simply a sexual attraction. He would admit a decided interest in exploring the softness of her breasts and the scent of her skin, but there was more to it than that. He liked talking to her. He liked looking at her. He liked—everything. Had he participated in this kind of banter with Sara? He didn't remember it. He didn't remember anything associated with Sara but anger and pain.

"Well, what do they say?" Sloan asked.

"Who?" he asked, puzzled.

"The Lucases. I get the feeling you have a whole committee of them you have to run things past."

"I don't know what you mean."

"Oh, yes," she assured him. "There's the wary Navajo Lucas, the one who thinks I have to be up to something because, historically speaking, white people are *always* up to something. And there's the how-is-this-going-to-look Lucas, erstwhile representative of tribal law and order *and* police department decorum. And, of course, just plain Lucas-the-man, whom I've only seen on a few fleeting occasions."

"No," he said pointedly, before they both got mad and the invitation went out the window. "I haven't had supper."

"We're having sandwiches again," she said, leading the way to the house. "You're welcome to join us. You know, I can't *cook* in Arizona. Can't bake. Can't boil. Nothing ever gets done. Patrick and Meggie have been about to starve."

"It's the—"

"I know, I know," she said, holding up one hand. "It's the altitude. You were kidding about the four a.m. thing, right?"

He had been kidding, yet another indicator of his weakness where this woman was concerned. He didn't tease white women. He didn't worry about them getting lost on the reservation, whether it complicated the job of the Navajo Tribal Police or not. He didn't go to their houses on pseudo-official business and stay for supper. And he didn't look forward to spending an entire day in their company.

In spite of all that, he enjoyed the supper of sandwiches and fresh fruit and ice water, and he enjoyed the company—which spoke well of the Baron hospitality. He'd been more than a little annoyed by Sloan's assessment of his multiple personalities, but he was still made to feel welcome at their table. The conversation was lighthearted and pleasant. He felt perfectly at ease. At ease enough to talk and laugh out loud. At ease enough to know that if he was not careful, the hunger he had for things other than food would show in his eyes. It was no wonder his mother worried about him.

Sloan and her entourage were ready and waiting the next morning when he arrived—not at four a.m., but at the more decent hour of nine-thirty. His volunteering to accompany her on an IHS mission had Becenti's wholehearted blessing. The captain was delighted that Lucas's presence at the *Kenaalda* would be official. Lucas would be able to ask a question here and there about Margaret Madman without causing any kind of panic, because he would arrive at the ceremony with Margaret Madman's white in-laws.

"How's the cold this morning, Patrick?" Lucas asked when Patrick came out.

"It's not a code," Patrick said through his congested nose. "It's—"

"An allergy!" Meggie and Sloan finished for him.

"Well, it is!" he said irritably. And he promptly settled down to sleep.

Lucas smiled, remembering when he was Patrick's age and how important it was for your family *not* to be right. He had forgotten, though, that nine-thirty could be the middle of the night for a boy this age. He chatted with Meggie over Patrick's immediate snores.

"I had to listen to that all the way from North Carolina," Meggie said, rolling her eyes.

And he was acutely aware of Sloan and of how some women smell nice apparently without having to work at it. There was no great cloud of celebrity or designer perfume surrounding her. Her scent was a subtle mixture of soap and hand lotion and *her,* and it lingered when she went into the house to get the rest of her supplies. She came out with a small six-pack-size cooler and a cardboard box. He noted that she was appropriately dressed for the occasion—jeans, athletic shoes, long-sleeved shirt. Her hair was pulled away from her face and intricately braided down the back of her head the way it had been the first time he'd seen her at the hospital. She had a red-plaid jacket she'd need when the sun went down thrown over one arm.

"What is it you're going to do today?" Lucas asked her as she stowed the box and cooler under Patrick's feet.

"Tuberculosis testing. Some of the families attending this ceremony have had active TB cases—only the IHS can't get the contacts to come in for testing."

"You want to give them some kind of shot?" he asked, because he could see a box of syringes.

"Yes. It goes between the layers of skin on the forearm. It'll show if they've been exposed to the disease."

He looked at her for a moment, hating to always be the bearer of bad news, but the fact was that the segment of The People they were going to see were very traditional. "You know this is going to be difficult," he said finally.

"I know there are taboos to get around—Meggie made me a list of things. You've got the list?"

"I got it," Meggie said, patting a pocket.

"And I know there is mistrust to overcome. I know I'm ignorant and it'll be a miracle if I don't offend somebody, whether I mean to or not. I know it's arrogant of me and the IHS to think I'm just going to waltz in there and do this." She finished buckling her seat belt and looked at him. "I think the word we're looking for here is impossible."

"Just so you know," he said.

"Then why are we going?" Meggie wanted to know.

"I get paid to give it my best shot," Sloan said. "Pardon the pun. And you get to see the *Kenaalda* regardless—unless I do something to get us run off."

"Oh, yeah," Meggie remembered.

Lucas was driving one of the tribal police sports-utility vehicles that the terrain they were about to challenge demanded. He glanced at Sloan from time to time as he drove, wondering if she would have really tried getting to this *Kenaalda* alone. Probably so. She was too uninstructed about the country and too determined to do what she was supposed to do not to try. But she understood a great deal more about the situation than he'd hoped. He was very reassured that she didn't seem to expect miracles.

Once they were out of Window Rock, he tried to look at the passing scenery through her eyes. He saw the buttes and the wild beauty of the land. She would see the secondhand house trailers and the abandoned cars and the makeshift plywood and corrugated tin corrals. The sun was very bright, glaring. He wanted to tell her that she needed to wear sunglasses. She was no longer in North Carolina, a place he imagined to be cool and shady and green. It was as if she had no respect for the differences in her country and his, and it annoyed him. She said very little, only a token question now and then.

Meggie filled in what could have been an awkward silence. She reminded Lucas of Nick Wager. Her interest knew no boundaries, and she was all rapid-fire questions, very much the way Nick had been the first time Lucas had brought him out to the reservation.

But that was a long time ago.

He kept checking the rearview mirror until they turned off the highway and onto a dirt road that was more gully than roadway. The tract was deeply rutted, and it took a good deal of concentration on his part to navigate the police vehicle through—too much to worry about whether or not he was being followed. Eventually, the ground smoothed out somewhat and they began a long incline to a hairpin turn and yet another upward climb.

"Where exactly are we heading?" Sloan asked, holding on to the door and the dashboard. She looked over her shoulder at Patrick, who was beginning to stir after the last two or three bounces.

"Higher," Lucas said obscurely. "The family who is holding the *Kenaalda* have moved to their summer home on top of the mesa. What do you think of it, Meggie?" he asked.

"I feel like I'm on the edge of the world. I feel like God can see me up here," she said, looking around.

Yes, Lucas thought. God. And perhaps her father.

He had to stop once and get out to look for signs that others had passed this way. He had told Sloan that getting to the right place was difficult, and he'd meant it. After a circle or two and some squatting down to study the ground—and some kibitzing from Patrick—he found the direction he wanted.

"Why hasn't there been more traffic through?" Sloan asked.

"We're coming in from the back side," Lucas said. It occurred to him that he'd never really been lost in his life—at least not for long—and he had enough vanity to give a small prayer that should that event occur, it not be now. He had his reasons for going at this the hard way. He wanted to see as much as he could—who had come to the *Kenaalda* and whether or not they had any connection to Margaret Madman—before word got around that a tribal policeman was there.

He suddenly slammed on the brakes, skidding to a stop on the edge of a drop.

"Road's washed out," he said, and Sloan gave him an arch look.

"If there was a road," he qualified, trying not to smile. "We'll have to walk from here."

She gave a small sigh, but she didn't complain. None of the Barons did, much to their credit, Lucas thought. They were as much a team as a family. Each of them took something from the vehicle to carry—medical supplies, food and water, aluminum folding chairs.

"Take your jacket," he said to Sloan. "It gets cold when the sun goes down."

Lucas led the way, and they walked for a time in silence, negotiating the rough terrain slowly to keep from dropping anything.

"I see a blue cardinal!" Meggie suddenly cried.

"That does it!" Patrick said, setting the cooler and the cardboard box on the ground. "A blue cardinal." He chased Meggie around until he'd gotten her in a headlock, then he turned her nose as if it were an on-off button. "I'm changing channels—nah, I'm turning this thing *off!*" He supplied all the appropriate sound effects and static noises, and he did it without malice. His silliness gave Meggie an acute attack of the giggles, and she gave him a token punch when he let her go.

"They're nice kids," Lucas said to Sloan as they walked ahead.

"Well, I can't take credit for that. My mothering skills are practically nonexistent. It's all been on-the-job training. I never know if I'm doing the right—" She abruptly stopped. "I shouldn't say that to you, should I? Not with things up in the air about Will the way they are."

He made no comment. The fact of the matter was that things weren't really up in the air at all. Unofficially, Will Baron's custody was already decided. Margaret Madman wasn't fit to mother anything, and the tribe wouldn't lose yet another child to some white woman's good intentions.

The land was becoming flat and grassy. A road appeared, this one actually visible.

"There it is," he said, pointing out the hogan and the log house and the numerous trucks and cars in a stand of trees in the distance. "Have you got a plan?" he asked Sloan, glancing at her. A few wisps of hair had come loose around her face. Her hair was golden, a kind of honey color. He found it most attractive.

"I thought I'd just say what I wanted to do and why and ask for permission," Sloan said, a bit disconcerted because he kept looking at her—as long as he thought she didn't know it. Her discomfort escalated because he abruptly laughed out loud.

"What?" she asked, trying to keep abreast of him.

"Nothing. It's just—" He chuckled to himself and shook his head.

"What?" she asked again.

"A representative of the United States government walking in and telling The People the honest-to-God's truth like that is liable to throw the whole crowd into shock. What's wrong, Ms. Baron, don't you have any big promises or trinkets and beads?"

Lucas stopped walking because she was no longer trying to keep up. He looked at her. She was staring at him, her face and her body communicating a single word.

Don't!

He didn't delude himself that he didn't understand, that he hadn't realized he was making her uncomfortable. He had the right to make her feel defensive and guilty for the sins of all those many white people who had arrived before her, and he wanted to exercise it. And it was to her detriment that she made him think of Sara.

He understood perfectly, and he realized, too, that she knew he did. But he made no apology and no attempt to justify his remark. He walked on, eventually waiting at the edge of a corral for the three of them to catch up. Some of the men working around the place had already begun to call out their greetings to him, waving for him to come join them.

"Ya-ta-hey!"

He gave them a gesture of acknowledgment, but he waited for Sloan. He felt no need to apologize to her, but he did feel a pang of regret at the disappointment he saw in her eyes.

And that made him angry.

What did she expect from him? He owed her nothing but the minimal courtesy required by his job. Even so, he realized that nothing was exactly what she *had* expected. No help. No encouragement. No understanding. Nothing. Not surprising, given her recent experience with her prodigal brother.

Her face was closed now. She had become the woman he'd first met that morning at the hospital. There were horses in the corral, and Meggie immediately ran forward to touch their noses. Used to the adoration of children, several of the horses whinnied softly.

"Who here today has the most clout?" Sloan asked him as she walked up.

"Me," he said without hesitation, and surprisingly, she laughed. He didn't fail to note how much it pleased him that she could appreciate his stellar wit, even when she was annoyed with him.

"*Besides* you, Singer," she said, still smiling.

"Oh, then that would be Dorothy Antonio—if she's here." He could think of no reason she wouldn't be, short of death, but if one believed in the mischief-maker Coyote on any level at all, there was always that possibility.

"Could we find her?" Sloan asked, forcing her amusement aside. She made a mental note to remember that she had to be on guard against this man's humor.

"Sloan, can I put this down now?" Patrick asked about the box and the cooler.

"I'll take them," she said.

"Can I go see what those guys are doing over there?" he asked.

"Can he?" Sloan asked, looking at Lucas.

"Go ahead," Lucas said. "If you get into any trouble, handle it the way you did that thing with Custer and your great-great-great-grandfather—kind of loose—but don't take any crap."

Patrick grinned. "Yeah, I can do that."

"What are you two talking about?" Sloan asked.

"It's a guy thing, Sloan," Patrick said, walking off toward a group of boys his age.

"Meggie, you stay with me," Sloan said, because she could see Meggie debating whether or not she should tag after Patrick. "I need you to help me."

"Maybe I can't read good enough to help," Meggie said, clearly worried by the prospect that whatever kind of help Sloan wanted involved the printed word.

"I don't want you to read. I want you to write down people's names for me."

"It'll take me forever," Meggie warned her.

"I'm not in a hurry," Sloan assured her. The fact was that she didn't expect to have anyone willing to have the skin test.

"Let's go look for Dorothy Antonio," Lucas said, taking the bag she was carrying and the box and the cooler Patrick had handed her and putting them in the shade of a small tree. "She's probably over there."

Sloan looked in the direction he indicated, toward an open, airy structure that appeared to be made entirely of brush and saplings or long sticks.

"That's where the family stays in the summer," he said to her. "It's cool and shady. They do their cooking out here, eat out here, sleep out here. Let me tell Dorothy what you're here for. And try not to butt in—"

"I'm not going to butt in," she interrupted.

"Try not to butt in," he repeated pointedly. "Dorothy may have questions but she won't be in any hurry to ask them. It's rude to be in a rush. Navajo people don't carry on conversations like white people. They take their time."

"So I've noticed," Sloan said, taking him off guard because he didn't quite know if she was teasing or being rude. "Does Dorothy speak any English?" she asked.

"She does but she won't."

"Will you translate what she says?"

"Yes."

"If I want to say something *then,* can I say it?"

"No," he assured her.

"How do I know you're saying the right thing?" she asked, glancing at a small pit that had been dug in the ground nearby.

"You'll just have to trust me. That's the pit for baking the corn meal cake for the *Kenaalda,*" he explained because she was looking at it closely. "They're probably still grinding the corn into meal—the girl the ceremony is being held for grinds the meal first and then some of the guests or her family help her grind it again. Then the women will make it into a special cake and they'll put it into the pit there and cover it with corn husks and build a fire over it. It'll take all night for the cake to get done."

"And then what?" Meggie wanted to know.

"And then it's eaten. I see Dorothy Antonio," he said, walking toward the summerhouse. "That's her sitting on the bench by the door. Don't look at her any more than you have to."

"I don't know what that means, Singer. How am I going to know—" Sloan managed to say before he shushed her.

"Dolly says it's rude to look at people," Meggie supplied helpfully.

Sloan and Meggie stood at a respectful distance while Lucas approached the elderly woman. She was wearing white tennis shoes and a navy blue and brown print skirt with a large flounce around the bottom, and a maroon print blouse that had pink cabbage roses and purple larkspur scattered over it. She had a number of barrettes in the front of her hair—one turquoise and silver and the rest plastic. She wore turquoise and silver dangling earrings and a heavy silver necklace. Her skin was deeply wrinkled, weathered by the sun, and her eyes watchful and serene. It was impossible for Sloan to guess her age.

Sloan waited quietly while Lucas spoke to Dorothy Antonio in Navajo, trying not to stare. She could feel the interest of the people nearby—the women in the summerhouse, men chopping a large pile of wood. She felt as awkward as someone dining in a restaurant alone with nothing to read.

"This is going to be an adventure, right?" Meggie whispered.

"Oh, I hope not," Sloan whispered back.

Lucas could feel Sloan's restiveness, but he still took his time, eventually telling Dorothy Antonio Sloan's simplistic but honest plan almost word for word the same as she had told him.

Dorothy listened and she looked to where Sloan and Meggie waited.

"She is paid to come here and do this?" Dorothy asked.

"Yes," Lucas said.

Dorothy made a monosyllabic sound of acceptance. *That* motivation she understood.

"Do you know what The People call her?" Dorothy asked.

Lucas knew the Navajo names for a few of the personnel at the IHS building. Some of them were immediately obvious—Blue Eyes, not to be confused with Blue Hair, and Red Glasses and Talks Too Loud. And some not so apparent, like Forgets the Ground, for the woman who walked so heavily it was as if she had lost track of the ground somehow, and it was always an inch or so closer than she had anticipated.

"I don't know," he said. "I think she hasn't been here long enough."

"Smiles At Children," Dorothy said, clearly pleased that in this matter she was ahead of him.

"Ah," Lucas said. He remembered someone describing Sloan in that way—Mary Skeets. He looked at Sloan. She did smile at children—at Meggie and Will and at the children at the receiving home. At the misbehaving Patrick. Now and again she even smiled at tribal policemen.

"She is the one who tries to steal Margaret Madman's baby," Dorothy said.

"She doesn't try to steal him. She is following the rules The People made to protect the children and she is working for the IHS to make money for her brother's white son and daughter."

"She is a white woman."

"She is the aunt of Margaret Madman's boy," Lucas said.

Sloan noticed that the don't-look edict apparently applied only to her. Both Singer and Dorothy Antonio were staring in her direction.

She gave a small sigh and tried to affect some kind of oblivious stance while the two of them continued to talk. And look. After a moment, Lucas motioned her over.

"Dorothy wants to know if the test is safe," he said.

"Yes, it's safe," Sloan said.

"And how does she know that?" Lucas asked on Dorothy's behalf, already anticipating Sloan's assurances.

"How does she know?" Sloan repeated, as the complexity of this problem sank in. She looked at the ground for a moment. "Because I say so isn't going to cut it, is it?" she asked, looking at him.

"No," Lucas assured her. That particular justification had been worn out a century or so ago.

"How?" she said again, this time under her breath. She looked off into the distance. "Well, there's only one thing I can do," she said, looking at him. "I'll take the test first—you'll have to give it to me."

"I can't do that," he said.

"You can if I give you my permission."

"I don't need permission. I don't know anything about giving somebody a shot," he said. And he didn't intend to learn, either. Some of the most traumatic experiences of his life at a reservation boarding school had centered around syringes and needles.

"I'll teach you."

"No, thank you. You . . . can give the test to me," he said. The offer was halfhearted at best, but at least one of them should know what she was doing.

"That won't work, Singer. For all she knows I'm out to get you, too. I'd do it on myself, but I don't think I can. It's intradermal—between the layers of skin. I have to make a raised place on the inside of my arm. It has to be done carefully because my test needs to look like everybody else's. I'm not sure I can do it with one hand. You have to do it for me."

"No, I don't."

"Singer," she said in exasperation. "Surely you've had some training in medical emergencies."

"I can deliver a baby and I can do CPR. This is not a medical emergency."

"Yes, it is. I'm the one on the receiving end here. If I'm willing, you should be."

"I don't want to stick you with a needle," he said, and he tried hard to subdue the suggestive mental analogies that particular choice of words precipitated.

"It's not that difficult. It's like sticking a butterfly's wing—in but not through it. You have to."

"No! If it has to be done, I'll help. Period. I can be your other hand."

She looked at him. Lucas could feel her mind working to find a more persuasive argument.

"Fine," she said, after a moment, apparently deciding there was none. "Help me carry the chairs, Meggie." She walked off toward the small tree where he had put everything. He didn't offer to help. He watched her go and return, trying to find some reason not to give his undivided attention to every move she made. But there was no excuse for a man who wanted to look.

She brought the cooler and the cardboard box with her, and she had Meggie set up the chairs close to Dorothy Antonio so Dorothy could see. Dorothy and a growing crowd of onlookers—mostly the elderly and the very young—watched with great interest as Sloan took a vial from the cooler and filled the needle and syringe.

"Don't you want to tell Dorothy what's happening?" she asked him pointedly.

"I can do that," he said, enjoying the am-I-going-to-have-to-do-*everything* expression on her face.

He told Dorothy what he suspected she already understood.

"Sit down, Singer," Sloan said, pulling the chairs close together.

"You're going to have to do this so the needle end doesn't point at anybody," he told her as she sat down. She handed him a packet with an alcohol swab in it, and then another, and she let Meggie carefully hold the filled syringe. He reached out and turned Meggie to the left so that the pointed end was directed toward a gap in the crowd and not toward any of The People.

"Why?" Sloan asked.

"Because you don't want to go pointing sharp things at people you're hoping not to offend."

"I'm going to be pointing this at *me,* Singer."

"Just so you know."

"I know," she grumbled. "I know I hate having to stick myself and I know you're a big sissy."

"Sticks and stones, Baron," he said, grinning. "Give me your arm."

"I don't want you to enjoy this, okay?"

"Okay," he said agreeably.

"Then stop laughing so I'll know you're not enjoying it!"

"Right. No laughing."

She took one of the packets with an alcohol swab and tore it open, swabbing down the inside of her arm. Then she took his hand and placed it firmly on the underside of her forearm. "Pull the skin tight," she said. "Syringe, Meggie."

Meggie offered it up with two hands as if it were some kind of holy relic or ceremonial sword.

"Don't miss," Lucas said as she took the cap off the needle with her teeth.

"Now there's an idea," she said around the cap, making a small fake thrust at his thumb. It was enough to make him jump and the onlookers laugh in appreciation.

"*Don't* do that," he said. "I have the dignity of the Navajo Tribal Police to uphold here."

"Ah, yes," she said, her eyes full of mischief and humor. "Dignity."

He took her arm again. It was soft and warm against his palm. She slid forward in the chair so Dorothy could see better, and she was careful of the direction the needle pointed. The entire procedure was very quick. A bump that looked like an insect bite was raised on the inside of Sloan's forearm as she gave herself the injection, and Dorothy made a soft ah sound.

"Tell her this place will disappear in a little while. Then, in twenty-four to forty-eight hours, if I or anyone who gets the test has the TB germ, the place will look like these pictures—and they need to come into the clinic ASAP."

Meggie was right on cue with the poster with color pictures of the different degrees of positive reactions, and Lucas didn't release Sloan's arm to make the explanation. He held it out for Dorothy and anyone else who was interested to make a closer inspection, partly because he knew they would be curious and partly because he liked touching Sloan Baron's warm arm.

Patrick walked up. "What's going on?" he asked, looking at Sloan's arm along with the rest of them.

"Don't ask," she said.

But it was Dorothy who asked, her eyes shifting from Patrick to Meggie. "Is this thing safe for children?" she said to Lucas in Navajo.

Patrick and Meggie both sat in the shade, fanning their recently tested arms long after they needed to. Sloan had to credit them for their ultimate willingness, in spite of the fact that Patrick was still complaining.

"Tommy Lee's aunt works at a doughnut place," he said. "She's always bringing him twenty-seven kinds of doughnuts. Chris's aunt works at the fried chicken place—she brings *him* big buckets of Buffalo wings. Do I get doughnuts and Buffalo wings? *No.* I get holes punched in my arm. And I've got a cold, too! Jeez!"

"It's an *allergy,* Patrick," Meggie chimed in.

"As soon as we get back, I'll take you to the clinic and we'll get a cast put on that arm," Sloan promised him.

"Very funny. I didn't come along to be a guinea pig, you know."

"I know. And I truly appreciate the sacrifice. Truly."

"Yeah, well, you'd better. You wouldn't have gotten anybody tested if I hadn't."

"I got tested, too, Patrick," Meggie said. "You're not the only one."

"I'm the one that counted," he said, dodging Meggie's swing.

Sloan went to work giving the skin tests to the few people who were willing—young mothers, a few elderly women and men. She wasn't entirely displeased with the light turnout, not when she'd expected no one at all. She was fully aware that she wouldn't have had any volunteers if it hadn't been for Singer, aggravating though he was. She glanced around, trying to see where he'd gone. Each time she located him, he seemed to be in a different place talking to a different person.

"Sloan, can I go see them put the stuff in the hole—the corn meal thing for the *Kenaalda?*"

"Yes—stay out of the way."

"I will," Meggie called over her shoulder.

Sloan sat down in the aluminum folding chair. She was tired suddenly. Her head hurt, and had for days—yet another consequence of the high altitude, the staff at the IHS clinic had assured her. Being this far above sea level seemed to affect her head as well as her cooking.

She was content to sit and wait for any more brave souls, showing her arm from time to time to the curious—children mostly, who wanted to check and recheck the consequence of the procedure with their own eyes.

But her thoughts kept going to Lucas Singer. She wondered what he was doing. She had no doubt that he was doing *something*. Not drumming up business for her, she decided, because some of the people he talked to had already had the test. A cheer went up behind her as a young girl suddenly burst from the hogan doorway and went running down the narrow dirt road that led away from the homestead. A crowd of children followed after her, Meggie among them.

"The young girl is running for a good life," Lucas said at her elbow. "She does that every day of the ceremony. The farther she runs the more good health she'll have. The *Kenaalda* will lead her to generosity and kindness and fertility, so she can walk in beauty always."

Sloan looked at him, and he sat in one of the chairs. "It's a good thing you're doing," he said.

"What? Offering something nobody here wants?"

"No. Not intruding here with your own agenda no matter how justified it might be. It's respectful and it gains *you* respect. The word will spread about Smiles At Children."

"Smiles At Children?"

"That's the name The People have given you."

"Smiles At Children," Sloan said. "I don't think it's true, but I like it. Could be a lot worse, couldn't it?"

"A *lot* worse," he said.

"How do you say it in Navajo?"

He said the name for her. She tried unsuccessfully to repeat it.

"Say it again," she said, watching his mouth. "I see," she said when he'd obliged. "The lips don't move."

No, he thought. *They don't. But they should. All over you—*

"I need to ask you something about Meggie," he said abruptly. "About her religion." He didn't look at her, forcing himself to ignore the things being close to her made him think and feel.

"I already know Meggie is firmly committed to several doctrines. Are you asking if I know she's well on her way to becoming a Baptist . . . Buddhist . . . Quaker?"

"Actually I think it's more Baptist Buddhist, Navajo Catholic, Quaker."

"You've got me there. I'm afraid to ask, but tell me."

Lucas told her about Meggie's plans for a Mass for her father.

"I didn't know," Sloan said.

"But you would know if Meggie's wanting a Mass is a problem," Lucas said. "Or if the reason she wants one is what's troubling her."

Neither of them said anything for a while. Lucas was acutely aware of the proximity of her body to his, just how far he would have to move to touch her. He wanted to touch her again. He wanted to run for his life.

"My mother also asks if you object to her teaching Meggie something about the Navajo Way. Meggie has a lot of questions when she comes to the receiving home. My mother wants to answer them. She doesn't want to offend you."

"I wouldn't be offended. Please. Thank your mother for her kindness."

Lucas suddenly smiled. "Dorothy is coming this way," he said, standing up. "I think you may be getting another customer. I'll leave you to it."

"Wait, aren't you going to translate?"

"Dorothy will speak to you in English if she wants to."

She didn't want to, but she did want to get the TB skin test, a conclusion Sloan made entirely without the aid of the spoken word. A number of other people followed suit, keeping Sloan busy for a time. She looked up once when Meggie returned, huffing and puffing.

"They—didn't care—if I ran—too," she said. "It was—great!"

"Catch your breath and tell me what you learned," Sloan said, injecting the last person and then finishing up the ensuing paperwork. Meggie talked at length, giving Sloan all the particulars she'd discovered about the *Kenaalda* ceremony.

"It's a real honor getting your first period out here," Meggie finished, and Sloan smiled.

"I learned something else," Meggie said.

"What?"

"I learned something about Officer Singer."

"What?" Sloan said, looking up from the papers she was shuffling.

"I heard this girl tell another girl that a white woman almost killed Lucas Singer once."

Lucas still had some people he wanted to see, questions he wanted to ask about Margaret Madman. So far he'd learned nothing about her whereabouts. It hadn't surprised him that Dorothy Antonio knew about Sloan's connection to Margaret. It did surprise him, however, that there had been anyone willing to take the tuberculosis test. Not that The People weren't essentially reasonable. Of course, it was difficult to find any duplicity in Sloan Baron when she had been willing to give the test to herself. He smiled a bit, remembering her annoyance with him for not being a more active participant. It was incredible to him that she would have actually trusted *him* to stick her arm.

He watched her now, crossing the yard to the fire over the pit where the *Kenaalda* cake was baking, and he felt once again the insistent rise of desire. It was still very disturbing to him how much he'd looked forward to today, how much he looked forward to *every* day because he might see her or talk to her, even when he supposedly did everything he could to avoid it.

She walked around the fire, listened intently to whatever Meggie was telling her, looking wherever Meggie pointed, smiling from time to time.

Smiles At Children.

It was a suitable name for her, regardless of what she thought.

Patrick suddenly stepped into his line of vision. "You want to tell me what the hell you think you're doing?" the boy said, clearly irate.

Lucas looked at him, not immediately understanding.

"You want to tell me what you're so upset about?" he countered mildly.

"Yeah, I want to tell you. What are you doing staring at Sloan like that?"

Patrick waited, fists clenched as if he actually expected an answer. Lucas could see several people nearby stopping what they were doing to listen.

"Patrick," Lucas said, trying not to smile. He was more amused than threatened. Patrick was the only male protector Sloan had. It was only right that he should be concerned about Lucas's or anyone else's intentions.

"I asked you a question, man!" Patrick said.

"And I'm going to answer it. You want to get out of my face first?" It was clear to Lucas that Patrick was not going to back down without some kind of satisfaction, just as it was clear his ire was not altogether unfounded. Lucas had been looking at Sloan "like that."

Lucas walked away a few paces. Patrick followed.

"Your aunt," Lucas said when they were out of the hearing of the onlookers, "is a pretty woman. Aside from that, she has a pleasant . . . joyful way about her. I didn't intend any offense to her—or to you. Men are going to look at her, Patrick."

"Yeah, well, it's not the *looking* I'm worried about," Patrick said, clearly not about to be fobbed off, even with the truth. "The Baron family has one half-breed Navajo bastard in the family already—we *don't* need another one!"

Chapter Ten

"Telephone, Sloan," one of the Indian health service secretaries called across the waiting area. The place was crowded with people waiting to see a doctor, and Sloan made her way carefully toward the hallway so as not to step on any children or diaper bags or purses. No one would be calling her here but Patrick or Meggie, and they were both visiting Will at the receiving home this afternoon. It was a great relief to her that the three of them seemed to get along so well—Will adored Meggie and worshiped his big brother, Patrick. She felt much less anxious knowing they were together at the receiving home while she was working. Until now, at any rate.

As soon as she was out of the waiting area, she walked swiftly to the nearest extension.

"Officer Singer," one of the nurses advised her as she picked up the receiver. "He came by while you were at lunch. Cute buns," she added in a whisper.

Sloan hesitated before she punched the only button with a blinking light. She hadn't seen Lucas Singer since the *Kenaalda* trip, which was just as well. She had allowed herself to become entirely too interested in his comings and goings, cute buns or not. And she had put entirely too much effort into trying to decipher what Meggie's cryptic tidbit of information about Lucas Singer and a white woman had meant. She was certain that the remark wasn't to be taken literally—though it might explain some of the wariness she'd sensed in him when they first met, still sensed in him. It didn't quite account for his sadness, however.

A white woman almost killed Lucas Singer once.

Suppose it was to be taken literally, she thought yet another time. Had it been an accident? A deliberate attempt? Did something happen in the line of duty? Or was it some kind of love triangle?

The truth of the matter was that she had no idea. The only person who could tell her was Lucas, and she wasn't about to ask.

"Ms. Baron," she said into the receiver.

"Sloan, it's Lucas," he said. "First—nobody's hurt. But you need to come down to the tribal police building—now."

"Lucas, you're scaring me," Sloan said, her hand gripping the telephone. "What's wrong?"

"Patrick was arrested. You need to come down here."

"Arrested for what!"

"I'll explain it to you when you get here. And don't speed. He's not going anywhere. I'll see you when you get here. Terry!" Lucas called as he hung up the phone. The other officer stuck his head in the doorway.

"I want to talk to the Baron kid," Lucas said.

"He's not talking to anybody. None of them are," the other officer said. "Can't get anything out of them but this huge, male-bonded, group silence."

"I know the kid. I want to give it a shot."

"Suit yourself. The man who owns the store is pressing charges, though. Big time."

The fact of the matter was that Lucas knew all the boys who had been brought in on some level. One of the Navajo boys had accosted Patrick in the restaurant the day he'd taken him there for chili. The other two he had questioned about Margaret Madman at the *Kenaalda.* Lucas would have guessed that all four of them had a common love of tall, four-wheel drive trucks—not vandalizing convenience stores. He picked up the folder with a copy of the arresting officer's report and walked into the hallway.

"Mary, call me when Ms. Baron gets here," he said to Mary Skeets in passing, and she held up her hand in acknowledgment.

The boys were in a huddle when he opened the door of the room where they were being detained, and they broke apart immediately. Lucas took the time to assess the array of bruised faces and scraped knuckles and torn shirts.

"All right," he said, slamming the folder down on the table. "I want to know what happened and I want to know *now!*"

They looked at each other—and said nothing.

"Do you have any idea how much damage you did?"

No one volunteered to guess.

"Did you call Sloan?" Patrick said finally, his voice only a little less sarcastic than the last time they'd spoken. It was clear that the boy saw this as an opportunity for Lucas to score some kind of points with his aunt.

"I did," Lucas said. "She's on her way. You know this is just what she needs from you—"

"It's none of your business!"

"You damn well better believe it's my business!" Lucas said, but they both knew that Patrick meant Sloan and not the incident at the convenience store. "I want to know what happened before she gets here." Lucas picked up the folder and tapped it on the table. "You gentlemen don't have anything better to do than to shame your families and make your mothers and your grandmothers and your aunts cry, is that it?" he asked quietly.

"It was an accident," Patrick said.

"You want to tell me how you can turn over *two* ten-foot free-standing shelving units and their contents *and* break a plate glass window by *accident?* Look, son. You are on the rez. The Navajo Tribal Police have jurisdiction here. You're *not* going to get off with a slap on the wrist."

"Okay, it was *my* fault!" Patrick said. "Satisfied?"

But his confession precipitated a loud protest from the other boys.

"Knock it off!" Lucas shouted into the din. "I appreciate your loyalty, but somebody better start talking. I'll do whatever I can to see you get fair treatment—maybe one of you will explain to Baron here how hard it is to get fair treatment in this part of the country when at least three of the accused happen not to be white. Now you think it over. I'll be back in five minutes and I want to hear it from the top."

He stepped out into the hall again. Becenti was standing near the door.

"What's the story?" he said.

"I don't know," Lucas said. "But it's not just vandalism."

"The Baron boy's aunt is here. She's pretty upset."

"I'll talk to her, but I want to have something to tell her when I do."

"I'm not having this kind of behavior from a bunch of young punks," Becenti said. "And I mean it!"

"Yes, sir," Lucas said, hoping Becenti's considerable voice had carried through the door to the boys on the other side. He went to his desk and made phone calls to some of the religious groups who evangelized and did charity work on the reservation. Then he filed several papers, making sure he took longer than the five minutes he'd allowed. Eventually, he walked back to the room, opening the door abruptly. This time the culprits weren't in a huddle. This time they all looked like the scared and miserable boys they were.

"Okay, let's hear it," Lucas said, perching on the edge of the table so that he was looking down on them. The folder had been moved. They had read the cold, hard facts of their crimes.

"Danny was trying to buy condoms," one of the boys said with his head down.

Lucas wasn't sure he heard right. "And?" he said in case he had.

"I got a new girlfriend," Danny—apparently the boy in question—volunteered. He glanced at Lucas, then stared at something in the far corner.

"I told him he better have condoms if he was planning anything," Patrick said. "Sloan told me all that stuff about AIDS and everything. And how you don't want to get a girl pregnant, not if you care anything about her."

"And?"

"And so Danny had the condoms and he was going to pay for them." Patrick looked at the other boys, aware suddenly that he had become spokesperson. "The guy at the cash register made this ... remark."

"What remark?" Lucas asked.

"About sheep," Patrick said, looking at Lucas.

"Sheep?" Lucas said.

"Yeah, sheep! I've heard some redneck remarks before, but this one took the cake."

"What did he say?"

"Something about how he didn't think you needed condoms if you only ... did it with sheep. He said there had to be *some* reason why the Navajo had herded sheep for so long. And he called Danny this ... name and he kept saying it. Danny wanted to just pay and get out. He said he was *used* to it, for God's sake. And then the guy said something about half-breeds and the first thing that popped into my head was Will. He's a good little kid, and here was this jackass—"

Patrick abruptly stopped, Lucas supposed because the boy hadn't until this moment realized the similarity of his own half-breed remark to whatever the store clerk had said.

"Go on," Lucas said.

Patrick glanced at the other boys. "Next thing I knew I had the guy pulled over the counter, because I'm *not* used to it—"

"Used to being on the *receiving* end, you mean," Lucas said.

Patrick looked at him for a moment before he answered. "Yeah," he said, looking at the floor. "And there were these other guys in the store—friends of his, I guess—that got into it. They ran out the back door when the officer arrived. It wasn't just us ganging up on a poor helpless store clerk like he said. The guy started it and we . . . finished it."

Lucas waited. This was *not* what he had expected. "Anything else anybody wants to add?"

"I sure hope Danny's new girlfriend is worth it," one of the boys said, and they all gave a nervous laugh.

"This is not a laughing matter, gentlemen!" Lucas said sharply.

"What are you going to tell Sloan?" Patrick asked.

"Nothing. You're going to be the one to tell her," Lucas said.

"I don't want her to know about this stuff. She . . . worries enough. And, yeah, I know I should have thought about that sooner than now. What's going to happen—to us, I mean?"

"I have no idea. It's not up to me. I'm going to go talk to Captain Becenti now. He's upset, by the way. This kind of stuff is bad for tourism. People don't want to spend their vacations trying to dodge a brawl. But I'll see what he says. Believe me, you'll be the first to know."

"Sheep!" Becenti said.

"Ah, yes, sir," Lucas said.

Becenti listened to the rest of the report in silence.

"I've talked to some of the Church groups already," Lucas said. "They're looking for some boys to help dig wells around the reservation in the next few weeks and they can always use some help chopping winter firewood for the elderly. I was thinking a good dose of community service would be—"

"That guy at the convenience store isn't going to sit still for community service."

"He might if he understood the situation. It's the tourist season. People come here to see Navajo Indians. Maybe he wouldn't want them to see Navajo Indians with signs picketing his store. Maybe if he knows we're *all* pretty sensitive about sheep remarks, he'd realize he wouldn't want a tribal boycott, either."

Becenti looked out the window. Lucas waited.

"Might work," Becenti said.

"You want me to talk to him?"

"No, Lucas, I want you to leave at least some of *my* job to me. This son of a bitch is a grown man. He thought he could get away with that kind of thing with a bunch of kids, and they kicked the hell out of him, and his friends, *and* his store. I'm going to enjoy pointing that out to him. The boys were totally out of line, of course, but for all the right reasons. Well-digging and wood-chopping sound like an appropriate enough punishment—if he agrees to it. It certainly helped me see the light a time or two when I was young. You found Margaret Madman? Or the FBI yet?"

"No, sir."

"Well, keep looking. Tell the Baron boy's aunt he's going to have to do some community service—unless I can't reason with this man. And then it'll have to go to court."

Lucas left Becenti's office, and he braced himself to talk to Sloan. As much as he welcomed the opportunity to see her—and even if Patrick's situation had the potential for turning out a lot better than it might have—he hated having to give her bad news. Again.

"Singer, you're rapidly becoming the Walter Cronkite of my life," she said when he walked up.

"Who?" he said, because he couldn't see any relationship whatsoever between a Navajo tribal policeman and a white television news anchorman.

"Walter Cronkite, the newscaster. My mother used to say she could stand any kind of bad news—wars, assassinations, you name it—as long as Walter Cronkite was the one who told her. What's happened?"

Lucas gave her the gist of the incident, leaving out the condom buying and the details surrounding it.

"I can't believe Patrick would have wrecked a store like that. I want to see him."

"He'll be released into your custody in a little while."

"Are you telling me everything?"

"Why do you ask that?"

"Because, Officer Singer, you're *not* telling me everything."

"I don't want to give you the details. Patrick can do that if he decides to."

"If he decides to!"

"Sloan, it's another—"

"Another what?"

"It's another... guy thing. It's embarrassing for him. It would be good if you didn't badger him about it. I will tell you that, regardless of the result, his motives were decent."

"Is that supposed to make me feel better?"

"Hopefully," Lucas said. He looked into her eyes. She was so distressed and tired. He wanted to put his arms around her. He wanted to find her a perfect peach or something to drink. He wanted to rub her back for her—anything that would make her feel better. And that was a revelation—that the flagrant lust he'd been feeling could be tempered with an equally flagrant need to take care of her. He actually wanted to take care of Sloan Baron, the most independent woman he'd ever met.

"His judgment was bad, his reasons were good, is that it?"

"Yes."

"He broke the Baron family golden rule, Lucas."

"Which is?"

"Behave or be *dead.*" She sighed heavily. "Of course it's the Baron women who made the rule. We made it, and the Baron men just go right on ignoring it. You know I'm ready to do bodily harm to my own flesh and blood here."

"I realize that. That's why I wanted to see you first."

"He was *supposed* to be at the receiving home with Meggie and Will."

"We didn't talk about that."

"No? You mean there's something he doesn't tell you?"

"Sloan—"

"I know, I know. I'm being unreasonable. I *feel* unreasonable, Lucas. What do you suggest I do?"

"Nothing—the only thing you can do with a boy this age. Take him home and feed him."

"I can't cook here!"

He tried not to smile. "Take him home. Cooperate with whatever community service they give him. Captain Becenti will let you know as soon as he knows something. And don't worry. Patrick is a good kid."

"Don't worry," she repeated. "Just like that."

"It's not going to do any good. Becenti is a fair man, but there are . . . circumstances."

"Lucas, Captain Becenti's back," Mary called to him.

Sloan looked up when Patrick was finally brought out, and she would have been fine if he'd kept quiet.

"Am I grounded?" he asked immediately, and her temper flared.

"Oh, yes, Patrick," she said. "*You* are grounded. Your wife and children are grounded. Your *grandchildren* are grounded. Now get in the car!"

He gave a long-suffering sigh, but he went.

She glanced at Lucas. "What!" she said, because he was trying not to grin.

"Oh, nothing," he said. The grin got away from him. "I'm just glad you're not a tribal judge."

"This isn't funny."

"It isn't," he agreed. "And it is," he added, grinning again. "Have a nice day, Ms. Baron."

But she never expected to have a nice day again—ever. And she wouldn't have if Patrick hadn't reminded her when she was almost home that she still had another child to pick up. She drove to the receiving home, angry and upset and incredulous that she could have completely forgotten Meggie, only to have it all dissipate in a shower of hugs from her and Will.

"I need one of your superdeluxe, really-bad-day hugs," she told them, and she got all she needed and more, until she felt relaxed and almost sane again. Even Patrick's poor-misunderstood-grounded-teenage-boy persona faded in the wake of Will's overt adoration. All three of them were unexpectedly invited to stay for supper with Will and the rest of the receiving home children, regardless of the fact that she'd missed the time when her tribal police escort would have been there, and she accepted, more aware than ever of how truly proud Will was of his relatives. She stayed long enough to read him a bedtime story, and it was well past dark when she got home. Lucas Singer was waiting in the driveway.

"Oh, no," she said by way of greeting, and he laughed.

"It's not a Walter Cronkite kind of visit," he said.

"Has Captain Becenti decided about the community service?"

"Not yet," he said. "I came by because I . . . need a favor."

"What kind of favor?"

"If you're not working tomorrow."

"What kind of favor?"

"I don't know any other medical person I'd want to ask.'

"Lucas! What kind of favor?" Sloan said pointedly. Neither Patrick nor Meggie had turned on the porch light, and Lucas was standing in the shadows. She could almost, but not quite, see his face.

"I want you to go with me to talk an old man into going to the hospital. He's sick and his daughter is worried enough about him to ask me if I'd go see him. His name is Hosteen Anagal. He's a medicine man."

"Is that why he won't go—because he's a medicine man?"

"I don't know. He's a traditionalist, but he's not stubborn or unreasonable—unless it's something new, part of his illness."

"He's a friend of yours?"

"He . . . helped me when I needed it."

"Okay," Sloan said. "I'm off this weekend. When do you want to go?"

He seemed surprised, as if he expected that talking her into going to see the old man would be more difficult.

"Early," he said. "I asked one of the nurses at the clinic to put together some things you might need—blood pressure cuff, the thing to check his blood sugar. I'll go by and pick it up if you want to do this."

"Okay," she said again. She could feel him looking at her in the darkness. "You want to tell me how early?" she prompted.

"I'd like to leave before five. We can drop Meggie off at the receiving home if you want. I've already talked to my mother. Meggie's welcome to stay there while you're gone."

"Could we drop Patrick off at the jail?"

He laughed. "That, too."

He said his goodbyes and left, and Sloan went inside, bumping into Patrick just inside the door.

"Patrick! What are you doing standing here in the dark?"

"Nothing," he said in a way that suggested exactly the opposite to anyone who dealt with a teenage boy on a daily basis. "Have you got something going with Singer?" he asked.

"He needs to try to talk an elderly man into going to the hospital. I'm going along."

"Going along where?"

"I don't know. I didn't ask," Sloan said, switching on the light.

"What do you mean you didn't ask? You're just going to go off someplace with him and you don't even know where you're going?"

"I'll find out in the morning. Don't worry—I'll leave you a note," she said pointedly to tease him, amazed by his parental tone. He sounded like *her.*

"Ha, ha," he said. "Very funny."

"I thought it was. Pretty dang clever, if you ask me. Notice how I just turned the tables there—got that little dig about the note in." She stopped, realizing suddenly that Patrick was completely serious. She also realized, when he'd asked if she had something going with Singer, he hadn't meant her travel plans.

"What's wrong?" she asked.

"Nothing!"

"This is where I came in, Patrick. Have you got something to say or not?"

"No, I don't have anything to say!"

But apparently he came to that conclusion a bit prematurely. "Well, what am I supposed to do while you're gone?" he called after her when she headed toward the bathroom.

"Be grounded," Sloan called back. "Or have you already forgotten?"

"I wish," she thought he said.

"Maybe you'd like to talk about *that*," she suggested. "Maybe you'd like to explain to me just how you ended up in a police station. You're going to have to sooner or later."

He didn't answer her.

"Is Patrick grounded?" Meggie poked her head out of the bedroom to ask.

"Yes," Sloan said. She rubbed a spot between her eyes that ached. Every bit of the harmony she'd found with Meggie and Will was gone.

"Is that why you needed me and Will to give you a superdeluxe, bad-day hug?"

"That's why."

"What did he get grounded for? I miss everything."

"I got arrested!" Patrick yelled from the living room.

"Did he?" Meggie asked, her eyes big.

"Yes," Sloan said.

"Well, why? Who?"

"Meggie, honey, it's a long story. I don't even know the details, and I'm too tired to go into it tonight. I have to get up early tomorrow." She told Meggie about the plan for her to stay at the receiving home while Sloan went with Lucas Singer to see the medicine man.

"That's cool," Meggie said. "I like to stay there. Sloan? Patrick isn't going to turn out like our dad, is he?"

"No," Sloan said firmly. "He isn't." She kissed Meggie good night, and she went straight to bed, falling asleep immediately in spite of the trials and tribulations of the day. And she woke up to a pounding on the back door.

"Oh, no," she whispered, trying to force herself to sit up, realizing that she hadn't set the alarm. She stumbled to the door in her nightgown. Lucas was standing on the doorstep, his arms folded.

"Five minutes," she said, peeping at him through a crack in the door.

His gaze traveled from her bare feet to her disheveled hair. "I don't believe in miracles, Ms. Baron," he said.

"Okay, *seven* minutes," she said. "Possibly nine."

"I'll wait," he said.

But he didn't wait. Sloan came out of the shower, hair still wet, to find him already gone.

"Well, where did he go?" she asked Meggie. "I've still got a good three minutes."

"He went to get breakfast," Meggie said, tying her shoe.

"Is he coming back?"

"I guess so. He wanted to know what you liked to eat. I said you didn't like egg anything."

Sloan hurried to the bedroom to find a T-shirt and jeans and to hunt for her denim shirt with the big pockets. She came back carrying her running shoes and a pair of socks. She sat down on the couch and tried not to fall asleep again. "I am not a morning person," she declared, putting her face in her hands for a moment. She reached over and gave Meggie a hug. "How come *you're* so chipper, Meggie Baron?"

"I'm just a kid," Meggie said, giggling. "And I like to stay with Will and Dolly and Jackie Begaye. I left Patrick a note—you said you'd leave him a note so I asked Officer Singer where you were going. It was hard to write—the name of the canyon sounds like s-h-a-y but it's got a *c* and two *l*'s in it. Officer Singer said I did it right, but he had to help me. He can help you spell good. Dolly says he might get to be a sergeant instead of an officer—he took some kind of test. She says if he passes, it'll show he got back in harmony. She said he was her best child—the kindest and the strongest and the best in college. She said he couldn't fail the test if his harmony was back. She said his harmony was gone for so long she thought he was lost."

"Lost?" Sloan said, looking up from putting on her shoes.

"That's what she said. I didn't know you took tests when you got grown up. I hate tests. Jackie Begaye says he does, too."

"You like Jackie," Sloan said.

"We got a lot in common," Meggie said.

Yes, Sloan thought. Lucas had told her. Both these children thought that their fathers hated them—and with good reason. She hadn't spoken to Meggie about the conversation Lucas overheard or about her wanting to have a Mass—another indicator of her stellar mothering skills. She'd always tried to teach Meggie that what a person did counted a lot more than what he or she said. How could she convince her that Mark had loved her when he hadn't even wanted to see her before he died? She couldn't, and coward that she was, she put off dealing with the problem.

She sighed heavily. And now there was this thing with Patrick. She had to be out of her mind to think that she could declare him grounded and then leave for the day.

"Here's breakfast, I bet!" Meggie said abruptly.

Lucas was already coming through the door when Sloan looked around. He handed Meggie a paper bag and sent her to the truck.

"What's wrong?" he asked as soon as she was gone.

"I was just worrying about leaving Patrick here," Sloan said truthfully.

"Don't," he said. "Some of the officers will check on him today. And the whole reservation knows he's grounded—unto the third generation," he added.

She tried not to smile, because she hadn't wanted to be reminded that she'd lost her temper.

"We should be back this afternoon," he said. He kept looking at her, and she realized suddenly that she was only borderline presentable—no makeup, her still wet hair pulled back and braided the best she could. He, on the other hand, looked quite nice—jeans and boots again and a pale blue linen shirt. She was close enough to be aware of his clean, masculine smell and to note that she found it entirely pleasant. Her eyes met his, and she tried to decide what precisely Dolly Singer had meant by "lost."

"All right," she said. "I can't stand over Patrick all the time, I guess."

Lucas had brought her a raisin bagel and a huge fresh peach that was ripe enough for her to peel with her fingers. And cold orange juice. She ate on the way to the receiving home. He wouldn't let her pay him for any of it or for Meggie's breakfast burrito. They dropped Meggie off at the receiving home in the gray predawn. Dolly met her at the door, waving to Lucas before she took a smiling Meggie inside.

"Your mother is up early," Sloan said.

"She follows the Navajo Way. She's always awake to greet the dawn and say her prayers."

"My mother used to do that, too," she said. "She used to say that she never wanted to miss when the birds started singing because she liked to send her prayers up with God's own musical accompaniment. A fanciful woman, my mother. I'm glad she didn't have to know about . . ."

She stopped, because she didn't want to think about anything unpleasant today.

They took a different direction out of Window Rock from when they'd gone to the *Kenaalda*. Lucas didn't attempt any further conversation, and neither did she. She wondered idly how it was he was able to drive a Navajo Tribal Police vehicle again when he wasn't on duty today—or at least he wasn't in uniform. After a time, he turned on the radio and tuned it to a country music station, cutting the volume down low so that it didn't interfere with the occasional transmissions on the police radio. She noted idly that he still wore his watch on his right wrist, and in spite of Patrick's admonishment, she didn't ask their precise destination. The truth of the matter was that she was glad to be with him today. She didn't care where they were going. She was aware, too, of a kind of mental list she'd been keeping, and that everything on it had to do with him. She noted that she had seen him cold and distant, angry, amused, annoyed, kind and perhaps a little sad. She noted that she had enjoyed his teasing, thinking one minute that it was the kind that indicated a man was more than a little interested in a woman and being certain the next that any sexual interest she'd perceived in Lucas Singer had been entirely the product of her celibate, old-maid mind. She had known for some time that she wanted his respect, but her growing need to remember exactly what he'd said and the way he said it made her realize that, regardless of her best efforts, she was beginning to want more. She was intensely aware of his closeness.

What exactly do I want? she thought, staring out the window. *Friendship? A love affair?* She had never had a lover and never wanted one—at least not a specific one. She'd never had the time for a lover—she didn't have the time *now*. She gave a small sigh. She was being ridiculous. She was considering the two possibilities, lover or friend, as if either of them was an option.

She was aware, too, that Lucas kept looking at her hair.

"What's wrong?" she asked bluntly. "I'm not going to scare Mr. Anagal half to death, am I?"

He let the chance she gave him to reassure her of her stunning, wet-haired beauty pass him by. "I was wondering if you could do something with the braid," he said.

"Like what?" she said, ready to be offended.

"Turn it under. I don't want Hosteen Anagal to know it's so short."

Sloan didn't think it was *so* short, but she hunted in her purse for an emergency barrette she kept for Meggie and clipped the braid under, so that its telltale shortness was less obvious. And then she waited.

And waited.

"Lucas, are you going to tell me why I did this or not?" she asked abruptly, and he looked at her in what could only be surprise. "I know it's polite to keep quiet and wait for the other person to say whatever they're going to say, but you never say anything else. You throw out these... tidbits and then you leave me dangling. It makes me crazy."

"You can ask whatever you want to know, Sloan," he said.

"I don't want to be a pest."

"We Navajo have a great capacity for overlooking a shortcoming."

"How nice. Are you going to tell me about the hair or not?"

"A traditional Navajo believes that a woman's wisdom is in her hair, so it's never cut."

"You mean the longer it is, the more wisdom she has?"

"Right. So if you have to offer a medical opinion, I want the old man to think you're wise enough to have one."

"Makes sense," she said, even though the situation was hopeless. She had admired the way some of the Navajo women arranged their long hair—kind of fan-folded at the base of the neck and tied in the middle. Her little turned-under nub of a braid wasn't going to impress Hosteen Anagal.

She watched the passing scenery for a while. Everything she saw reminded her of Mark—and therefore Will and Patrick and Meggie—and therefore Patrick—and therefore Will—

"I do have some questions," she said to keep from thinking about the things that worried her so.

"Ask."

"Why do you wear your watch on your right wrist? You're not left-handed because you wear your gun holster on your right hip, unless you're ambidextrous, of course."

Lucas looked at her, a little surprised that a thing like that had caught her attention. It was something Sara had never asked him about, and what was even more surprising to him was that he wanted to tell her.

"When I was a little boy—" he began.

"How little?" she said.

He was beginning to understand that her interruptions were not so much a white person's rudeness as an intense need she seemed to have to understand a situation exactly. "About Meggie's age. When I was a little boy, the Hubbell Trading Post had a guess-the-number-of-beans-in-a-jar contest. The prize was a genuine, self-winding Timex watch. I won it. It was one of the biggest thrills of my life—even if I had no use for a watch whatsoever. I never had to do anything by a certain time, except at boarding school, and they were always ringing bells to get you places. I didn't know that most people—white people—put them on their nondominant arm. I wore the watch until it fell apart. By that time I was used to having it on my right wrist. I still wear my watch there to remind me."

"Of what?" she asked.

He turned his head to look at her. "Of where I started and how far I've come. I don't want to ever forget who I am."

"Did you like boarding school?"

"Boarding school was little-Navajo-boy hell," he said matter-of-factly. "I don't know why I didn't die. Most of the time I was sure I was going to."

"Things have a way of not killing us sometimes."

Yes, he thought. *Like boarding schools. And Sara Catherine McCay. And worthless brothers.*

"I want to ask you about . . . my brother," she said, as if she'd heard his thoughts. "I know it's taboo to speak about the dead, but I don't know who else to ask. I don't know the people at the clinic well enough—and I'm getting used to hearing bad things from you." She glanced at him, as if she was trying to assess whether his silence gave her permission. "I wanted to know what exactly he did at the community college. Do you know?"

"Yes, and it's not bad. I'm told he taught an automotive course," Lucas said. He hadn't realized that she still knew so little about her brother's life here or that she had been mindful enough of the taboo not to ask. "He'd beg an abandoned car from somebody on the rez. He and his class would take months to restore it and get it running. The boys—and some girls, I understand—learned about motors and simple welding and patchwork and paint jobs. Then, when the car was as finished as the school could afford to make it, he'd raffle it off. The students who fixed it up got a chance to win it. I bought a ticket once on a turquoise and white Edsel. The money they raised went to the school."

"I'd forgotten," she said after a moment, "that he always liked to work on cars. It's good he was doing . . . something he enjoyed."

Lucas suspected that the dead teacher was an expert at that, but he didn't say so. "Hosteen Anagal is at his summer hogan on the mesa above Canyon de Chelly. We're going in the shortest way," he said.

"With or without a road?" she asked mildly.

"With," he said. "Most of the way," he added. "It'll take a least an hour to get there. Sleep if you want."

She took him up on the invitation, pulling her legs up and leaning against the door in a way that reminded him of the first time he'd seen her, asleep in the intensive care waiting room at UNM Hospital. He took the opportunity to look at her as much as he could and still drive, the question *he'd* wanted to ask foremost in his mind.

Who is waiting for you in North Carolina?

Was she married or about to be? Divorced? He didn't know anything about her personal life and he wanted to. He wanted to know very badly.

Sloan roused at the noise of barking dogs and Lucas's hand on her shoulder. The truck had stopped.

"Wait here," he said. "I'm going to go see where he is, then I'll call you."

She nodded and promptly dropped off to sleep again, but a final, loud bark close to the truck door woke her up again. She raised her head to look around her. They were parked under some cottonwood trees not far from another, now familiar-looking Navajo homestead. She could see Lucas walking along with the dogs toward a red-roofed hogan. He spoke to them as he walked, patting the nearest ones on the head.

Sloan sat up and stretched her legs. She took the time to examine the box of supplies Lucas had had someone at the clinic put together. It was more than adequate for this kind of home visit. She could at least check the old man's blood pressure and do a screening test for an elevated blood sugar. She'd already seen a number of newly diagnosed cases of diabetes among the Navajo patients at the clinic.

There was an envelope containing some lancets and a few alcohol swab packets in the box. She took the envelope out and folded it as small as she could and put it into her shirt pocket. She looked in the direction Lucas had gone. He was standing in front of the entrance to the hogan, waiting, it seemed, but then he disappeared inside. She waited a moment, then opened the truck door, bringing the dogs immediately. They yapped around her as she got out.

"I know you're hungry," she said softly, "but I don't have anything but bagel crumbs and a peach pit. *I* am not on the menu, got it?" She held the box down so they could all sniff it. Apparently satisfied that they had done their duty, they milled about, still giving an occasional yap but with their tails wagging.

She looked at the sky. The sun was just coming up, turning the grayness to pink. A cool morning breeze rustled the leaves in the cottonwoods, and she turned her face into it, savoring the feel of it against her skin. She could hear bleating sheep and tinkling bells nearby. And birds. One sounded like a mourning dove. Did they have mourning doves in Arizona, she wondered?

She smiled to herself. Maybe it was Meggie's blue cardinal.

"Sloan!" Lucas called from the doorway of the hogan. He motioned for her to come. She and the dogs hurried forward.

"He's very weak," Lucas said. "I need to get him outside so he can see the sun come up."

She put the box on a bench beside the hogan door, moving a snuff tin and jar of roofing nails to make room.

"Are you sure you want to move him?" she asked, following him inside the hogan.

"I'm sure," he said.

It took a minute or two for her eyes to adjust, before she could locate the old man lying on a folding aluminum chaise longue against the far wall. Lucas spoke to him in Navajo, stepping forward to help as the old man attempted to get up out of the chaise. Lucas caught him before his knees buckled, and Sloan moved closer to take the old man's other arm.

The old man said something in Navajo that was clearly an inquiry.

Who is this person? Sloan imagined that he asked, because he looked at her and then at Lucas.

Lucas answered him, and the old man made a monosyllabic sound of understanding. Together, she and Lucas took Hosteen Anagal outside. She had to move the snuff can and the jar of nails again so the old man could sit down. He sat with his eyes closed, his chest heaving. She glanced at Lucas. After a moment, he helped the old man to his feet.

"What . . ." she started to ask, but Lucas held up his hand.

"He needs to say his morning prayer," he said, and she realized suddenly that the old man was indeed praying, a kind of whispered chanting that took more breath than he had. She moved a few steps away, because it seemed wrong to crowd him now, even if she only intended to help.

She remembered what Lucas had told her at the *Kenaalda*—not to look at Dorothy Antonio any more than she had to, and she supposed that the same held true for Hosteen Anagal. She took the time now to make her visual assessment, while he was otherwise engaged. She could see nothing but an aged frailness and his devout belief as he prayed, that, and Lucas's gentleness with him.

She realized that Lucas was praying, as well, and she stood awkwardly, feeling every bit the outsider she was. His voice was stronger and just as sure. She felt a keen sense of Mark's loss suddenly. She had to fight down an intense urge to cry as she witnessed their reverence for an event she had always taken for granted. She looked away, staring with them toward the place where the sun was about to rise, realizing that Lucas's wanting to leave so early was likely because he knew that his help with this morning ritual might be needed. When the prayer was finished, he assisted the old man to the bench, then disappeared inside the hogan, returning after a few seconds with a cup of water. The old man drank thirstily.

"Come closer, Sloan," Lucas said. "I've told him why you're here. What do you want to do first?"

"I'd like to take his blood pressure and listen to his heart," she said. "And then I'd like to check his blood sugar. I need a drop of blood from his finger to do that."

Lucas spoke quietly to the old man in Navajo, then listened to his reply.

"Okay," Lucas said.

She stepped forward, waiting until the old man had unbuttoned his shirt. Then she listened to his chest for a time. She took his blood pressure quickly, noting again the regular rhythm of his pulse as she watched the gauge. She was surprised at how good the reading was and that his heart was so strong and regular.

"Your blood pressure is fine," she said directly to Hosteen Anagal. "Your heart sounds strong." She returned the blood pressure cuff and the stethoscope to the box and took out the things she would need to check his blood sugar, forgetting for a moment that she'd put the lancets and the alcohol swabs in her pocket. She reached for Hosteen Anagal's hand when she was ready, but he hesitated, saying something instead to Lucas.

"He apologizes for his hands," Lucas told her.

"There is no need," Sloan said, taking the old man's hand into hers. She recognized immediately that this man was a farmer. "He has hands like my grandfather's—a working man's hands," she said, glancing into the old man's eyes. "He dug in the earth, too, to make things grow."

She cleaned his fingertip with an alcohol swab and stuck it with the lancet, then collected the blood she needed for the test. The only adhesive bandages in the box were the ones with cartoon characters for children. Hosteen Anagal studied the one she put on his finger carefully, then said something to Lucas.

"He says he's seen these people before on his granddaughter's television set in Chinle. He says they fall down a lot and they aren't very smart."

Sloan smiled and turned her attention to the test. The old man's blood sugar was alarmingly high, much worse than she expected. She looked up to find both men watching her.

"This isn't good," she said, showing each of them the reading. "Ask him if he's thirsty all the time, if he pees a lot, if he has to get up at night to go."

Lucas translated. "Yes," he said after the old man had answered.

"I think he's probably diabetic, Lucas," she said. "He needs more testing to be sure. And he needs treatment now. He needs to go into the hospital today."

Lucas translated again; Sloan didn't need any help to determine the old man's response.

No.

"Lucas, tell him I think he may die if he doesn't go."

"No," the old man said again, without Lucas's translating.

"Tell him he's hardheaded like my grandfather, too," Sloan said in exasperation.

Lucas apparently did, because the old man abruptly laughed, shaking the hand with the bandaged finger at Sloan.

"I'm going to feed his stock," Lucas said after a moment. "He needs time to think about this. And it'll help him to know his animals are taken care of."

Sloan stood there for a moment, then sat down on the bench beside Hosteen Anagal. She watched Lucas drag a bag of dog food from the hogan and mix it in a bucket of water for the dogs, sending them all into a frenzy of anticipation. Then she picked up the box she'd brought and began to rearrange it. The box didn't need rearranging; she needed some busywork so she could decide what to do. If worse came to worst, she and Lucas both were bigger than Hosteen Anagal. Surely, they could take him.

"Young woman," Hosteen Anagal said in English, startling her. His voice was dry and raspy, but pleasant. She looked at him, realizing that speaking or not speaking English on the reservation must be a kind of ace in the hole.

"Why do you trouble yourself about an old man?" he asked.

Sloan pondered the question. She could give some kind of standard, I-live-to-serve nurse reply, except that it wouldn't be true. It took her a moment to decide exactly what *was* true. She sensed very strongly that this man wanted specifics.

"Because Lucas is troubled," she said, knowing that that was the heart of the matter. "He asked me to come with him, to help you if I could. I think he trusts me to know what to do. I think you're very sick. I want you to go to the hospital because you're important to him. I want you to go to the hospital because..." She hesitated, then gave a small shrug. "I don't want to fail in his eyes. I don't want him to think I'm useless."

The old man said nothing. Sloan had no indication of whether or not he even understood. They sat in silence until Lucas had finished feeding everything that required feeding. Hosteen Anagal spoke to him at length when he returned to the hogan. Lucas squatted down by the bench to listen. Sloan could tell nothing from either of their faces.

"He wants me to check his corn," Lucas said to her finally.

"What corn?" Sloan said. She hadn't seen any corn growing.

"It's down in the canyon."

She hadn't seen a canyon, either.

"It'll take at least an hour to get down there and back," Lucas said. "I know you're worried about Patrick."

She shook her head. "You can't reason with a man who's worried about his corn. You have to do it."

Hosteen Anagal said something in Navajo.

"You have to do it, too," Lucas said. "He says to take you with me."

"How do I know I want to go?" Sloan asked. The old man took the box out of her hands and put it on the bench.

"You do," Lucas said. "It's beautiful. *Yeibichai* lives there—Talking God."

"Talking God?" she asked as he stood up.

She looked at Hosteen Anagal, who was shooing her away with both hands. She stood, and she had to walk fast to catch up with Lucas because she expected him to go toward the truck and he took off in the opposite direction.

"*Yeibichai* is the spokesperson for God Himself," Lucas said over his shoulder.

She suddenly realized that they were going down into this canyon on foot. She looked at Hosteen Anagal. He waved.

She followed along after Lucas until he came to a down-sloping track.

"Oh, my Lord," she said when she caught sight of the canyon itself. "Are you sure we can get down there?"

"I'm sure," he said, his eyes filled with mischief.

"Alive, I mean," she qualified.

"It's been done," he said.

She wasn't particularly reassured.

They followed the path downward as far as it went. There was a considerable drop to the next ledge.

"There are footholds cut in the rock," Lucas said, pointing. "Step where I step."

"If I fall, I'll take you with me," she said, trying to be practical.

"If I go first, I'll scare away the snakes," he countered.

"After you," she said demurely, and he laughed.

They continued to make their way downward. The track appeared again, making the walking easier. Even so, Sloan felt breathless and light-headed. Lucas looked back at her from time to time. She tried to appear more athletic than she felt, and she tried not to think about the return trip. She just followed along, dogging his steps, trying to keep up and not step on his heels. At one point, she stopped walking, struck by the incredible stillness of the place as they wound lower into the canyon. It was indeed beautiful, and she felt such a sense of the past suddenly, of people who were no longer alive, and yet they *were* here on some level, still traveling as she traveled, using the same ancient footholds and paths.

She started violently as a bird flew upward from the ground.

"What's the matter?" Lucas asked, shading his eyes to look in her direction.

"Nothing—my mother wasn't the only fanciful Baron woman, I guess. I feel as if I have to be careful so I don't step on some spirit's toes," she said, walking again.

"Yes," was all he said.

The angle of descent smoothed out until they were on nearly level ground. She followed along, and she stared at his back, at his shoulders and his hips. She stared at the way he walked and the back of his head.

What are you doing? she kept asking herself. She had no business being here in the first place. She should be in Window Rock doing laundry and buying groceries. No. She should be *home,* for God's sake, with her two jobs and Mark's children—*all* of Mark's children—and not lusting after Lucas Singer. And there was no doubt that she had crossed the fine line from admiration to lust. At this particular moment, she wanted to crawl all over him just because of the way his hair lay on the back of his neck. And if that wasn't bad enough, she'd all but told Hosteen Anagal that she did.

She gave a heavy sigh. Lucas looked at her over his shoulder.

"It's not much farther," he said, and she nodded as if the distance to wherever it was they were going was her sole concern. She wondered if he had any idea of the thoughts she was having.

No, of course he didn't. How could he? She'd only just realized herself.

The ground slanted sharply downward again.

"Did your grandfather really grow corn?" he asked after a time.

"Yes. And he really was a hardhead. He loved Silver Queen white corn—the man who had the neighboring field loved yellow corn. Neither one of them would give an inch, and every year we ate white corn with big yellow polka dots. Why?"

He was smiling. "I just wondered."

"Why? Did you think I wasn't telling the truth?"

"No, not exactly."

"What then?"

"I was surprised."

"Why? Because you didn't think white North Carolina grandfathers grew corn?"

"No. Because it was exactly the right thing to say."

They reached the canyon floor. She basked in what she perceived as a genuine compliment—left-handed though it may have been. She wasn't pleased that he would "not exactly" think she was lying. But it was a better compliment than if he'd assured her that she was simply gorgeous with her hair wet.

Finally, they reached the canyon floor. She could see a wide, shallow stream up ahead and what must be Hosteen Anagal's field of corn. They walked forward. The ground turned level again, and sandy and soft.

"Who lives there?" she asked, because she could see another hogan.

"It belongs to Hosteen Anagal. He lives down here part of the year—late spring—until he gets his corn planted. You can see he plants the old way, in a kind of spiral," he said, pointing to the circles of corn.

"What exactly are we looking for?" she asked, and she was careful not to get too close to him.

"We're checking the corn tassels. He wants to know that they're strong and full of pollen. The corn pollen has religious significance for us. It looks good from here," he said.

Sloan followed him into the field. The corn looked nothing like her grandfather's. His had been planted precisely spaced and in rows. This corn grew in clumps. She watched Lucas go from stalk to stalk, shaking the tassels so that the pollen fell into his hand. He touched his forefinger to his tongue, then dipped it into the pollen and stuck it into his mouth. Then he offered his pollen-filled hand to her. She did the same without hesitation, trying to identify the taste. It tasted, she supposed, like . . . pollen.

The wind blew softly, and somewhere overhead an eagle cried. She lifted her eyes to ask him a question, and she realized immediately that in spite of her best intentions she had come too close. His eyes were waiting, and whatever query she wanted to make completely left her mind. She stood there, lost, needing to say something, to do something, struggling to keep herself and him in their discrete places well away from any emotional harm.

"Lucas," was the only thing she managed, his name barely a whisper, his name somehow becoming everything all at once—her loneliness and her sadness and her desire.

He reached for her then, his mouth coming down hard on hers. She could feel his hunger and his need, and she responded in kind. He pressed her into him, and his hand cupped her breast. She gave a small whimper of desire, her mouth opening under his. She clutched the back of his shirt. The wind rustled the corn.

She loved the smell and the taste and the feel of him. She loved—

He suddenly held her away from him, his hands gripping her arms, his fingers hurting. "I won't do this again," he said. "I will *not* do this again!" He abruptly let go of her.

She didn't understand. She held out her hand to him, but he stepped back, leaving her standing, trembling, among the cornstalks. He went crashing away from her, unmindful of Hosteen Anagal's fine field. And he didn't stop until he reached the shallow stream.

She struggled for composure, her breath still ragged with desire. She had pollen all down the front of her shirt. She stared after him, watching him standing alone and implacable by the quietly moving water.

I don't understand! I don't understand you! I don't understand this place! I don't understand me. . . .

She began to brush at the front of her shirt, trying to get the pollen off, but it was useless. She felt the envelope that had held the lancets in her pocket. After a moment, she took it out and begin to blindly collect another batch of pollen, this time for Hosteen Anagal. He was supposed to be the reason she came. He should see the status of his corn for himself.

She folded the envelope and put it into her shirt pocket. When she looked up, Lucas was waiting.

"I'm not going to explain," he said, his face as closed as it had been the first day they'd met.

"And I'm not going to feel ashamed," she answered quietly. She stepped past him, walking in the direction they had come.

But she *did* feel ashamed. She felt as if she had offended him somehow, as if her very willingness had sullied him in a way she didn't begin to understand. She felt it so acutely that it was all she could do not to cry.

He took the lead when they reached the track that led to the canyon rim, and once again she followed after him, neither of them talking. When they reached the footholds, he offered her his hand. She didn't take it. If there was something about her that he found distasteful, she wouldn't inflict herself on him again. She made the climb as she did everything else—alone.

She was exhausted by the time they reached the hogan yard. Her head pounded. It was all she could do to stay on her feet. Hosteen Anagal was still sitting on the bench, waiting. She removed the envelope from her pocket and held it open, sitting down heavily and offering the contents to him. He went through the same pollen-tasting ritual Lucas had, beaming with pleasure. He kept showing the envelope to Lucas, telling him something in lengthy Navajo. Lucas glanced at her from time to time, but he made no attempt to translate. They were both very careful not to meet each other's eyes.

There was a lull in their conversation, and when it began again, it seemed to Sloan that it was more subdued and serious.

This time Lucas did explain. "He says he'll go to the hospital now."

Sloan couldn't keep from smiling. "Good," she said, picking up the box of medical equipment. "The sooner the better."

She offered Hosteen Anagal her arm, but he refused, standing up clumsily by using a cane he produced from under the bench. She didn't hover around him. She walked ahead to carry the box to the truck, briefly meeting Lucas's eyes before she turned away.

Lucas watched her go, his mind in turmoil, his harmony completely gone.

"You need to take some clothes with you, my grandfather," he said to Hosteen Anagal.

"Already in the truck," the old man said, and Lucas laughed in spite of the misery he felt.

But his laughter quickly faded.

Sloan!

He had wanted her so badly. He still did. His body ached for her. If he hadn't stopped himself, he would have taken her right there on the ground.

He looked around to find the old man watching him.

"Tell me, my son, how long have you wanted to look after this woman's sheep?"

"She doesn't have any sheep, Grandfather," Lucas said, pacing his stride to the old man's shuffling.

"Where is her man?"

"I don't know," Lucas said.

"Maybe she hasn't got one."

"I don't know," Lucas said again.

"Maybe you should find out. The People think all the whites are the same—this one isn't the same. This one isn't like the other one."

Lucas made no reply. He didn't have to. He knew precisely which other one the old man meant. Hosteen Anagal took his arm when they reached the truck.

"No sheep," the old man said sadly. "Ah, well. Perhaps she has something else for you to look after."

Chapter Eleven

"But we *have* to!" Meggie said, pulling on Sloan's hand.

"No, we don't *have* to."

"Sloan, please! Please, please, please, *please!*"

"Meggie!"

"We need something to celebrate, you say that all the time. This is something to celebrate."

"I'm sure it is, but Officer Singer—"

"Sergeant!" Meggie interrupted. "He passed the exam."

"The sergeant," Sloan qualified, "has his own family and friends. He isn't going to want to celebrate something as important as this with us." *With me,* she almost said.

"Yes, he is. I already asked him."

"Meggie Baron!"

"I didn't think you'd care. You like for us to do things together at the receiving home. That's where I said we'd do it—so Will could come. He's crazy about Officer—Sergeant Singer. And Patrick can come to something like that at the receiving home even if he's grounded, if he's back from well digging. And Dolly can be there even if she's working. And Jackie Begaye says Lucas Singer is his friend. It'll work out good, Sloan. Honest!"

"Does it work out good as to where we'll find the money?"

"It's ice cream and cookies—how much money can it be? Please!" Meggie wrapped her arms around Sloan's waist. "I'll eat toast for a week—that'll save money! Please, please, please!" she begged, nearly toppling Sloan over.

"Meggie . . ."

"*Please*, Sloan! Think of all the disappointed little children, of which *I* am one!"

"All right!" Sloan cried. "We'll have a party!"

"Do you mean it?"

"Yes!" Sloan said. "I mean it!" And God help her, she thought. The last thing she needed was to try to celebrate something—*anything*—with Lucas Singer.

Someone knocked loudly, and Sloan looked around. A woman stood on the other side of the screen door, peering into the house. Meggie got to the door ahead of her, opening it wide to let the woman come in.

The woman smiled at Sloan, her eyes taking in Sloan's cutoff shorts and bare feet in one sweep. The woman, on the other hand, was wearing jeans—some kind of perfectly tailored designer jeans—and a white silk blouse with French cuffs and black and gold cuff links. She had on a black and white plaid blazer with gold buttons, and heavy gold earrings, and very expensive black leather shoes. Her hair was pale blond, smooth and sleek. She was simply gorgeous, and her whole look reeked of money. "I'm trying to find Lucas Singer," she said, her voice at a low octave Sloan suspected was more learned than natural. "They told me at the tribal police station he might be here."

Who in the world told you a thing like that? Sloan almost said. But she already knew. Mary Skeets. Mary asked about Lucas every time they ran into each other.

"No, I haven't seen him today," Sloan said. Or yesterday. Or the day before that.

"Oh," the woman said, clearly disappointed.

"We're having a party for him Saturday afternoon," Meggie, ever helpful, told her. "You want to come? It's at the receiving home. He passed the sergeant's exam and we're—"

"I'm not sure I'll be here then," said the woman, cutting Meggie off short. "Well," she said, glancing around the kitchen as if she thought he might be hiding somewhere. "Thank you."

"You want us to tell him anything?" Meggie asked as the woman turned to go. "I can give him a message."

"No, thank you, dear," she said.

"I can tell him your name."

"No," she said. She glanced at Sloan. "I'm sure I'll catch up with him."

I'm sure you will, Sloan thought. This was clearly a woman who was used to getting her way.

"Are you a...friend of Lucas's?" the woman suddenly asked. She was looking at Meggie but the question was for Sloan—even Meggie realized it.

"No, I'm more his worst nightmare," Sloan said, and the woman gave a small laugh. "Have you tried the—"

"I've tried *everywhere,*" she said sweetly. "This was my last resort."

"Ah, well, he'll turn up."

The woman smiled and turned to leave. A sweaty, work-stained Patrick tried to get in the door as she went out. She was careful not to brush up against him.

"Who's the babe?" he asked, opening the refrigerator and sticking his head in it.

"Beats me," Meggie said. "Patrick, you stink!"

"Get over it, Meg-head. If you'd been digging a hole all day, you'd stink, too."

"Shut the refrigerator door, Patrick. Did you find water?" Sloan asked.

"Nope. You know when Grandpa Baron showed me how to dowse? I think I'm going to take something along tomorrow and try that—a coat hanger like he did. We got any extra coat hangers around here? Look at this," he said, flexing his arm. "All that carrying pipe and stuff, I think my muscles are getting bigger."

"They are—all the ones between your ears, muscle head," Meggie told him, squealing and running out the door when he took off after her.

"Shut the refrigerator door!" Sloan yelled to an empty kitchen.

There was more squealing and the sound of running feet across the porch. The screen door rattled on the heels of a loud shriek.

"Patrick, leave Meggie alone!" she yelled, closing the refrigerator door.

"It's not Patrick," Lucas said, and she whirled around.

Oh God, she thought. She was angry with him, hurt by him. It was incredible that she could be this happy to see him.

Lucas, go away, she thought in desperation. *Go away so I can stand it.*

"I hear congratulations are in order," she said lightly.

"That's what I came about. I don't want you to think that you have to do anything at the receiving home."

"I don't mind," she interrupted. It was a lie. She did mind. But not as much as she would mind having him refuse the gesture. "It's for the children. It's good for them to celebrate when someone in the tribe succeeds." She sounded like a page from White People's Platitudes 101.

"I don't want you to go to any trouble."

"It's no trouble. Meggie has everything planned."

"I couldn't say no to her."

"Lucas, it's okay. It'll be fine."

They stared at each other across the room.

"And good for all the little Navajo children," he said with a finely edged sarcasm she had to admire.

"Yes," she said. She forced herself to look into his eyes. "Someone came here looking for you just now."

"Who?"

"She didn't say."

"Probably my sister, Lillian. She's down from Santa Fe. I've been missing her all day. She's never been one for hanging out with the family, but she's always been supportive of my career milestones. Probably wants to buy me lunch."

"I didn't know you had a sister."

"There are a lot of things you don't—" He stopped, but he didn't look away.

"This woman wasn't Navajo," Sloan said.

"What did she look like?"

"Blond. Three-hundred-dollar purse. Four-hundred-dollar shoes."

"Ah," he said. "A woman with her price tags showing."

Sloan had to force down a smile. "She didn't want to leave a message in case we saw you. She didn't want to leave her name. She said she'd catch up with you."

"Hosteen Anagal asks about you," he said, apparently dismissing the mystery woman.

"Does he?"

"He worries that you don't have any sheep."

"Oh, I have sheep. I feel like Bo-Peep all the time—only my sheep have two legs and two of them have red hair. The other one I can't get into the flock no matter how hard I try." She turned away and opened the refrigerator door she'd just closed, taking out the large glass jar she'd recycled to hold cold water. She took off the lid and poured a glass, fully aware that he watched her.

"Could I have some of that?" he asked, and she took down another glass.

"It's a novelty for me," he said when she handed him the filled glass. Their fingers touched lightly.

"Water is a novelty?"

"Water like this, kept in a refrigerator, the kind we had with the sandwiches the other night."

"You don't keep water in the refrigerator?" she asked inanely, watching him tilt back his head and swallow.

"Never occurred to me," he said.

What are you doing? she thought, looking into his eyes again. *Why are you reminding me that there was a time when you were welcome here?*

"It must be a Southern thing," she said, glancing away. "You couldn't open a refrigerator where I come from without finding a cold water jar."

He drained the glass. "You'll let me know the time, then? For the thing at the receiving home."

"Meggie will."

He hesitated. "Sloan—"

"She can leave word with Dolly," she interrupted.

"Yeah," he said, turning abruptly to go. "Thanks for the water," he called as the screen door slammed behind him.

So now you know, she thought, watching him go down the steps and out into the yard. She gave a heavy sigh. *What* did he know? That she was no pushover? She, who would have rolled on the ground with him in the cornfield?

"Lucas, I don't know what you want," she said aloud. She didn't know what *she* wanted. She didn't know anything, except that she needed to get Mark's son and get out of here. She'd been away too long already. She had two employers to pacify. She needed to check on the house and the mail, pay bills, find the money to outfit Meggie and Patrick for school when it started again in the middle of August.

And, in spite of all that, she stood there wondering who the mystery woman who'd come looking for Lucas had been.

Letting the receiving home children be a part of celebrating his promotion was a good idea, Lucas realized, regardless of his sarcasm with Sloan. It *was* good for them to share in a tribal member's success, and share they did. The ice cream feast in his honor had been more than enjoyable. He had particularly appreciated their boisterous rendition of "Happy Sergeant To You"—except for the fact that Sloan hadn't been there to help sing it.

He sat at the picnic table, wondering why she had missed the party. Was she working late? Ill? He could have satisfied his curiosity by simply asking Meggie or Patrick or even his mother for the information they'd all been too busy to volunteer. But he hadn't done it. His pride and his instinct for survival had required that he maintain some measure of control in this situation. And he could still ask—except that Patrick had already gone home and Meggie was inside watching television with Jackie Begaye.

Well, perhaps he couldn't have asked Patrick, he decided. The boy was obviously still suspicious of Lucas's motives, and with good reason, it would seem. He had thought about coming here, seeing Sloan again, all day. He had thought about it more than he'd thought about Sara and her recent, highly visible quest to locate him. He had no doubt that she was the woman Sloan had described. It was just like her to affect some kind of mysterious and dramatic air, to pointedly avoid saying to any number of people who she was and what she wanted—or to simply pick up the telephone.

Poor Nick, he thought.

He looked down at the tugging on his sleeve.

"You need somebody on your lap," Will told him, rubbing his eyes.

"You are one tired boy, aren't you?" Lucas said, picking him up.

"No," Will assured him. "I don't want to take a nap." He curled himself against Lucas's chest, touching his badge for a moment with his fingers, and the top of the pen Lucas had in his pocket, and finally the pocket flap, before he dropped off to sleep.

Lucas sat quietly, knowing he should take the boy inside and knowing, too, that when Sloan arrived—if she arrived—Will would be the first person she'd want to see.

Sweet boy, she called him, much to the child's delight.

Ah, Sloan, he thought. *This is going to break your heart.* It had been wrong to let her get so close to Will Baron, wrong for her and for the boy.

"Is the party over?" someone whispered, and he looked around sharply. "Better late than never," Sloan said, sitting down beside him at the picnic table. She reached out to gently touch Will's hair. "Too much for him?"

"Let's just say it's a good thing I don't make sergeant every day."

She smiled. "I'm sorry I missed it. All hell broke loose at the clinic right at quitting time." She leaned forward and rested her head on her arms for a moment. He couldn't see her face, only her ear, the small gold earrings she wore. "I feel like I've been pulled through a keyhole backward," he thought she said. "So how was your day?" she asked abruptly, lifting her head to look at him.

Are we going to sit here and make small talk when it's all I can do not to—

Yes, he thought. Apparently they were. He had himself to blame. He had set the tone.

"My day was full of grave robbers," he said. "They got into a major burial site up near Dorothy Antonio's. Scattered the bones everywhere, some of them babies and children. They took some of the skulls. I despise the sons of bitches. One of these days I'm going back East and dig up some white graveyard and scatter the bones and say I'm looking for clay pots so it'll make it all right." He stopped, not because she wasn't listening, but because she was. "Sorry," he said.

"Why?"

"Because I—" He suddenly realized that he wasn't thinking about grave robbers anymore. He was thinking about being with her in a cornfield, about the way she'd felt and tasted and the way she'd looked at him when he pushed her away. "I hear Patrick's taking his community service like a man," he said, trying to keep the desperation he felt out of his voice. This was not the time to discuss what had happened in the cornfield. What could he say? *I wanted you so much I couldn't stand it—so I ran like some kid Patrick's age?*

"Like a man? Yes, I suppose he is, whatever that means."

A car pulled into the receiving home parking lot. It was maroon, new, a Japanese make, and contained one person—female, the law enforcement part of him noted. Sloan had been entirely right about his doing everything by committee. After a moment, Sara got out of the car and walked purposefully toward them. He had forgotten how beautiful she was, beautiful and completely self-absorbed. He could see it on her face as she approached.

"Hello," she said pleasantly to Sloan. "Lucas, I need to talk to you." Her eyes went to Will, who still slept peacefully in his lap.

"I'll take him inside," Sloan said, standing up and reaching to take Will from his arms.

"You don't have to leave," he said.

She gave him a small half smile. "Yes, Lucas, I do."

The boy roused as she lifted him. "An' Swone," he murmured.

"What, sweet boy?" she said softly, her eyes meeting Lucas's over the child's head.

"Did you miss your boy?"

"Yes, yes, yes," she said. "I missed my boy all over the place."

"Patrick, um, called, said *he's* the Big Bro'," Will said sleepily. "Patrick said I'm a Poco Bro'—I'm not a *poco*. Did you see my daddy now?" he asked.

"No, Will. I didn't see him." She kissed his cheek and carried him toward the back door, looking at Lucas once before she went inside.

"Is that her child?" Sara asked.

"Her brother's," Lucas said. "He was killed out here a few weeks ago."

"Too bad," she said. "It's nice you can help out. I didn't realize how much you liked children."

He stared at her, unable to believe she would say something like that to him. Was she that callous? No, he decided. It was just that she was that unaffected by what had gone on before. "Sara, what do you want?"

She was wearing the perfume she always wore, the same perfume he remembered from all those times they'd made love together. "What do I want? Lucas, I'm *worried* about you. Nick and I both are."

"Why?" he said obtusely.

"*Why?* Nick told me you're in some kind of trouble with the FBI."

"I'm not in trouble with the FBI."

"Nick says you are, and he says you aren't taking it seriously enough. I can see he's right."

"So what do you and Nick suggest I do?"

"I don't know! Something—go see them."

"Yeah, right. Did you forget *everything* you learned out here?"

"Be careful, then."

"I'm always careful."

She gave a heavy sigh and looked toward the receiving home. "And I wanted to see if you're all right about my marrying Nick."

"I'm fine about your marrying Nick," he assured her, a bit surprised because at some point and with little or no conscious effort on his part, that statement had become entirely true. "You can send me a wedding invitation."

"Would you bring *her?*" she asked lightly.

"Who?" he said, his obtuseness still intact.

"That woman. The one who just left—"

"*Her* name is Sloan Baron."

"Would you bring Sloan Baron?" she asked with a slight smile, looking into his eyes. "She is the one who took my place, isn't she?"

"No," he said truthfully. "She didn't take your place. She didn't take anybody's place. She has a place of her own." He stood up. "Anything else I can do for you?"

She caught his arm. "Lucas—"

He put his hand on top of hers for a moment. "Best wishes for a happy marriage, Sara. I have my doubts, but I really do hope you and Nick have a great life. He's a good man."

He left her sitting there, and he didn't look back. He walked toward the dusty parking lot. He needed some time to think, to get used to the truth he'd just told her. As much as he'd resisted it, as much as he denied it to himself even now, Sloan Baron did have a place in his life. And that fact would likely make both of them miserable.

He looked up as the driver of a battered, no-color truck parked across the street started the engine. The gears scraped and the engine strained as the person tried to pull away from the curb at a speed that was beyond the truck's capabilities. As it swung out into the street, he caught a glimpse of the driver's face. He recognized her immediately—the elusive Margaret Madman.

Chapter Twelve

Lucas waited for Sloan to come to the telephone. The receiver at the IHS clinic had been laid on a counter somewhere. He could hear the background conversation quite clearly.

"Who is it?" Sloan asked the woman who had answered the phone.

"Sounds like the tribal policeman, the one with the cute buns."

Lucas frowned. That was all he needed—to become known around the reservation as Cute Buns. He supposed that in the future, when he had to go to the IHS clinic, he'd have to back around the walls.

"I'm very busy here," he heard Sloan say.

"You know, we're all wondering why he calls here so much—comes by—and just since *you* started working here, too. *I* wonder. Dr. Pellam wonders. Susanna and Jane wonder..."

"I get the picture," Sloan said.

"Well, are you going to talk to him?"

"I'm very busy here," she said again.

There was a rustling as someone picked up the receiver again. "I'm so sorry," the woman said. "Ms. Baron is *extremely* tied up at the moment. Can I—"

"Tell her it's Walter Cronkite," Lucas said.

"He says it's Walter Cronkite," the woman whispered loudly.

"Oh, my God," Sloan said. "Lucas," she said into the phone. "What's wrong?"

"Meggie stole a horse."

"She did not!"

"I'm afraid she did. She and Jackie Begaye."

"But—"

"You need to get down here. Now."

Lucas hung up the phone and stared across his desk at the two culprits. Meggie looked incredibly worried, the old hand, Jackie, nonchalant. He waited a long time before he said anything. Jackie picked at the edge of his shoe sole. Meggie gave a wavering sigh.

"I don't have to tell you I'm surprised at this," he said finally.

"It was *my* horse," Jackie said.

"That's not what your cousin says."

"He a liar. My uncle gave it to me. He said if I take care of it, it's mine. I took care of it. I took care of it *good*. He's *my* horse. I don't know how you found out about it, anyway," Jackie complained.

"I found out about it because your uncle reported the horse stolen. I found out about it because a Navajo boy and a carrot-top, redheaded white girl make a pretty conspicuous pair. I found out about it because everybody I talked to from here to Fort Defiance remembered seeing the two of you *and* the horse. And I can tell you right now—if you and Meggie are headed for a life of crime, you'd better pick different sidekicks."

"Was Sloan real mad?" Meggie asked timidly.

"*Real* mad," Lucas said.

She sighed again.

"She just wanted to help me get *my* horse, man," Jackie said.

"Sergeant Singer to you—and be that as it may," Lucas answered. "The horse was reported as stolen property." He understood Jackie's motivation perfectly. Jackie was entirely capable of getting the horse by himself, but he'd wanted to show off. It was Meggie's motivation he didn't understand. Maybe Jackie was taking her to hunt down a priest.

"Where were you going?" he asked.

Neither of them answered.

The phone on his desk buzzed. He picked up the receiver.

"Singer."

"Sloan Baron is here," Mary said.

"Show her the way, will you?"

He stood up and opened the door.

"Where is she?" Sloan asked as she came down the hallway. She still had on her lab coat, and a lavender stethoscope hung around her neck.

"In here," he said.

She stepped into the room, glancing at both children. She didn't say anything to either of them.

"Can Meggie go now?" she asked when he'd told her the situation.

"Yes," he said. He wanted to look into her eyes. She wouldn't let him.

"Am I going to have to dig wells like Patrick?" Meggie felt brave enough to ask.

"No," Sloan said. "This is the Southwest. They *shoot* horse thieves in this part of the country."

"Aw, I'm just a kid," Meggie said.

"So am I," Sloan assured her. "Or I was until a few days ago when you and Patrick started turning me old before my time. Do I have to sign anything?" She glanced at Lucas, still carefully avoiding his eyes. If he'd any doubts at all that they had turned some kind of corner since the party at the receiving home, his phone call to the clinic ended it. She had made some kind of decision where he was concerned, and she was making a conscious effort to carry it out.

"No, she's ready now," he said.

"What did you do to keep busy all day before the Barons arrived?" she asked, and he smiled.

"This and that," he said. "It was pretty dull, actually."

The phone buzzed again.

"Excuse me," he said, reaching to answer it.

"Lucas, Jackie's uncle called," Mary said. "He says since Jackie is the one who got the horse, he'll drop the charges."

"Okay," Lucas said. "The charges are dropped," he said to Sloan, eliciting a cheer from both children. "There's still the matter of running away from the receiving home," Lucas said pointedly, cutting the cheering short. He moved Sloan into the hallway. "Are you . . . okay?"

"No, but I'll get there," she said, and she still wouldn't quite look at him. "I've done too much delegating of *my* responsibility, Lucas. I'm going to take Meggie home. She and Patrick and I are going to sit down and have a long talk. Let's go, Meggie."

Meggie stood up and came carefully around the chair. "I'm sorry, Sloan," she said with her head down.

"I know you're sorry. You're sorry, and Patrick's sorry, and I keep having to come to the police station. I am trying to get custody of your little brother here. Do you think they're going to give him to somebody who can't keep the other two children from getting arrested all the time?''

Meggie looked up at her, her bottom lip trembling. "I'm sorry!" She flung herself into Sloan's arms. "I'm sorry," she said again.

Sloan gave a heavy sigh. "I know, Meggie. But you and Patrick are going to have to remember what the agenda is here. We want to get Will and we want to go home to North Carolina just as fast as we can." She glanced at Lucas.

Meggie sniffed loudly.

"I need a favor, Lucas," Sloan said. "I need to go through my brother's things. Do you know where they are? If they're still at the house he was using, do you know where I could get the key?''

"I'll find out," he said.

"Thank you." She seemed about to say something else, then didn't. "Let's go, Meggie.''

He stood and watched her walk down the hall. She spoke to several other officers along the way, and he frowned, feeling a pang of what could only be described as jealousy. He had forgotten that her visits to the receiving home had to be supervised and that while he'd been so busy trying to avoid running into her there, she must have gotten to know any number of the Navajo Tribal Police Force by name.

"Hey, Sloan!" one of the younger officers called to her as she went by. "Did you put in a good word for me?"

"Yes, Carlos."

"Well, what did she say?"

"Carlos, I told you—the girl is engaged!" she called back to him on her way out.

"So what are *you* doing Saturday night?" he yelled down the hall, and Lucas could hear her laugh as the door closed behind her.

His frown deepened. He was annoyed by the officer's familiarity much more than he wanted to admit.

He looked around into Jackie Begaye's grin.

"You got it bad, man," he said.

He did have it bad. He had it so bad that he didn't care if Jackie Begaye recognized it. "Mind your own business and wait outside," he said to the boy.

"What are you going to do about me running off from the receiving home?''

"Nothing," Lucas said. "I'm going to let Dolly Singer handle it. You remember her—that very traditional Navajo lady you fooled. I tried to fool her once, and look what happened to me. You're in for it now, Begaye. She'd going to find enough chores for you to last until you're fifty. You'll be the oldest kid *ever* in a receiving home."

"That's not funny, man," Jackie said on his way out, and Lucas laughed.

"Hey, Lucas," someone said, and he looked up.

"Yeah, Carlos, what?"

"I got something, I think, about the FBI agents on the rez."

"What is it?" he said, surprised. What with hitting on IHS nurses, he didn't see how Carlos had the time to ferret out any agents.

"I've been seeing this same beat-up car around—a black 1988 Firebird—with two white guys acting a lot younger than they really are in it. One of them wears a red bandanna and mirrored sunglasses. The car looks like hell. It's dented up, rusted out, left front parking light busted, but the motor's in top condition. And I mean top. It doesn't fit, you know? This really great motor in a junk car, and these guys acting like a couple of kids when they're past it, loud and mouthy like they don't care if you see them. And they don't care a little too much, you know? Even if they were kids, the kids out here don't want big motors—they want four-wheel drives like their friends have got so they can go tear up the ecology in a riverbed somewhere. Feels all wrong."

"Where did you see them?"

"Different places around Window Rock. Once at the chili joint, yelling at the girls who went in and out. And then once when I was on my way to baby-sit Sloan—the Baron woman—at the receiving home. They were kind of cruising the other side of the street."

"You get a license number?"

"No, I'm always coming in the wrong direction or they get away too fast."

"You say anything to Becenti?"

Carlos grinned. "I figured you'd want to do the chain of command thing."

"Anybody else see these guys?"

"I don't know."

"Ask," Lucas said. "Let me know." There was a chance that these two were FBI agents, he thought, particularly since they *and* Margaret Madman were apparently hanging around the receiving home. He'd already made sure all the receiving home staff had seen Margaret's picture. He couldn't imagine why she'd have been there in the first place. Margaret Madman was *not* the motherly type. In any event, he still wanted to talk to her about that surveillance list—what exactly she'd done to get herself on it, and what the two of them could possibly have in common that would cause the FBI to include him. It occurred to him that if these men were federal agents, then he wasn't the Lucas Singer on the list, because he hadn't seen the car or them, and he'd certainly been visible enough around Window Rock to attract their attention if they'd wanted to follow him.

He took the rest of the afternoon to locate the dead teacher's belongings. They were still in the reservation house where he'd been living, but Lucas waited until Friday to take Sloan the keys, until he had the afternoon off, because he had every intention of making the trip to Chinle with her. The woman at the community college who had given him the keys had insisted that Sloan shouldn't be allowed to go through the contents of the house unattended. He had offered his opinion that Sloan Baron was no thief, but the woman had been adamant. He wondered idly how much having a white daughter-in-law had to do with the woman's suspicious nature. Having to escort Sloan was no problem for him. He wanted an excuse to see her again. He wanted an opportunity to be with her, whether she wanted him along or not. And he didn't expect that she would. When she'd come to pick up Meggie at the police station, she'd had that look, the same one he remembered from the hospital, the one that said quite plainly that she wouldn't allow herself to need anyone's help or comfort or company—least of all his.

He was relieved to see Sloan's car when he arrived at the house. She was in the kitchen when he knocked on the back screen door. For a moment, he thought she might be glad to see him, but the moment quickly passed. She hesitated before she came to the door, and he thought she wasn't going to let him come inside.

She was wearing a yellow print dress, one that buttoned up the front and came down long and hung loose. He didn't mind the loose fit. He fantasized that she wore little under it, and that her body would be warm and firm and smooth if he lifted the dress to touch it. He already knew that her skin would smell of something delicately rose-scented, the way it had in the cornfield. He could smell the roses when she finally held open the door, and it made him forget everything except how much he wanted her. He had to force himself not to look at her mouth or the soft swell of her breasts.

"I have the keys to your brother's house," he said as impersonally as he could manage. "We can go this afternoon if you want."

"I'd rather do this alone, Lucas," she said. She looked up at him. He could almost feel the effort it took for her to do it.

"That's not possible," he said.

"Why? I'm sure you have other things to do. Or are you afraid I'd make off with the silverware?"

"*I'm* not," he said truthfully.

"I see. And you're the one exception. Lucas, this is going to be hard for me." She abruptly moved farther away from him. "I . . . I'm probably going to bawl my head off. I don't want you to see me. Do you understand?"

"I understand."

"Good."

"But I'm still going."

"I don't want you to."

"That's the way it is, Sloan. You don't have to worry. I'm civilized enough not to intrude."

"I never thought you weren't," she said stiffly. "All right. Now is a good time to go. Meggie's helping wash windows at the receiving home. I guess you know she gave herself community service. She's staying to have supper with Will so she'll be there until six. Patrick is off well digging overnight. If we could stop by a pay phone, I'll call Meggie and tell her where I'm going."

He drove to the nearest pay phone and waited in the truck while she made the call. She didn't seem to mind that they were going in his fifteen-year-old, not air-conditioned vehicle, but she was very quiet. No questions. None of the teasing remarks he'd come to expect. He had missed being with her, talking to her, having her make him laugh. He had missed it a great deal.

As she was walking to the truck, he caught a glimpse of a noisy black car in the side mirror. He looked around sharply, opening the door so that he could see.

"What's wrong?" she asked.

"Nothing. I thought I saw a car we've been looking for."

"What did they do?"

"Nothing, as far as I know. It's a gut feeling. It's one of those—"

"Guy things," she finished for him.

"Police things," he corrected, and she smiled.

Better, he thought. *Much better.*

He turned onto Highway 264 toward Ganado and tried to make conversation so she wouldn't retreat from him.

"Have you seen Will today?" he asked.

"Yes," she said. And that was all. No report on what he'd said and done, as she might once have given him.

"Did you hear anything from the tuberculosis testing you did?"

"Dorothy Antonio has it."

"Too bad," he said, and he was fast running out of topics. "Are you still matchmaking for Carlos?" he ventured, and she looked at him briefly.

"No," she said. "Carlos is about as subtle as a sledgehammer. Matchmaking for him is apt to get me trampled." She was looking at the sky. "Would you stop for a minute?" she asked.

"Here?"

"Please," she said, still looking.

He pulled onto the shoulder of the road, and she immediately got out and stood looking toward the horizon. He tried to see whatever it was she was staring at, but he saw nothing but open sky scattered over by a long expanse of high, white clouds.

After a moment she got into the truck. He pulled onto the road again, and he kept waiting for her to explain, glancing at her from time to time as he drove along.

"What were you looking at?" he asked finally.

"A memory," she said. "A sky like this. It's one of the few things I remember from being in this part of the country when I was a child. My brother and I thought the sky out here looked like some kind of hallway, because the clouds seemed to go on and on to some other place we'd never even heard of before. We'd ride in the car all day, day after day, and still never get to the end of it."

"You don't have skies like this where you come from?"

She looked at him. "No," she said. "Nothing as immense as this. You'd hate North Carolina," she added.

"Would I?" he said, surprised that he was offended by the assertion. "Why?"

"Because it's so open out here. I've hardly ever seen the horizon at home—except when I've been to the coast. You'd feel smothered in North Carolina."

Yes, he thought he probably would, but he still didn't want her to just arbitrarily decide that for him. Maybe he would like her home in spite of the claustrophobic landscape. Maybe he would like anyplace where *she* was.

"I've put off doing something about my brother's things too long," she said after a long period of silence.

"It's understandable," he said.

"Understandable or not, I should have done it when I was still numb." She gave a quiet sigh. "Oh, I hate the thought of this."

"Are you sure you want to go?"

"I have to. I need—"

"What?" he asked, because she didn't go on.

She looked at him, and he could feel her making up her mind as to whether or not she wanted to tell him. "I need to look for legal papers," she said finally. "Marriage license. Birth certificate." She glanced at him. "One of the nurses I work with has a nephew in law school. He says I need some proof that Will is my brother's son."

He didn't think it would make a difference in the final outcome of Will Baron's custody, except perhaps in that Sloan would be able to satisfy herself that she'd done everything she could. He contemplated the idea of preparing her for the very real possibility that she would lose the case. He cared about this woman. He cared enough not to want her hurt. But then he dismissed the notion altogether. Sloan, regardless of her open-mindedness, didn't understand the tribe's collective memory of the years of white persecution that would come into play in this situation, and he chose not to try to explain. How could he, when she had no point of reference? He hadn't yet told her that he'd seen Margaret Madman hanging around the receiving home. He wouldn't tell her sad times weren't over. It was unavoidable, part of the natural pattern, because she loved her brother's Navajo son.

"How far away is the house?" she asked abruptly.

"It's this side of Chinle. You won't be able to stay long if you're going to get back by six."

"No, I don't have to be back. Meggie asked for permission to go home with your mother. Dolly's been showing her how to weave rugs. Meggie is thrilled."

"Then my mother is, too. My sister, Lillian, wouldn't touch a loom, not even when she was a little girl—and there aren't any grandchildren to teach."

Why not? Sloan almost said. She wanted to know what had happened to the one *he* would have given her. She had realized from the first that Lucas and the woman who'd come looking for him had a history—even before Meggie had filled in some of the details that afternoon at the receiving home.

"Dolly's worrying," Meggie had said, looking over Sloan's shoulder at Lucas and the woman before Sloan had realized she was there. "I think that must be her."

"Who?" Sloan asked, in spite of herself. She'd seen Lucas's face when the woman walked up, the emotion he'd almost but not quite been able to hide.

"Sara Catherine McCay, the anthropologist," Meggie said. "Dolly won't talk about her."

"Meggie, for heaven's sake, you didn't *ask.*"

"I have to ask people stuff," Meggie said reasonably. "I can't find out anything if I don't. Dolly said I shouldn't talk about sad things if I'm going to be helping her work her rug loom—it'll go into the rug and it won't be good to have around. Jackie said there was supposed to be a baby, Lucas Singer's baby. Jackie said Sara Catherine McCay was rich and white and she got rid of him *and* the baby. She probably left it with somebody like my dad left me and Patrick, don't you think?"

It was a question Sloan couldn't answer, then or now.

I won't do this again! Lucas had said.

She thought she understood his behavior in the cornfield now, at least on some level, and it only made their relationship all the more complicated. She was as determined as he was to keep some distance between them. And how typical of life's little quirks that she should become infatuated with a man who was so unavailable. It was not because of their different cultures or the fact that they lived thousands of miles apart, but because he had been in love with another white woman. She thought he still was, and she didn't need that kind of grief. She didn't miss the irony of the situation, either. She waited so long to find a man for whom she could feel that exquisite blend of respect and desire—and he was in love with a woman who had supposedly almost killed him. She had to stop thinking about Lucas and start focusing on the most important thing at hand—getting Will and going home to North Carolina.

The trip to the house where Mark had lived took less time than she expected, perhaps because she wanted—enjoyed—Lucas's company regardless of what she'd told him about wanting to do this alone. She had to mentally brace herself to get out of the truck and go inside. She did *not* want to do this, but as always, she had no choice. She was aware that Lucas kept looking at her, and not in an admiring way. Instead, he was assessing her level of distress the same way he'd done that first day in Albuquerque. She waited for him to find the right key. There were other houses and several house trailers not far away. The place looked very similar to the rest of the reservation she'd seen, except for a stunning view of a dark mesa in the distance.

"What is that?" she asked Lucas.

"Black Mesa," he said, and she supposed that a Navajo deity must live there, too, as one did in Canyon de Chelly. It looked more than appropriate for metaphysical beings.

He unlocked the door finally, and he went in ahead of her.

"Wait here," he said, but she didn't wait. She doubted that there was anything inside that would make her feel Mark's presence any more than she already did, and she just wanted this quest for legal documents to be over.

The house was hot and stuffy from being shut up for so long. Lucas walked through, opening windows and turning on the fans he found. The living area was much neater than Sloan would have expected, knowing Mark. Perhaps someone had come in to clean. There was a couch and an easy chair, both of them covered in brightly striped blankets, and a portable television that sat on a small wooden table that had been covered with a red-checked plastic tablecloth. In winter, the room would have been heated by an ornate wood stove of a kind she hadn't seen since she was a child. A rug loom sat in the corner with a small, partially finished rug in it. She wondered who would have been working on that—not Mark, surely. Will's mother? Or perhaps a woman who had taken her place.

She walked into the kitchen and opened the refrigerator door. Someone had had the foresight to empty it, except for the glass jar of cold water Mark must have kept. The jar was half full, and she stared at it a long time, until she became aware that Lucas was watching her.

She gave a small sigh and closed the refrigerator door, then looked around for someplace Mark might have kept important papers. She opened all the kitchen drawers and cabinets, finding nothing. There was a small desk in the far corner of the living area. She walked to that and began searching through it. It was crammed with old bills and receipts and letters—her letters—and some pictures of young people she didn't recognize, pictures that had been taken here on the reservation. She stuffed everything in the canvas tote she'd brought with her.

Don't cry! she admonished herself.

"I'll wait outside," Lucas said, but she didn't want to do this alone after all.

"Would you . . . mind staying?" she asked, trying not to sound as shaky as she felt. She knew she was perhaps asking him to violate some personal taboo, but being here among Mark's things was harder than she expected. Much harder. There was no sense of anticipation about the place, as if Mark was about to return, but more a sense of finality and abandonment and utter waste that made her want to cover her face and weep.

"All right," Lucas said, and she looked at him gratefully.

"Thank you," she said, turning abruptly away and going into the bedroom.

The bed was made. A pair of Mark's shoes sat in the corner. She took a deep breath and slid open the closet door. His clothes hung neatly at one end, and there was an empty space at the other. She supposed that Will's things had been hanging there and that they'd been taken to the receiving home. She looked through the pockets of Mark's jackets and shirts, and in all the shoe boxes on the floor, finding nothing but shoes and pocket lint. She closed the closet door and walked to a small, unlevel bureau that rocked when she touched it. One drawer was empty. Again she supposed it had held Will's things. The other drawers contained more of Mark's clothes. She wondered what could be done with them. She didn't want them and she doubted that Patrick would. She wouldn't put the question to Meggie. Meggie would need to keep everything. She should find some keepsakes for them, she thought, whether Patrick wanted anything or not.

She heard Lucas talking to someone—a man—in the other room. The man's voice grew louder. They were both speaking Navajo. She walked to the doorway to see what was going on. A Navajo man in dirty clothes was trying to get past Lucas, but he was unsteady on his feet, obviously drunk, and clinging to a large, cardboard box Lucas apparently wanted. Lucas wrestled the box away and the man sat down hard on the floor, rocking and holding his head and making a loud keening sound.

"What's wrong?" she said, coming forward.

"Stay away, Sloan," Lucas said sharply. To the man, he said something equally sharp in Navajo.

"What's wrong?" she said again, alarmed because the man toppled over.

"Stay away!" Lucas said. "He's shameful enough without you watching!"

He dragged the man to his feet and all but carried him out of the house. She followed after them, stepping around the box that had been dropped on the floor. The man still made the keening sound.

"Lucas—"

"Sloan, for God's sake, mind your own damn business!" He dragged the man out to the truck and thrust him inside, then he got in on the driver's side and drove away. She stood there, staring after the truck, feeling as she had so often when it came to Lucas Singer—completely at a loss. She made her living being sensitive to other people's feelings and needs and it was incredible to her that she could keep offending this one man when she wanted so desperately not to. Clearly, the harder she tried, the worse she became—at least in his eyes.

Lucas wasn't gone long, and he was still angry when he returned. The pocket on his shirt was torn.

"Where did you take him?" she asked when he came into the house.

"Someplace to sleep it off. It's one of the things I do for a living. Take drunk Indians someplace to sleep it off."

"He wanted to give me this?" she said, ignoring his sarcasm and holding up the cardboard box she still hadn't opened. It was addressed to Patrick and Meggie.

"Yes."

"Why didn't you just let him?"

"The man was drunk, Sloan."

"I've seen drunks before."

"You mean it didn't matter at all to you that he was in that condition?" he said, coming closer than she wanted him to be. She had only to reach out her hand to touch him. She was fully aware that she should move away and fully aware of the reason she didn't.

"No, I mean I think you should have just let him give me the box."

"The man was drunk," he said again. "It mattered to *me*, all right? I was ashamed of him. And for him. I didn't want you to have to deal with it."

She would rather have dealt with the man's drunkenness than with Lucas's defensiveness and anger, she thought. It was Lucas who was so difficult for her to understand. He had always kept some kind of wall between them. The only time she'd been able to breach it had been that brief moment in the cornfield—and what a disaster that had been for them both. There was no accounting for the times like now, when she knew that he was being completely candid with her, and the time in the cornfield when he'd categorically refused to explain.

He was the first to look away, and she didn't say anything. She turned the box over and tried to pull the tape off the top flaps, finally accepting the pocketknife Lucas handed her. She slit the tape and opened the box. It was nearly empty—except for two brightly wrapped Christmas presents.

Chapter Thirteen

The sun was low in the sky. They rode past the turnoff to Hubbell Trading Post, the place where he'd so skillfully guessed the number of beans in a gallon jar when he was a boy. He needed some of that skill now in trying to second-guess a dead man. Sloan had been so quiet since they'd left her brother's house, staring out the truck window at nothing, as far as hc could tell. The box with the Christmas presents sat jammed between the seat and the dashboard. Once she reached out to touch the edge of it, the only indication he had of her distress.

"He could have forgotten to mail them," Lucas ventured finally.

She looked at him. In spite of her self-control he could tell how badly she wanted to cry, not because of the sorrow she'd anticipated, but because of her frustration and anger.

"You don't forget to mail your children's Christmas presents, Lucas. If he didn't mail these, then it was deliberate and it was...crazy." The last word was barely a whisper. "You don't know how disappointed they were. Patrick tried to pretend it didn't matter to him, but Meggie—Meggie *believed,* you know? And it wasn't a present she wanted, it was never that. She just wanted to know Mark still cared about her or that he at least *remembered* he had her. She'd wait and she'd wait for the mail to come. She'd tell me she was sure her Christmas package from her father must be lost and it would turn up, she just knew it would. But nothing ever came, not even a card. And finally she quit talking about it.... What am I supposed to do? Am I supposed to give them these presents *now?*"

A white car came up fast behind them, following too close. Lucas couldn't tell the make—only that it was something big out of Detroit and probably new. He slowed down to let the car pass. It didn't. Annoyed, he accelerated to put some distance between them.

"There has to be a reason, Sloan."

"Yes, and I'm all worn out with trying to find it—and all the rest of the *reasons* my brother had to have. I don't know why he did this. I don't know why he did anything."

"Somebody may know," he said. "Maybe Charlie Nez, the man who brought the box. He may know when he's sober. Or Will's mother, maybe."

"And where is she?"

"She's around," he said, glancing at her and at the car behind them. "I saw her the other day parked across from the receiving home."

"You didn't talk to her?"

"I couldn't catch her. She took off when she saw me and she'd disappeared down a side street somewhere by the time I got on the road to look."

"Do you think she's going to try to get custody of Will?" she asked quietly.

"I don't know. But it would surprise me if she did, particularly since there's nothing in it for her."

"She's his mother."

"Well, I don't think that's made much of an impression on her so far."

He glanced into the mirror again. The car was farther back now. He fought the impulse to reach for Sloan's hand.

"Lucas, if..." she began.

The car behind accelerated suddenly and pulled out to pass. But, instead of going around, it cut sharply in front of them, blocking the way. Lucas swore and slammed on the brakes, causing the truck to veer and slide off the road in a cloud of dust. The car reversed and swung around in front of them again, both doors flying open. Two men jumped out. Lucas lost sight of them in the dust, but then the doors of the truck jerked open. He had no time to say anything, no time to keep Sloan from being dragged out on the passenger side. He was forced out of the truck, his feet swept out from under him as soon as they touched the ground. He fell hard, facedown in the sand. The barrel of whatever weapon the man carried clipped him hard above the ear.

Dazed, he tried to roll over. "Wait— What—"

"Shut up!" the man said, shoving him. "Hands on the back of your head! Now! *Now!*" Lucas did as he was told. After a moment, the man brought Lucas's arms down and caught both his wrists in a loop and pulled hard. The strip of plastic cut into his wrists, and his fingers began to tingle. He tried to turn enough to locate Sloan and the other man.

She cried out suddenly on the other side of the truck.

"Don't hurt her, man!"

"He doesn't like what you're doing over there, Chuckie," the man said. "Get her around here so he can see her. On your knees—slow and easy," he said to Lucas, dragging him upward. "Did you find it?" he called to the other man.

"It's not here!"

"What do you mean it's not here! Look in the box!"

"It's not here, I told you! There's nothing but Christmas presents."

"Well, look in those! Have I got to tell you everything?"

"There's a bunch of CDs and a Walkman and a book of fairy tales. That's it!"

"You son of a bitch!" the man hissed in Lucas's ear. "What did you do with it?"

The other man all but carried Sloan around from the other side of the truck, an automatic weapon in one hand, his free hand almost but not quite cupping her breast. She was terrified, but she was talking to the man who held her. Lucas couldn't tell what she said, only that she was making him listen.

"You see her now, don't you?" the man said in his ear. "She's fine, and if you want her to stay fine, you tell me where it is."

"In my wallet, my hip pocket," Lucas said, his eyes locked on Sloan.

The man kicked him hard in the ribs, causing him to sprawl facedown again. A rock dug into his left cheek, but he couldn't turn his head enough to get off it. "Wrong answer, son! What I'm looking for doesn't fit in a wallet. Let's try again. *Where is it?*"

"Aw, now you ought to let the man show you his badge," Chuckie said. "Them tribal police badges might be hard to come by."

Lucas had dirt in his mouth. The pain in his side was excruciating. These two men were in the wrong kind of car, and there were no red bandannas and no mirrored sunglasses—but he was still sure. "Tell you what," he managed to say. "Why don't you just show me yours. You two ever heard of illegal search and seizure? How long have you clowns been with the bureau anyway?"

"Damn it, I told you!" Chuckie said. "I told you the other day that son of a bitch of an Indian cop made us."

"Shut up, Chuckie!"

"Chuckie's right," Lucas said. "The son of a bitch of an Indian cop made you. A damn rookie right out of the academy. The bureau sent you out here to practice, I guess. How many times did it take you to pass Undercover 101, anyway?" He stopped because of the pain in his ribs. He felt light-headed, hungry for air. "You know, I was almost an FBI agent once."

"Yeah, right. The minority quota full that day?" Chuckie asked sarcastically.

"Couldn't get past the background check," Lucas said. "Too many ancestors plotted to overthrow the United States government. And, of course, my parents were *married—*"

"Lucas!" Sloan cried, because the last remark got him another kick in the ribs. He writhed in pain on the ground.

"Funny man! You're a real comedian, Mr. Tribal Policeman!" the kicker said, dragging Lucas to his knees again. "I am sick to death of you people! I want to know where the stuff is!"

"I don't know what you're talking about!"

"The shipment is missing, son! The late Mr. Baron knew where it got to, but apparently he wasn't talking. *Your* name was the first name to turn up at the hospital after somebody tried to take him out."

"What do you mean?" Sloan cried. "What do you mean?"

Lucas only half heard what the man answered. A wave of nausea washed over him, and his ears rang.

"Car coming," he thought Chuckie said before he pitched forward.

It was very quiet. The truck engine had been running. He didn't hear it anymore. He opened his eyes and turned his head slowly to keep the vertigo at bay. Sloan was on her knees beside him.

"Hold still," she said. "I don't want to cut you."

He could feel her sawing away. It took her a long time, but the plastic strip around his wrists suddenly broke.

"Where are they?" he asked, trying to sit up. She held out his pocketknife, but he couldn't take it. His hands were completely numb.

"Gone," she said, shoving the knife into his pocket for him. "A van full of schoolchildren came by and all but stopped. I guess it scared them away." She reached to steady him. He jerked his arm out of her grasp.

"Which—way did they go?"

"Toward Ganado. Lucas, you need a doctor."

"No, I don't." He needed to do something with the rage he was feeling. He needed to get into the truck and go look for these two men—to ride all night if he had to.

Damn the arrogant sons of bitches!

No probable cause. No nothing. They had arbitrarily decided he was guilty, and that had been enough. What was a cracked skull or a broken rib or two if the perpetrator happened to be a reservation Indian? Tribal policeman or not? It was a small matter to attribute that kind of injury to resisting arrest. They didn't have to explain the fact that they'd been utterly wrong, because out here, there was no one to whom they were answerable. He considered himself lucky to be alive—and Sloan.

Ah, God, Sloan!

He hadn't been able to do anything to keep her from being manhandled. If they'd wanted to do worse, he couldn't have stopped them. He couldn't bear the thought of what might have happened to her.

He managed to get to his feet, even to walk a few steps before the pain in his side doubled him over.

"Lucas, you're hurt," she said, trying to take his arm again.

"Don't!" he said sharply.

"Lucas, you need—"

"Don't tell me what I need. Leave me alone! I don't need your help!"

She let her hand fall. "I'm sorry," she said, her voice husky, barely audible. "I thought you did." She abruptly turned and walked away, disappearing on the other side of the truck.

He swore and hobbled after her, holding the place in his side that hurt. She was sitting on the ground trying to smooth the bent pages of a book of fairy tales. The book had been quite beautiful before it had been ground in the dirt, leather bound with gold lettering. *Antique Fairy Tales.* Meggie would have loved it.

Sloan didn't look at him. She kept turning and unbending pages. "I don't want to play this game any more, Lucas," she said, glancing at him. "And don't look at me as if you don't know what I mean! You've been doing it since the first day we met! I can't help what happened to your people—what *keeps* happening, if this is any indication. I can't help what some other white woman did to you. I'm not a racial bigot and I'm not Sara. I'm not going to suffer for somebody else's transgressions when my only sin is trying to get my nephew out of this place and worrying about you. No, I take that back. I guess it *is* my fault—something my brother did was bad enough to cause all this.'' She held her hand out to include the debris scattered around her—Christmas presents and the contents of her purse and the canvas tote she'd filled with the letters from her brother's desk. "Lucas, you're hurt, damn it! And I can't stand it!"

She bowed her head, and all the anger went out of him.

"You don't understand," he said.

"No, and you're not about to explain it to me, are you?" She looked at him. "If I don't understand, it's not from lack of trying, Lucas."

He dropped heavily to his knees beside her. She knew about Sara. Of course, she did. Everybody on the reservation over the age of ten knew.

"It's not what you think—"

"I don't think anything, Lucas. I don't *know* what to think."

"You think it has to do with my being Navajo and going head-to-head with the United States government and not being able to win—even when I haven't done anything wrong. It doesn't. It has to do with...whatever is between us, Sloan. You and me. And don't pretend that you don't know what *I* mean," he said when she was about to interrupt. "It has to do with dignity and pride and being a man." He was so tired suddenly, but he was still going to tell her. "No man wants his woman to see him with his face down in the dirt like that. Is that so hard to understand? I don't want your token concern. I don't want your medical expertise. What I want from you right now—the kind of comfort I need—you wouldn't be willing to give."

She sat there for a moment, then she moved away from him and began picking up the rest of the things that had been turned out on the ground. She didn't look at him. When her hands were full, she walked to the truck and threw everything into the box that had apparently precipitated all this.

"Sloan," he said to make her look at him, and he asked the question he should have asked before now. "Are you all right?"

She glanced at him. "They didn't hurt me, if that's what you mean." Her voice wavered.

He made it to his feet again. "Come here," he said. "Let me lean on you."

She stood for a moment, then came to him, sliding her arm around him when he reached for her. She pressed her face into his neck. Her hand clutched the front of his shirt. He could feel her trembling.

"My God, Lucas," she said. "What did my brother do?"

Sloan drove the truck to Window Rock, her mind filled with one question.

Now what?

Lucas had declared that there was something between them, and she hadn't disputed it. End of discussion. She glanced at him from time to time because he wasn't saying anything. She knew he was in pain, too much pain to manage a straight-drive truck without power brakes and steering. She was in a different kind of pain, the kind that was all too familiar to her. The kind that came from following after Mark all her life and picking up the pieces. What had he done? Whatever it was, if she could believe men who behaved the way those two agents had behaved, it had been bad enough to cause his death.

"I have to go see Becenti," Lucas said when they reached the outskirts of Window Rock. "Turn here, and then right at the next road. And stop worrying."

"You could have a broken rib," she said in her own defense.

"I could, but I don't. I've had broken ribs before, and this isn't it."

She looked at him doubtfully.

"I used to rodeo some to make extra money when I was in college. I know what a broken rib feels like."

"Lucas—"

"Next driveway," he said pointing.

"I'll wait here," she said as she parked the truck.

"You can come inside with me, Sloan."

"No. I'll wait here."

He didn't press her. He got out of the truck.

"Sloan," he said when he was about to shut the door. "I think you should know I want you to stay with me tonight. I'm not joking and the invitation isn't for anything Platonic."

He slammed the door closed and walked off. She sat with her hands on the steering wheel, watching him try to make his way to the Becenti front door as if nothing hurt.

Well, yes, Lucas, she thought, stunned. I guess I *should* know that.

A woman came to the door, a woman who gave a soft cry at the sight of him. Lucas clearly hadn't realized that his face was bruised, but he immediately turned and directed the woman to the truck where Sloan sat.

"Lucas," she said under her breath as the woman approached.

"My name is Mae Becenti," the woman said pleasantly. "Lucas says I'm to bring you inside if I have to carry you. He says he'd do it, but he needs all his strength to talk to my husband. He's a very good man, my husband, but he's been known to shoot the messenger." She opened the truck door. "Please," she said. "You look a bit frazzled."

Sloan managed a smile and got out of the truck, surprised at how weak her knees had become. "I'm Sloan Baron."

"Yes, I know," Mrs. Becenti said, smiling. She said something in Navajo. "Smiles At Children," she translated. "That's a good Navajo name to have, Sloan Baron."

It took a certain amount of effort to follow Mae Becenti up the sidewalk. Her adrenaline high had dissipated in spite of Lucas's announcement. Mae held open the storm door for her to go inside. The house was neat and cool and decorated in the Southwestern style. Sloan could immediately hear Lucas's voice in another room. She looked around to find Mae watching.

"He's all right," she said. "I've seen him worse. And I didn't really mean that my husband would shoot him."

Sloan managed another smile. *When?* she thought as she followed Mae into the kitchen. *Was he worse when he used to rodeo? Was he worse when Sara got finished with him?*

She sat at the kitchen table while Mae poured her a glass of cold lemonade. The lemonade was wonderful, exactly what she needed. Mae poured two more glasses to take into the other room. "Now I have to go assure Lucas that *you're* all right," she whispered on her way out.

Sloan sat alone, staring at nothing.

I want you to stay with me tonight.

Now what?

Letting oneself be carried away by the heat of passion in the middle of a cornfield was one thing. Deliberately deciding whether or not she would accept Lucas Singer's invitation to bed was something else again. She thought of all the women and young girls she'd encountered in her work who'd absolutely refused to accept any responsibility for their situation—for their unwanted pregnancy or their disease or their broken heart. How many times had she heard, "It just happened!"

It wasn't going to "just happen" with Lucas. He'd made sure that there could be only token self-recriminations in the cold light of day. Tonight would happen only if she wanted it to.

She looked around because she heard his voice closer, and Mae came into the room.

"He's telephoning," she said. "He says these men don't care who they question or how. He wants to make sure that Meggie is all right. And he's going to ask the dispatcher to send one of the officers in the area where Patrick is to check on him."

"And Will?" she asked.

"The little one at the receiving home? I'll see if he's calling there," Mae said, going out again. She returned almost immediately and sat down at the table. "First place he called," she said.

"Thank you for the lemonade," Sloan said. "It's wonderful."

"Old family recipe," she said. "Sloan, my husband doesn't know about you and Lucas."

"There's nothing to know," Sloan said. She met the woman's eyes. Mae Becenti didn't believe her.

"It shows, Sloan," she said kindly. "Particularly in Lucas—in his concern for you and for your brother's children. He's glad to be alive again. I think it's your doing. I'm telling you this because when my husband does know, he may not be happy because of what happened before."

Lucas came in carrying an empty glass, and she didn't go on. Sloan immediately made up her mind. The situation was entirely too complicated. She and Lucas were going to have to maintain the status quo of being neither friends nor lovers for both their sakes—and that's all there was to it. There was no point in disrupting both their lives. Any kind of involvement would do neither of them any good.

Firm in her conviction, she looked up at him, recognizing immediately from the closed expression on his face that the talk with Becenti had been as difficult as Mae had hinted. He studiously avoided her eyes, making small talk with Mae about the weather and how soon it would rain. When he finally did look at her, the desire she saw in his eyes took her breath away.

Lucas!

Her lips parted, and her belly grew warm and her breasts heavy. He was standing very close to her chair. She could feel the effort he was putting into not touching her, regardless of the fact that Mae Becenti was there chatting away.

"Meggie and Will are okay," he said, his neutral-sounding voice completely belying what she saw in his eyes. "Somebody will call

me at home as soon as they check on Patrick. Are you ready to
go?''

She nodded, and she must have said something to Mae and to
Captain Becenti on the way out. She had been brought up to be
polite, to acknowledge another's hospitality, to say thank you.

But she remembered nothing about leaving. Lucas drove this
time, if somewhat jerkily. He kept looking at her, as if he was expecting her to protest the direction he was taking. He reached for
her hand, dragging his thumb across her palm. Her fingers clung
to his, but she didn't move any closer to him. She was afraid to.

He drove quickly, still holding her hand, letting go only to make
the final turn into the driveway where he lived. He opened the
truck door. "Do we need to talk about this?" he asked, catching
her hand again.

"No," she said.

The sun was down, the twilight soft and edged in orange and
purple. She could hear a faint roll of thunder in the distance, feel
the stirring of a breeze. She got out of the truck and walked with
him to the front door, aware that there were other houses nearby
where any number of people might be watching. She could smell
someone's supper cooking—fried potatoes, she thought—and
hear country music.

She stood awkwardly while he unlocked the door.

I don't know how to do this, she thought. *I don't know what the
rules are. I don't even know if there are rules.* She should tell him
she didn't, before she made some blunder that would ruin everything. She was only certain of one thing—that she wanted to be
with this man. She didn't want to think about anything but him.
She didn't want to feel anything but him. She wanted to lie with
him all night and wake up in his arms in the morning. And she
wanted him to be the one. Her first lover. Her last.

Had he ever brought Sara here? No, no, she didn't want to think
about that.

He pushed the door open and she stepped inside. She stood
waiting, her arms over her breasts as if she was cold. Lucas
reached for her as soon as he'd closed the door, and she went to
him, trying to be careful of his ribs. He kissed her mouth, and
then her eyes, and then her mouth again.

Then he took her by the hand and led her into the bedroom. The
bed had been stripped. He opened the windows. The wind had
picked up and the room was immediately filled with the smell of
rain. He got sheets and pillowcases out of the bureau drawer, and
they made the bed together. She found the act of preparing a place
for them to lie both intimate and incredibly arousing.

"I'm going to shower," he said when the bed was done. "Come in with me."

Come in with me?

He didn't wait for her answer. He opened the closet door and handed her one of his shirts. "Best I can do," he said.

Sloan swallowed heavily. He nuzzled her cheek and left her standing. In a moment, she heard water running in the shower.

She looked down at her dress. This was no time to play the shy old maid. The memory of being held against her will this afternoon was strong. She needed to wash away the feel of another man's hands on her body; she needed to have him do it.

She stripped quickly and put on his shirt. It came down to her thighs. She didn't button it. When she came into the bathroom, he was naked. She went immediately to him, careful of the mottled bruises on his left side.

Lucas was surprised that she'd come in. She had looked so startled when he'd made the suggestion. She wasn't startled now. She was beautiful and she was more than a little scared.

But she let him take away the shirt. And she let him look at her. He was immediately aroused. His hands trembled when he reached for her.

"You are so beautiful," he said against her ear.

"Am I?"

There was nothing coy in the question. He was about to become her lover, and she wanted to know if he was pleased.

He stepped into the shower, pulling her along with him, letting the water run over them both, letting his mouth taste hers—only taste, because he was aching with desire and he couldn't stand any more than that. He reached for the soap and turned her away from him, putting his arms around her and letting her lean against him so he could lather both their bodies. How pale her skin was in contrast to his.

Slowly. Go slowly.

He pressed himself against her. Her hands rested on top of his. He soaped her arms and her belly, and she gave a sharp sigh when his wet, soapy hands cupped her breasts. When he slid his hands between her legs, her head arched back and she gave a soft "oh" sound.

It was nearly his undoing.

He gave her the soap and turned away, letting her stroke his back, savoring the feel of the water running over him. Her hands were firm, stronger than he would have thought and very careful of the bruises. He closed his eyes and let her do this however she wanted, giving a grunt of pleasure when her hands slid around to touch him in the same way he'd touched her. He turned around again, his mouth coming down on hers hard. Her lips parted, giving him access. He was so hungry for her. How long had he wanted to do this? How long?

Sloan!

He reached blindly to turn off the water, stepping out of the shower, all but carrying her in spite of the pain in his side. He lurched into the bedroom, tumbling onto the bed with her. He had a towel in his hand he didn't remember getting, and he tossed it aside, rummaging frantically in the nightstand for the condoms he'd bought—for her—after that day in the cornfield. He tore the packet open with his teeth, his hands trembling, his breath ragged. He realized that he needed to be more subtle than this, but he couldn't slow down, most assuredly couldn't stop. It had been too long since he'd been with a woman. If he didn't do it now, he'd die—

She helped him. With the condom. With his entry into her body. She was so tight. *Too* tight. It was only at the last second that he realized why. It was too late then; he was too far gone. His body thrust against hers and then again, deeper. He knew that he hurt her but he was completely unable to hold back. He thrust again, his release violent and oblivious to any need but his own.

"Why didn't you tell me?"

He had waited for what seemed a long time for her to come back to bed, and he lay beside her now, listening to the last remnants of the thunderstorm outside the window, his mind in turmoil. He hadn't expected that she would be a virgin—not for one minute. He had known she was afraid, but making love with someone for the first time was always frightening. How could he have guessed that she'd never been with a man like this before? He couldn't, damn it, and she'd just let him go at it, as if she didn't matter to him and he'd paid for the privilege.

"Why didn't you say something?" He raised up on his less injured side, reaching out and grabbing her by the wrist. "I want to know, damn it! Why me? Surely you could have found somebody else to take care of this for you. My God, your compassion is boundless, isn't it! There's nothing you won't do for the hopeless and downtrodden—"

"Lucas, don't," she said, rolling against him. She wanted to put her arms around him. He wouldn't let her. He didn't mean somebody else, and she knew it. He meant somebody white.

"I thought you knew what you were doing," he said. "I thought you knew what you were getting into with me. You didn't, Sloan! You should have told me so I—"

"What, Lucas? So you could run away from me again? I did know what I was doing, and I knew you'd hate it. I knew you'd think I was some kind of walking emotional trap, that I'd make you responsible for me and my *lost* virginity. I didn't lose it, Lucas. I *gave* it to you. I didn't feel sorry for you. If anything, I felt sorry for *me*. You're the only man I've ever trusted enough to go to bed with. I had begun to think there was something wrong with me. I wanted *you*. If that makes you uncomfortable, I can't help it."

He swore and sat up. "You should have told me," he said. "This wasn't any good for you. Your first time shouldn't be like that."

How should it be, Lucas? she almost asked.

He got up and disappeared into the bathroom. She lay there, waiting, expecting him to tell her to get out and go home the best way she could, or to leave himself.

A man wants to be a woman's first. A woman wants to be a man's last. Where had she heard that? A piece of grandmother's wisdom she'd picked up somewhere along the way that was completely wrong.

She lay in his bed listening to the rain. How upset would he be if he knew she loved him? She'd skirted all around *that* revelation. He hated that there was anything between them at all. From the first day she'd met him, he had been so determined there wouldn't be.

She closed her eyes, remembering what it had felt like, having him inside her.

I love you, Lucas. I wish I didn't—

No, she thought. That wasn't true. She was glad about it, no matter what happened.

She opened her eyes to find him standing by the bed.

"I hurt you, didn't I?" he said.

It *had* hurt at first, but then not so much. She had almost but not quite understood what making love could be like. "I'm all right," she said.

The rain outside came harder, another storm approaching. She could see the flash of lightning, hear the roll of thunder. The air had turned cold, and she shivered. He slid into bed beside her and gathered her close, spoon fashion, to keep her warm.

"I did know what I was getting into with you, Lucas," she said quietly. "I don't want anything from you. I know this is just—"

His arms tightened around her suddenly, and he pressed his face into her shoulder.

"Sloan..."

Her name was a whisper she barely heard, but she turned to face him, moving closer to him in an invitation as old as time, gently kissing his mouth again and again. Her hand slid downward to touch him.

He gave a sharp intake of breath and kissed her hard, his hand moving purposefully to cup her breast. "Sloan—you're not used to this."

"Make me used to it, Lucas," she whispered.

She had been quiet a long time; he had thought she was asleep. But then she reached down to take his hand, sliding her fingers between his.

"I didn't know it could be like this," she said.

He lay beside her, sated, exhausted, in pain, and now he smiled, infinitely pleased. It had been better the second time, much better—because he'd truly made love to her, patiently letting her feel how much he wanted her, needed her.

Loved her.

But he hadn't said the words, and he wasn't sure why. Sloan Baron was his woman—in his mind and in his heart.

She gave a quiet sigh. "Lucas," she said, "did you ever bring Sara here?"

His smile faded. "No."

"Tell me about her."

"I..." *Don't talk about her,* he was about to say, but he found suddenly that he wanted to tell Sloan about this unhappy part of his life. "I was in love with her," he said quietly. He raised up to reposition the pillow, then positioned her so that her head was on his shoulder. "I was incredibly stupid where she was concerned. I thought she meant what she said—otherwise, why say it? We were lovers. She got pregnant. She left and went back East without saying anything to me, not even goodbye. She just disappeared. She had an abortion. I found out about it well after the fact. I didn't handle it very well. I started drinking, and I nearly ruined my career. I would have ruined it if it hadn't been for Becenti and the old man—Hosteen Anagal. Everybody on the reservation knows about it. End of story."

"Not quite. She's come back looking for you."

"No," he said.

"There's unfinished business between you."

"Not for me," he said truthfully. "Because I finally understand her. I remember the pain. I remember that I loved her, but it doesn't mean anything anymore. I understand the kind of person she is. I understand that what she is, she can't help." He reached to tilt her face upward so that he could kiss her mouth. "Go to sleep now," he said, smiling in the dark. "So I can."

She laughed softly and curled herself against him.

But he didn't sleep. He lay there listening to the same car drive slowly past the house for the third time.

Chapter Fourteen

Someone was pounding on the front door. Sloan stirred in his arms as the racket escalated.

"Go back to sleep," Lucas whispered to her, gently kissing her shoulder and her ear. She reached up to touch his face.

Reluctantly, he got out of bed and put on his jeans, looking at her sleeping face a long moment before he went out.

I love you, Sloan.

The words lay so easy in his mind and in his heart, but he still couldn't say them.

The pounding came again. He looked out the window, then jerked open the door.

"Damn if you don't look like a man who got lucky," Carlos said, grinning from ear to ear.

"What do you want?" Lucas said, ignoring the comment and the grin. The sun was barely up, and his side was killing him.

"I need to see Sloan," he said, trying to look into the house over Lucas's shoulder. He had an envelope in his hand.

"Why?" Lucas said. There was no point in pretending that she wasn't here, when it was obvious the reservation grapevine had informed Carlos otherwise. Or perhaps his had been the vehicle that had gone by the house so many times last night.

"Becenti sent me," Carlos said. "He wanted this hand-delivered—"

"I'll give it to her."

"I can't do that, Lucas. He said *I* was to personally make sure she got it."

"Why?" Lucas said again.

"Lucas, I'm just the legman. All I know is what he said. He said he didn't want this in the hands of any officer who might have his own agenda."

"What the hell is that supposed to mean?"

Carlos sighed. "Don't give me a hard time, man. Just let me give the letter to Sloan. And I need to tell her something. Mary Skeets wants me to tell her something about the oldest boy, Patrick."

Lucas only realized this minute he hadn't received a phone call verifying that Patrick was all right.

"What about Patrick?"

"Lucas, let me talk to Sloan, okay? I can do what Becenti wanted me to do and I can get Mary Skeets off my back and *you* can get back to whatever you were doing. Let's just say you owe Mary big time, okay?"

"Carlos—"

"What's wrong?" Sloan said behind him. She was awake and dressed and quite beautiful, Lucas thought.

"Good morning," Carlos said cheerfully. "I'm sorry to bother you so early, Sloan." He glanced at Lucas, giving him a look of frank envy.

The telephone rang, and Lucas stepped inside to answer it. "Give her the letter, Carlos," he said.

"What letter?" Sloan said, moving to let Lucas get by. Their eyes met briefly. He was annoyed—worried?—about something. She took the letter Carlos handed her. It had a tribal council return address. She opened it and read it quickly, aware of Lucas's brief telephone conversation behind her and that Carlos was apparently waiting.

"Am I supposed to answer this?" she asked him.

"No. I just have to know you got it and read it."

"The custody hearing is scheduled," she said to Lucas when he returned. "First thing Monday morning."

"What else did you want to tell her, Carlos?" Lucas said, looking at the young officer.

"Sloan, Patrick came home early last night—the camp where he was staying got rained out. He was pretty upset that he couldn't find anybody. Mary Skeets talked to him. She was at the receiv-

ing home when he called looking for you. She told him you were
staying with a . . . friend. She told him she'd get in touch with you
if he wanted. I guess he didn't. Anyway, Mary thought you ought
to know so you'd . . . know what to say," he finished lamely.

"Thank you, Carlos," she said, looking down at the letter. Her
nephew had been upset and looking for her while she'd been off
with her lover. She should be feeling a lot more guilty than she did.

"Well, I'll be going," Carlos said awkwardly.

"No, wait," Lucas said. "I need a ride in."

Carlos seemed about to comment, but apparently thought better of it. Lucas closed the door, leaving Carlos outside. Sloan
moved immediately into his arms.

"I have to go in to see Becenti," he said, kissing her forehead.
"You take the truck to your place. I can pick it up later. Are you
all right?" he asked, because whatever respite they found last night
from the real world was about to end.

She nodded, then leaned back to look at him. "I wish I'd found
Will's birth certificate or a marriage license or something. I should
have been looking long before now. Was that Becenti on the
phone?"

"Yes," he said, and now was the time to tell her that no legal
document was likely going to make a difference in the decision the
tribal council would make. But he looked into her eyes and he
couldn't do it.

"He knows I stayed here last night, doesn't he?"

"Probably," Lucas said. If Carlos and Mary Skeets did, then
everybody did.

"I'm sorry. I didn't want to cause you any problems."

He abruptly grinned. "The kind of problems you cause me, I
know exactly how to fix."

She smiled in return—and blushed. He hugged her to him,
laughing, marveling at how good she made him feel.

"Sloan, you aren't sorry we . . ."

"No," she said, lifting her head to look into his eyes. "I'm not
sorry."

"Sergeant Singer—Lucas?" Carlos called pitifully from the
other side of the door.

"I have to go. What will you tell Patrick?"

"The truth, if he asks," she said. "That I was here with you.
I've never lied to him or Meggie."

"Good," Lucas said. "He might as well know. Everybody
might as well know."

* * *

Patrick was still asleep when she got home, and she was more than a little relieved. She had told Lucas she would tell Patrick the truth, and she would—but it was just one more thing on her list of things to dread.

She went out to Lucas's truck to bring in the box with the Christmas gifts, wondering if they were even salvageable. Meggie would be thrilled regardless of the bent pages. Patrick would probably burn the Walkman and the CDs whether they still worked or not.

Apparently, he had heard her come in the first time. He was sitting at the kitchen table when she carried in the box, his arms folded. He'd had a restless night, if the sprigs of hair that stood up all over his head were any indication, and he'd either dressed quickly or he'd slept in his clothes. She understood his being upset, regardless of the fact that he'd stayed alone any number of times before. This time he hadn't known she wouldn't be here. She realized suddenly that he was about to cry.

"You should have told Mary to find me," she said, putting her hand on his shoulder. He immediately shook it off.

"I didn't have to tell Mary to find you," he answered. "I knew where you were. You were shacking up with Lucas Singer."

"Patrick—"

"You think I'm a dumb kid, but I'm not. I knew you'd go off with him the first chance you got. I thought we were supposed to be a family! I thought you wanted us—Meggie and me—to remember that we were trying to get Will. Well, what about *you*, Sloan! How do you think what *you're* doing looks! Everybody's going to know, Sloan. You think Meggie won't find out about it? Meggie hears everything."

"Patrick, I want to tell you something," she interrupted. "I haven't told anyone this—not even Lucas—but I'm telling you so you'll understand and not be so upset."

"What!"

"I love Lucas, Patrick."

"I don't want to hear this!" he said, standing up so quickly the chair tipped over backward. "I'm going! I'm going over to Danny's! See, I told you where I'll be, so don't go sending one of your little tribal police friends out looking for me!"

"Patrick, wait. We need to talk—"

The screen door slammed behind him, and he walked angrily across the yard to the street.

"Call me peculiar, Sloan, but I don't want to talk about Lucas Singer!" he called over his shoulder. "He *likes* white women, Sloan! You know that, don't you!"

"We need to talk about your father—"

"Nice try, Sloan! Oh, look! *Nice* set of wheels!" he called over his shoulder, one hand making a sweeping gesture toward Lucas's truck.

She let him go because they both needed time to calm down. Her revelation had only made matters worse, and she might as well get used to it. The truth of the matter was that she couldn't think of anyone who would be happy to hear she was in love with Lucas Singer, not even Lucas.

She stayed close to home, waiting for Meggie to return and for Patrick to get back from Danny's and for Lucas to come for his truck. She spent the time going through the papers from Mark's desk more thoroughly, reading all the letters she'd written to him, some part of her looking for something she might have said in one of them that would have kept him away. But there was nothing she regretted having told him, nothing that made her feel guilty. And if there were any legal papers pertaining to Will's birth or Mark's marriage, he hadn't kept them in the house where he'd been living. With Mark, who knew where they could be. She put the box in another room until she decided what to do about the Christmas presents. Her mind went immediately to Lucas. She had been so afraid for him yesterday. She hadn't been ready to admit on any level that there were still places in this country where innocent people could be treated so badly. She was still afraid for him. Facedown in the dirt, his hands bound, he hadn't for a moment given in. Those two men hadn't been able to intimidate him. Lucas had been brash and insolent. A part of her had been undeniably proud of his refusal to yield. But she was fully aware that those men were still around someplace and that the kind of contemptuousness Lucas had exhibited could easily get him killed.

Meggie returned shortly after lunchtime, full of enthusiasm for the craft she was learning from Dolly Singer.

"You have to leave a way out," Meggie was saying.

"What?" Sloan said, because she was worrying about Lucas again and she'd only been half listening.

"A way out of the rug," Meggie said. "When you work on something that hard, your spirit gets hung up in there so you have to leave this different piece of yarn running to the outside of the pattern when you get it done so it can get out." She came and threw her arm over Sloan's shoulder. "Do you think that's true?"

"It is if you believe it is," Sloan said.

"Yeah, that's what I thought."

They both looked up as Patrick came in. He didn't say anything to either of them, heading for the refrigerator as he always did and then going outside again.

"I think I'll go outside, too," Meggie said. "And bug him."

"No, not today," Sloan said. "You can go outside, but don't bother Patrick, okay?"

"Why?"

"He's upset with me," she said.

"Again?" Meggie said, and she smiled. It must seem to Meggie that she and Patrick were always at odds.

By late afternoon, Lucas still hadn't come for his truck. She toyed with the idea of driving to the nearest pay phone and calling Mary Skeets to find out where he might be, but she didn't. She wanted to see him. In lieu of that, she wanted to hear his voice—but she wouldn't embarrass him with her unsolicited worry, no matter how justified it might be.

They had an early supper. Patrick was talking more, but not to her. Someone knocked on the screen door while she was cleaning the table. She turned around, expecting—*hoping*—to see Lucas. There was a woman standing on the porch, a briefcase under her arm.

"I'm looking for Sloan Baron," she heard the woman tell Meggie.

"I'm Sloan Baron," she said as Meggie ushered the woman inside. The woman made a sweeping assessment of the room and walked immediately to the half cleared kitchen table. "This will do," she said, picking up a napkin and wiping a spot clean to put her briefcase. She looked around for a place to throw the napkin, and Sloan held out her hand.

"Thanks," the woman said, opening the briefcase and unloading some papers.

Sloan glanced at Meggie, who shrugged.

"Excuse me," Sloan said. "Do I know you?"

"Lillian Singer," the woman said, glancing up from the papers. "And this is Meggie and Patrick, right?" she said. "I need to talk to your aunt privately, please," she said to them. She waited until both children had trooped out—neither of them very happy about it. "I take it my brother didn't tell you I was coming. I see his truck outside. I thought he might be here."

"No, he didn't. I haven't—"

"I'm a lawyer, Ms. Baron," Lillian interrupted. "Lucas called me early this morning. He says you need one."

"I don't need a lawyer."

"Are you or are you not trying to get custody of your brother's half Navajo child?"

"Yes."

"And the hearing is Monday morning."

"Yes, I just got the—"

"Then you need legal counsel, Navajo legal counsel, somebody who understands what's going on here and can explain it to you. Whether or not you have a lawyer isn't going to make a damn bit of difference in the final outcome of the case, of course, but—"

"What?" Sloan said, completely bewildered.

"My brother didn't tell you that, either, I take it." She gave a sharp sigh. "Ms. Baron, this is what my brother tells *me*. He says you don't understand this situation. He says you're used to custody cases where having a responsible, upstanding petitioner for custody is a rarity—therefore, when there is one and that person is a relative, the case is found in that party's favor. That is not the case here. The truth of the matter is you don't stand a snowball's chance in hell of getting that boy. If you were his natural mother, or if he'd been living with you since birth, you might have had a shot at getting some kind of joint custody. As it is, we're just going through the motions—and Lucas should have told you that."

"Yes," Sloan agreed. "He should have." She looked at Lillian Singer. "I've had Mark's other children for several years. I'm not somebody who just wandered in. I'm the boy's aunt."

"Maybe you are and maybe you aren't. I've checked vital statistics in Santa Fe and in Phoenix. There's no birth certificate on file for a Will Baron approximately three years old. In any event, you're a white woman. My people are rather touchy about handing over our children to well-meaning white people."

"Yes," Sloan said. "That much Lucas did tell me."

"So are you and Lucas lovers?" she asked bluntly.

Sloan was completely taken aback—and even if she hadn't been, she wouldn't have answered the question. She said nothing.

"You know, that's exactly what Lucas said," Lillian said, nonplussed. "Well, that lets out our calling him as any kind of character witness. Everybody in Window Rock is going to know. His involvement with you will discredit anything he might say in your behalf. What I can't understand is what is it with you white women and my brother. Can't you find any of your own kind to ruin? Sit down. I need some information."

"Ms. Singer, why—"

"Lillian," she corrected.

"Why are you doing this?" Sloan said, ignoring the invitation to use the woman's given name. "If I can't win, why are you even bothering? I certainly can't afford to pay you—except in installments. Very *small* installments."

"Sit down," Lillian said again. She waited until Sloan sat. "I want you to know exactly what we're up against. We don't have any proof that you're an actual relative. It *looks* as if you are, but that won't hold up in court. Essentially, we're going before the tribal judges with nothing but my brother's hot reputation for getting involved with white women."

"Then why are you doing this?"

"Lucas wants it. We're a lot alike, Sloan. You and I both will do things for our brothers we wouldn't do for anyone else."

Yes, Sloan thought. She could understand that.

"Any questions?" Lillian asked.

"Just one," Sloan answered, because she felt as if she'd just gone head-to-head with a steamroller. "Are you related to Inez Yazzie?"

Surprisingly, Lillian Singer threw back her head and laughed.

Mary Skeets headed Lucas off the minute he walked into the building.

"If you've got a uniform in your locker, you better put it on," she whispered.

"Why? I'm off duty."

"Do it!" she said. "I'll give you five minutes and then I'll tell Captain Becenti you're here."

He went and put on his uniform—as bad as Mary might be with the telephone messages, she knew the ins and outs of Captain Becenti's moods. Then he stood where she could see him. She gave him a thumbs-up and pointed toward Becenti's office.

Becenti was waiting with two FBI agents out of Albuquerque, one older, ready to retire, and clearly tired of all this crap, the other one itching to set the world on fire. Lucas decided immediately that he had no intention of becoming the kindling.

"Come in, Lucas," Becenti said. He made the introductions and pushed the door shut, immediately dashing the hopes of all the eavesdroppers in the hall.

"Is this the extent of his injuries?" the younger one said to Becenti, looking at Lucas's face.

"No, it isn't," Lucas said, surprised at how quickly his anger over yesterday's humiliation returned. "He has some more, but he's not running them out for some FBI jackass who's already decided they were caused by tripping over a gopher."

The older agent bit off a grin.

"Lucas, that's enough," Becenti chided.

Apparently, Becenti had filed a formal complaint, which surprised Lucas. Last night he hadn't been sure Becenti even believed him.

"They want you to look at some file photos," Becenti said.

"Fine," Lucas said. It took him a very short time to locate the right ones. "These two," he said, tossing the photographs on Becenti's desk. "This one the other man called Chuckie."

The younger agent picked up one of the photographs. "This man is deceased," he said, tapping the photograph with his forefinger.

"If he is, he died sometime after seven o'clock yesterday," Lucas said, refusing to be rattled. "These are the two men. They've been on the reservation for some time. They usually play dress-up—mirrored sunglasses and red bandannas—and drive around in a rough 1988 black Firebird with a big motor, left front parking light broken out."

"License plate number?" the younger one asked.

"I don't know," Lucas said, giving him a point.

"You don't know," he repeated.

"That's right. I don't know."

"It seems to me that ought to be the first—"

"Did either of these men tell you why they pulled you over?" the older agent interrupted.

"They didn't pull me over. They cut me off and ran my vehicle off the road."

"Did they ever say what they were looking for?"

"Yeah," Lucas said. "The deceased guy called whatever it was 'it' and 'the shipment.'"

"What happened to your wrists?" he asked, overtly making an inspection.

"Ty-rap," Lucas said, referring to the plastic strip that had been used to bind his hands.

"Is that what they used?" the younger one asked in a tone of voice that suggested Lucas might be into deviant sexual practices.

Lucas chose not to respond.

"The woman who was with you—was she hurt?" he persisted.

"More emotionally than physically," Lucas said.

"Emotionally," the younger one repeated, as if a word with that many syllables had to be beyond Lucas's grasp.

"Yes, emotionally. She feels the same way your woman would feel if she'd been dragged out of a vehicle for no apparent reason and had a .357 Magnum held to her head and been felt up by some FBI piece of—"

"Gentlemen!" the older agent interrupted. "Sergeant Singer, you are understandably upset by this thing. But if we could just stick to exactly what happened."

They went through it all again. And then again. Lucas said nothing about the dead schoolteacher until the older agent specifically asked, then he told him the only thing he knew—that their agent indicated Mark Baron's death hadn't been an accident. Then they went through it all again—how Sloan Baron, sister of the deceased schoolteacher, happened to be out here and how Lucas's name happened to have been left at the intensive care unit to be notified of any changes in Mark Baron's condition—until even Becenti had to be satisfied that he did *not* have an officer involved in a felony. It took an adjustment in thinking on Lucas's part to accept the fact that apparently it wasn't his association with Margaret Madman that had put him on a surveillance list, but his association with Sloan.

He was exhausted by the time the interview was over. His side hurt, and he needed sleep, and he needed Sloan. He wanted to be with her, to lie down on a bed somewhere with her and sleep for a while and then make love.

He knew perfectly well that Becenti had let him walk into this interrogation cold, and that if there had been any holes in his story whatsoever, Lucas Singer would have been hung out to dry.

"Is that all, Captain?" he asked. He fully intended to find Carlos and buy him a big bowl of chili and a beer. The rookie had been right on target all the way with his identification of undercover FBI agents—even without the license plate number. And startling *four* agents with information the tribal police shouldn't have, instead of only two, was always a preferred goal.

"No, it isn't," Becenti said. "You handled yourself well just now, Lucas, and I appreciate that, but I'm sending you out of Window Rock for a while."

"Why?"

"I think you know why. I don't want another scandal like the last one. You're going to Shiprock."

Lucas ignored the heavy-handed allusion to Sara Catherine McCay. "I would rather not be sent to Shiprock at this time, sir."

"I'm sure you wouldn't, but you're going. I want things to settle down around here. You and the Baron woman need to get over what happened to you yesterday. It's understandable that the two of you might feel a certain bond after a thing like that. But a little distance between you and a little time can give both of you a new perspective—give you back your harmony."

Save the already tarnished reputation of certain Navajo Tribal Police personnel, Lucas thought but didn't say.

"Sir, the Baron child's custody hearing is Monday. I'd like to be here for that. It's going to be difficult for the Baron family."

"She's going to have to get through it without you," he said. "This custody hearing is none of your business. People are going to be talking enough without you lining up on the wrong side."

"I don't think it is the *wrong* side. The child loves his aunt, all his white family."

Becenti stared at him across his desk. "You go to Shiprock and you go now. And you don't make any side trips on your way out of town. I've already made the call, and they're expecting you. And I don't have to remind you that the rules that were bent to keep you in the tribal police after that other incident didn't set a precedent, do I? This department is *not* taking the brunt of your mismanaged personal life again. There are worse places for a tribal policeman to end up than Shiprock."

No. He didn't have to be reminded. He left immediately as ordered, looking through the building on his way out for Mary Skeets or Carlos, somebody he could ask to take Sloan a message.

Chapter Fifteen

Sloan got a visit from Carlos shortly after ten o'clock on Sunday morning. Her first glimpse of a tribal police uniform through the window set her hurrying to the door, only to be disappointed, and visibly so. She'd heard nothing from Lucas since she'd left his house yesterday. His truck still sat in the driveway—a source of great irritation to Patrick. Seeing Carlos now, she expected the absolute worst.

"It's me again," Carlos said, and she managed a smile. "Will's got another ear infection, Sloan," he said quickly, as if he realized she was worried by his visit and he wanted to set her mind at ease. "They want you to come over to the receiving home if you can. Dolly's gone someplace and he keeps crying for you. The doctor's seen him, but he feels pretty bad, I guess. I used to get those things all the time when I was a kid. I still remember how bad they hurt."

"Thank you, Carlos. I'll go on over now."

He didn't leave; he stood there looking out into the yard and then at her. "Well," he said. "I'd better get busy. I've got a couple of errands to run before I meet you at the receiving home. But you can go on now—they trust you."

She watched Carlos walk to the patrol car. They had gotten through their conversation without either of them mentioning

Lucas. She hadn't asked about him, in spite of how badly she'd wanted to, and what an empty victory it was. Nothing had happened to Lucas. She was reasonably certain of that. Lillian would know if he had been hurt or arrested or attacked again by renegade FBI agents. He was simply elsewhere, and when everything was said and done, she didn't think he was off someplace suffering a bad case of regret. She wondered if it was humanly possible for any woman to go to bed with a man without expecting him to become a part of her life, to *be* there when she needed him.

As unaccustomed as she was to depending on another human being, she wanted Lucas here now. She wanted to talk to him about the hearing. She wanted to know why he'd never bothered to explain to her what a futile gesture her petitioning for Will's custody would be. Surely he'd known how important this was to her. On some level she thought perhaps she *did* understand. In his culture, it was vital to maintain one's harmony. Her harmony—what little she possessed—would have been long gone if she'd known with this much certainty that she couldn't have Will. On some level she knew that he hadn't told her for the same reasons he wouldn't have told Sara Catherine McCay. He simply didn't trust her response.

Still, she wasn't surprised that she hadn't heard from him. She had told him she understood what she was getting with him. She did—a night of sexual intimacy and no emotional involvement. And, apparently, his very assertive sister and his truck.

She spent the rest of the day at the receiving home. Carlos was in and out, and one of the other young officers who apparently wasn't experienced enough to be trusted with anything more serious than monitoring her visits.

Will had been miserable when she arrived, feverish, crying, refusing to eat and unable to keep down what little he drank. He was only satisfied on Sloan's lap, and she held him constantly, rocking him in the receiving home rocking chair, sponging him off with a wet washcloth from time to time to keep him cool. She sent Patrick and Meggie out to find some Popsicles, her old standby for feverish, nauseated children. And she rocked. And sang.

"Sing me, An' Swone," he said at the end of every song.

"What do you want me to sing you, sweet boy?" she asked, and he'd name his version of something from the 1940s World War Two hit parade, the official list of Baron lullabies he'd learned from Meggie, the ones Sloan had learned from *her* mother and grandmother when she was a child. The Baron matriarchs had apparently firmly believed that "Slow Boat to China" and "Sunday Kind of Love" did wonders for a restless child, and Sloan must have sung them to Will a hundred times, finding particular significance in the lyrics of the latter. It suddenly occurred to her that *she* was the Baron matriarch now.

It was after eight o'clock when Will finally went to sleep for the night. Carlos came wandering through.

"I think you want to go out the back way," he said as she picked up her purse to leave.

"Why?"

"Because," he said significantly. "Meggie and Patrick are waiting in the car out front. You need to go out the back. And walk fast."

She looked at him. He grinned.

She frowned and went out the back door into the cool night air, stepping directly into Lucas's embrace.

"I thought you were never coming out," he said.

She laughed as he lifted her off the ground. "You're going to hurt your side. Are you hiding out here?"

"Yes," he answered. "I have to. I'm not supposed to be here. Kiss me quick. I've got to go."

She gave him the quick kiss he asked for.

"You weren't listening," he murmured against her ear, his hands sliding over her, a lover's hands, impatient with desire.

"You said quick," she whispered, her breath catching as he cupped her breast.

"That wasn't the key word," he said, his mouth seeking hers in a needy kiss that took her breath away. "I've got to go—you didn't see me—kiss me again."

Then he was gone, running by the sound of it, and she stood there chuckling, happy to have seen him even for this brief moment before reality came crashing in on her again. Her smile faded, and she gave a wavering sigh.

Lucas, what am I going to do about Mark and Will? What am I going to do about you?

Regardless of the outcome of the custody hearing, regardless of the fact that nothing concerning Mark had been resolved, she would have to go home soon. How could she bear to leave Lucas *and* Will behind?

It took her a very long time to get to sleep, and she woke up well before the alarm went off. At Lillian's request, she and Patrick and Meggie arrived early for the hearing, only to have it immediately delayed for an hour. She wore the dress she'd worn to bury

Mark, because she didn't have anything else that satisfied Lillian. She hadn't ever wanted to wear the dress again.

The hour delay came and went, and nothing happened to keep her from thinking about Lucas and the smoothness of his skin, the warmth and the weight of his body.

I'm too far gone, she thought. She gave a sharp sigh and scanned the faces of the people as they entered the courtroom. A few people came from the IHS clinic, both staff and patients. Hosteen Anagal came in, shuffling along and holding a young woman's arm—his granddaughter in Chinle with the television? Sloan wondered. She went to speak to him.

"*Ya-ta-hey,* Hosteen Anagal," she whispered to him. "You're looking fine this morning."

He smiled and patted her hand. "You got any sheep yet?" he asked.

"Ah, no. No sheep," she said, smiling.

"Too bad," he said sympathetically.

She moved on to speak to her IHS coworkers and to thank them for coming.

"You know Hosteen Anagal?" Lillian asked when she returned.

"Yes," Sloan answered. "Lucas took me out to his place."

"Well, I'm impressed," she said. "Let's hope the judge is. I wish I knew who was presiding over this case."

More people came in—Dolly Singer and Inez Yazzie.

Meggie reached for Sloan's hand. "I'm scared, Sloan," she said.

So am I, Sloan thought, hugging Meggie tightly for a moment, but she didn't say so. She glanced at Patrick. She had been more than a little surprised by Patrick's cooperation. He was still upset with her, but to his credit, he was participating today.

"Stop looking for Lucas," Lillian said under her breath, and Sloan glanced at her, more than a little annoyed.

"I'm not looking for anyone," she said.

"Don't lie to your lawyer, Ms. Baron," Lillian said. "He's going to turn up sooner or later, but don't look for him here."

"He has to turn up sooner or later," Sloan said absently, scanning the crowd one more time. "I've got his truck."

Not a fair exchange, she thought. She had his truck; he had her heart.

"Nobody seems to know exactly where he is," Lillian said. "My mother doesn't know. Mary Skeets says she doesn't know. I think Becenti sent him someplace. Knowing Becenti, it probably involved a plane ticket and at least three time zones—except that he's such a tightwad. Stop looking for him! It doesn't look good. People will think you want to find him because you think he can do you some kind of favor."

"Aren't they going to notice *you* sitting here?"

"That's different. They won't know how I got here—you could have hired me. I'm an exceptionally good lawyer. Word of my expertise could have reached South Carolina."

"It could, except that I don't live there. When is this thing going to start?"

Patrick, in his nervousness, was jiggling his leg and making at least three chairs around him shake. She reached out to punch him in the arm to make him stop. A side door opened suddenly and a judge entered, taking his place in front of the great seal of the Navajo tribe. A woman immediately came forward to give him a stack of folders. He looked through them, and after a moment he asked her a question, the answer to which she apparently didn't know. She left the room for a time and returned, telling him with a shake of her head whatever he'd wanted to know. They conferred for a moment, then he rapped sharply with a wooden gavel.

"Here we go," Lillian said.

Sloan was immediately lost, because the proceeding was being conducted in the Navajo language. She assumed that both sides were presenting their petitions, Inez Yazzie and then Lillian, but she had no way of knowing for sure. Both the presentations were lengthy. Lillian, at least, *looked* eloquent. At one point, she made a sweeping gesture toward Sloan that drew comment from Hosteen Anagal and those of her coworkers who understood Navajo.

"What's happening?" Sloan asked when Lillian finally sat down.

"I said you were worthy—and you're going to get to see my brother, after all. He's been called to testify. The judge wants to hear from somebody who knows you. This is not good, Sloan. Lucas's reputation and the rumors about the two of you are going to precede him right to the witness podium. His judgment as to your character is going to be suspect, at best."

"But he's not here—"

"He's on his way. That's why there was a delay. The judge is asking for a report on Will's home situation before your brother was killed, and whatever information there is concerning Margaret Madman. Inez is going to do that, and Lucas should be here by the time she finishes."

Sloan knew when Lucas arrived without turning around, because of the buzz in the room. She had to fight hard to comply with Lillian's earlier admonishment and not turn around to look for him.

Inez finished, and Lucas was called immediately. He went to the podium, and he only glanced in the direction where Sloan sat. He looked tired and resigned. She supposed only she and Carlos knew that this was his second trip from wherever he'd been banished in just a few hours.

The judge began to ask Lucas questions.

"He's asking how long Lucas has known you, and how he met you. Things like that— Oh, great," Lillian said under her breath. "Let's just cut to the chase."

"What is it?" Sloan whispered.

"The judge wants to know if Lucas intends to help you take a Navajo child away from the tribe."

"What?"

"Sh! Lucas says you aren't trying to take away a child you have no right to. He says you're the boy's aunt, his Navajo mother abandoned him, none of her family has come forward, and his father is dead.

"The judge wants to know if helping you is important enough for him to lie at this hearing. Lucas says that he is Navajo, and he's spent the last fourteen years of his life trying to help The People. He says a Navajo child is important to all of us. What is best for a Navajo child is important.

"The judge is asking again if he would lie."

Lucas suddenly looked in Sloan's direction, his eyes holding hers, his voice strong.

"No," Lillian translated. "He says he would not lie."

The questions and answers went on, but Lillian wasn't translating anymore.

"What are they saying?" Sloan whispered, frantic to know what was happening.

"Lucas just said that you have your brother's other children and you have no money."

"Wait a minute!" Sloan whispered. "Lillian, do something! Tell him I'm working as hard as I can!"

"Sh!" Lillian said. "That's a compliment to you. We believe any man who has money to throw around can't be looking after his family the way he should. The poorer you are, the better it speaks for your commitment to your relatives. Wait," she said because Sloan was about to interrupt again. "He just asked Lucas if he'd personally witnessed any racial bigotry in the Baron family."

"No, he hasn't," Sloan said firmly.

"Are you sure? My brother isn't answering."

"Yes, I'm sure!"

"Well, Lucas isn't. There's something behind the question, or the judge wouldn't have asked it. He wants to know if Lucas has heard anyone make any kind of disparaging remark about the fact that Will Baron is half Navajo."

"He hasn't—"

Lucas was finally answering.

"My brother is avoiding the question, Sloan," Lillian said. "He says that *you* are not a bigot. The People who have had dealings with you at the IHS clinic know that you aren't.

"The judge just asked specifically about Meggie. If he's heard Megan Baron, the alleged half sister of Will Baron, make any remark."

"Meggie wouldn't!" Sloan whispered fiercely.

Lillian held up her hand. "Lucas says no. He says Meggie only sees a person's heart and never the color of their skin.

"The judge wants to know about Patrick. I think he already knows the answer, Sloan. I think he knows something about Patrick and he's going to make Lucas tell him in court."

Sloan looked around at Patrick. His eyes met hers, guilty eyes that had heard enough of Lillian's translation to know what was about to happen. He leaned forward as if to speak to her, but she turned away. She had known he'd been upset when he first knew about Will, but his anger had been directed toward his father and toward the *idea* of a biracial half brother—never toward Will himself, and particularly once he'd met him. No big brother could have been kinder. Or so she'd thought.

Patrick!

"Damn it all," Lillian said. "One of you should have told me about this."

"I didn't know," Sloan whispered. Lucas was speaking again, and Lillian began to translate.

"He says that Patrick is young and he was very angry at the time. He says that Patrick has defended his half Navajo brother against such remarks. The judge wants to know if Lucas means yes, he has heard the boy make racist remarks."

Lucas took a long time to answer, his eyes on Sloan.

"The judge is asking him again—have you heard this boy make a racist remark about Will Baron being half Navajo? My brother's caught, Sloan. And he's going to have to tell him, or the rest of what he said will have no credibility whatsoever."

The judge waited; Sloan looked into Lucas's eyes. She saw no apology there, only a certain regret, perhaps, that, like Sara Catherine McCay, she couldn't understand him or his people.

"Yes," Lucas said in both languages, causing a murmur of response among the spectators.

"That's the ball game," Lillian whispered. She stood to ask Lucas several questions. Even Sloan recognized that they were only token ones at best. Finally, Lucas stepped down.

The judge was addressing Lillian. "He wants to ask you a question," she said, and Sloan stood up.

"Ms. Baron," he said in English. "How do you feel about a child growing up on an Indian reservation?"

Sloan took a moment to answer, and she answered truthfully. "I don't think *where* a child grows up is as important as whether or not he or she has a caring, supportive family."

"I agree, Ms. Baron," the judge said. "I find it admirable that you are so willing to shoulder your brother's responsibility. By all reports you are a stable and competent person, but you know nothing of the Navajo Way—"

"I do, sir," Meggie suddenly interrupted. "I'm learning all the time. Dolly Singer is teaching me—and Will—together. I can teach Sloan what Dolly teaches me. I already have. She knows about harmony and stuff like that."

"And that is very commendable, Megan," the judge said. "But the subtleties of his Indian heritage, William Baron can only learn here. And, unfortunately, *all* of young Will's family is not so supportive. Ms. Baron, no child, regardless of his race, can escape the remarks people outside the nuclear family may make, but he shouldn't ever have to hear them at home—particularly a biracial child who will have a difficult enough time finding his place in life even in the best of circumstances. Will Baron's alleged half brother has made his feelings known—in public and in the hearing of a number of The People. I can only assume that his lack of reticence is an indicator of how deep these feelings run. In light of that fact and the fact that you, Ms. Baron, have only known this child for a short time—"

"Will Baron *is* my brother's child, regardless of how long I might have known him."

"Perhaps so. The boy's mother is not available to confirm or deny that. The proper course in this matter seems clear to me, and I see no reason to prolong your uncertainty by delaying my decision. No amount of deliberation on my part will change the facts as they now stand. I will not allow William Baron to be placed in a detrimental environment—"

"No, wait," Patrick said, interrupting. "I didn't mean it! It wasn't like that. What I said didn't have anything to do with Will! Sloan, it wasn't like that!"

But the judge wasn't listening, and Meggie began to cry.

"William Baron will remain at the receiving home until such time as his natural mother can be located and notified of her last opportunity to prove her fitness—or until he is declared a tribal ward and put up for Navajo adoption. This hearing is adjourned."

"I can still see him, can't I? Lillian, find out if I can still see him!" Sloan cried, holding onto Meggie.

Lillian immediately approached the judge. The conversation was very short.

"You can see him," Lillian said when she returned, her expression grim. "With supervision. He expects you to prepare the boy for your leaving."

"Lillian—"

"Sloan, I told you how hopeless this was."

"I know. I know you did."

She hid her face against Meggie for a moment, then looked around for Lucas. He was no longer in the courtroom. "Let's go," she said to Patrick, putting her hand on his shoulder. He didn't seem to hear her. "Patrick," she said again. "Let's go."

He got up slowly, as if he was in a dream. Finally, he looked at her. "So tell me," he said. "Do you love Lucas Singer *now?*"

"Lucas told the truth," she said sadly. "What exactly did *you* do?"

He looked away without answering.

"Take Meggie to the car," she said. "Go on, Meggie. Go with Patrick. I have to talk to Lillian."

"What can I do?" she asked when Patrick and Meggie had gone. She felt stunned, disoriented, and the only way she could deal with it was to fix her attention on some alternative plan.

"Nothing," Lillian said.

"There has to be something!"

"There isn't. Sloan, there isn't any proof even that you're his aunt."

"Can't we appeal?"

"And say what? Yes, Patrick is into racial slurs but he won't do it anymore? Or that you aren't quite as non-Navajo as you look? Too many of our children have been taken away, Sloan."

"You agree with the judge, don't you?"

"It doesn't matter whether I do or not. But Will would lose half of himself if he went with you—can you teach him what he needs to know about his Indian heritage? I'm sorry for the pain this has caused you—I even think my brother's taste in white women has improved considerably—but you have to look at the—" She abruptly stopped. "Hosteen Anagal is waiting to speak to you."

Sloan looked around, trying not to cry.

"The thing called Lucas away," the old man said, and she shook her head, not understanding what he meant.

Hosteen Anagal made a motion as if he was pulling something off his belt. Then he drew a small rectangular shape in the air with his two forefingers and held the imaginary shape in one hand. "The thing called him to the receiving home. Lucas says for you to come there."

Chapter Sixteen

Sloan drove to the receiving home as quickly as she could.

"Are his ears hurting worse?" Meggie asked on the way. She was still wiping her eyes from time to time, but she was no longer actively crying.

"Blow your nose," Sloan said, her eyes on the traffic. She glanced into the rearview mirror. She could see Patrick clearly. He was careful to avoid her eyes.

"Is it his ears or not?" Meggie said, reaching for the box of tissues. "I *hate* earaches."

"I don't know," Sloan said. She didn't know anything except what Hosteen Anagal had told her—and that they wouldn't have needed Lucas for an earache.

There were several tribal police cars parked in front of the receiving home when she arrived. She got out and went inside, her eyes briefly meeting Patrick's as she closed the car door. He didn't say anything, and neither did she. It was clear to her that the participation he'd provided earlier this morning was over. Lucas was standing just inside the receiving home door. He came immediately to her, but he was businesslike and official, very much the tribal policeman and not Lucas her lover or even her friend.

"What's wrong?" she said, looking into his eyes. He glanced away. Meggie came and stood beside her, putting her arms around Sloan's waist the way she did when she was worried or scared.

"Patrick says he's walking home," she said.

Sloan was about to protest, but then she let it go. She was too upset to deal with more than one problem at a time. She looked at Lucas.

"We think Margaret Madman's taken Will," he said.

"You *think?*" Sloan said incredulously.

"Nobody saw anything except Jackie Begaye. He saw a woman matching Margaret's description sitting in a truck on the other side of the street earlier. She wasn't doing anything. He thought she was waiting for somebody at the receiving home to get off duty or something like that."

"I'm going to talk to Jackie," Meggie said abruptly, and Sloan let her go.

Sloan moved closer to Lucas so that he would have to look at her. "Margaret Madman just walked in and took him?"

"Apparently so."

"The boy is sick, Lucas."

"I know that, Sloan. Margaret is his mother. She didn't need much of a chance. There's no reason Will wouldn't go with her if she wanted him to, particularly if he wasn't feeling well."

"Are you telling me you won't be looking for him? Because she's his mother?"

And she's Navajo?

"No, I'm telling you that any mother, even a bad one, is better than no mother at all. I know you're... upset."

She ignored his acknowledgment of her distress. "Where would she take him?" she asked. She pressed her lips together to keep them from trembling.

"I don't know. All the law enforcement agencies in the area have been notified. We *are* going to look for him." He could say that with all certainty, but not because Margaret Madman had taken her child. He could say it because she was wanted for questioning by a federal agency.

Sloan looked at him a long moment, wishing that for once in her life she could ask for comfort from another human being, that she could go to Lucas and have him put his arms around her and tell her that everything would be all right. But her problems were not his and never had been. It all came down to that same old equation, the one she and a million other women never seemed to be able to learn—one night of intimacy never equaled a lifetime of commitment. She abruptly walked away because she was going to cry and she didn't want him to see her. "Fine," she said over her shoulder. "You do that."

"Sloan," he called after her. "Where will you be?"

"North Carolina, if I have any sense," she said sarcastically. But then she turned to look at him. She was every bit as bad as Captain Becenti when it came to shooting the messenger. "Here, unless they throw me out. I'll be waiting here. I'm . . . going to try to find somebody who can tell me how Will is feeling today. He was so miserable yesterday."

She disappeared into the dayroom, but it seemed to Lucas that she wanted to say more. He stared after her. It had been all he could do not to ask the question.

What do you want, Sloan?

He had no idea what she expected. Did she expect him to apologize for what had happened in court today?

No, he thought. He knew her better than that. She didn't expect him to lie for her and she didn't expect him to apologize. She didn't expect anything at all, and in that context, he might have been a complete stranger, someone she'd never even met before.

I wanted you, Lucas.

He had believed her the night they made love. She clearly didn't want him now. He realized that she must think they were embroiled in the game again, the one where she suffered the consequences of all those sins white people had committed long before she got here.

He looked down because Meggie was standing at his elbow.

"Jackie wants to tell you something," she said.

"What?" Lucas asked, looking around at the boy.

Jackie stood with his arms folded, staring at the ceiling. He did *not* look like someone who was about to volunteer information.

"Tell him," Meggie said. "Please, Jackie."

"My family doesn't tell cops anything," he said. "And you weren't supposed to go running to him—"

"Tell him or we're not friends anymore *ever*."

Jackie glanced at Meggie, apparently trying to decide if she meant it.

"I'm leaving. I mean it, Jackie Begaye," Meggie said. She waited a moment, then abruptly headed for the door.

"Wait!" Jackie said. "Okay, okay, I'll tell him."

"Jackie, if you know something about this, you'd damn well better say so," Lucas said.

"Okay," Jackie said. "I . . . know that woman."

"You know Margaret Madman?"

"Not to talk to. Just when I see her. I know the man she's living with. He's got a trailer up around Fort Defiance."

"Easy to find or not?"

"Not," Jackie said. "My old man used to go up there to get his whiskey. Bootleggers ain't easy to find, man."

Tell me about it, Lucas thought.

"You think Margaret's going to go back there?"

"Where else is she going to go?" Jackie said. "If she's been living with him, she ain't got no money. That's what he wants women for—to get him cash."

Lucas didn't have to ask how getting the cash came about. And Margaret was taking Will into that. "Wait right here," he said.

"Why?"

"Because you're showing me the way to this trailer."

"No, I'm not. Aw, man, maybe I don't know where it is anymore."

"Maybe you don't," Lucas said. "But maybe you'd better think about it so you'll remember that it's Meggie's little brother we're looking for. Maybe you'll remember he's sick. Damn it, Jackie, you've been kicked around enough to know what can happen to a little kid like him if he gets in the way. And he *will* get in the way, Jackie, just because he *is* a little kid. Maybe you'll even remember Meggie's your friend and you owe her something for that trouble with the stolen horse. And while you're at it, maybe the way to that trailer will come back to you."

"I'm going to find Sloan," Meggie said. She gave Jackie a long look, a silent plea for him not to be angry.

"What? No more blackmail?" he asked sullenly.

"I don't have to," Meggie said. "I know you'll help Will. I know you'll do the right thing."

Jackie gave a sharp sigh and watched her go. "What can you do with a woman like that?" he said to Lucas. "Next thing you know, I'll be going to church and joining the Boy Scouts."

Lucas considered taking Jackie with him but decided it would be too dangerous. He would have to trust the boy to draw him a map of sorts instead.

"I'd better be able to find this," he said, looking at Jackie's handiwork.

"*Anybody* can find this," Jackie said. "Even a cop."

"Is the trailer in the open? How close can I get to it without being seen?"

"You can't, man. You think a bootlegger is going to live in a place where a tribal cop can walk up on him any time he feels like it? You're going to have to wait until dark. Or maybe this guy will come out at sunup like a good Navajo and you can get him then."

"How far up the track can I drive before he sees me?"

Jackie thought about this for a minute. "There's this big sandstone rock, looks sort of like the side of a man's face—"

"The profile, you mean?"

"Yeah, the profile. It's got a nose and the bottom lip looks stuck out like this." Jackie showed him with his own bottom lip. "Don't go past that. Get out and walk."

"Is there another way in and out?"

"I wasn't looking for another way in or out, man. I was there to get my old man a couple pints."

"Has this man got dogs?"

Jackie rolled his eyes, and Lucas fought down a grin.

"Let me rephrase that. How many dogs *has* he got?"

"You better take plenty of Alpo," Jackie said. "They ain't mean, but they're loud. He couldn't afford to have dogs that bit the customers. This bunch can be bribed, I think, if you throw out something."

"The man's name?"

"I don't know his name," Jackie said. "My old man didn't tell me and I didn't ask."

Lucas didn't necessarily believe him, but he didn't press him for any more information. He took the map and left the receiving home without speaking to Sloan again, regardless of how much he wanted to. She was sitting outside at the picnic table with Meggie and one of the receiving home workers. She watched him go, her face pensive and sad. Once again he felt the urgent need to do something for her—to feed her, rub her back, hold her until she felt better again. The best he could do was in keeping with Hosteen Anagal's idea of their relationship—he would try to take care of her sheep, the little one she couldn't get into the fold no matter how hard she tried.

He needed to talk to Becenti. Lucas had had nothing to do with being called back to Window Rock to testify, so he didn't anticipate the captain's being upset that he wasn't in Shiprock. He suspected that his precipitous return had been Inez's doing and probably without Becenti's knowledge or blessing. But Lucas intended to stay, now that he *was* here, and look for Will Baron, either officially or without pay.

Becenti was in his office when Lucas arrived. He didn't keep him waiting; he had Mary send him directly in. Becenti even let him say everything he wanted to say about Margaret Madman's whereabouts and the situation she was probably taking the boy into.

Then he sat tapping the eraser end of a No. 2 yellow pencil on the desktop.

"You better take somebody with you," he said finally. "Take Carlos. He knows the area, and the bootlegging business. And he listens to what you tell him. I want you to bring Margaret in so the FBI can talk to her. This man she's living with—he may not be happy that you're trying to disrupt one of his major sources of income. You watch yourself, and take one of the utility vehicles. Who knows what kind of place you'll have to get into."

"Yes, sir," Lucas said, turning to go.

"Lucas," Becenti said when he reached the door. "I want you to get that child out of there."

Lucas nodded. He had every intention of getting Will.

He made a copy of the map Jackie had drawn and got the keys to one of the four-wheel drive utility vehicles.

"Find Carlos *now*. I need him," he said, handing the copy of the map to Mary on his way out. "This is where we'll be going. I'll wait for Carlos outside."

"I know where he is," she said. "I'll get him. Lucas!" she called when he was about to go through the door. "Patrick Baron's looking for you."

"Where is he?"

"Around here somewhere," she said.

Lucas didn't have time to hunt for him—and he didn't have to. As he unlocked the vehicle, he saw Patrick standing in the parking lot.

"Patrick!" he called and immediately wished he hadn't. The boy was obviously upset, and Lucas had neither the time nor the inclination to try to assuage him. "Mary says you're looking for me. What do you—"

He didn't even get the sentence out before Patrick jumped him. The boy was strong, and Lucas was taken completely by surprise. He tried to pin Patrick's arms down, but he got a well-placed elbow in his already bruised side.

"Damn it, Patrick, what's wrong with you!"

Patrick took a swing at him, then another. Lucas managed to sidestep both of them. Furious, the boy made another dive for him. They both fell on the ground. Tribal police officers came running out of the building, grabbing Patrick and pulling him off. It took two of them to hold the boy back.

"I told you!" Patrick yelled. "I told you to leave her alone!"

"Patrick, I am going to say this but one time! Whatever is between Sloan and me is none of your damn business!"

"You son of a bitch!" Patrick yelled, still trying to get loose. "You damn—" His voice broke, and suddenly the boy was crying. He let his body sag, let the officers who restrained him hold him up.

"Patrick," Lucas said, coming closer. "Let him go," he said to the officers.

"Are you sure, Lucas?" one of them said.

"Let him go," Lucas said again. "I want to talk to him. Patrick—come over here," he said, all but dragging the boy out of earshot of the others and letting him lean against the back of somebody's truck. He stood waiting, giving the boy time to pull himself together.

"You want to tell me what this is all about?" he asked finally.

"You know what it's about! You told the judge what I said and you know it didn't have anything to do with Will. It was between me and you. It was about Sloan."

"And what did you expect me to do? Did you want me to tell the judge—to say in front of all those people that you only made the remark because you thought I was trying to get into Sloan's pants?"

"Yeah, and you didn't have to try very hard, did you?" Patrick said sarcastically.

Lucas grabbed him by his shirtfront. "You don't talk about Sloan like that, understand? Not ever! Understand?" Lucas said, giving him a shake.

"Yeah! I understand!"

"Good. Now, I'm telling you. The judge already *knew* what you'd said, Patrick. The *words* are what mattered, not the reason you said them. He wouldn't have asked me so specifically if somebody who'd been at the *Kenaalda* hadn't already told him."

"We—Sloan—lost Will because of you!"

"Patrick!" Lucas said in exasperation. "This situation is more complicated than you can ever imagine. And it's not about what I said in court, son!"

"I'm not your son!"

"I am *not* taking the blame for the custody hearing!" Lucas said, fully aware that the officers who had begun to file into the building were on their way back again. "If you want to blame somebody, you go look in the mirror! I don't have time to fool with you. Go home. Or do you want to get yourself locked up again so we can put Sloan through another ordeal today?"

"Lucas!" one of the officers called, and he walked in that direction, trying not to limp although his side was killing him.

"Mary says Carlos is in the middle of an arrest. It's going to take him at least an hour before he can get here. Becenti says it's your call—wait, take somebody else or go alone. He wants to know what you're going to do. You okay, Lucas?"

"Yeah," Lucas said, lying. He had alienated his woman, and her nephew, when she didn't even know he thought of her as his and wouldn't stand for it if she did. He had no harmony and no hope of any—for himself or her. And he didn't miss the irony of the situation; he didn't miss Coyote's practiced hand. He'd wanted to take care of Sloan Baron, and he'd essentially made her life—both their lives—hell.

He reached into his shirt pocket because he realized he no longer had Jackie's map. He must have dropped it in the scuffle with Patrick. He didn't see it anywhere on the ground—the thing had probably blown halfway to Gallup by now. He went inside to make another copy and to tell Becenti that he'd go alone.

He didn't see Patrick when he came outside, and he put the boy out of his mind. It was admirable, he supposed, that Patrick was so protective of his aunt, but he was still a nuisance.

Lucas drove out of the parking lot, intending to head north out of Window Rock. He focused his attention on trying to drive and memorize the copy of Jackie Begaye's map. And where he could get some cheap cans of dog food. And how he was going to get Margaret Madman and Will out of that trailer. He tried not to think about the way Sloan had looked at him. Even with his mind so occupied, he spotted the black vehicle in his rearview mirror before he was a mile out of town.

He missed the second turnoff—because he was following the tracks of somebody who'd gone through earlier and not Jackie's map. He had to back down a steep slope to get to the place where he should have turned. It was only a short distance from there to the rock that looked like a man's profile. Jackie Begaye was a damn good mapmaker; Lucas made a mental note to tell him that when he got back. He stopped close to the rock and got out, trying to decide if he could back into a small niche on the far side of the monolith and get himself and the vehicle out of sight. He'd still be partially visible to anyone coming in the same way he had, but not to anyone coming from the opposite direction. It would give him a slight advantage if the black vehicle was still following.

The fact of the matter was that he wasn't entirely sure he *was* being followed. He had been sleep-deprived long enough not to be sure of anything. Whoever it was never seemed to get any closer whether he slowed down or not. He wasn't even sure what kind of vehicle it was—car or truck. He was only sure of the wary feeling it gave him, seeing that black whatever-it-was constantly in the rearview mirror—not surprising, given his recent encounter with the FBI. Chuckie and his deceased friend could still be trying to catch him at something and using the black Firebird this time to do it.

It took a lot of maneuvering and gear shifting to back into the niche, but he managed it finally and with only a few minor scrapes to the paint job—which Becenti would still probably notice.

He waited for a long while, giving the black vehicle a chance to catch up, but he could hear nothing that sounded like someone trying to drive up the track. He got out again, taking the rifle, the canteen and the binoculars with him. He needed to find out how much he could see and how close he could get. He realized immediately that Jackie had been right. There was very little cover. The trailer was in a big open space with a few scrubby cottonwoods that were hardly bigger than a man. He lay on his belly and looked through the binoculars. One vehicle—a no-color pickup truck—with the left rear tire flat. Margaret and her friend wouldn't be going anyplace in that. He could see a small corral, a privy, the dogs, no people. The sun was hot, beating down on his back and head. His head ached and his eyes burned from lack of sleep, regardless of the fact that he was very happy about the way he'd been kept awake. He tracked a dust devil across the open ground, watching it kick up the dust until it abruptly disappeared. When he was just about to retreat, a woman came out of the trailer. Margaret Madman. He could see her clearly. She was hardly bigger than a child herself, and she was carrying Will. She took the boy to the privy. He cried all the way there and back and a long time after she'd taken him inside the trailer—until he abruptly stopped.

Now what? he thought, wiping his sweaty face on his shirt sleeve. Walk in? Drive in? Wait until dark? Either way, Jackie Begaye had been right. The location of the trailer left an expanse of open ground to cross. There was no way he was going to sneak up on them without a great deal of luck. He had no idea how difficult confronting Margaret would be. Will's crying could be getting on her nerves by now. She might be glad for a tribal policeman to show up and take him off her hands. The man was the problem. If he thought Lucas was there because of the bootlegging, all hell could break lose. Lucas had been shot at enough times not to expect calm and rational thinking from a man who sold something illegal for a living.

He jumped, because the dogs suddenly bolted out from under the trailer, barking furiously—but not in his direction. He scanned the yard with the binoculars, looking for the reason. A black truck with big tires came driving up from the far side. It stopped, then backed around so that it was heading in the direction it had just come, and parked. Two boys got out and came walking into the yard—customers of Margaret's or the bootlegger's or both, he guessed.

"Son of a bitch!" he said out loud. No, by God, they weren't customers. He identified the boys immediately, because one of them still hadn't learned his lesson about picking conspicuous redheaded accomplices.

Jackie Begaye and Patrick Baron.

Jackie had avoided answering directly when he'd been asked about there being another way in and out, and Lucas hadn't pressed him—which he apparently should have. There was another way, all right. And when in the hell had these two hooked up with each other and where had Patrick gotten a black truck?

"Son of a bitch!" Lucas said again, because the two little jerks were going to walk right up to the door and knock—and say what? *Good afternoon, my name is Patrick Baron and I'd like my half brother now?*

No, he thought. Jackie was going to do all the talking. Jackie the former customer.

Patrick stood out of the line of vision of whoever answered the door, and Lucas had to credit the two of them with a little sense. A pair of little legs suddenly worked to get down out of the trailer—Will wearing nothing but his underpants.

Lucas had never felt so helpless in his life. The mere sight of a tribal police uniform would be enough to send a bootlegger reaching for his shotgun. There were three too many children in the way.

Jackie was still talking. He casually opened the door a little wider. Will tiptoed barefooted around on the rough wooden boards that someone had nailed together to make a kind of high step, doing his little boy dance to the edge and finally getting down on his hands and knees to slide off the side. The second his feet touched the ground, Patrick grabbed him and Jackie slammed the door closed. Both boys were off and running back the way they'd come, the dogs in hot pursuit.

Lucas was up and running, as well, toward the trailer instead of away, throwing off the binoculars and the canteen as he ran, saying a prayer that Coyote was inattentive and elsewhere at this moment.

"Patrick!" he yelled. He could hear Will crying again, and he managed to reach the yard as the man burst out of the trailer.

"Don't!" Lucas yelled at him, raising the rifle, and the man skidded to a stop, his eyes darting wildly around for a way out. "Stay where you are and keep your hands where I can see them!" Lucas said. "Margaret! Get out of the trailer—get out *now!*" he yelled, moving to the left a little so he could watch the half closed door. He could hear her moving around in there, and, after a moment the door squeaked open just far enough for him to see probable cause in reference to the bootlegging.

"Margaret!"

She finally appeared, leaning against the doorjamb, her arms folded as if she hadn't a care in the world. She gave him her best seductive smile.

"Well, well, well," she said. "Officer Singer. What's new, Lucas?"

But her attempt at bravado was completely unsuccessful. Her mouth began to tremble and she suddenly covered her face with her hands.

Chapter Seventeen

It was still daylight, but the lights at the receiving home were on. Sloan's car was in the parking lot. Lucas reached out to touch Will Baron, who slept soundly on the front seat, in spite of the seat belt and his upright position. The boy felt hot.

"Can I take him in?" Patrick asked.

"Go ahead," Lucas said. Patrick had been very quiet on the ride back to Window Rock. To his credit, he hadn't made excuses or tried to convince Lucas that he hadn't done anything wrong. He'd merely sat in the back seat, reaching over to comfort his little brother from time to time as best he could, as best either of them could.

He made no move to get out. "Sloan is never going to forgive me for what I did," he said finally. "Never."

"Patrick—"

"She taught me better than to say things like I said to you. It wasn't you, man, you being an Indian or anything like that. It was because I was scared. Sloan never paid any attention to anybody before—no guy, I mean, not the way she did you. She just took care of me and Meggie no matter what. She was different with you—happy. I was scared maybe if she wanted you, she wouldn't want us anymore. She's all we got, man." Patrick got out and opened the front door on the passenger side, lifting Will ou without waking him. "Lucas," he said, bending down to look inside the vehicle. "Sloan...told me she loved you. I guess you ought to know that. It would be just like her not to tell you—especially now."

"She what?" Lucas said, but Patrick was already halfway to the front door. In any event, the revelation came too late.

He gave a sharp exhalation of breath and got out of the vehicle, walking toward the back of the receiving home. He needed to talk to his mother before he saw Sloan. This incredibly trying day was far from over.

Sloan looked up at the sound of footsteps on the gravel path.

"Lucas," she said, because he didn't immediately see her. She got up from the picnic table and walked toward him. "Did you find Will? Is he all right?"

"I found him," he said, but he didn't come any closer. He looked so tired. It was all she could do not to reach for him. She tried to see his eyes so that she would know precisely which Lucas she was dealing with, but his eyes told her nothing. She felt as if she was looking at the man she'd first met at the trauma center, the one she had never kissed and lain with all night.

"Is Will all right?" she asked again.

"How can he be all right, Sloan? He's like that kid in your Bible—the one with King Solomon—only this kid's being pulled three ways instead of two. You want him. Inez wants him on behalf of the tribe. All of a sudden Margaret decides *she* wants him. There's no wisdom here. No harmony. Just this scramble to see who's going to get that boy, regardless of what *he* needs. Do you know what it does to a little kid to see his mother arrested? He thought I was hurting her, and I had no choice. I had to bring Margaret in—and her sorry boyfriend. I'm out there trying to do that and trying to keep Patrick from getting into any more trouble than he's already in. Margaret *and* Will were both in hysterics by that time—and all I can think about is how crazy this is. No, I wouldn't say he's all right."

He tried to walk away, but Sloan caught him by the arm. "Where is he, Lucas? What has Patrick got to do with this?"

"Patrick and Jackie Begaye stole Will from Margaret before I could get to him—and no, there aren't going to be any charges. I don't know how to charge two kids for having more guts than they've got brains. Will is here, Sloan. Carlos took Margaret and her boyfriend in—and Jackie, because Becenti needs to put the fear of God in him for walking off from the receiving home again. I came on here with Patrick and Will because I'm damned crazy enough to—"

"To what?" she asked, because he didn't go on.

"To want to look after your sheep," he said, and he walked off toward the back door, leaving her standing.

She frowned, trying to understand the shift in the conversation and what seemed to be some kind of unhappy declaration of his intent. "Lucas," she said, but he didn't stop. "Lucas, wait!"

She followed him inside, but he still didn't wait for her. He kept going, regardless of the fact that Patrick stood in the kitchen with Will asleep on his shoulder.

"Patrick, what have you done?" she said, letting Lucas go, because she still could only handle one problem at a time. She was upset, but she was more relieved, and she abruptly hugged Patrick and Will both. For once, Patrick suffered the gesture without protest.

"It's a long story, Sloan," he said, glancing in the direction Lucas had gone.

"Oh, I'm sure it is. Like the story that goes with what happened in the convenience store. Patrick, I want to know what you did and I want to know *now*."

"It's no big deal, Sloan. I ran into Jackie in the law enforcement building parking lot—"

"Why were you there?"

"I just *was*. Do you want to hear this or not?"

"Go on."

"I ran into Jackie and we sort of decided to look for Will."

"How? On foot? Are you telling me the truth?"

"I borrowed Danny's truck. It's still up there where we went to get Will. We're going to have to go bring it back because Lucas made me come back with him. And yes, I'm telling you the truth!"

"Then stop looking over your shoulder like you're afraid Lucas is going to hear you."

"I'm not—"

"Yes, you are. I want you to tell me what happened."

"I'm trying to! See, Jackie knew the way to this trailer where Will was, and we got him—Jackie and I did."

"His mother just handed him over."

"No—see, we didn't exactly know Lucas was already there somewhere. We sort of knew he was on the road ahead of us, but that's all. See, Will came out by himself and we had the chance to get him, so we got him. End of story. Except Lucas thought we could have really messed things up or got hurt—but we didn't. mean we got Will all right, and nobody shot a gun or anything.'

"Patrick, did it occur to you that you had no legal right whatsoever to—"

"No, ma'am, it didn't. Oh, and we stopped by the clinic to let the doctor check Will out on the way here. You want to know what the doctor said, I guess—he's still got the ear infection. He's missed so many doses of his medicine, they gave him a shot at the clinic. Man, he cried. The doctor said to give him something for his fever when we got to the receiving home, but not aspirin. Can you take the poco bro' here? I got to go to the bathroom."

He unceremoniously handed the sleeping Will over.

"Patrick, wait—"

"I got to *go*," he said over his shoulder.

Will began to cry, and she swayed back and forth, rocking him gently, crooning to him. He didn't stop crying. Perhaps Lucas had been right. The real mother, bad or not, was the mother of choice.

Someone said something in Navajo, and she turned to see Dolly Singer motioning her to follow. Surprisingly, Sloan thought that she understood what Dolly had said—her Navajo name, Smiles At Children. She took Will in the direction Dolly wanted, into a small room with a table and a basin of water and clean towels and pajamas. Together they stripped Will out of his dirty clothes and gave him a quick, cool bath. Then they put him into clean pajamas and Sloan gave him something for the fever. Will cried the entire time, even after Meggie had come in.

"Can I rock him in the rocking chair for a while?" Meggie asked, holding out her arms to him. Will went immediately to her, and he still cried.

Sloan, knowing that she was here only on sufferance, looked to Dolly Singer for permission.

Dolly nodded. "Go be with the boy," she said in English. "You and Meggie—and Patrick. All three of you. Go be together."

Sloan wanted to ask if Lucas was still here, but she didn't. She did as Dolly wanted, following Meggie and Will to the dayroom and the rocking chair, sitting close by while the two of them rocked. The television was on—a Fred Astaire movie. A bath and clean pajamas, something for the fever, and a Fred Astaire musical seemed to have done wonders for Will. He was cheerful again in spite of his ears and his ordeal. He asked nothing about his mother or Mark. He sat contentedly on Meggie's lap, watching Fred Astaire in a shoe repair shop dancing with half a dozen come-to-life pairs of shoes. He pointed at the screen, laughing when Fred tried to control the runaway shoes with a broom, calling Patrick when he appeared in the doorway to come see.

Sloan kept watching the door for some glimpse of Lucas, but she didn't see him. From time to time she thought she heard his voice. After a while, she stopped looking for him. He knew where she was if he wanted to talk to her.

Other receiving home children, fresh from their baths, wandered in, sitting in a circle on the floor in front of the television to watch Fred Astaire dance. Dolly came with apple juice for them all, and after only a few swallows, Will was nearly asleep. Sloan left the dayroom to go turn down his bed. Lucas was in the hallway talking—arguing—with Inez Yazzie. Carlos stood off to one side, apparently waiting to hear the outcome. The conversation abruptly stopped when she appeared, regardless of the fact that they had been speaking in Navajo and there was no way she could have understood.

"What's wrong?" she said, glancing from one of them to the other. She had no doubt that something was happening. She had only to look at their faces. "I think you'd better tell me."

Lucas said something else in Navajo to Inez, who apparently, albeit grudgingly, agreed.

"Inez is here to take Will, Sloan," Lucas said to her.

She glanced at Inez. "Take him where?"

Lucas didn't answer her.

"Take him where, Lucas?"

"Sloan, the boy has been through enough," he said. "Inez is going to take him to another place where he can settle down."

"Away from me, you mean. Are you going to tell me where you're taking him? Am I going to be allowed to see him?"

No one answered her.

"Sloan," Inez said finally. "We don't want to risk Margaret or somebody she knows taking the boy off again. He was in a potentially dangerous situation today. And it's no kindness to let him get any more attached to you and your family. You know that—"

"*He's* my family," Sloan said, her voice rising. "Can't you understand that? *He* is my family!"

"Sloan," Lucas said, reaching for her. He put both hands on her shoulders. She tried to move away, but he made her look at him. "There is nothing you can do about this. There's nothing you can do to stop it. The judge has made his ruling and Inez has the authority. It's my job to see that it's carried out. Do you understand?"

"No, I don't understand. Please, don't take him away. Not yet—I need more time, Lucas! Please! I need time to explain to Meggie—this is going to break her heart. Lucas—" Tears slid down her cheeks. Lucas's arms went around her. He held her tightly and she hid her face against his chest.

"I can't stand this," she whispered.

"Yes, you can," he answered. "Don't cry. Don't," he said, his voice gentle and quiet. "It's better that you're here—better than coming tomorrow and finding him gone. You have to make it as easy for him as you can, Sloan. It won't do him any good to see you crying. I know how strong you are. I know you can do this."

"I love him, Lucas."

"I know you do," he said, still holding her. "That's why you'll do what's best. Inez has agreed to let you handle this part of it—but you have to do it now. Now, Sloan."

She lifted her head, wiping furiously at her eyes with the backs of her hands. But the tears only came harder. She took a deep breath and struggled for control, trying desperately to think of some alternative.

There was none.

"All right," she said after a moment, her voice husky and tremulous. "All right."

"If you can just bring him out, Sloan," Inez said, her tone incredibly kind. "It will be worse for everyone if I—we—have to go in and get him."

She looked at Inez for a long moment. Lucas was right. There was nothing to be done. She couldn't take the boy and run with him the way Margaret had. He wasn't hers and never had been. Her only recourse was to make it as easy for him as possible.

"It's better if he doesn't see me," Lucas said. "I...think he may be afraid of me after the thing with Margaret this afternoon. I won't be here when you come out."

She looked at him, but she didn't reply. She didn't trust her voice. He put his arms around her again.

"I never seem to bring you anything but grief, do I?" he whispered so that no one else could hear. Then he walked away.

She took another deep breath, and another. She had to stand outside the dayroom for a moment before she could force herself to go in. Fred Astaire still danced, Will still dozed on Meggie's lap. He opened his eyes as she came closer, and he smiled.

"Come here, sweet boy," she said, reaching to take him. He came willingly, resting his head on her shoulder for a moment. She hugged him tightly, savoring his just-bathed little-boy smell. "Guess what?" she whispered.

"What?" he murmured sleepily.

"A friend of yours is here to take you on a trip."

He lifted his head, rubbing his nose hard with the back of his hand. "Who?"

"Inez. You remember Inez."

"I don't want to go to the doctor."

"Patrick already took you to the doctor."

"Is it a special trip or... um... plain?"

"Oh, special, I think. You need to say bye to Meggie and bye to Patrick now and give them a kiss."

He did so dutifully, still not quite awake. Meggie got up out of the rocking chair to come with her. "Wait here, Meggie," Sloan said quietly.

"But I want to—"

"Wait here, Meggie," she said again. Her eyes met Patrick's. She gave him a pleading look.

"You heard the woman, Meg-head," he said. "Ours is not to reason why. Give me a he-man hug, too, poco bro'," he said to Will, half standing up to get his hug.

"Be a good boy, Patwick," Will said before Patrick got the chance.

"*You* be a good boy, short stuff. I'm *always* good."

"You got to dig wells," Will said.

"Shh!" Patrick said, waving his hands around to keep him from telling his terrible secret.

"Shh!" Will echoed, laughing.

Sloan hesitated, struggling again for composure, then she carried him toward the door.

Will kept looking at her face. "Don't cry, An' Swone," he said.

"I'm not," she said, her mouth trembling.

"Are you just kidding?" he asked. "Or are you crying?"

"Just kidding," she said lightly.

She stepped into the hallway. "I love you, sweet boy," she whispered. He put his arms round her neck and it was all she could do not to sob. Inez and Carlos stood waiting by the door. Lucas had moved to the far end of the hall.

"Don't *cry*," Will said, patting her gently on the shoulder with little, uncoordinated pats. "It'll be all right. I'll come back," he promised her earnestly. "Then you can be *happy*."

"Yes," she managed, trying hard to smile. "Then I can be happy."

She stopped in front of Inez and briefly closed her eyes, because it took every ounce of strength she had to hand Will over.

But he went into Inez's arms without protest. He was, after all, Mark Baron's son and used to change.

"Thank you, Sloan," Inez said. "I'm truly sorry."

"I like a special trip," Will said to Inez.

"Yes, I know you do," she answered, turning away as if she expected Sloan to suddenly change her mind. "That's why I thought of you."

Sloan stood watching them go, her fingers pressed against her mouth, body trembling with the effort it took not to weep out loud. As Inez carried him through the door to the outside, Will suddenly leaned over her shoulder and held out his hand in Sloan's direction.

"Bye-bye, Sweet Sugar!" he called.

Chapter Eighteen

Someone knocked at the front door. Sloan moved quickly, because she was hoping to see Lucas this morning. She hadn't had the opportunity to say anything to him after Will had gone; it had been all she could do to deal with Patrick and particularly Meggie.

She looked out the window. Inez Yazzie stood on the doorstep.

"I'd like to talk to you," Inez said when she opened the door.

"Why?" Sloan asked bluntly. Inez Yazzie was the last person she wanted to see today.

"I'm not your enemy, Sloan. I need to speak to you about two things. Are you going to let me come in or do you want me to do it from here?"

Sloan looked at her for a moment, wondering if she could handle any more unhappy developments. "Come in," she said finally, holding open the door. "Don't tell me, let me guess. My services are no longer required at the clinic and I am no longer going to be allowed the use of this house."

"I told you, Sloan. I'm not your enemy."

Sloan gave a soft sigh. No. Inez wasn't her enemy. She understood Inez Yazzie's position perfectly. But understanding didn't lessen the pain.

"Is Will all right?"

"Yes. When I left him last night, he was quite all right. Your niece—Meggie—how is she this morning?"

"She's asleep. She cried most of the night."

"I'm sorry," Inez said.

"Are you?"

They stared at each other.

"Sloan, I'm going to see Margaret Madman this morning before the FBI does whatever it is they're going to do. Lucas told me you have a lot of questions about your brother that perhaps Margaret can answer. I came by to see if you want to go with me."

Sloan looked at her in surprise. "Yes. I do. I need to tell Patrick so he can stay here with Meggie—" She stopped because Meggie was standing in the doorway. She was still wearing her nightgown and she had the album of family pictures Sloan had let her bring along clutched tightly over her chest.

"Meggie," Sloan said. "I didn't know you were awake."

"Can I ask Mrs. Yazzie a favor, Sloan?" she asked. Her eyes were still puffy and red from crying.

Sloan looked at Inez.

"Of course," Inez said. "I . . . may not be able to do it, but please ask."

"It's this album," Meggie said. "It's got Baron pictures in it—me and Patrick and Sloan. And my dad. I want to know if you'll keep it for Will, and not let anything happen to it. He's too little now—" She gave a strained smile. "He'd probably try to color it with a crayon or something. But when he's bigger, will you give it to him to keep—maybe look at it with him sometimes until then? I don't think I'm going to get to see him anymore. I don't want him to forget us. He *will* forget us if he doesn't see a picture. I know because I forgot my mom—I don't know what she looks like now because I can't see her and I don't have a picture. Please, Mrs. Yazzie. Will you keep this for my little brother? He shouldn't forget us just because we're not the best thing for him."

Inez hesitated, looking at Sloan. "Is it all right with you?" she asked, and Sloan nodded, not trusting her voice. She knew how precious the album was to Meggie.

"Then I'll take it, Meggie," Inez said. "And I promise I'll do my best to keep it safe for him."

"Thank you, Mrs. Yazzie," Meggie said politely. "Now I don't have to worry." She looked at Sloan. "Can I go with you to see Margaret Madman? I won't get in the way. I can sit out front and talk to Mary Skeets. I like Mary Skeets. She likes kids and I'm a kid. I can get ready fast. Okay? Okay, Sloan?"

"Hurry, then," Sloan said, and Meggie bolted from the room. Sloan glanced at Inez, who was quietly looking at the Baron pictures. "What was the second thing?"

Inez looked up from the album. "Lucas is being questioned by the FBI again. He's been shut up with them since late last night."

The law enforcement building was very quiet when they arrived. Sloan wondered if Becenti was bending any rules in letting Inez speak to Margaret Madman before the FBI did. Perhaps they didn't know Margaret was in custody, and that was how he managed it. Perhaps he'd notify them after they finished with Lucas. She was so worried about Lucas's being questioned again. She had seen firsthand the method they used to get information on the reservation. There was no one around she could ask about him—if he was still being questioned or if he'd finally been let go.

"This way," Inez said, and Sloan followed her to a small side room with nothing in it but four chairs and a table. After a short time, Margaret was brought in. She was pretty, and Sloan was surprised at how petite she was. Her hair was dark and parted in the middle. She wore a denim jacket and a tan suede skirt with a fringe and no jewelry of any kind. Margaret looked like the sort of woman who would wear the traditional turquoise and silver and a lot of it. Sloan assumed it must have all been taken from her for safekeeping.

Margaret smiled broadly at them both, a bold attempt to cover up the fact that she was so scared. She sat down at the table, making a lot of noise with the chair, and Inez began to speak to her in Navajo. If Margaret was even listening, she gave no indication. She stared at the far wall.

Inez stopped talking; Margaret appeared not to notice. Then she abruptly brought her fist down on the table. "I'm not giving up my kid. You two can just forget that!"

Inez spoke sharply in Navajo. Margaret gave her a surly look.

"Please," Sloan said when she thought the exchange had ended. She waited until Margaret looked at her. "My brother is dead. I have so many things I want to know. Will you help me?"

"Why should I?"

"Because you're the only one who can, Margaret. You and I are linked together—by your son."

"Are we? Everybody tells you what *I* am, don't they? And you don't even ask who the boy's father is, woman."

"I don't need to ask about that, Margaret. It's enough for me that my brother treated Will as if he was his own. But I need to ask what happened to my brother out here. It would give me peace to know, and it would give peace to his other children. No one knows the truth but you. There is no one else who can tell me."

"I can't speak of the dead," she said. "His *chindi* will come."

"You can tell me the events and not say his name. Please."

Margaret stared at the far wall again.

"Please," Sloan said, and Margaret looked at her.

"People say you're Lucas Singer's woman," she said.

"Yes," Sloan said without hesitation, knowing that Margaret only wanted to show off, to feel at least some power in this situation. "I've heard that they do."

"Are you?" she persisted.

"Yes," Sloan said again.

"Well, well, well," Margaret said. "That Lucas. Did you know about them, Inez?"

Inez replied in Navajo, and Margaret laughed.

"Inez says I should act like I had relatives to teach me how to behave, and mind my own business." Her laughter abruptly faded. "Do you know where my son is?"

"No," Sloan said.

"You're a liar."

"No. I don't know where he is."

"Then Inez is hiding him from both of us, I think."

Sloan didn't reply. She waited, as Lucas had taught her to wait, fighting down the need to try to badger the information she wanted out of this woman.

Margaret attempted another smile. She didn't quite make it. "My . . . son. He likes you. He says you sing to him and you call him sweet boy. It makes him laugh—sweet boy." She sighed and looked away. "Okay, my son's aunt," she said, looking at Sloan. "What do you want to know?"

"Everything you can tell me. From the beginning."

Margaret gave another sigh. "Okay. Everything. But you remember when you don't like it that you *asked.*"

Lucas was asleep. Sloan sat on the side of the bed watching his quiet breathing. He didn't know she was coming here; she hadn't known herself until she suddenly began to make arrangements for Meggie and Patrick so that she could have this time—this last time—with him. She had gone to see Becenti to talk to him about commuting Patrick's community service sentence to time served. She'd gone to the cemetery to make her only visit to Mark's grave, and to the IHS clinic to resign. Then she'd come here, come into

Lucas's house without knocking, entering quietly through the unlatched screen door she'd promptly latched behind her. She'd walked through the rooms, finding him asleep, lying on top of the bed, a small electric fan turning back and forth, blowing the air across his body. The shades were pulled only halfway down, leaving the room semidark. She could hear children laughing and playing somewhere outside, hear a radio tuned to the inevitable country music station. He was lying on his back and he was wearing nothing but white boxer shorts, his arms flung out in complete repose. Mary Skeets had told her that he was exhausted when the FBI had finally let him go, and so he was. She let her eyes linger over him, his smooth muscular body, the bruises he'd gotten ostensibly because of her, because she'd asked him—a stranger—for a favor.

What's going to become of us? she thought, knowing full well that there was no *us*. And what kind of man was this, who wouldn't compromise his obligation to his people and yet would send his sister and Inez Yazzie to help her? She wanted to touch him so badly. She even reached out her hand to do it, stopping herself at the last moment, because when everything was said and done, she had no idea if he'd want her here or not—and that was another serious problem. As different as they may be, they were exactly the same in one aspect, at least. Neither of them could reveal their true feelings.

She suddenly lost her nerve, and as she moved to get up from the bed, he opened his eyes.

"Sloan? What—" He caught her hand to keep her from leaving. "What is it?"

"Nothing," she said, reaching out to lightly touch his face, because he looked so worried. "Everything," she immediately amended. She bowed her head for a moment, then looked at him. "I'm so tired, Lucas," she said, moving to lie down beside him. "I just want to be here with you a little while. All right? Just a little while—"

He made room for her, giving her part of the pillow, putting his arms around her so that they were lying face to face. She closed her eyes and felt the soft kiss he placed on each eyelid.

"Go to sleep," he said. "We'll sleep for a while and then we'll talk."

"I don't want to sleep, Lucas. I don't want to talk."

She moved closer to him. In spite of his fatigue, the feel of her body and her soft rose scent immediately piqued his desire. Roses. Where had he, hogan-raised in the desert, ever learned to identify the scent of roses? He didn't remember. He only knew that for the rest of his life it would remind him of her.

He looked into her eyes, trying to see if what Patrick had told him was true.

Sloan told me she loves you.

Her eyes were so sad.

"We never should have met, Lucas," she said. "Our lives should never have become tangled together." She reached up to touch his face again. "But I need this now. I need *us*, Lucas."

She lifted her mouth to his. He kissed her slowly at first, so slowly, letting their breaths mingle, letting his body grow heavy and aching with desire. Then he kissed her harder—perhaps too hard, because he was suddenly overwhelmed by the loneliness and the longing he'd tried all this time to suppress. He had the sensation of events accelerating beyond his control, of being out of the natural pattern, of losing his harmony—and her—and never being able to get either of them back again.

He, too, didn't want to talk. He didn't want to hear her say the things he knew in his heart to be true. That there was no hope for them. That, body and mind, they each belonged in an altogether different place. He didn't want to think about the fact that Will Baron had gone from her life and that he'd done nothing to help her. He didn't want to think about anything but being with her now, like this.

He moved so that he was lying nearly on top of her, and he worked to pull her T-shirt out of the waist of her skirt, sliding his hand under it to run along her ribs and touch her breast. Then he leaned back once again to look into her eyes. Had she come here for this?

"Lucas," she whispered, her eyes searching his. "Lucas."

Yes, he thought. Incredibly, she had, and that knowledge filled him with urgency. He wanted her naked. He wanted to suckle her breasts and hear her soft cries. He wanted to lose himself deep inside her. He rolled over, pulling her on top of him so that he could take the T-shirt off. She helped him with that, then she lay back on the bed, watching him take away the rest of her clothes and his, letting him look at her and touch her, completely unselfconscious under his gaze.

His hands trembled with desire. He was hard and aching. He knew the secrets of a woman's body. He knew precisely what to do for her and how. But she had learned, as well—from him. She was no longer the passive virgin. She was his woman—*his* woman—and when she clung to him, when she returned touch for touch and kiss for kiss, he could feel her need for him and more. He could feel her saying goodbye.

Wait, he thought. They *did* need to talk. He had to know the real reason she'd come here—but her mouth eagerly sought his and her body rose under his hand. His desire for her drove everything else out of his mind. He pressed his hardness against her; her fingers slid downward between them, stroking his belly, moving over him, moving lower. He made a low, needy sound in the back of his throat when she touched him, stroked him, and he lifted himself upward to give her better access, his arms trembling with the strain.

"Wait," Sloan thought he said. But she didn't wait. She moved under him, reaching up to bring him to her. She was afraid, but not of this. She had to remember everything—his taste and his touch, the smooth warmth and the masculine scent of his skin, the feel of his body on hers, in hers—because she was going to have to live the rest of her life without him.

I love you, Lucas.

Impatient now, he knelt between her thighs and drove himself into her; she lifted her hips to meet him. He slid his hands under her, holding her tightly. Her head arched backward as he began to move; with each thrust she gave a soft cry. He reveled in the sounds she made. He wanted to do this for her and he wanted to make it last.

But he couldn't hold back. He thrust harder, fierce in his need for her, completely lost in the exquisite sensation of her tight heat around him. Her body suddenly arched against his. He could feel her climax, feel the spasms of her release, and he let himself go, let the pleasure that was akin to pain overtake him and peak and shatter.

At the very last moment, he was finally able to say the words.

"I love you, Sloan!"

He poured himself into her, until he no longer existed except as a part of her, knowing that their oneness meant nothing and that she would still want to go.

Don't leave me!

The shadows were long when Lucas abruptly woke. He was lying apart from her, facedown on the bed. He had no idea how long he'd slept. She was lying on her back, and he shifted his weight slightly, trying not to disturb her. She immediately opened her eyes. He didn't ask if she was all right, because he knew that her harmony was long gone and that their lovemaking would not have restored it. He moved to her so that he could touch her, keep her as long as he could.

"Yesterday," she said quietly, looking into his eyes. "When you brought Will back to the receiving home you knew that Inez would be coming for him."

It wasn't quite a question, and there was no recrimination in her tone. He thought it was more that she was trying to understand.

"Yes."

"And Dolly. She knew, too. You told her."

"Yes," he said again, and she gave a soft sigh.

"She was very kind to me... afterward. Even if..."

"Even if what?" he asked when she didn't go on.

"Even if I'm white. Even if I'm hurting you."

"You're not hurting me, Sloan."

"Yes, I am. I don't mean just this—that I'd come here like this and everybody will be talking about it. I mean the mess my brother got himself into. It wasn't intentional, my getting you involved in his trouble, but it hurt you just the same. I am sorry for that."

"There's nothing for *you* to be sorry for."

"Lucas, do you know where Will is now? Do you know where Inez took him?"

"No."

"Can you find out?"

"Sloan, don't ask me that."

"I'm sorry. I'm sorry," she said, holding on to him because he would have moved away from her if she hadn't. "I know better than to ask. I know you won't tell me. It's just—I can't believe he's *gone* out of my life and there's nothing I can do about it. It doesn't matter at all that Margaret says Will *is* my nephew, does it?"

"No."

"I can't..." The rest of whatever she was going to say gave way to a wavering sigh.

"You saw Margaret Madman," he said, because he thought she was going to cry. She had been strong last night; he had been proud of her strength. But it had been nearly all he could do to withstand her tears, and he didn't want her to cry again. "Tell me what else she said."

"My brother was a grave robber, Lucas," she said bluntly, and, taken by surprise, he made an involuntary sound of disgust.

"It gets worse. He was in it with another man and Margaret. Margaret was supposed to show them where the burial places were. If she didn't actually dig and didn't actually go there, she thought she'd get around the taboo. But the money wasn't nearly equal to the amount of work it took to get something worth sell-ing, so Margaret and the man found themselves another job without telling—''

She was about to say her brother's name and Lucas pressed his fingers lightly against her lips to warn her. "Sorry," she said. "Margaret said she met a man who wanted someone to pick up cocaine shipments that were being air dropped in the desert. He offered a tremendous amount of money to whoever would do it, a lot more than she could ever resist. So she went to work for him. She found the drop sites in the dark, and my brother's grave robbing friend did the rest. She said they didn't tell my brother what they were doing, because he'd already refused to desecrate any more burial sites—that's one thing to his credit, I guess. Anyway, they thought he might not be too receptive to becoming involved in smuggling cocaine. He was living in Gallup then. Margaret said he wasn't like any man she'd ever met. She wanted him and they became lovers and when she got pregnant, he married her. She said he was always kind to her—she thought he was *too* kind. She said he—'' She abruptly stopped, hiding her face in his shoulder.

Lucas waited, gently stroking her back. "Tell me all of it," he said, prompting her before she was ready, because she needed to talk about this more for herself than for him.

She sighed. "Margaret...said that my brother's first wife— Patrick and Meggie's mother—haunted him. He wouldn't stop talking about her, especially when he was drinking. It was almost as if she was telling me about somebody else, Lucas. He never drank very much before. I never knew what happened to Meggie and Patrick's mother—except that she died. Margaret said she never asked him, because she was afraid the *chindi* would haunt her, too. But whatever it was, she said my brother felt responsible for it, and that he must have thought that being kind to *her* would keep his first wife's *chindi* away. It was a kind of second chance to do better, I guess. Margaret said she was happy with him, but they needed money after Will was born. She went back to picking up the shipments and she started keeping part of them to sell herself. My brother's grave robbing friend—her partner in the cocaine business—didn't know. Then *he* was murdered because of what she was doing. She was really scared—so she ran away. She left Will with my brother, since she couldn't run with a baby. She doesn't know what happened then. She thinks the FBI came to talk to him, and maybe the people she'd been cheating, too. She said when she finally saw him again, he was really angry. He said he was being watched and followed and he could never see his North Carolina family again—because of the danger she'd put him in. He took the job at the community college and he moved onto the reservation—she said because Will was half Navajo and people wouldn't notice him so much there—but they would notice any strangers asking questions.''

"That must have been right after he bought the Christmas presents," Lucas said. "He bought them, then he didn't mail them. Maybe he was afraid to. Maybe he didn't want these people Margaret had gotten herself involved with to know he had family in North Carolina and go looking for her there."

"It . . . makes sense, I guess. You don't know how much I want to believe he had a reason for neglecting Patrick and Meggie the way he did. He was certainly upset with me just before he died. He kept insisting that I take them and go home. Maybe that *is* why... Oh, I don't know. I just keep going around and around with this, and I don't get anywhere." She moved closer to him, her eyes searching his face. "Are *you* all right? Inez said you'd been with the FBI all night."

He smiled and brushed her hair from her face. "It's been worth it. They're in the wrong and they know it—and they know Becenti knows it—but they just had to give it one more shot. The backpedaling has been something to behold. And you're off the hook."

"Me?"

"Inez told them you didn't know where your brother was until she called you, and they had the bank records. Your withdrawals all across the country verified your whereabouts, and the recorded telephone calls to the Navajo Tribal Police dispatcher seemed to satisfy them that you weren't doing anything criminal."

She shook her head in disbelief, then rested it on his shoulder again. He waited for her to continue and he waited for what seemed a long time.

"Lucas," she said finally. "I . . . love you, too."

"Then when were you going to tell me?"

"Tell you?"

He abruptly moved away from her and sat up on the side of the bed. "I'm on duty in a little while," he said. "I'm going to have to go."

"Lucas—"

"Damn it, Sloan! I've been through this before! Believe it or not, I'm a little smarter this time around. You think I don't know a farewell—"

"Don't!" she interrupted.

"—when I get one?" he finished anyway.

"Don't," she said again. "I'm not *her,* Lucas."

"You're leaving," he said. He hunted for his shorts and put them on. "You're going home. Were you going to tell me or were you just going to do this and disappear?"

"I have to go home, Lucas. You know that."

"No, I don't know it, Sloan. I don't want you to go, damn it!"

He was still sitting on the side of the bed, and she moved behind him, wrapping her arms around him. He could feel her bare breasts against his back, and he closed his eyes against the rush of feeling.

"I have to," she said. "I don't belong here. I have another life. I have a job—two jobs—or I did. I may have been fired from both of them by now. I have bills and obligations—and a house to see about. I have to think about Meggie and Patrick. It's nearly time for them to start back to school. And there's Will. I don't know what to do about him. I don't know what to do about—about you. I believe you when you say you love me, and I know you hate it."

"I don't—"

"Yes, you do, Lucas! Do you think *I* can't tell how unhappy caring about me has made you? Sometimes I think you can't tell us apart—me and Sara Catherine McCay. Our problem was never that I wanted to take a child away from the tribe and you might have to take sides. Our problem was—*is*—that you're ashamed to have people know you've gotten involved with a white woman again. You love me, and you still expect me to behave exactly the way she did. I still have to suffer the consequences of what *she* did. It's that same old game."

"All right! In the beginning I thought it was some weakness of mine—the feelings I had for you. That's not true now. I'm not ashamed."

"Then what are we going to do? What *can* we do, Lucas? I've been in an impossible situation I don't even begin to understand. My brother's dead and buried here. His son's been taken away from me and Patrick and Meggie, and I'm still not sure why, not really. I've never had anyone think I was a bad influence on a child before. I've never been a reason for a man to feel ashamed."

"Sloan—"

"I don't know how to handle it, Lucas! I have to get away from all this so I *can* understand." She abruptly let go of him and began searching for her discarded clothes and blindly putting them on.

"Do you have to get away from me?" he asked quietly.

"No! Not from you."

"What am I to you? Tell me that."

She put on the last of her clothes, and she came to sit beside him on the bed. She slid her hands into his. "Lucas," she said, her eyes never leaving his face. "Lucas, you're the love of my life."

"Then don't go! I told you yesterday this thing with Will is all wrong. There has to be some way to find the harmony."

"I have to go home. And you have to do what you asked me to do for Will. You have to help me—" She suddenly bowed her head.

He reached for her then, holding her fast. "If you go, I think you'll never come back," he said against her ear, his voice gruff with emotion. "What we have is too new. It isn't strong enough yet, Sloan."

She clung to him for a moment, then leaned back to look at him, and she managed a wavering smile.

"I think it is. The highway runs in both directions, Lucas. If I don't make it back, you come and get me."

Chapter Nineteen

"I'd like to take a week off this Christmas—tomorrow until the twenty-eighth," Lucas said, causing Becenti's head to come up as if he'd announced the building was on fire.

But he stood his ground, refusing to waver under Becenti's steady gaze.

"You want to tell me when exactly you started observing *that* holiday?" the captain asked. "What are you doing asking me at this late date?"

"I don't observe it—"

"You know we're shorthanded this time of year—"

"—Sloan Baron does," he said as if Becenti hadn't interrupted.

"Sloan," Becenti repeated, as if he needed to make sure he heard right. He picked up a pencil from his desk and began to tap—not a good sign, in Lucas's opinion. "I thought that thing had run its course."

"No," Lucas said.

Becenti continued to tap. "Is she coming back out here?"

"No, I'm going to North Carolina. I need the time to get there and back."

"She know you're coming?"

Lucas didn't answer. Becenti put down the pencil.

"All right," he said. "But I don't like it."

"Yes, sir," Lucas said.

"I don't like it one damn bit."

"Yes, sir," Lucas said again.

"Now get out of here so I can get some work done," Becenti said by way of dismissal.

Incredibly relieved, Lucas was only too happy to oblige. Mary Skeets and several tribal police officers were suspiciously close to Captain Becenti's door when he opened it.

"Well?" Mary said pointedly when he would have walked by.

"I'm going," he said, deciding not to be coy. Half the reservation would soon know that he intended to go all the way to North Carolina to see Sloan Baron.

"Tell her I said hello," Mary called after him. One thing Lucas could say with certainty—Mary Skeets had always been in favor of his relationship with Sloan Baron.

"Okay," he said without stopping, fervently hoping that it was going to be that kind of visit, one where he would be welcome and where he could leisurely give her all the news and well wishes that came from Window Rock. The truth of the matter was that he didn't know. He hadn't been able to tell her he was coming. He hadn't heard from her in over two weeks—when he'd gotten at least one weekly letter from her and he had made a phone call a week to North Carolina for the past four months. Since her last failed attempt to establish some kind of legal ties to Will Baron, his mailbox had been empty, and he hadn't been able to get her on the phone. And Lillian, who was still handling the legalities, had told him that Sloan was more discouraged than she'd ever been.

And then the terse note from Meggie arrived yesterday.

Dear Lucas, it said in her childish hand. *Can you tell me what to do? Sloan's harminy is all gone.*

If Meggie was worried, then so was he. He had some news for Sloan, good news, he thought, but it had been Meggie's letter that had precipitated his sudden decision to go. And he'd felt the pressing need to hurry all day, as if Coyote was hard at work someplace, and if he didn't see Sloan very soon, everything would be lost. He hit the door to the outside at a near run, but he didn't get ten feet.

"Lucas!" Mary called after him. "Telephone!"

"Mary, I'm not here!" he said without looking back.

"It's your friend Nick Wager!"

He swore, but he made an about-face to go into the building. Better to take the call now than to try to figure out Mary's phone message later. She held up two fingers to let him know which line when he came through the door.

"Nick!" he said into the receiver. The caller answered in Navajo. He looked at Mary who suddenly held up an additional finger.

"Nick?" he said, punching another line.

"Lucas! Damn if you're *still* not hard to track down," Nick responded, and Lucas laughed.

"What can I do for you, Nick?" Lucas said, looking at his watch. "How's married life?"

"It's . . . good, Lucas. In fact, that's sort of why I'm calling. We . . . hadn't heard from you since the wedding."

Lucas looked at his watch again, and he could hear someone— Sara?—whispering in the background. "Well, you know how it is. I've been pretty busy here."

"Actually, I—we—just wanted to make sure you were all right. You know, after that thing with the bureau . . . and everything."

Nick Wager still had no guile, Lucas thought, even on the telephone. He hadn't wanted to do this, and Lucas suspected it was the "and everything" part that was the crux of this call. Sara wanted to know if he was devastated by her marriage.

"I'm fine, Nick. I'm better than fine. I'm hoping to take the plunge myself."

"You're getting married?" Nick cried.

"Only if I can talk her into it," Lucas said.

"Well, who is she, man?"

"Look, Nick, I'm on my way to see her now. Sara has met her. She can give you the details."

"Yeah, well, that's great, Lucas! Good luck!"

"Thanks, Nick," Lucas said, knowing how much he would need it. "Thanks for calling."

He stood there for a moment after he'd hung up the receiver. He had known—admitted—for a long time that he wanted Sloan Baron, but he wondered exactly when he'd decided so definitely on attempting a marriage. It must have been some time ago, because he felt completely comfortable with the idea, impossible to achieve as it might be.

Sloan, Sloan, he thought. *You told me to come and get you.*

He drove all night, slept four hours in an economy motel well off the interstate, and drove again, completely losing track of the time, of everything except the road signs and the fact that he was presuming a great deal in coming to see Sloan unannounced. He stopped trying to get her on the phone after he crossed the Mississippi River. After he'd come this far, he had no intention of turning back, regardless of what she might say to him.

It started to rain as he crossed the mountains into North Carolina, a driving male rain, the kind Sloan must see here all the time and the kind that made him, desert-raised as he was, want to get out of the truck somewhere and look up and marvel. It was still raining in the early evening when he reached the town where Sloan lived. The place hadn't been that difficult to find, even in the downpour and the dark, but he had no idea where to look after that. Sloan's address was a post-office box. He'd never asked her precisely which street. He had no idea *where* to look, but he did have an idea how. He spotted the small police station as soon as he drove into town, and he pulled in there. The place was quiet enough when he walked in, quiet and clearly not accustomed to having inquiries from Native Americans on a regular basis. When he stepped inside, everybody in the place looked up.

He introduced himself to the first officer he came to, a considerably overweight young man whom Becenti would have had in his office to discuss low-fat foods and self-discipline. It wasn't cost effective to have an officer in such bad physical shape, just as it wasn't cost effective to have one who was in bad shape mentally. Which was why Lucas was standing here in the first place. Becenti wanted him to get whatever this thing was with Sloan Baron out of his system once and for all, regardless of the fact that his four-month separation from her had had no ill effects on his job performance whatsoever.

The officer looked at Lucas's credentials a second time and apparently decided that whatever he represented was likely beyond his authority and expertise.

"Wait here," he said, getting up and handing Lucas his identification.

Lucas waited, and looked around at the Christmas decorations interspersed with the wanted posters. The building was old and to the point. He rather liked the succinct gold lettering on the huge plate glass window—Police Department. In a few moments the overweight officer returned with an older, Becenti-type officer who clearly found whatever was transpiring potentially very interesting.

"Come on back here, son," he said to Lucas, leading the way to a small office. "Sit down—what can we do for you? You Cherokee?" he asked before Lucas could answer.

"Ah, no. Navajo."

"Navajo," the man said, delighted for some reason. "That Fred," he said, gesturing in the general direction of the overweight officer's location. "He's a good old boy, but he don't part with a lot of information, you know what I mean? You got to *pull* it out of him. You with the Navajo Tribal Police, then?"

"Yes," Lucas said, surprised that the man would know about the tribal police if Fred hadn't told him. Lucas still had his identification in his hand, and the man took it, checking it far more closely than he wanted it to appear.

"I had an uncle that was a marine in World War Two," he said, giving the shield back. "He was a bodyguard for one of your code talkers when he was in the Pacific—both of them weren't nothing but little old boys, but there they was stuck in a war together. And you talk about an unlikely pair. I reckon they kept in touch until my uncle died a few years back. He was a good old soul, my uncle, but he had a *bad* drinking problem—man, he used to keep us nephews spellbound with his war stories about him and his Navajo code talker. I'm proud to meet you, son," he said, shaking Lucas's hand vigorously. "Now what can I do for you?"

"I need directions," Lucas said. "I'm trying to locate someone—Sloan Baron."

"Sloan! I reckon you must be here about Mark's littlest boy then. She told me something about that. That kind of trouble can put you between a rock and a hard place, now, can't it? Well, son, you just missed her. She's gone. Won't be back for a while yet—"

"Gone where?"

"Off to the beach, she said. We're checking on the house while she's gone."

"I still need directions to wherever she is," Lucas said.

"Yeah, we can do that. Libby!" he suddenly yelled. "Where's that address Sloan Baron gave us in case her house catches on fire—or a Navajo tribal policeman is looking for her or something like that?" he asked, still yelling. And he gave Lucas a mischievous grin.

"Stuck on the bulletin board where you put it!" the invisible Libby answered. "And quit asking me where everything is!"

"Man, she is testy *today*," he said, moving over to his bulletin board. "And can't never get a message straight. Hell, I ain't half known for sure where I was supposed to be going or why in twenty years—you ever have that problem?"

"All the time," Lucas said, watching him peruse the board.

"Makes life interesting, I reckon. Here it is." He unpinned a slip of paper and copied the information down on another sheet. "Here you go. You got a map? Well, it ain't hard to get to the beach where she is whether you do or don't. You go down here a couple miles and you get on Highway 52. Then you get on 74—74 and 74-76 will take you right to the water about two hundred miles, Wrightsville Beach.''

"Wrightsville—not Crescent," Lucas said.

"Nope. Wrightsville."

Two hundred miles, Lucas thought as he took his leave, but there was no question of his not going—if his reservation truck still had that many more miles in it. His worry about Sloan escalated as he drove the extremely understated "couple miles" to get to the right highway. A Christmas at the beach. Clearly, Meggie hadn't exaggerated. Sloan must be completely without her harmony if she'd gone looking for it in her childhood.

At least four more hours of driving, the code talker's bodyguard's nephew had said, and Lucas soon realized that the man had been telling the truth. There was a huge difference between two hundred miles flat out on a straight desert highway and two hundred miles through innumerable small Southern towns on a dark, rainy night.

The rain ended in stages, downpour to drizzle to nothing. He was fighting sleep hard by the time the moon came out, and he rolled the truck window down in spite of the cold. He could smell the ocean a long time before he got there—salt water and something else he couldn't identify.

The highway that was supposed to take him to the water did exactly that, ending in a small, poorly lit plaza between a motel and some kind of boardwalk. There were parking spaces with meters, and he pulled into one of those. He was exhausted. In spite of his need to find Sloan, his body and mind wouldn't function anymore and he immediately dropped off to sleep, waking as the sun was about to come up. He was cold and hungry and he had a stiff neck, but he wanted to see where he was. He got out of the truck. He could hear the sound of the waves and he walked into the sand toward the beach. There were a few people about, fishermen, he guessed, and the early morning runners, all of whom looked at him curiously.

He gave a small intake of breath as he came upon the vast expanse of water. It was gray, not green or blue as he'd supposed, but as gray as the early morning sky itself. The wind was cold and stiff, and the sea gulls hung stationary in the air currents. He could taste the salt on his lips. Had he ever suspected that? That you could stand on a windy beach and taste the ocean?

The tide was out, and he started walking along the wet sand. He needed to think. He needed to greet the dawn here in this place and he needed to ask for strength and guidance, because he was filled with doubt. How could he expect Sloan to leave *this* for him and a desert?

The morning chant rose in his mind and in his heart, the chant as old as The People, as old as time itself. He stopped walking and faced the horizon, his entire focus on the first rays of the sun, his scattered thoughts and his disharmony swirling away in the chanting and the sunrise.

When he was done, he stood there a moment longer, then shivered in the cold wind.

"Lucas?" Sloan said behind him.

He abruptly turned and she leapt into his arms, dispersing all his fear that she wouldn't be glad to see him. She clung to him; he could feel her trembling.

He leaned back to look at her, to cup her face in his hands and kiss her mouth again and again. "Sloan, how did you find me?"

"Last night, the police department here brought me a message from the police department at home. It was about a representative of yet another police department being on his way down here. Then I saw your truck parked on the street. It's a one-of-a-kind truck, Lucas. I saw *you* down the beach—you're pretty one-of-a-kind, too. And you law enforcement guys really network, don't you?" she added, and he laughed.

She grabbed him by the hand. "Come on, come on," she said, pulling him along. "Let's get out of the wind."

But she only went a few steps before she was in his arms again. "I'm so glad you're here, Lucas," she whispered against his ear, holding on to him tight. "I waited all night for you to get here. I thought you'd gotten lost or changed your mind."

"I came to see if you'd changed yours," he said, and she lifted her head to look at him.

She made no comment, and they began walking up the beach again.

"I love you," she said after a time.

"That's not the question. The question is whether or not you've changed your mind. Where are we going?"

"Back to the house. It's a friend's place. She felt sorry for me and let me use it." *So I could decide what to do,* she almost said.

"Patrick and Meggie will be there, won't they? I'd rather say everything I need to say out here."

Sloan looked at him, her eyes searching his. "All right," she said. She was afraid suddenly. She had wanted to convince herself that they were too different, that they had different goals and ideals and that they could never understand each other. It wasn't true. Lucas Singer understood the state of mind she was in. He understood perfectly.

She would have let go of his hand, but he stuck her hand into his jacket pocket with his as they began walking again. His fingers were strong and warm around hers. She forced herself to be quiet, to wait and not ask him any questions. She had learned that much from working among his people and loving him—to at least try to let him say whatever he had to say in his own good time.

The gulls cried overhead. They walked past a group of fishermen on their way to the pier.

"Not too many Indian people in cowboy boots go walking here, do they?" he said after the third double take.

"Not too many, no," she agreed.

"This is going to be all one-sided," he said.

She looked at him, more afraid now. "What do you mean?"

"I mean there's a way for us to be together, but you're the one who'll have to make all the concessions because I can't ever live anywhere but the reservation. You know that, don't you?"

"I know," she said.

"It isn't fair, but it's the way it is. Being a tribal policeman isn't just what I do, Sloan. It's what I am."

"I know that, too, Lucas."

"Yes," he agreed. "And that's why you've changed your mind."

Once again, she didn't deny it. She glanced at him. He was looking at the Christmas lights strung on the entrance to the fishing pier.

"I read the letter," he said, looking at her. "The one your brother had in his pocket the night he was hurt. You wrote to him about a Christmas at the beach when you were little. I didn't have any concept whatsoever of what that entailed. I still don't."

"Lucas—" she began, but he wouldn't let her talk.

"I told you I'd try to find a way. I'd try to find the harmony. This is hard, Sloan, because I don't have anything to give you. If you were Navajo, and you were traditional, I could have my uncle speak to your family. I could bring you some token of my intent—a string of really fine horses or something. And if you were willing, we'd marry." He gave a slight smile. "I'd look after your sheep. We'd have children and grow old together. But I can't do any of that. The only thing I can do is ask you to completely disrupt your life for me. To put up with bigotry and with the remarks people would make—my people and yours. And in return you'd get nothing. Except me—a low-paid tribal cop who might fall off the wagon again if things got really bad."

"Don't, Lucas," she said.

"I just want to make sure you know the way things are, Sloan. I'm not ever going to be anything except what I am right now, and I'm not unhappy about that. In spite of everything I could do, I love you—with all my heart, for whatever that's worth. I care about your family. As far as I'm concerned, your brother's children would be *my* children. I want you to know this truth first, Sloan. I want you regardless of what happens with you and Will. I have some news about that, and what scares me is that you might think of me as a means to an end. I don't want you to think you'd have to marry me to get the boy. You wouldn't. One thing doesn't have anything to do with the other. As far as I'm concerned, if you stayed with me just for Will's sake, it would be worse for me than never seeing you again."

"Lucas, I don't understand what you're telling me."

"I went to the Peacemaker Court after you left. It was my mother's idea. She wanted me to see what could be done about you and Will. She said that The People in the Peacemaker Court were very wise. She said they had helped her when she had lost the Beauty Way and perhaps they could help you.

"I tried to explain to her that what had been done about Will Baron was legal. Legal, yes, she said. But *not* wise. The Peacemaker Court has been deliberating ever since you left. A few days ago, they gave me and the tribal judges their decision."

Sloan stopped walking.

"And something else has happened," he said. "No one from Margaret Madman's clan has ever come forward to petition for custody of Will, and Margaret has asked—I think Inez may have had a part in this—Margaret has asked that the tribe share the custody of her son with you. She says she didn't have relatives who cared enough to teach her. She doesn't want that to happen to Will."

Sloan abruptly looked away, giving a furtive wipe at her eyes as if they were tearing from the wind.

"What all this means, Sloan, is that you would have to come back to the reservation to live so that the tribal council would have indication of your sincerity and your intent."

Lucas waited, giving her the time to speak. But she didn't say anything. He was encouraged by her silence, and he plunged on. "The Peacemaker Court says that if you did this, Will Baron would be able to live with his relatives who want him—with you and Patrick and Meggie—and that the tribe would be on hand to see that his Navajo upbringing wasn't neglected. They said the boy is ours—*and* yours. They think we can all work together for the good of the child to teach him the best of both his worlds. They think that you wouldn't have any trouble finding a job at one of the clinics again—you could find the kind of work *you* love. You already know that The People need what you know how to do. It would be a good way to live, Sloan. Reservation life isn't just the poverty and all that goes with it. It's learning from The People about harmony with nature and harmony in oneself. It's learning about an entirely different culture. It's a good way to live," he said again, "if you don't care anything about money. And you don't," he assured her. His assurance made her give a tremulous smile.

"What else?" she asked, wiping at her eyes again.

"Patrick and Meggie both seemed to like Window Rock. Their father's work was respected at the community college. Living there would give them a chance to learn about a positive side of his life they didn't know before."

"What else?" she asked again, her eyes never leaving his face. He wasn't offering her anything so tangible as a string of horses. He was offering her much more. He was offering her the chance for the two of them to grow old together, after all. He was offering her—and Mark's children—a new life, and she wanted to hear every aspect of it.

"What else? Nothing else," he said, a bit panicked because his mind was suddenly blank. Had he said everything there was to say? He didn't know. He could only look into her eyes. She had told him once that he was the love of her life; there was no doubt in his mind that she was his. "Except for what you already know. I love you, Sloan Baron."

"Lucas," she said, putting her arms around him and resting her head on his shoulder for a moment. "There's one more thing." She lifted her head to look at him, and she smiled. "If I understand this correctly—my *husband* would be there."

* * * * *

A Note From the Author

Selecting a place for *One of Our Own* wasn't difficult. I have a faded sepia photograph of a smiling six-year-old standing in the hot sun in the Painted Desert. Me. Every time I look at it I remember yet another place, yet another people who somehow stayed in my heart until the time came when I would write. (Those of you who have read *A Crime of the Heart* and *The Prisoner* know I have a penchant for such things.)

Anyway, the moment I saw the picture again, I knew it was time for the Southwest story. And I knew that in order for Sloan Baron to be that special woman in my mind, she'd have to be modeled after the kind of strong woman I've been fortunate to encounter so many times in my life, both among my family and friends and in my other profession—public health nursing. So I mixed the two vigorously until suddenly I was *there* with Sloan and Lucas and the others. Once again, let me say thank you for joining me in that wonderful game of let's pretend.

Dark secrets, dangerous desire...

Lovers
DARK AND
DANGEROUS

Three spine-tingling tales from the dark side of love.

This October, enter the world of shadowy romance as Silhouette presents the third in their annual tradition of thrilling love stories and chilling story lines. Written by three of Silhouette's top names:

LINDSAY McKENNA
LEE KARR
RACHEL LEE

Haunting a store near you this October.

Take 4 bestselling love stories FREE

Plus get a FREE surprise gift!

MONTANA Mavericks

Stories that capture living and loving beneath the Big Sky, where legends live on...and the mystery is just beginning.

This September, look for

THE WIDOW AND THE RODEO MAN
by Jackie Merritt

And don't miss a minute of the loving as the mystery continues with:

SLEEPING WITH THE ENEMY
by Myrna Temte (October)
THE ONCE AND FUTURE WIFE
by Laurie Paige (November)
THE RANCHER TAKES A WIFE
by Jackie Merritt (December),
and many more!

Wait, there's more! Win a trip to a Montana mountain resort. For details, look for this month's MONTANA MAVERICKS title at your favorite retail outlet.

Only from *Silhouette®* where passion lives.

The Loop™

Is the future what it's cracked up to be?

This August, find out how C. J. Clarke copes with being on her own in

GETTING IT TOGETHER: CJ
by Wendy Corsi Staub

Her diet was a flop. Her "beautiful" apartment was cramped. Her "glamour" job consisted of fetching coffee. And her love life was less than zero. But what C.J. didn't know was that things were about to get better....

The ups and downs of modern life continue with

GETTING IT RIGHT: JESSICA
by Carla Cassidy in September

GETTING REAL: CHRISTOPHER
by Kathryn Jensen in October

Get smart. Get into "The Loop!"

Only from *Silhouette*®

where passion lives.

THE PARSON'S WAITING
Sherryl Woods

A life of harsh assignments had hardened correspondent Richard Walton. Yet his heart yearned for tenderness and warmth. He'd long ago given up the search for these precious qualities—until town parson Anna Louise Perkins entered his life. This courageous, loving woman's presence could be the cure Richard's soul so desperately sought....

Don't miss THE PARSON'S WAITING, by Sherryl Woods, available in September!

She's friend, wife, mother—she's you! And beside each Special Woman stands a wonderfully *special* man. It's a celebration of our heroines— and the men who become part of their lives.

Don't miss **THAT SPECIAL WOMAN!** each month— from some of your special authors! Only from Silhouette Special Edition!

Silhouette
SPECIAL EDITION
™

WHAT EVER HAPPENED TO...?

Have you been wondering when much-loved characters will finally get their own stories? Well, have we got a lineup for you! Silhouette Special Edition is proud to present a *Spin-off Spectacular!* Be sure to catch these exciting titles from some of your favorite authors:

HOMEWARD BOUND (July, SE #900) Mara Anvik is recalled to her old home for a dire mission—which reunites her with old flame Mark Toovak in *Sierra Rydell*'s exciting spin-off to ON MIDDLE GROUND (SE #772).

BABY, COME BACK (August, SE #903) Erica Spindler returns with an emotional story about star-crossed lovers Hayes Bradford and Alice Dougherty, who are given a second chance for marriage in this follow-up to BABY MINE (SE #728).

THE WEDDING KNOT (August, SE #905) Pamela Toth's tie-in to WALK AWAY, JOE (SE #850) features a marriage of convenience that allows Daniel Sixkiller to finally adopt...and to find his perfect mate in determined Karen Whitworth!

A RIVER TO CROSS (September, SE #910) Shane Macklin and Tina Henderson shared a forbidden passion, which they can no longer deny in the latest tale from *Laurie Paige*'s WILD RIVER series.

Don't miss these wonderful titles, only for our readers— only from Silhouette Special Edition!

Silhouette

SPECIAL EDITION

WILD RIVER

Maddening men...winsome women...and the untamed land
they live in—all add up to love!

A RIVER TO CROSS (SE #910)
Laurie Paige

Sheriff Shane Macklin knew there was more to "town outsider"
Tina Henderson than met the eye. What he saw was a generous
and selfless woman whose true colors held the promise of love....

Don't miss the latest Rogue River tale, A RIVER TO CROSS, available
in September from Silhouette Special Edition!

SEWR-5